D1604361

Roll On, Columbia

ROLL ON, COLUMBIA

A Historical Novel

BOOK ONE
To the Pacific

BILL GULICK

UNIVERSITY PRESS OF COLORADO

Copyright © 1997 by Bill Gulick
International Standard Book Number 0-87081-425-7

Published by the
UNIVERSITY PRESS OF COLORADO
P.O. Box 849
Niwot, Colorado 80544

The University Press of Colorado is a cooperative publishing enterprise supported, in part, by Adams State College, Colorado State University, Fort Lewis College, Mesa State College, Metropolitan State College of Denver, University of Colorado, University of Northern Colorado, University of Southern Colorado, and Western State College of Colorado.

The paper used in this publication meets the minimum requirements of the American National Standard for Information Sciences—Permanence of Paper for Printed Library Materials. ANSI z39.48-1984

Library of Congress Cataloging-in-Publication Data

Gulick, Bill, 1916–
    Roll on, Columbia / by Bill Gulick.
    p.   cm.—(To the Pacific: bk. 1)
    ISBN 0-87081-425-7 (alk. paper)
    I. Title. II. Series: Gulick, Bill, 1916– To the Pacific: bk. 1.
PS3557.U43R65   1997
813'.54—dc21

10 9 8 7 6 5 4 3 2 1

Roll On, Columbia

Folk song by Woody Guthrie

Green Douglas firs, where the waters cut through,
Down her wild mountains and canyons she flew;
Canadian Northwest to the ocean so blue;
It's roll on, Columbia, roll on!
  Roll on, Columbia, roll on!
  Roll on, Columbia, roll on!
  Your power is turning
  Our darkness to dawn,
  So roll on, Columbia, roll on!

Tom Jefferson's vision would not let him rest;
An empire he saw in the Pacific Northwest;
Sent Lewis and Clark and they did the rest;
So roll on, Columbia, roll on!
  Roll on, Columbia, roll on!
  Roll on, Columbia, roll on!
  Your power is turning
  Our darkness to dawn,
  So roll on, Columbia, roll on!

At Bonneville now there are ships in the locks;
Waters have risen and cleared all the rocks;
Shiploads of plenty will steam past the docks;
It's roll on, Columbia, roll on!
  Roll on, Columbia, roll on!
  Roll on, Columbia, roll on!
  Your power is turning
  Our darkness to dawn,
  So roll on, Columbia, roll on!

And on up the river is the Grand Coulee Dam;
The mightiest thing ever built by a man,
To run the great factories and water the land;
It's roll on, Columbia, roll on!
Roll on, Columbia, roll on!
Roll on, Columbia, roll on!
Your power is turning
Our darkness to dawn,
So roll on, Columbia, roll on!

Used by permission
"Roll On, Columbia"
Words by Woody Guthrie
Music based on "Goodnight, Irene" by Huddie Ledbetter and John A. Lomax
TRO © 1936, 1957, 1963 Ludlow Music, Inc., New York, New York

Author's Note

In 1941, the Bonneville Power Administration paid folksinger Woody Guthrie $266.66 to spend a month writing twenty-six songs in praise of the development of government water and power projects. The ballad "Roll On, Columbia" was one of the songs he composed.

Used as background music to the twenty-minute documentary movie on the building of Grand Coulee Dam, it has been heard by millions of visitors to the site since that time, so has proved to be a real bargain as a musical score.

Though I never met Woody Guthrie, I long have been an admirer of his songs. As I researched and wrote this book, I came to realize that we had a number of things in common. We both were raised in Oklahoma during the Dust Bowl and Depression years of the 1930s. I spent two years working for a private utility that was building electric lines to serve rural Oklahoma areas in need of power, flood control, navigation benefits, and irrigation water, just as he later worked for BPA, which was doing the same thing in the Pacific Northwest.

Called a "Radical" in his day, all Woody Guthrie asked of the politicians was a job for a decent rate of pay. Coming to know construction workers as I did, I found them to be the salt of the earth and the strength of a nation in peace and war, just as he proclaimed them to be in his ballads.

Some fifty years ago I settled in the heart of the Columbia River watershed near its juncture with its largest tributary, the Snake. Since then, all my writings have dealt with some aspect of the past, present, and future of the two rivers. During these years, I have followed, reported on, and taken part in controversy as to what uses should be made of the waters of the legendary "River of the West."

In planning what probably will be my last book on the Columbia River, I decided that the best way to tell the story of what man has done to the river was from the viewpoint of six generations of white and Indian families whose fictional lives were closely entwined with

BILL GULICK the use and development of the Columbia from the establishment of Astoria in 1811 down to the present day. All other characters in the book are real.

Some twenty-five years ago in the introduction to my nonfiction book *Snake River Country*, I wrote: "Somewhere along the way I learned that a great river influences the lives of the people in its watershed just as surely as the acts of those people influence the life of the river. Without water, people die. Without people's concern, a river dies. Thus, this book ..."

That statement still holds true today. So to all the river people I have known—both real and fictional—over the years, as well as to the memory of Woody Guthrie, this book is dedicated.

—BILL GULICK

Roll On, Columbia

1.

HIGH IN THE MAINMAST RIGGING of the *Tonquin* as the ship lay at the lower East River dock September 8, 1810, Ordinary Seaman Ben Warren paused at his task of tidying up the lashings of the furled sail. Staring down at the squat figure of John Jacob Astor, who was saying a grumpy farewell to the commander of the three-masted vessel, Captain Jonathan Thorn, he found it hard to believe that the richest, most politically powerful man in North America was standing just thirty feet below him, an easy target for a grommet dropped by a butter-fingered young sailor or the heedless excretions of the big white seagull soaring a few feet overhead.

Though he had no intention of dropping a grommet, Ben Warren hoped that the seagull would be equally careful. If the bird cut loose and befouled the great man's shiny beaver hat, black broadcloth coat, or white silk stock, the simple fact that a sixteen-year-old seaman was standing in the spar safety loops above would direct immediate attention to him, Ben knew, for aboard ship blame for anything bad that happened always seeped down to the bottom, the Ordinary Seaman, who, by definition, was the lowest form of life afloat. As his father, Third Mate Thomas Warren, had warned him:

"Aboard the *Tonquin*, laddie, you must remember that Captain Thorn served ten years in the American Navy. Even though his first command is a commercial ship, he'll run it with strict naval discipline. You'll have to toe the mark, boy, whatever happens, with no help from me. From this day on, I have no son aboard."

"I'll ask no favors, sir. From this day on, I have no father aboard."

Below, Mr. Astor now had moved down to the main deck and was shaking hands with his four senior partners in the Pacific Fur Company: Alexander McKay, Duncan McDougall, David Stuart, and his nephew, young Robert Stuart. To Ben, Astor's heavy, Germanic accent was so thick it could barely be understood.

"Haf a goot trip oudt to de Oregon Country, gentlemen. In troubled times like dese, only brave, far-seeing peoples like us dare take big risks vhich vill make us big fortunes."

"You speak God's truth, Mr. Astor," Alexander McKay agreed, his Gaelic accent almost as thick as Astor's. "We'll certainly do our best."

Glancing up at the quarter deck, where the muscular, stocky, ruddy-faced Captain Thorn stood scowling down at the disordered chaos of men and belongings strewn helter-skelter across the poop deck, Mr. Astor waved a chubby hand.

"Gott-speed und fair vinds, captain. Let noddings stand in your vay."

"Aye, sir!" Captain Thorn answered briskly, clicking his heels together and responding with a crisp, naval salute. "Be assured, I shall follow your written orders to the letter."

Though in time past Ben's father had commanded far larger ships than the *Tonquin* and was twice Captain Thorn's age, Third Mate Thomas Warren had been very close-mouthed with his own son when it came to talking about the ship's destination and the epic adventure about to begin. Thus, what little Ben had learned about both had been gleaned from the gossip of crew members and passengers. Coming to America from Germany twenty years ago, Astor first had been a butcher, Ben knew, then a musical instrument salesman, and finally a gatherer of furs in upstate New York and eastern Canada.

As a fur trader, he had made a fortune so vast that he had no difficulty gaining the attention of expansion-minded leaders like Thomas Jefferson. After pushing the Louisiana Purchase through Congress in 1803, President Jefferson had sponsored the Lewis and Clark Expedition to the Pacific and back in 1805–6, then, after its return, had listened sympathetically to a proposal made by John Jacob Astor that was so broad in its scope only a man with President Jefferson's vision could have agreed to it.

If the government of the United States would give him an exclusive charter for his proposed Pacific Fur Company, Astor told the president, he would equip by-sea and by-land parties that would journey west to the mouth of the Columbia, establish a trading post there, and collect all the furs from the western half of the continent. Following this, he would develop a trade with China and the Far East that would make the United States a major world power, directly challenging England's domination of the seas and the three-way, rum-tea-spice trade that long had been the cornerstone of the British Empire.

"Chust gif me de charter, Mister Jefferson," Astor grunted, "und I vill do de rest. It von't cost de United States a single dollar."

As one of the last acts of his presidency in 1808, President Jefferson had granted the request, exclaiming:

"The charter is yours, Mr. Astor. God bless you in your high endeavor! Strong, far-sighted men like you will help me achieve my dream of a nation stretching from sea to sea!"

Though current President James Madison was not nearly as expansion-minded as Jefferson had been, Astor's plans were too fully developed to be stopped now, even if Madison had tried. Journeying north to Montreal, Astor proposed to the Canadian leaders of the North West Company that they join him as partners and split up the Western world in an international fur combine that would put the Hudson's Bay Company out of business. Rebuffed by the Nor'westers—who felt they could destroy the H.B.C. without any help from an upstart German-American ex-butcher—Astor did the next best thing, using his money and his hammer-blunt logic to persuade six experienced North West Company men to desert their country and employer and go to work for or with him.

In talking to young Robert Stuart and the still younger French-Canadians, Gabriel Franchere and Alexander Ross, who were half-share partners, Ben Warren gathered that whether they were working "for" or "with" Mr. Astor depended upon how one interpreted their contracts with the Pacific Fur Company. Of the sixty men aboard the *Tonquin*, twenty-five were members of the ship's crew, while the remaining thirty-five were in the employ of the fur company whose supplies and trade goods were being transported around Cape Horn to the mouth of the fabled River of the West. Eventually to be reinforced by a sixty-five-member overland party led by Wilson Price Hunt, the Astor enterprise would be the first American settlement on the Northwest Coast.

Following the departure of Mr. Astor from the still shore-linked ship, Ben Warren climbed down out of the rigging and spent the increasingly warm forenoon doing whatever chores First Mate Ebenezer Fox, Second Mate John Mumford, and Third Mate Thomas Warren told him to do. For the most part, this consisted of attempting to make the badly hungover French-Canadian voyageurs, who, if they did understand English, pretended they did not, to stow their gear below decks in the cramped forecastle crew quarters, rather than hanging their capotes and caps on belaying pin racks where they would be in the way of gear used to raise or lower sail. Already it was clear from the contemptuous way the Astor party voyageurs, clerks, and mechanics treated the crew and the hostile way the crew regarded them that there was going to be serious trouble between the two groups.

Watching the confusion from the height of the quarter deck above the ship's stern, Captain Thorn scowled in growing irritation. From what Ben had experienced of the captain's discipline during the three weeks he had been a member of the crew, he suspected that the fur company employees were in for a rude awakening, once the *Tonquin* put to sea, for Thorn ruled his ship with an iron hand.

As two of the senior partners, Alexander McKay and David Stuart, mounted the ladder and started to walk across the quarter deck, Captain Thorn blocked their way.

"Where, pray tell, d'ye think ye're going?"

"Why, just to the other side of the boat in order to get a better view of the lower harbor," Alexander McKay said politely. "Is there anything wrong with that?"

"This is a ship, Mr. McKay, not a boat."

"As you will, Captain. All I care about is that it floats."

"Don't you know the first thing about courtesy aboard ship, Mr. McKay?"

"How is it different from courtesy ashore, Captain?"

"This is *my* ship and *my* quarter deck!" Captain Thorn exploded. "By my leave, you and the other partners may walk on the port side of the quarter deck in fair weather. In foul weather, you'll not set foot on the deck without my permission. In any kind of weather, the starboard side of the quarter deck is mine—and mine only. Is that clear?"

Alexander McKay's face darkened as he stepped belligerently forward toward forbidden territory, only to be stopped by David Stuart's restraining hand on his forearm.

"I was under the impression, Captain Thorn, that the Pacific Fur Company had chartered this ship," Stuart said quietly. "Therefore, you are in our employ."

"Mr. Astor is my employer, sir. It's only his orders I'll obey."

"Did he tell ye where the quarter deck should be divided?" McKay demanded. "Did he put it in writing?"

Captain Thorn's wind-reddened face turned bright crimson. "I'm in command of this ship, sir! You'll obey my orders or I'll put you ashore!"

Passing along the lower deck within earshot, Ben Warren marveled at how childish the argument had become and how quickly it had escalated into something personal and nasty. He saw David Stuart take McKay by the elbow, turn him aside, and murmur: "*Nae so muckle o' it*, Alex …"

Apparently this was Scottish for "Don't make too much of it... " As a result, Alexander McKay shrugged and descended the ladder to the lower deck with David Stuart, where both men moved to the starboard rail and stared broodingly into the distance as they continued to discuss the incident in Gaelic.

"Mister Fox!" Captain Thorn called down to the First Mate.

"Aye, sir?"

"There's an offshore breeze stirring. Cast off the lines and move the ship across the bay to Staten Island. We'll spend the night anchored there. If the wind is right with the ebb tide tomorrow morning, we'll move out toward Sandy Hook and the open sea."

"Cast off it is, sir. Mr. Mumford! Mr. Warren!"

"Aye, sir?"

"Prepare to cast off the lines. Lay men aloft to shake out a close-reefed mains'l. Set the jib for steering way. We're crossing to Staten Island for the night."

As the mooring cables came in and the offshore breeze began to fill the sails, the ship became a living creature, quivering with anticipatory eagerness. At the first ripple of motion, the voyageurs lounging on deck leaped to their feet and scampered to the nearest rail, chattering and laughing like delighted children experiencing a new sensation. Most of them had never been aboard an oceangoing ship before, Ben knew, for their adult lives had been spent paddling and portaging canoes on inland waters in Canada and upstate New York. From the way Captain Thorn glared down at them, Ben guessed he was mentally wagering that, familiar with white-water rapids and inland rivers though the voyageurs might be, they would get sick as dogs once the *Tonquin* began to pitch and roll in heavy seas. When that happened, Thorn would show them no mercy.

5

Outside the protected harbor, Ben knew, warships of the British Navy were prowling, impressing American seamen and capturing American ships on the thinnest of pretexts. Under these conditions, it was highly risky for a small ship laden with valuable supplies and manned by crewmen of mixed nationalities to venture on a long sea voyage. But off Sandy Hook, the pride of the American Navy, the U.S.S. *Constitution*, stood ready to meet all adversaries in the undeclared war. While still in the shadow of her protection, Captain Thorn no doubt intended to get a running start on the high seas in a southerly direction, depending upon his skill as a navigator and sailor to evade being overtaken and captured.

In addition to flight, the *Tonquin* appeared to be very well armed for her size, boasting gunports for twenty-two eight-pound cannons. Carrying out a deception planned by Captain Thorn, the ship's armorer, Stephen Weeks, and his brother, ship's carpenter John Weeks, had filled ten of the ports with real cannons and the other twelve with fakes made of wood. The fakes looked so real they could not be detected at any distance; so for all intents and purposes, the 269-ton ship appeared to be bristling with guns.

"We'd not last long agin' a frigate-of-war carrying twenty-pounders," Armorer Stephen Weeks told Ben. "But we've got enough sting to make smaller vessels think twice before tackling us. Should it come to a fight, we've got four-and-a-half tons of gunpowder stowed below decks, so agin' anything close to our size, we can fight all day."

"Captain Thorn served ten years in the American Navy, I understand."

"Aye, that he did. A tougher, cockier little rooster never lived. Before he'll give up this ship—which is his first command—blood'll run ankle-deep in the scuppers, I'll guarantee you that. Why, he might even give me the order to blow up the *Tonquin* with all that's left aboard, rather than surrender."

"Would you carry out such an order?"

"I'd have no choice, lad. Might as well be dead by my hand as his—for he'd kill any man that disobeyed an order, quick as he'd kill a fly. That's his naval training."

2.

ROM THE WAY First Mate Ebenezer Fox and Second Mate John Mumford treated his father, it was clear to Ben that both men had known Thomas Warren long before he signed on as Third Mate of the *Tonquin*. Though superior in rank to him now, they seemed to regard him with respect, even as he deferred to them without seeking special favors. In all probability, both officers were more familiar with his father's past than Ben himself, for they had been seafaring men for many years while Ben's saltwater experience had been limited to a year's sailing on coastal waters.

Four years had passed since the terrible wreck that had ended Captain Thomas Warren's career as a master mariner. Sailing out of Gloucester, Massachusetts, February 4, 1806, in command of one of the newest whaling ships in the New England fleet, the *Cotton Mather*, Thomas Warren had taken his wife, Sarah, and their three oldest sons, George, nineteen, Peter, seventeen, and Emil, sixteen, aboard ship to keep him company during the long voyage around Cape Horn, then north to the Sandwich Islands and a season of profitable whaling in the cold waters of the North Pacific.

At least the well-to-do owners who had supplied fifteen thousand dollars to build and equip the ship had every reason to expect that the venture would be profitable. In New England, those days, sperm oil was fetching such a high price that it was not uncommon for a two-year whaling voyage to repay the cost of building and outfitting a vessel three times over in a single trip. Captain Warren would share in the profits, of course, if the voyage were successful. In exchange for the services of his three strong sons as able seamen, his wife as mistress of supplies and supervisor to the ship's cook, and his own skill as master, his family held a quarter-interest in the enterprise, whose total value for underwriting purposes had been set at twenty thousand dollars. Being just twelve years old at the time and too young to go to sea, Ben Warren had been left behind in the care of his mother's older sister, Flora Partridge, who had been widowed by the sea three years ago.

Exactly what had happened during that stormy night off Cape Horn, Ben Warren never learned. All he knew was that the *Cotton Mather* foundered with a terrible loss of life. Among the drowned had been his mother and his three brothers, while only his father, nine crew members, and First Mate Matthew Robinson had survived. Because of his youth, Ben had not been permitted to go to the hearings and court trials that had accused his father of drunkenness, incompetence, and dereliction of duty, eventually costing him his captain's license and a share of the underwriter's settlement, all of which went to the owners of the vessel.

Among seafaring men, later gossip accused the owners of greed and First Mate Robinson of blaming his own faults and failures on a captain too stunned by the loss of his wife, his three sons, and his ship to put up an adequate defense of his actions at a time of great stress. Because Thomas Warren was too grief-stricken to make more than a token attempt to repair the damage done to his career, he incurred the further punishment of being forced to spend three bitter years ashore without employment at his trade. By then, the only position he could obtain was on small vessels in the coastal trade. Finally three weeks ago he had secured the low-pay, high-risk berth of Third Mate aboard the *Tonquin*, which stood a good chance of being lost at sea either to the hazards of Cape Horn or to war with Great Britain. Since Ben had gotten his papers just a year ago and would also work cheap, he had been hired as an Ordinary Seaman.

"All I know about the *Tonquin*," Thomas Warren told his son, "is that she's one of a dozen or so three-masted square-riggers built on the East Coast during the late 1790s and early 1800s in shipyards between Maine and New York."

"One of the sailors told me she was built specifically for the fur trade on the North West Coast."

"Most of those ships were, lad. They run from one to three hundred tons, carry crews of thirty to sixty men, handle well in tight waters like those to be found on the North West Coast of America, and are sturdy enough to withstand the storms off Cape Horn."

"Have you ever been on the North West Coast?"

"No, I haven't," Thomas Warren answered, shaking his head. "I'm told it's like no other, so far as being stormy is concerned."

Aboard ship, the relationship between Ben and his father must be strictly professional, his father warned, with Ben doing his level best to learn his trade as quickly as possible with a minimum of questions. Which was fine with Ben. He wanted no coddling.

Since hiring on, both Ben and his father had learned more about the history of the *Tonquin*. Seeking a ship suitable for a journey around Cape Horn to the mouth of the Columbia, then to the Northwest Coast, China, and on around the world, John Jacob Astor had purchased the relatively new vessel for $37,860, her final registration papers being made out to him on August 23, 1810.

"Her designer and first master was Captain Edward Fanning," Thomas Warren told his son, "a good friend of mine and one of the best sea captains in the business. He supervised the selection of her timbers and the laying of her keel in the New York shipyard of Adam and Noah Brown in early March 1807, building her specifically for the China trade. From the beginning, she proved herself to be a sweet sailer."

The *Tonquin's* first certificate of registration described her as being ninety-four feet long, twenty-five feet wide, and twelve feet deep. Her burden was 269 tons. Though her hull was pierced for twenty-two guns, she never carried more than ten, the remaining ports being filled with dummy cannons.

"On her maiden voyage, she left New York on May 26, 1807," Thomas Warren told Ben, "bound for Canton, China. I'm told she made her first round-the-world circuit in ten months, which was not a record but still mighty good sailing. A year or so later, she made a second trip in just as good a time. When Astor bought her, he wanted Captain Fanning as her master, but he wasn't available. So he settled for Jonathan Thorn."

After spending the night riding at anchor off Staten Island, dawn's first light and a rising offshore breeze brought Captain Thorn's order to weigh anchor and set sail. Scampering aloft to free the mains'l, Ben stood watching the ship's snow-white canvas fill with wind as the *Tonquin* gathered way and moved out toward the open sea. On the deck below, the voyageurs, clerks, and mechanics of the Astor party shouted, chattered, and laughed exuberantly for a while, thinking it all great fun. Then, when the ship dipped her bow into the oncoming seas, took a bone in her teeth, heeled ten degrees over, and began to yaw sickeningly to leeward, the laughter and shouting died, several members of the party turned green, staggered to the nearest rail, and lost their breakfast.

By mid-afternoon, the shoreline off Sandy Hook was barely visible in the thin, early September haze. Two miles ahead, the U.S.S. *Constitution* lay at anchor, rocking to and fro with seas rolling inshore from across the breadth of the Atlantic. Seeking shelter in the lee of the great warship, the *Tonquin* lowered sail, dropped bow and stern anchors, and lay under the protecting wings of the larger ship.

Descending to the deck, Ben saw Captain Thorn come out of his cabin, raise a hand to shade his eyes, and squint across the intervening distance toward the *Constitution*. From head to toe he looked every inch the master of a commercial ship, his black boots polished till they shone, his dress trousers and coat pressed, his black ribbon tie neatly in place, and his billed cap squarely centered on his head. As Ben watched, Captain Thorn made a curt gesture and spoke sharply to First Mate Fox. In response, the officer gave him a good imitation of a naval salute, turned to the waiting five-man boat crew of coxswain and oarsmen, and cried:

"Now hear this! Captain Thorn is paying a courtesy visit to the admiral of the fleet aboard the *Constitution*! Make ready to lower the long boat!"

Descending the ladder from the quarter deck, Captain Jonathan Thorn stepped into the long boat, then waited with stiff-necked dignity as it was lowered from its davits and touched the heaving surface of the sea. No drums rolled and no bugles sounded, but to Ben the leave-taking was impressive just the same. Demonstrating the quality of their training, the four oarsmen and the coxswain performed flawlessly, catching the swell just right, then moving across the interval between the two ships without an oar blade flicking so much as a drop of water on its passenger in the bow.

"*Mon Dieu!*" one of the voyageurs exclaimed. "Ze capitan of zis tiny ship makes a courtesy call on ze Admiral of ze American Navy? Why, zat is lak a commoner calling on ze King of England!"

"Not quite," a voice nearby said softly. "In this case, they're old friends."

Ben realized that the speaker was his father. With all the crew and passengers aboard the *Tonquin* now watching the progress of the long boat and impressed with the importance of the occasion, Senior Partner Alexander McKay regarded Third Mate Thomas Warren with unconcealed curiosity.

"Captain Thorn served in the American Navy, I understand."

"Aye, that he did, Mr. McKay. For ten years."

"Why did he resign?"

"That I cannot tell you, though it has been said it was Mr. Astor himself who requested a leave of absence so that he could command the *Tonquin*. As you may have noticed by now, he runs her like a military ship."

"Indeed, I have, Mr. Warren," Alexander McKay said dryly. Filling and lighting his long-stemmed redstone pipe, he gazed out across the water for a time, then spoke thoughtfully. "As a Scotchman and a citizen of Canada, I have serious gaps in my knowledge of American history. But I do know that the United States Navy did very well in the affair at Tripoli in 1801. Even the British give your country credit for that."

"As they should, Mr. McKay. If President Jefferson hadn't taken the action he did, all the seafaring nations of the world would still be paying tribute to the Bey of Algiers—just as I was forced to do on one occasion as captain of a merchant ship."

Dimly Ben recalled a time as a child of four when the town of Gloucester had been alive with tales of their ships and seamen being captured and held for ransom by the Barbary pirates in some distant port on the North Africa coast. Like the other wives who had husbands at sea in the area, his mother had been very worried for a while, then, after months of suspense, relieved when her husband and the other Gloucester family heads had finally come home. Seeming to regard the adventure as simply another hazard of life at sea, his father had never talked about it much to his family, though in taverns along the waterfront the happenings of those days still remained vivid in the memories of many men.

"Were you captured by the pirates?" young Robert Stuart blurted.

"Aye, that I was."

"What did you do?"

"Why, I sat in their stinking jail with the rest of my ship's crew until the owners of our ship paid ransom."

"Ah, *M'sieu* Warren," Gabriel Franchere exclaimed, "I have read of these stirring times when French, British, American, and all other ships of the civilized world were being held for ransom by the Bey of Algiers! But never before have I met a man who actually was there. Please, *M'sieu* Warren, tell us about it."

"Pray do!" Alexander Ross said enthusiastically. "It's a piece of history every colonial ought to be proud of."

Of the ship's officers and crew, only First Mate Fox and Third Mate Warren were old enough to be regarded as tellers of tales, a pastime indulged in aboard ship during those rare interludes when there was no pressing work to be done and the captain of the vessel was absent on a visit to another ship. Ben saw his father gaze questioningly at the First Mate, whose privilege it would be to take over the tale-telling himself, if he so desired. Mr. Fox nodded in deferral to him.

"We've time on our hands, Mr. Warren, and it is indeed a tale worth telling."

"You experienced part of it."

"Aye, but not as much as you. If ever a person lived who should tell the story, you're that man. Start at the beginning, Thomas, and tell it all."

By now, Ben Warren was acutely aware that he was part of a historic time. During recent weeks, much had been made in the local and regional newspapers of the increasingly belligerent attitude being taken by England toward the rights of American ships and seamen on the high seas. Still smarting from the loss of the United States forced upon them by the treaty that ended the Revolutionary War, the British were ruthlessly enforcing their version of maritime law, seeming to feel that though they could not defeat the colonials on land, they could throttle them on the sea. Time and again the American government had warned Great Britain that it would go to war once more in order to protect the rights of its seamen and shipping. Time and again England had ignored the warnings. Now it seemed inevitable that a clash of arms soon must take place.

If hostilities did break out, the Canadian partners, the voyageurs, clerks, and mechanics of the Astor enterprise, the captain, officers, and members of the ship's crew, the *Tonquin*, and the U.S.S. *Constitution* all would be players in the game, with the lives of their people at risk. The men listening to Thomas Warren knew that, so they paid close heed to his tale.

Following the outbreak of war between England and France in

1793, Third Mate Warren said, the newly born American government realized that, without a navy to protect its shipping, unprincipled governments could force its overseas commerce to pay tribute to their superior power. Among the worst of those governments were the piratical countries along the North African coast. To remedy this unhappy state of affairs, Congress authorized the building of six frigates-of-war, of which three—the *United States*, *Constellation*, and *Constitution*—were begun in 1796, with the other three to wait until more funds were available.

Designed by master shipbuilder Joshua Humphreys, the *Constitution* was planned to be a big ship capable of carrying 450 officers and men, a large store of powder and shot, 50,000 gallons of freshwater, and enough supplies for a six-month cruise. She would be built, Humphreys said, of prime liveoak, cedar, pine, and locust cut in the virgin forests of states ranging from Maine to Georgia, every piece of timber in her the best available. Her heavy batteries would be cast in the foundries of Maryland and Connecticut, while Paul Revere of Boston would supply the copper rivets and spikes used in her construction, which he promised he could furnish "as cheap as anyone."

As designer Humphreys pointed out, her armament would be the newest and finest on the high seas. Most frigates at that time mounted 16-pound cannons; hers would be 24-pounders. Though he originally had designed her as a forty-four-gun frigate, he made enough improvements after her keel was laid that by the time she was launched she mounted fifty-four guns, weighed 1,576 tons, was 204 feet long, and had a 43-foot 6-inch beam. When she went into battle, she carried thirty long 24-pounders on her gun deck, sixteen 32-pound carronades on the quarter deck, six 32-pounders on her fo'c's'le, and two 12-pounders as bow-chasers. Costing $302,718, she could justly be called one of the most formidable ships of war afloat.

Launched in October 1797, she went to sea under the command of Captain Samuel Nicholson, seeking French privateers said to be operating in the area of her shakedown cruise, which ranged along the Eastern Seaboard and as far south as the West Indies. She found none, but the voyage did give her crew a chance to get acquainted with her capabilities. Soon enough, a challenge worthy of her talents came along.

Since 1785, Barbary Coast pirates sailing out of Morocco, Algiers, Tunis, and Tripoli had been taking a heavy toll of the world's merchant shipping. If a tribute were not paid, the pirates would seize the ships, confiscate the cargo, and take the crew prisoners as slave labor until a stiff ransom was paid. Being a young, weak nation, the United States alone had paid more than one million dollars a year to the Bey of Algiers before 1800, in addition to a personal tribute of $22,000 annually.

Annoyed because the Bey was extorting more money out of the United States than he was, the Pasha of Tripoli ordered that the flagstaff outside the American Consulate there be chopped down and the American flag burned. Growing still more arrogant, he then declared war against the United States. This was on May 14, 1801.

But by then recently elected President Thomas Jefferson had had enough. In a ringing statement broadcast to the rulers of all the countries along the North African coast, he declared:

"We will pay millions of dollars for defense—but not one cent for tribute!"

Now under the command of Commodore Edward Preble, the *Constitution* and a squadron of American vessels set sail for the Mediterranean, with orders to blockade the port of Tripoli. Everything that could go wrong, did go wrong. While in hot pursuit of a Tripolitan ship, the thirty-six-gun frigate *Philadelphia* went aground on a reef just within the harbor. Captured by the pirates with all her crew, the American frigate was refloated by jubilant enemy sailors, who then began making her ready for action against her former owners.

By this time, the *Constitution* had arrived on the scene. Eagerly backed by seventy-four officers and men—all of whom volunteered for the hazardous duty—Lieutenant Stephen Decatur proposed a daring plan. Embarking in a native ketch they had captured, he and a dozen American sailors would stain their faces, dress like pirates, approach the anchor chain of the *Philadelphia*, and request permission to come aboard. Hidden below decks and among scattered trash aboard would be sixty uniformed naval fighting men, armed to the teeth, who would secure grappling hooks, climb up rope ladders, overwhelm the pirate crew, and retake the ship. Would Commodore Preble approve the plan?

He would—and did.

Shortly after dusk, next evening, the ketch slipped into the harbor of Tripoli and came alongside the *Philadelphia*, which lay anchored under the protection of the big guns of the shore forts. Securing a line to the warship's anchor chain, one of the American sailors sang out what he hoped was a reasonably accented request for permission to come aboard. Grudgingly, it was granted. Moments after the first of the American sailors swarmed up the ladders and landed on the deck, the alarm was sounded, the pirates tried to defend themselves, and a fierce, hand-to-hand battle with cutlasses, daggers, and pistols began.

It did not last long. Killed, tossed overboard, or jumping over the side of the ship to save themselves, the pirates were soon defeated. Lieutenant Stephen Decatur and his gallant band now controlled the ship. But with the shore batteries firing and neither time, tide, nor favorable wind to aid raising sail and maneuvering the *Philadelphia* out toward the open sea, the boarding party had no choice but to set fire to the ship, get back into the ketch, and return to the safety of the *Constitution*, which was lying out of reach of the shore forts' big guns.

There, they were greeted as heroes, for, even though a fine American fighting ship had been lost, the boarding party had made sure that the enemy could not use her.

"That was the beginning of the end for the Barbary Coast pirates," Thomas Warren said as he concluded his tale. "When the Bey of Algiers sued for peace, it was made on our terms. We've never paid tribute to a foreign nation again. Nor is it likely we ever will. Not even to England."

Grumpy-faced partner Duncan McDougall had exchanged strong words with the master of the *Tonquin* last night, Ben knew, because of Thorn's order that all cabin reading lamps be extinguished at eight p.m. in order to conserve whale oil and prevent the ship's lights from being seen by British patrol boats. Clearly, he disliked the American captain. But like many colonials, he hated the British, too. He looked dourly at Ben's father.

"Dinnae accuse me of approving the British practice of impressing American seamen, Mr. Warren, for we Scotch-Canadians are colonials oursel's. But I am curious about your Captain Thorn. Was he in the American Navy at the time of the Tripoli affair?"

"Aye. As a young midshipman."

"Was he in the party that boarded the *Philadelphia*?" Robert Stuart asked.

"So I've been told. He was right behind Lieutenant Stephen Decatur when the boarding party hit the deck, they say, a saber in one hand, a pistol in the other, and, for all I know, a dagger between his teeth."

"How old was he?"

"He enlisted as a midshipman a year earlier, when he was just the age of Ben here—sixteen. So he was seventeen years old when he fought with Lieutenant Decatur in the Battle of Tripoli." Gazing out across the sea at the *Constitution*, Thomas Warren shook his head. "He has many friends aboard yon warship, I imagine. Whatever his faults may be, a lack of courage is not among them."

From his talks with Robert Stuart, Gabriel Franchere, and Alexander Ross, who were close enough to his own age to share shipboard gossip with him, Ben knew that the Senior Partners were chafing under the restraints Captain Thorn was placing upon them.

"He keeps telling them he has written orders from Mr. Astor, saying they can't do this or that," Robert Stuart said peevishly. "If those orders are in writing, why doesn't he show them to us? Does Mr. Astor think he can control everything that happens during the two years we'll be out of touch with him by sealed orders kept in the strongbox of a pig-headed captain?"

Having no answer for what was obviously meant to be a rhetorical question, Ben gave none. But he was beginning to realize that this was going to be a long, difficult voyage for more reasons than adverse weather.

Dusk was at hand and the wind had died before the long boat was sighted returning to the *Tonquin*. Even though the four oarsmen and the coxswain conducted themselves just as smartly as they had done several hours ago, the appearance of Captain Jonathan Thorn had changed drastically. As the long boat pulled alongside, Ben saw the captain standing up in the bow, his cap set askew over his left ear, his tie undone, his coat unbuttoned, and no semblance of dignity in his bearing. As a matter of fact, he was so drunk that the nearest crew member had shipped his oars and risen to his knees, keeping a desperate hiplock on him in order to prevent him from falling overboard.

"Bless my soul!" David Stuart exclaimed. "He's loaded to the gills!"

"So he appears to be," Thomas Warren said quietly. "A nip too many with his old shipmates, I'll wager!"

Concluding the ribald ballad he was singing, Captain Thorn took another swallow out of the half-empty bottle of rum he was holding in his left hand, awkwardly saluted the quarter deck with his right hand, and shouted mushily:

"Ahoy the goddam ship! Cap'n requests permishun to come aboard!"

"Aye, sir, permission granted!" First Mate Fox answered smartly, returning the salute. Out of the side of his mouth, he muttered to Ben's father. "Help me get him aboard without mishap, Mr. Warren. Drunk though he is, he'll not forget an insult to his dignity."

Standing just as straight and saluting just as smartly, Ben's father murmured, "Never fear, Mr. Fox. I've handled many a drunk captain."

In a miracle of perfect timing, the long boat was raised and secured to the davits and the captain was brought aboard without accident. Once set down on deck, Thorn stood stiff-legged and tottering for a moment, then he blinked owlishly and said:

"Now hear this, Mr. Fox!"

"Aye, sir?"

"We sail under escort of the *Constitution* at dawn. She'll stay with us till we're well on our way. Should any goddam British warship come snoopin' around, my old shipmates in the U.S. Navy'll blow it out of the goddam water! D'ye understand what I'm saying?"

"Aye, sir, I do."

"An' you, Mr. Warren? D'ye understand how important the United States government thinks this voyage is to our country? D'ye understand that?"

"Aye, Captain Thorn. I certainly do."

"Good! Now, if you two gentlemen will be so kind, please escort me to my cabin. I've had a long, busy day."

3.

$\mathcal{K}$EPT BUSY ALOFT with the sails next morning, while the *Tonquin* took a southeasterly course before a stiff following wind, Ben Warren made a point of staying high in the rigging as the bustle and confusion on the deck below got straightened out. Most of the voyageurs were desperately seasick, he saw. Though First Mate Fox, Second Mate Mumford, and Third Mate Warren had their hands full making the undisciplined French-Canadians stow their personal baggage below decks and choose bunks in the dank, cramped, fo'c's'le crew quarters, these officers' problems were relatively mild compared to the bitter conflict going on between the Astor Company partners and Captain Jonathan Thorn. The gist of their argument, Ben gathered, was that the partners were insisting that the clerks and mechanics be treated as passengers while the captain stubbornly claimed that they were part of the crew.

"By God, this may not be a naval ship," Thorn declared crustily, "but I intend to run it like one. Which means I'll have no slackers or dead lumber aboard."

"These people have contracts with the Pacific Fur Company," Alexander McKay protested. "You can't force them to work like common sailors."

"The devil I can't! To you they may have special rank, Mr. McKay. But to me they're just sweepings you hired out of Montreal gutters and gave high-falutin' titles such as clerks and mechanics. Far as I'm concerned, they're grass-green sailors who's going to work their way or be tossed overboard."

"Ye'd not dare do such a thing!" Duncan McDougall exclaimed.

"The hell I wouldn't! This is *my* ship, Mr. McDougall, where *my* word is law! Aboard it, I'll do as I please!"

"That's an outrageous statement, sir!" Alexander McKay cried angrily. "Before we'll let you tell us what to do, my people will take strong measures to defend our rights as part owners of this enterprise."

His face several shades redder than usual and his head no doubt throbbing because of his overindulgence the day before, Captain Thorn appeared to be on the verge of an explosion. Shaking a balled fist under McKay's nose, he grunted in a tone so deadly that there was no question he meant exactly what he said:

"Now hear this, Mr. McKay! I swear I'll blow the brains out of any man who dares disobey any order I give aboard *my* ship. Put that in your long-stemmed Indian pipe and smoke it!"

Again, it was Senior Partner David Stuart who counciled caution, putting a hand on Alexander McKay's elbow and muttering something in Gaelic. Starting to turn on his heel and walk away, the captain stopped, wheeled around, and demanded: "What did you say?"

Observing the effect of David Stuart's remark in the strange tongue, Duncan McDougall laughed harshly, then added a crude Gaelic comment of his own. Since it was obviously meant as an insult, Captain Thorn seemed on the verge of demanding a translation. Thinking better of the impulse, he stalked up the ladder to the quarter deck, where he picked up a spyglass and trained it on the distant hulk of the *Constitution*, which was barely visible in the distance off the port beam.

"Mr. Fox!"

"Aye, sir?"

"The *Constitution* has raised a signal flag saying she's pulling away. Prepare to make a proper response."

"What shall I say?"

"Say we thank her for the escort and wish her well."

"How do I do that, sir? I'm not familiar with the navy's signal codes."

"Where have you spent your life, Mr. Fox?" Captain Thorn snorted contemptuously. "Alternately lower and raise the colors three times a quarter of the way down the mainmast—that's all you have to do."

"Aye, sir. Lower and raise the colors it is."

With all sails set and filled with wind, Ben Warren no longer had any excuse to stay aloft; still, he lingered a minute longer as he watched the American flag atop the mainmast of the *Tonquin* fall and rise three times in response to the signal from the distant warship, which was heeling away smartly now on the starboard tack and turning back to the north. A shiver of excitement mixed with dread rippled over the surface of his skin as he realized that from now on the *Tonquin* was on her own, with only her speed, her captain's sailing skills, and her not very substantial defensive abilities to protect her from being over-hauled and captured.

So long as the *Constitution* had been in sight, no British man-of-war would have dared come close to the *Tonquin*, for the United States had made it clear that any attempt by the British to board an Ameri-can merchant ship and demand that its sailors prove they had not de-serted from nor owed duty to the British Navy would be regarded as an act of war and would draw a proper response. But in the large ex-panse of the Atlantic Ocean between here and Cape Verde Island off the African coast, on down to the Falkland Islands off the coast of South America, around Cape Horn, and then north to the Sandwich Islands in the Pacific, the *Tonquin* would be alone and without protec-tion. If a British man-of-war hailed her in those waters, her only choice would be to surrender or fight. When that time came, the cru-cial decision would be made by a single man: Captain Jonathan Thorn.

Did the sealed orders given him by Mr. Astor cover that eventual-ity? Ben suspected they did. But until the crisis actually came, he guessed that the proud, patriotic captain would stubbornly refuse to reveal what his choice would be until the very moment he made it …

As the ship made its southeasting day after day before favoring winds, the weather grew balmy and pleasant, though there was no thaw in the chilly relationship between the Pacific Fur Company partners and Captain Thorn. The term "compromise" did not aptly describe the change which had taken place in that relationship, though the word "accommodation" could be applied. On the status of the voyageurs, clerks, and mechanics, for example, Captain Thorn remained inflexi-ble, insisting that they live in the cramped, stifling crew quarters under hatches before the mast, stand watches in turn with the rest of the ship's sailors, and accept the iron-handed discipline of himself and the ship's officers.

Of these, the reluctant sailors soon learned that First Mate

Ebenezer Fox was a kind-hearted, humane man; that Second Mate John Mumford was a pompous, stuffed shirt; and that Third Mate Thomas Warren knew more about merchant ship sailing techniques than anyone else aboard, though he was careful never to exceed his authority.

In the Astor party, Alexander McKay was nominal head of the shipboard partners, for he was a man with years of experience in dealing with the Indians, French-Canadian trappers, and voyageurs employed by the North West Company. Next in rank was dour-natured Duncan McDougall, who was not as well-liked or trusted as Alexander McKay, though his fierce manner and reputation for violent action demanded that he be respected.

David Stuart, the oldest of the Senior Partners, was mild-tempered and reasonable, while his nephew, Robert Stuart, who was also a full partner despite his youthful age of twenty-five, was brash, impulsive, and quick to take offense at any insult to his dignity. Scotsmen all, they spoke English with a thick, burred accent, often switching into Gaelic when Captain Thorn was within hearing distance for no other reason than that it irritated the captain, who suspected they were plotting against him in a language he could not understand.

Alexander Ross, who was Irish, and Gabriel Franchere, who was French, were in their early twenties and had begun the voyage as half-share partners, meaning that they had signed contracts to work five years for one hundred dollars and expenses annually, after which time they would be brought into the Pacific Fur Company as full partners entitled to share in the profits on an equal basis with the Senior Partners.

Following the example of his father, Ben was careful never to be caught talking to any of the Astor Company employees under circumstances that Captain Thorn might judge disloyal to him. But he could not help seeing and hearing events of the running feud between the partners and the captain.

For example, the partners had given in when Captain Thorn insisted that the rank and file of the Astor party live and work as common sailors. But after the first night's curfew of "lamps out" at eight p.m. to conserve whale oil and prevent the ship's being sighted by British patrols, sour-natured Duncan McDougall declared he'd burn the lamp in his cabin as late as he damn well pleased. When Captain

Thorn demanded he turn it out as ordered, McDougall replied that, like all Scots, his cabin was his castle, with no man powerful enough to tell him how to live in it.

"Try me, if ye dare, Captain Thorn," McDougall grunted morosely, "and I take oath I'll put *your* lights out!"

Backing off from enforcing the "lamps-out-at-eight" order on Duncan McDougall, Captain Thorn endured the indignity of seeing all the other partners burn their lamps as late as they pleased, too. In retaliation, when a spell of bad weather made the ship roll and toss so violently that the four Senior and two Junior Partners became as seasick as the voyageurs had been, the captain gave them no sympathy. Instead, he advised them to leave their stuffy cabins, come on deck, take some vigorous exercise in the fresh sea air, and soothe the heavings of their bellies by eating solid meals of ship's biscuit, boiled beans, and fat salt pork.

"Ye'll not get well lyin' in your foul-smellin' bunks sippin' weak tea and thin meat broth," he told them sarcastically. "Get out and about the deck, gentlemen! Behave like men—and ye'll start feelin' like human bein's again, I guarantee."

Bluntly rejecting the advice, the partners profanely replied that they'd get seasick when and where they damn well pleased, and they'd thank the captain to mind his own business.

To the bored and weary passengers, the prospect of a landfall at Cape Verde Island, where the casks of freshwater would be refilled, loomed in their minds like a dream of heaven. But a week's voyage short of the African coast, Captain Thorn suddenly changed his plans, gave the order to alter course from southeast to southwest, and set sail for the Falkland Islands, two months' travel away. When they heard about that decision, Alexander McKay and Duncan McDougall went storming angrily up to the quarter deck, though they took care not to cross to the starboard side.

"Don't you know we're low on freshwater?" Alexander McKay demanded.

"Aye, I know."

"Then why the sudden change in plans?"

"We're in dangerous waters, Mr. McKay. Around Cape Verde Island, British patrols will be thicker than barnacles on an old ship's bottom. With all the Tories I'm carrying, I can't risk being hailed and boarded."

"What are we going to do for water?"

"Being low on fresh water ain't the same thing as bein' out," the captain answered curtly. "By my reckoning, if we reduce the ration to a pint-and-a-half a day per man, we'll still have two months' supply. Which will be plenty to take us to the Falkland Islands, even if we get no rain along the way—as we usually do."

"Good Lord, Captain Thorn!" Duncan McDougall muttered, "we're only ten degrees north of the Equator. This is early October and the temperature is ninety-four degrees. Why, I myself sweat a pint-and-a-half of fluid by noon! What am I to do for water the rest of the day?"

"As I see it, you have two choices, Mr. McDougall. You can stop sweating—or go below decks and suck bilgewater. Now get off my quarter deck and let me sail my ship."

Between the time the ship changed course on October 10 and the day it sighted the Falkland Islands December 7, the *Tonquin* sailed from 10 degrees north to 53 degrees south across as empty a stretch of ocean as existed in this part of the world. On a happier ship, a ceremony with a lot of foolishness by King Neptune and his court would have initiated the sailors and passengers crossing the Equator for the first time into the ancient and honorable order of mossybacks; but both the need to be alert for hostile sails and the friction between the Astor people and Captain Thorn kept the horseplay at a minimum. Even so, Ben and a number of first-timers got their heads shaved, were anointed by King Neptune, and were declared members of the club.

Twice during the two months spent southwesting, other ships were sighted in the distance, but their identities were unknown. The first vessel appeared to be a merchant ship quite a bit larger than the *Tonquin*, which, soon after being seen bow-on, sheared away and fled from the smaller American ship as precipitously as the *Tonquin* avoided it. The second, seen a week later, had the lines of a man-of-war and was thought to be Portuguese, British, or French. When she altered course to sail in a parallel direction, indicating either curiosity or a desire to close and board, Captain Thorn ordered every stitch of canvas set, altering course twenty degrees to port to run directly with the wind at the *Tonquin*'s best speed. At the same time, the gunports were cleared and the crew under Armorer Stephen Weeks prepared for action.

Though the two ships sailed in sight of each other from noon till an hour before sunset, with the stranger getting no nearer, a violent rain-squall dropped a blanket of clouds between the two vessels from then until well past dark. When the next day dawned clear, the stranger was gone—which was good news for the *Tonquin*, Thomas Warren told Ben, for she'd not have been able to fend off a well-armed attacker for long.

"If a man-of-war did order us to lay to, do you think Captain Thorn would obey or fight?" Ben asked his father.

"God knows. He's a proud, stubborn man."

"The partners call him pig-headed."

"Aye, he's that, too. But whatever he chooses to do, our duty is clear, lad. We obey *him*."

Situated in a cold, gray sea two hundred miles off the east coast of South America just north of the Strait of Magellan, the Falklands were a bleak, forbidding place. Steep mountains of gray and rust-red rock rose sheer over shorelines with few safe anchorages. No trees or people lived on the Falklands, Ben's father said, though from time to time parties from passing ships seeking freshwater or game spent a few days in tents or shacks made of driftwood or whalebone as they foraged on the islands, whose only decent harbor had been named Port Egmont Bay. Though Third Mate Warren was aware of that fact, Captain Thorn apparently was not, for his first landfall was on the far side of the islands, where there was neither a decent anchorage nor a source of freshwater. Disgusted at the failure to find water, Thorn called the shore party back aboard, beat out to sea, and spent three days circling the islands until finally anchoring in Egmont Bay.

"Why didn't you tell the captain that the best anchorage and freshwater are here?" Ben asked his father.

"Because he didn't ask me."

"But you'd been here before and he hadn't. You knew and he didn't. You could have saved him three wasted days."

"There's a shipboard rule you'll learn to live by, lad. Never show you know more than your captain does—even if you do."

Back in Gloucester at this time of year, Ben recalled, winter would be at hand, but here at fifty-three degrees south latitude these were the first days of spring. Treeless and barren though the sand dunes above tide level appeared to be, a bubbling freshwater spring three hundred yards inshore, a large expanse of gray saltmarsh grasses and pale green shrubs, large flocks of ducks and geese, a number of seal, and a colony of pompous-looking king penguins gave the ship-weary passengers three delightful days of exploring, hunting, and frolicking ashore.

Assigned to the crew working under the direction of Second Mate Mumford and the ship's carpenter, John Weeks, to clean, fill, and seal the freshwater casks, Ben was happy to join the party camped in tents on a hummock of sand a quarter of a mile from the beach. Each day, Duncan McDougall and David Stuart, who were avid hunters, roamed over the lowlands killing ducks, geese, seal, and—just once, a penguin—which the two voyageurs they took along as bearers cleaned and carried back to camp. After the penguin proved to be too tough and stringy to eat, they concentrated on more edible game.

Captain Thorn came ashore only once, Ben noticed, and, when he did, took offense at what he regarded as a deliberately contrived trick aimed at destroying his dignity. What happened was that an Astor Company clerk named Thomas Farnham caught a large gray goose, which he tied to a rock near the landing place, thinking he and his hunter friends would have some sport with it later on. Not aware of this, Captain Thorn saw what he thought was a loose goose as he disembarked from the whale boat that had brought him ashore, excitedly ran back to the boat, seized a shotgun, and fired at the goose from a distance of twenty feet. Not being much of a shot, he missed it the first time, hurriedly reloaded, and fired again.

This time he at least wounded it, for the goose started flapping around on the ground with a loud squawking, the sound of which brought all the men in camp running from every direction. Getting there just in time to see the flustered captain grabbing the tethered, wounded goose, and getting covered with blood, feathers, and embarrassment, all the members of the shore party hooted with laughter. Dropping the goose as if it were hot, Captain Thorn stalked down to the whale boat, got aboard, and had himself rowed back out to the ship, never setting foot ashore again.

Whether it was the captain's foul mood or Duncan McDougall's misunderstanding of what he was told that led to the confusion as to when the ship would sail, Ben never knew. With the freshwater casks filled, sealed, and taken aboard in the whale boat on the afternoon of December 10, McDougall spent the night aboard the *Tonquin*. When he came ashore in the pinnace, next morning, he told the people camped there that Captain Thorn would not sail until the morning of the 12th; therefore, the nine persons now ashore did not need to come aboard until the night of the 11th. Glad to have a day with little to do ashore, Ben spent the morning exploring with Alexander McKay and several other Astor party members, while David Stuart, Duncan McDougall, and their two voyageur bearers went for a last hunt a mile or so inland.

Disturbed by a grave-marker he had found the day before, Ben guided Mr. McKay and the others to the site, showed them the grave-marker, then asked permission to tidy up the site.

"This is such a lonely place to die and be buried," he said wistfully to McKay. "Can't we do something to show we care?"

"Aye, lad, we'll do the dead one last kindness." Mr. McKay answered gently. Peering down at the bleached wooden marker, he shook his head. "Your eyes are sharper than mine, boy. Can you tell me what the inscription says?"

Stooping, Ben read the inscription, which proclaimed:

> *William Stevens, aged twenty-two years, killed by a fall from a rock on the 21st of September 1794.*

> *Benjamin Peak, died of smallpox on the 5th of January 1803, ship* Elenora,

> *Captain Edmund Cole, Providence, Rhode Island.*

Straightening up, Ben said quietly, "That's my name, sir, and my part of the country. It seems only decent I tidy up the grave."

"Aye, lad—and we'll help you. Mayhap, when you write home, you can tell your namesake's people in Providence, Rhode Island, what you've done, for whatever solace that may be to the relatives."

By the time they finished recarving the names on the board and setting a cross over the grave site, it was two o'clock in the afternoon. Not knowing what faith the deceased had been, Mr. McKay said that bared heads and a few moments of silence would be all the show of respect they could or should offer. As they stood in this bleak spot half a world away from home, Ben heard the distant boom of a cannon. Turning, he and the other men stared down the hill at Port Egmont Bay, where the *Tonquin* lay at anchor.

"*Mon Dieu!*" one of the voyageurs exclaimed. "They're calling us back to the ship."

"So they are," Mr. McKay said calmly. "But we've plenty of daylight left before we have to go aboard."

Walking leisurely down the hill to the camp, from which David Stuart, Duncan McDougall, and their two game-carriers were still absent, the members of the party took down the tents, packed up the tools, cooking utensils, and gear they had used ashore, and carried it down to where the pinnace was pulled up on the shore. Barely twenty feet long, the boat was going to be crowded, Ben thought, for it would be carrying nine men, their camping gear, and all the game killed during the past couple of days by the hunting party—which included a 150 pound seal.

From the *Tonquin*, another plume of white smoke blossomed from a port-side gunport, followed by another boom of a cannon.

"Run up to the top of yon dune, lad," Mr. McKay told Ben. "See if you can spy the hunters and hurry them along. Captain Thorn seems anxious to get us aboard."

Scampering over the soft, crusted sand to the crest of the dune, Ben saw the missing hunters a quarter-mile away, headed in this direction. He waved to them in a beckoning gesture meant to speed them along. Whether it did or not, he could not tell, for his attention was suddenly distracted by a shout from the direction of the beach.

"The ship's off!"

Indeed, that incredible thing was happening, for the anchor had been raised, sails hoisted, and the *Tonquin* was underway. Frantically, the shore party prepared to follow. It took half an hour for the hunting party to arrive and all the gear, game, and people to be stowed in the pinnace. Meanwhile, the *Tonquin* was moving briskly out of the bay under full sail, until by the time the pinnace was launched it was at least three miles away.

"He can't be leaving us!" David Stuart cried. "He wouldn't dare!"

"He'll do whatever he wants to do, that villain will!" Duncan McDougall muttered harshly. "Row, lads, row! Put your backs and guts in it!"

Of the nine people aboard, three were Senior Partners with little experience in rowing a boat; four were voyageurs, who were more familiar with paddles, which meant that Ben Warren and another Ordinary Seaman named Edward Aymes were the only sailors aboard able to manipulate the four sets of oars with any degree of skill. Being strong-backed and familiar with canoes, two of the voyageurs will-

27

ingly picked up the other two pairs of oars and quickly caught the rhythm of it, making the small boat literally skim along over the water. But even after the dead seal was pushed overboard—as Mr. McKay soon insisted be done—the gap between the pinnace and the ship continued to grow.

As the afternoon wore on, the wind freshened, the seas grew rougher, and the overloaded boat began to take on water. Grimly putting all his breath and energy into pulling at the oars, as Aymes was doing, Ben winced at the growing tenderness of the palms of his hands, which were not used to this kind of labor and starting to blister. In a confused babble of French and Gaelic, a voyageur not engaged in rowing found the bailer and began tossing water over the side, only to be sworn at by Mr. McDougall, who accused him of tossing more water back into the boat than he was throwing out. Snatching the bailer out of the voyageur's hand, McDougall started doing the bailing himself—with even worse results. Swearing at him, the voyageur tried to retrieve the bailer, McDougall jerked it away, and, as they struggled for its possession, the bailing bucket fell overboard.

Picking up a loose oar, another voyageur attempted to spear the bailer as it floated past the boat. David Stuart tried to help him, stepped on the oar, and broke it squarely in two. Watching the bailer and the oar float away, the two men cursed both the lost tools and each other in two languages.

With the wind rising, the seas running higher, and the ship they were pursuing well out of the sheltered harbor now, there was nothing the men in the small boat could do but keep rowing in hopes that the wind would change and give them a chance to catch up or that Captain Thorn would have a change of heart, lay to, and wait for them. Finally, after six hours of desperate pursuit and with darkness beginning to fall, one of the voyageurs cried:

"*Voila!* The ship! She is laying to!"

Indeed, the *Tonquin* had lowered sail, turned back, and now lay waiting in the growing dusk for the small boat to come alongside. Whatever sort of revenge Captain Thorn had intended to take on the shore party for the wound inflicted on his dignity by the tethered goose incident, he apparently had decided that the lesson had gone far enough. Even so, when the pinnace finally pulled into the lee of the ship, making contact with the violently heaving hull and getting the small boat's passengers aboard without mishap was a touchy business requiring all the skill, timing, and luck that the two sailors and the voyageurs could muster to achieve the transfer without mishap.

As the first man to be deposited safely aboard the *Tonquin*, David Stuart was greeted by his nephew Robert with a bear-hug embrace and a fervent exclamation:

"Thank God, you're safe, Uncle David!"

"Weel, it's nae credit to Captain Thorn that I am! Where is the villain?"

"In his cabin—sulking."

"Sulking, is he?" Duncan McDougall grunted indignantly. "After the game he played with us, he crawls into his cabin and sulks!"

"It was nae a game, Mr. McDougall. He had every intention of leaving your whole party on the Falklands. To die, for all he cared. But I persuaded him to change his mind."

"How?" Alexander McKay asked quietly.

"With sweet reason—and a loaded pistol. I backed him to the starboard side of the quarter deck, put my pistol to his head, and told him if he didn't lay to he was a dead man."

The last of the party to leave the boat, Ben Warren was being given a hand by his father as Robert Stuart answered Mr. McKay's question. Though Ben's feet were now solidly on the deck of the *Tonquin* and he needed no more support, Third Mate Thomas Warren still was tightly clasping his right hand. Even in the fading light, Ben could see that his father's mouth was compressed into a straight line, and that his lean, tanned, weathered face was several shades lighter than usual.

"So that's what happened!"

"Aye, lad," Thomas Warren murmured. "Young Robert Stuart threatened to kill the captain if he didn't lay to. But between you, me, and the Good Lord who saved me from an act of mutiny, if he hadn't put a pistol to the captain's head, I would have done it myself. I'll not lose the last son I have to a madman like Captain Thorn."

4.

$\mathcal{T}$HOUGH THE PARTNERS had not been permitted to read the sealed orders from Mr. Astor upon which Captain Jonathan Thorn claimed all his actions were based, the captain made no secret of the fact that he was reporting every detail of what he regarded as their misbehavior to the wealthy merchant in New York. This took the form of a running letter, which he dictated as time allowed, to the ship's clerk, James Lewis. The report could not be sent, of course, until the *Tonquin* reached the Sandwich Islands, where it would be entrusted only to an American vessel bound for New York.

Since the Sandwich Islands were still two months away, with any American vessel encountered there probably going on around the world by way of China, it would be at least a year before Mr. Astor received the report. Another year would pass before the partners could receive whatever instructions he might choose to give them. By then, the trading post at the mouth of the Columbia would have been established, with the partners as completely in control of their destiny on land as Captain Thorn judged himself to be aboard the *Tonquin* at sea.

Still, he would have made his report and his point, for whatever *that* was worth.

Leaving the door to his cabin open as he dictated to Clerk Lewis in a loud voice, Captain Thorn made sure every person within earshot heard what he was reporting to Mr. Astor. Shortly after the voyage began, he had complained about the "lubberly" character of the men the partners had hired and had expressed great concern for the sanctity of Mr. Astor's property, which he considered to be at the mercy of "a most heterogeneous and wasteful crew."

As to the employees, he pronounced them mere pretenders, "not one of whom had ever been among the Indians, nor farther northwest than Montreal, nor of a higher rank than barkeeper of a tavern or marker of a billiard-table, excepting one, who had been a school-master, and as foolish a pedant as ever lived." This last reference apparently was to James Lewis, the very clerk to whom Captain Thorn was dictating the report.

Even after what had happenened yesterday, the partners found it difficult to believe that the captain really had intended to leave the shore party marooned on the Falkland Islands. But in his dictation to Clerk Lewis, he made it crystal clear that was exactly what he had meant to do, for he declared to Mr. Astor:

> Had the wind unfortunately not hauled ahead soon after leaving the harbor's mouth, I should positively have left them; and, indeed, I cannot but think it an unfortunate circumstance for you that it so happened, for the first loss in this instance would, in my opinion, have proved the best, as they seem to have no idea of the value of property, nor any apparent regard for your interest, although interwoven with their own.

Curiously enough, he made no mention of the fact that young Robert Stuart had been holding a pistol to his head at the moment "the wind hauled ahead." But aboard the *Tonquin*, everyone knew the truth and was prepared to tell it as soon as the ship reached port.

"Just make sure you're not one of the gossips, lad," Thomas Warren quietly warned his son. "It's not our quarrel or concern."

What did concern his father, Ben knew, was the imminent passage around Cape Horn, for of all the officers aboard the ship he had faced its terrors more often than anyone else, having logged three west-to-east passages and four attempts from the other direction, on the last of which the *Cotton Mather* had foundered. Though Thomas Warren still did not like to talk about the disaster that had cost him his captain's license, his ship, his wife, and three of his sons, First Mate Ebenezer Fox, who knew several of the survivors and had discussed the tragedy with a number of knowledgeable mariners, told Ben that his father had in no way been responsible for the loss of the ship.

"She's a ship's graveyard, the Horn is, and no man alive can beat her when the weather turns against him. What happened to your father, lad, was a combination of wind and seas so fierce there was nothing he could do to whip them. Even runnin' before the wind as fast as her sails would take her, the *Cotton Mather* could not stay ahead of the monstrous followin' seas. So she got 'pooped.'"

"That's a term I've never heard before, sir. What does it mean?"

"Why, lad, when huge followin' seas overtake a ship and dump such a big load of water on her poop deck that she can neither dump it nor carry it, her bow fails to rise to the next sea. Because she's carryin' such an unbearable weight of water, she's literally driven under to her doom. Or pooped, as we say."

"Does it happen often?"

"Only where winds top a hundred knots and waves crest over a hundred feet—which they now and then do in the China Sea, the Indian Ocean, and below Cape Horn. When them things happen together, all a seafarin' man can do is run before the wind and seas and pray."

According to Gabriel Franchere, who was keeping a detailed journal and sharing the information he was recording with Ben, a SSW course was set upon leaving the Falkland Islands. On December 14 at 54 degrees South Latitude, the high mountains of Tierra del Fuego came in sight and remained visible until evening, when the weather thickened and the view was obscured. A furious storm raged a few days later, driving the ship south to 56 degrees, forty-five miles off Cape Horn. A dead calm followed, during which an onshore current carried the *Tonquin* within fifteen miles of the Cape itself. Gazing at the rugged, bleak rocks as the ship drifted slowly toward them, Ben's father said:

"Cape Horn's a place where the devil made the biggest mess he could. Even the names given it by early-day navigators show how much they feared it: Desolate Bay, Deceit Island, Mistaken Cape, Fury Harbor, Hately Bay, Dislocation Harbor."

"Franchere says some ships try to sail west to the Pacific through the Straits of Magellan, instead of going around Cape Horn. Is that route safer?"

"Only when wind, current, and weather are favorable. If you make one mistake in the Strait, your ship is doomed. Sailing further south around the Cape, you've at least got some sea room for maneuvering. There, you can turn and run before a storm, with water instead of rocks under your keel if your luck turns bad. Either way you go, you usually wish you'd gone the other."

Helped by an offshore breeze, the *Tonquin* beat out to sea and

maintained a southerly course until it was well clear of the tip of South
America. At this point, Franchere told Ben, the ship had sailed 9,165
miles from New York and had reached Latitude 58 degrees, 16 minutes South.

Though this was midsummer in the Southern Hemisphere and the days were as long as they were back in Gloucester on June 21, floating icebergs now became a hazard to be watched for and the air during the brief nights was bitterly cold. Noting that the thermometer registered four degrees below zero on December 23, Gabriel Franchere said facetiously:

"Yet they call this Tierra del Fuego—Land of Fire! Where do you suppose the natives go to get warm when winter comes in July?"

According to veteran seamen who had made the Cape Horn passage before, the *Tonquin*'s journey was relatively easy and brief this time compared to what it might have been. As a Christmas Day present, the contrary winds changed, swinging around to the south, permitting the *Tonquin* to raise sail and make her westing until well past the Horn, swinging north then before cold but favorable winds, until by January 1, 1811, she recorded her position at 40 degrees South Latitude. At long last, she was in the Pacific Ocean.

To Ben Warren, the six weeks it took the ship to sail northwest to the Sandwich Islands were a sailor's dream of what life at sea should be. In this upside-down world south of the Equator, the midsummer days were so long that the sun seemed barely to set before it rose again, the increasingly warm southeast trade winds drove the *Tonquin* briskly along on her course, and it was a pleasure just to be alive. As his father had advised him, he carried no tales regarding either side of the quarrel between Captain Thorn and the Astor people, though he could not help observing that friction still existed between the two parties.

In his running report to Mr. Astor, the captain began to hint at a new development to the plot they were concocting against him. He had every reason to believe, he dictated to Clerk Lewis, that the Canadians were secretly disloyal to their employer; that if, when they reached the Sandwich Islands, they heard news that England and the United States had gone to war, they would foster a mutiny, seize the ship, put the American captain and crew ashore, and use the stores

Mr. Astor had provided to establish a trading post at the mouth of the Columbia under the British flag. Knowing that his father had a fair understanding of Gaelic, Ben asked him if this were true.

"Not from what I've heard of their talk," Thomas Warren answered with a quiet chuckle. "The worst they've said is that the captain is pig-headed, vain, and stupid. I'll not give you the Gaelic words they used, for you've no need of them."

Running under a full spread of sail before a brisk wind on an early February day, the ship and crew experienced an hour of intense excitement when the twelve-year-old cabin boy, Guilleaume Perrault, attempted to climb to the top of the mainmast and fell overboard. Fortunately for him, the ship was quartering before the wind, with her lee rail canted so far over that it was almost awash. As a consequence, the boy fell into the sea rather than onto the deck, where he surely would have been killed outright. Even so, his chances for survival seemed slim, for, though the cry "Man overboard!" was immediately made, with the helmsman putting the ship about and the people on deck throwing everything loose that would float over the side in hopes the boy would catch onto something and stay above the surface until he could be rescued, this was a big ocean with high seas running. The chances of finding the lost boy seemed very poor.

But after an hour's search, he was found, his limp body draped over a door ripped off its hinges and thrown overboard, which he had seized and clung to tenaciously, though he now was unconscious and showed no signs of life. Brought aboard, he was rolled over a barrel, pummeled, and pumped, until finally to everyone's surprise he began to gasp and sputter and breathe again. Two days' rest brought him a complete recovery, after which he took a solemn vow never again to climb any higher than he could go while still keeping one foot firmly in contact with the deck.

Making landfall at Oahu off the Sandwich Islands February 15, 1811, the *Tonquin* dropped anchor in the beautiful, mountain-surrounded harbor. During a two weeks' stay, the freshwater casks were refilled; fifty hogs, two dozen sheep, two roosters, a number of laying hens, and a large supply of sugarcane stalks with which to feed them were purchased and brought aboard. In addition, twenty "Kanakas," as the Hawaiian natives were called, were hired on three-year contracts to work as sailors aboard the ship and as laborers ashore when the trading post was built at the mouth of the Columbia.

Suspiciously watching the handsome, laughing, brown-skinned native men and the beautiful, smiling, bare-breasted native women as they circled the ship in their canoes, swam, dove, and cavorted like fish in the warm water, Captain Jonathan Thorn found it impolitic to deny access to the deck to the native chief, King Kamehameha, and his consorts, or to restrict shore leave to the ship's sailors. This was a nation ruled by an absolute monarch, Senior Partner Alexander McKay warned the captain, whom the master of a foreign ship dared not insult by violating local rules of hospitality.

"Make no mistake, lad," Thomas Warren told his son, "King Kamehameha has more power in these islands than King George has in England. The person who violates one of his taboos is sure to lose his head."

"What's a 'taboo'?"

"An unwritten law that decrees a certain thing must not be touched, said, or done on pain of death. In some cases, there are places not to be walked on or even looked at because of the king's taboo."

"His Majesty certainly looks harmless enough—so fat, jolly, and happy."

"Why shouldn't he be jolly and happy when he lives in the world's finest climate, can have as many wives as he wants, and needs only express a wish to have it granted?"

"That's an odd name—'Sandwich Islands.' Where did it come from?"

"The British explorer, Captain James Cook, named the islands for the Earl of Sandwich when he discovered them back in 1778. But today, they're usually called the Hawaiian Islands."

"Didn't the natives kill Captain Cook a year or two after he discovered the islands?"

"Aye, that they did. Cooked and ate him, too."

"You mean, they're cannibals?" Ben said in horror.

"I'm told they used to be, lad, though I don't think Kamehameha eats foreigners today. As a matter of fact, his chief adviser is said to be a British sea captain who came ashore ten years ago and liked the Islands so well he's made them his home ever since. His name, I'm told, is Reginald Barker."

"If the United States and Great Britain go to war, will he try to persuade King Kamehameha to favor England?"

"From what I've heard about Captain Barker," Thomas Warren

answered, shaking his head, "he'll advise the king to play one nation against the other, getting the most trade from each as his price for staying neutral. It was the captain's scheming that helped Kame-hameha end centuries of warfare among the petty chiefs in the outer islands, bringing them all under the king's control. As a reward, I've been told, Reginald Barker was given the king's oldest daughter as a wife, a palace of his own, and the title 'Most Exalted Minister to His Royal Highness' or some such name."

Going ashore for the better part of a day with the young Irish half-share-partner, Alexander Ross, Ben got a close-up view of how the natives lived. Each morai—as the villages were called—was composed of several miserable-looking huts. Passing by all the smaller ones, they finally reached the king's morai, which Ross said was supposed to be the grandest one of the place. It consisted of five low, gloomy, pestiferous houses, huddled close together. Alongside the principal one stood an image made of wood, resembling a pillar, about twenty-eight feet high, in the shape of a human figure, cut and carved with various devices. The large, rather crude sculptured head on its top appeared to be the likeness of a human face, topped by what Ben judged to be a black cowl.

Hearing that King Kamehameha's eldest son, Tatooirah, had been exiled to this morai in disgrace for having gotten drunk and talked back to his father, Alexander Ross thought it would be amusing to pay a visit to the prince, slip him a pint of rum, and pick up some court gossip. But half a dozen paces outside the border of the morai, a pair of husky, mean-looking natives armed with long-blade spears blocked the way, grunting:

"*Taboo! Taboo! Taboo!*"

"What d'ye suppose that means?" Ross said with a crooked grin, having already taken a nip or two out of the rum bottle.

"It means we better not go any further," Ben answered nervously, for he had not touched the rum. "This ground is tabooed by the king's orders. If we trespass on it, we may lose our heads."

"Well, it certainly smells bad enough. Just look at all that awful stuff lying around."

Counting the bodies of four dogs, two hogs, five cats, and a number of other carcasses too decomposed to be identified, as well as a very ripe collection of rotting fruits and vegetables, Ben supposed the highly odiferous materials had been placed there as some sort of sacrifice or penance which was part of Prince Tatooirah's punishment.

36

Whatever their purpose, neither he nor Ross saw any reason for risking Kamehameha's wrath by visiting his out-of-favor son.

Shortly after Ben Warren and Alexander Ross returned to the ship in late afternoon a tremendous offshore gale forced the *Tonquin* to slip her cable and move out to sea rather than risk being driven aground in shallow water. Because of the large number of hogs, sheep, and chickens confined in temporary pens built on the poop deck, working the ship was a messy, smelly business for the sailors, in which only the happy-go-lucky Kanakas, who were used to such things, found anything to laugh about. Staying high, dry, and free of slimy manure and odor on his privileged strip of quarter deck, Captain Thorn indicated from the number of times he removed his handkerchief from his sleeve, held it to his nose, and sniffed disdainfully that it was only because of Mr. Astor's orders authorizing the purchase and transport of the animals to the new trading post that he endured having the pristine, hoylstoned deck of his ship turned into a stinking pigsty.

With the storm abating, the *Tonquin* moved back into the harbor the morning of February 27, where the crew and shore party finished loading the sugarcane stalks, freshwater casks, and other supplies, all of which were brought out to the ship by native canoes. Sending two of the ship's boats to the beach late in the evening to pick up sailors ending their shore leave, Second Mate John Mumford found three sailors missing when the time came to return to the ship. As Mumford came aboard, Captain Thorn called down from the quarter deck:

"Three men are missing, Mr. Mumford. Who are they?"

"Seamen Adam Fisher, Peter Vershel, and Edward Aymes, sir."

"Log their names for proper punishment. Ten lashes on bare backs, then into the brig in irons on bread and water until the ship sails."

"Aye, sir."

Hearing a hail from the direction of the beach, Second Mate Mumford turned, saw two of the sailors piling hastily into a native canoe, waved up at the captain, and called, "Two of the men are coming now, sir. They barely missed our boat and are being brought out in a native canoe."

"They're late just the same. Carry out the punishment."

"But, sir! Only five minutes—"

"You're insubordinate, Mr. Mumford. It's the brig in irons for you, too."

Standing beside Second Mate Mumford at the rail, Ben Warren saw the man's face turn pale and his lower lip tremble. Until now, Ben had not liked John Mumford, who seemed pompous and arrogant. But his quick defense of the two tardy sailors and the captain's harsh punishment of him for it made Ben suddenly sympathetic to the man, who he felt deserved better treatment. Impulsively, Ben started to reach out and pat Mumford on the shoulder, only to be restrained by his father's iron grip on his forearm.

"Belay that, lad! It's not your affair."

"But, father, it's such a rotten thing for the captain to do!"

"Keep your mouth shut, son, or you'll get the brig too."

Aware of the fact that his father was right, but resenting him for it, Ben turned away and stared stonily out across the darkening harbor as Second Mate Mumford was taken below decks to be placed in irons. The two tardy sailors, Adam Fisher and Peter Vershel, came aboard. As soon as their feet touched the deck, they were seized, stripped to the waist, and shoved toward the mainmast, where their arms were raised and their wrists lashed above their heads.

As the ten lashes were administered by the husky bosun, John Anderson, Captain Thorn watched closely from the quarter deck to make sure the blows fell smartly. Wincing inwardly at each stroke of the whip, Ben stood frozen, trying to control his anger. Aboard ship, a captain had a right to administer discipline; Ben did not need a lecture from his father to make him accept that. But should not the discipline be tempered by justice?

Beside him, Robert Stuart, Alexander Ross, and Gabriel Franchere made no effort to conceal their contempt for Captain Thorn, expressing their displeasure in three languages.

"The bloody bastard!" Ross exclaimed. "You should have shot him, Robert, when you had the chance!"

"I wish I had!" Robert Stuart muttered. "Well, a few weeks more and we'll be rid of the monster."

The punishment given the two sailors that evening paled in comparison to the physical abuse meted out by Captain Thorn next morning when the last missing seaman, Edward Aymes, came out to the *Tonquin* shortly after dawn in a large native canoe loaded with sugarcane stalks. A small-statured, thin, wizened man with a strong Cockney accent, he stood up in the bow of the canoe as two natives were securing it to the side of the ship, cupped his hands around his mouth, and shouted:

"Ahoy, the ship! Can I be 'avin' a word with First Mate Fox?"

Coming to the rail, Ebenezer Fox called down sternly: "You were due aboard before dark yesterday, Aymes. What have you got to say for yourself?"

"Only that I'm sorry, sir. I was only fifteen minutes late gettin' down to the beach. By then, both the shore party boats and the native canoe that brought Fisher and Vershel out to the ship were gone. The tide was turnin', sir, an' try as I might, I could not hire a native canoe to bring me out. That's God's truth, sir! These native blighters 'ave no sense of time. Not one of 'em would lift a paddle for me till now. Gor' Blimey, if they would! So I had to wait—"

"You're a deserter, Aymes!" Captain Thorn shouted from the quarter deck. "You meant to jump ship!"

"Oh, no, Captain! I swear I never meant to do that!"

"You're a liar, Aymes! You're scum! You deserve to be left on the beach to rot like a piece of garbage!"

"But, sir—!"

Coming down from the quarter deck to the side of the ship up whose rope ladder Seaman Aymes was starting to climb, Captain Thorn shouted angrily at First Mate Fox:

"Don't let him come aboard, Mr. Fox! If he tries to climb up that ladder, take a belaying pin and knock him off!"

"Aye, sir."

"Please, Captain, give me another chance! If you'll just take me aboard, you can punish me any way you like—"

"Punish, you say?" Captain Thorn roared, his face turning bright red and his eyes flashing fire. "I'll show you what punish means when I'm in command!"

To the astonishment of Ben Warren, his father, the ship's crew, and the Astor people, Captain Jonathan Thorn scrambled down the rope ladder and stood face to face with Seaman Edward Aymes in the bow of the sugarcane-laden boat. As Aymes cringed before him, the captain picked up a heavy stalk of cane as thick as his wrist, raised it high, then brought it down on the sailor's head with all his strength. Falling to his knees, Aymes groveled and pled for mercy. But Captain Thorn had gone completely berserk, bringing the stalk of sugarcane down time and again on the sailor's shoulders, upper arms, and head until he was at last beaten unconscious. Straightening then, the captain gave Aymes a contemptuous kick in the ribs, while the two natives stared at him with open-mouthed amazement. Thorn ordered:

39

"Throw the bastard overboard!"

Gazing first at Captain Thorn, then at each other, the pair of brown-skinned Hawaiians shook their heads uncomprehendingly.

"Wassamatta *paakiki malihini?*"

"Why crazy man captain say toss *haole sailor in kai?*"

"Don't you understand English, you goddam niggers? Throw him over the side! Then unload your goddam sugarcane and get clear of my ship!"

Reluctantly obeying the captain's gestures, the two natives picked up the still unconscious man, called out a request to other Hawaiians who were paddling their smaller canoes a short distance away, then tossed the unresisting body into the sea. Climbing back up the ladder by then, Captain Thorn did not notice that moments after Aymes disappeared under the surface of the water, two natives dove out of their boat, came up supporting his body, loaded him into the boat, and rowed him in the direction of the beach. From his movements, it appeared that he had regained consciousness.

"As God is my witness!" Duncan McDougall muttered harshly, "the man is stark, raving mad! He ought to be judged insane and locked up!"

"It's right ye are, Laird McDougall," David Stuart said bleakly. "But where's the court and who's the judge that will try him?"

Neither court nor judge could be found in this port, Thomas Warren told his son, for this was a sovereign nation in which King Kamehameha's whim was law. Whether the sailor was a deserter from or abandoned by the *Tonquin* did not matter an iota to this absolute monarch, who controlled the life of every person in the Islands.

"What will happen to Aymes?" Ben asked his father.

"He won't starve or lack for shelter," Third Mate Warren said, shaking his head. "The natives in these islands are the most hospitable people in the world. In fact, he may like it so well here, he'll decide to stay in Hawaii for the rest of his life."

"But he's a member of the *Tonquin*'s crew, sir. Captain Thorn has no right to abandon him half a world away from his home. According to fo'c's'le talk I've heard, the Seamen's Guild rules give all sailors certain rights—"

"The law of the sea is not made in the fo'c's'le, lad, nor do Seamen's Guild rules matter a tinker's dam to a man like Captain Jonathan Thorn. Aboard his ship, law begins and ends with him—with no appeals allowed. Don't you ever forget that."

By late afternoon, all the cargo had been brought aboard, the relatives of the Kanaka sailors who had signed on for a three-year stint of employment with the Astor Company had embraced their loved ones with a mixture of laughter and tears, and the last of them had dropped into the canoes circling the ship as she weighed anchor and made preparations to leave the port. Rowed out from the beach by a native in a small canoe, Sailor Edward Aymes made one final appeal to be taken back aboard.

"Please, Captain Thorn, don't leave me in this God-forsaken, heathen land! Punish me as you will! But in the good Lord's mercy, take me aboard!"

Standing high on the starboard side of the quarter deck, Captain Thorn did not even bother to glance down at the sailor, deliberately turning his back to the bow of the ship, near which the canoe was being held against the ebbing tide. Getting no response from the captain, Aymes appealed to First Mate Fox, who stood on the port side of the lower deck just above the small canoe.

"I beg you, sir—"

"Mr. Fox!" Captain Thorn shouted, without turning around.

"Aye, sir?"

"Tell that piece of stinkin' Liverpool scum that if he ever sets foot on the deck of my ship again, I'll kill him! Tell him that!"

"Aye, sir."

Standing a few feet away from the First Mate, Ben saw Fox turn and gaze down at Sailor Aymes, an unspoken sympathy in his eyes. He said quietly, "You heard what the captain said, Aymes?"

"Aye, I did, sir," Aymes answered humbly. "I won't try to come aboard, where I ain't wanted. But the least he could do is give me my clothes and protection papers. He's got to do that, sir. It's in the Seamen's Guild rules."

According to the fo'c's'le talk Ben had heard, merchant ship sailors of the United States, England, and most European countries belonged to an organization that guaranteed them certain things. Among these rights were that they could not be discharged in any country other than their own against their will; and that each sailor must be given a paper stating where, when, and by whom he had been hired, with the "protection" that he could not be set ashore in a foreign port and left unemployed and penniless.

If these rights were violated, fo'c's'le talk had it, even an Ordinary Seaman could take legal action against the master and owners of the ship. Exactly how, where, and when this legal action could be initiated, Ben did not know. But the right existed.

"Seaman Warren," First Mate Fox murmured without turning his head.

"Aye, sir?"

"D'ye know where Aymes bunks?"

"In the fo'c's'le crew quarters, sir. His berth is next to mine."

Glancing up at the quarter deck to make sure Captain Thorn's back was still turned, First Mate Fox took a folded piece of paper out of a jacket pocket and unobtrusively handed it to Ben.

"These are Aymes's protection papers, which I knew he'd be wantin'. Go quietly, lad, without appearin' to hurry. Wrap his clothes and belongin's into his slicker and tie it into a small bundle, with the papers inside. Mind ye do it on the sly."

"Aye, sir. What do I do with the bundle?"

"Look to me for signal when you come back on deck. If the captain's not watchin', I'll give you a thumbs-down sign. Drop the bundle over the side, where a native canoe will be waitin'. Go softly, now."

Going below decks, Ben did as instructed, pausing momentarily when he came back on deck and peering through the growing tropical twilight at First Mate Fox. Near the stern of the ship now, Sailor Aymes had removed his hat and was waving it hysterically up at the quarter deck, where Captain Thorn stood with his back turned in contempt and scorn.

"You ain't heard the last of this, Cap'n Thorn!" Aymes was shouting. "Not by a damn sight, you ain't! Oh, I'll 'ave the law on you good an' proper, I will, claimin' damages and a pile of money for desertin' me in a foreign port! Damn your eyes, Cap'n Thorn, I'll make you sorry for the way you went off and left me—!"

Noting that the thumbs-down sign was being given him by First Mate Fox, Ben dropped his package overboard, where it was caught before it hit the water by a smiling native in a small canoe. The Hawaiian called up softy:

"*Aloha, haole!* Good-bye, my white friend! *Hele me ka hau 'oli!* Go with joy!"

"*Mahalo, aloha!*" Ben replied, waving in return and using the only two native words he had learned during his stay in Hawaii. "Thank you—and good-bye till we meet again!"

5.

O F THE TWENTY Kanakas that had been employed under three-year contracts at a one-hundred-dollar annual wage, half were to work ashore for the Astor Company, while the others were to become sailors. Since they spoke no English and had not the faintest notion of discipline aboard a merchant ship, Captain Thorn left the job of training them to the ship's officers, First Mate Ebenezer Fox and Third Mate Thomas Warren, both of whom had a working knowledge of the Hawaiian tongue. What was more important, both men had the patience to show rather than merely tell the Kanakas what they wanted done, repeating a task several times themselves until the easygoing natives understood what was required of them.

"They're as nimble as monkeys in the rigging," Thomas Warren told Ben. "It's impossible to drown one when the water and weather are warm. Cold weather is another matter, of course. I doubt if there's a man among them who's ever seen ice or snow."

The transition from the mild climate of Hawaii to the colder region off the coast of North America was a relatively brief one. For the first two weeks, warm, light airs came steadily from the south, then on March 16 at 35 degrees North Latitude and 138 degrees West Longitude, the wind shifted to SSW and blew so violently that the *Tonquin*'s topgallants and topsails had to be hauled in, forcing the ship to run before the gale with only her foresail set, scarcely six feet of surface exposed to the wind.

The rolling of the ship was far greater than Ben had experienced in all the preceding storms, but by now everyone aboard was past getting seasick; both crew and passengers reveled in the good headway the ship was making. Knowing that the Northwest Coast was not far away, Captain Thorn took the precaution of laying to for two successive nights rather than risk being driven aground on a lee shore.

By then, there was not a happy person aboard the ship, even though the end of the six-month-long voyage was in sight. Released from the brig the day after the *Tonquin* sailed, Seamen Adam Fisher and Peter Vershel nursed lacerated backs and angry feelings, while Second Mate John Mumford suffered from wounded pride made worse by the fact that the happy-go-lucky Kanakas paid absolutely no attention to any order he gave them, apparently feeling that the time he had spent in irons below decks made him unfit to command them.

Bewildered and numbed by the freezing gale, driving snow, and ice freezing in the rigging, the Hawaiians lost their good humor, refusing to go aloft when ordered to do so, seeking refuge and warmth in the cramped fo'c's'le, where they climbed into their hammocks, pulled up all the covers they could find, and lay shivering and whimpering, declining to move. Needing hands to work the ship, Mates Fox, Mumford, and Warren again called upon the French-Canadian voyageurs to climb the ice-crusted lines, only to have them sullenly rebel because of a lack of cold-weather gear.

"*Mon Dieu*, *M'sieu*, we cannot be asked to do sailor's winter work when we have no winter clothes," Basile Lepensee protested vehemently to Senior Partner Alexander McKay. "Zis is inhuman!"

"I agree."

Climbing the ladder to the quarter deck, McKay pounded on the cabin door, which had been closed against the icy wind.

"Captain Thorn! We've got to talk."

After what apparently was intended to be a deliberately long silence, Captain Thorn opened the door and stood blocking it, not inviting Alexander McKay to come in out of the cold.

"What d'we have to talk about, Mr. McKay?"

"You can't ask men to do winter work without winter gear."

"Didn't they bring along their jackets?"

"They've had no need of jackets till now. But we've got plenty of warm clothes packed in the boxes we're taking to the Columbia River trading post. I suggest you open them."

"Mr. Astor gave me special instructions regarding those boxes, Mr. McKay. They're not to be opened until the trading post is built."

"Nonsense, Captain Thorn! I'm sure Mr. Astor never intended to let my people freeze to death."

"Nevertheless, those are his orders—which I intend to obey."

Moving up the ladder behind McKay, Duncan McDougall thrust out his chin like a belligerent bulldog straining at his chain.

"If he'll nae listen to reason, Alex, we'll have to use force. I've a musket in my cabin, which won't take long to load. And Robert Stuart has a brace of pistols—"

"Goddam it, I won't be threatened aboard my own ship!" Captain Thorn exploded. Reaching behind him into the cabin, he pulled out the shotgun with which he had missed the tethered gray goose on the Falkland Islands two months ago. "Stay away from those boxes, gentlemen, or I'll fill your butts with buckshot!"

Again it was David Stuart who played the peacemaker, suggesting that Captain Thorn be permitted to work the ship with the sailors who did have foul-weather gear or would loan theirs to those voyageurs willing to stand brief watches when deck chores or tasks aloft needed to be done.

"We've put up with the pig-headed ass this long. Surely we can stand him for another week or two. *Nae sa muckle o'it*, friends. Dinnae start a battle wi' him so late in the voyage."

As the ship neared the mouth of the Columbia, the weather grew worse. On the 17th, in Latitude 37 degrees North and Longitude 137 degrees West., a violent gale rose, which increased almost to a hurricane and lasted four days without intermission. While it lasted, great difficulty was experienced in maneuvering the ship, which had sprung a leak and become waterlogged. At times she simply scudded before the wind; at times she lay to; at times she moved groggily under one sail, then under another. All the people onboard were weary of the sea and anxious for the long voyage to end.

During the brutal storm, everything on deck was carried off or dashed to pieces. Half the livestock was either killed or washed overboard. The weather was so bad—first with rain, then with sleet, hail, frost, and snow—that all the rigging froze stiff, with the ropes and sails becoming so iron-hard that there was no coiling or bending them.

When the storm finally eased up, the leak below decks was repaired and the ship became more manageable. On March 22, 1811, land was sighted in the gray mists ten miles to the northeast. On a nearer approach, it proved to be the three-hundred-foot-high headland guarding the north entrance to the Columbia River, Cape Disappointment.

When Ben asked his father the origin of the name, Third Mate Thomas Warren shook his head and said he did not know, for he had never visited this part of the coast before. But First Mate Ebenezer Fox knew the region's history well, for he and his uncle, who had also been a sailor, had visited it several times. He told Ben:

"Big as the Columbia River is, lad, many a bold explorer passed by its mouth without markin' it down on a map. First, a Spaniard named Bruno Hecata sailed past it in 1772, noted a lot of freshwater pouring into the sea from between two mist-shrouded capes, and guessed that what geographers then called the 'River of the West' must disgorge there."

"Did he try to enter it?"

"Neither wind nor tide favored that, he wrote in his log, so he sailed on north and told a British sea captain named Meares where he thought the river's mouth was located. A few months later, Meares came south lookin' for it, saw the headland but couldn't find the river, so gave it the name it now bears, Cape Disappointment."

"Who did discover the mouth of the river?"

"An American sea captain named Robert Gray, sailing the ship *Columbia*. The way it happened was this: Like Hecata, Captain Gray saw what appeared to be the mouth of a great river while sailin' north up the coast in April 1792. In the Strait of Juan de Fuca a while later, he ran into the famous British explorer, Captain George Vancouver, who was cruising around discovering islands and mountains and naming them after his fancy English friends like Admiral Hood and Lord Rainier.

" 'Look here, Cap'n Vancouver,' Gray says, 'I think I've found the mouth of the River of the West, which geographers have been looking for so long.' When he told Vancouver where he thought it was, the great British explorer just smiled and said: 'Captain Meares proved years ago no river was there, thus the name of the headland, Cape Disappointment. Best stick to commanding your ship, my boy, and leave discovering rivers, mountains, and islands to people who know their business.'

"Well, sir, Cap'n Gray apologized for bein' so green at the discoverin' business. But just out of curiosity, he sailed south again, found the mouth of the river that wasn't there, and by stubbornness, luck, or good old Yankee sailin' skill, crossed what later would be known as the most dangerous bar in the world and went up the river for twenty-five miles. Not bein' acquainted with people in high places like Captain George Vancouver was, he named the river 'Columbia' after his ship, then went on about *his* business, which happened to be sailin' around the world by way of China."

At one-thirty in the afternoon, March 22, Captain Thorn ordered the sails furled and the ship laid to well off the coast until he satisfied himself that this was indeed the mouth of the Columbia. Knowing that First Mate Fox was the only person aboard the *Tonquin* who had ever been in this area before, he ordered Fox to take the ship's smallest boat and a crew of four men and see if he could find a safe passage across the bar. Disliking both the boat and the crew chosen for him, the First Mate protested strongly:

"You're giving me only one sailor, sir, three Canadian lads unacquainted with sea service, and a very old Frenchman with a lame back and failin' eyesight. That's a poor crew for such dangerous duty."

"These are the only men I can spare, Mr. Fox."

For the first time during the six-month-long voyage, Ben's father criticized an order given by the captain, though Thomas Warren did it in such a low tone of voice that only Ben heard him.

"What in God's name is the captain doing, sending Fox out into such wild seas with that kind of boat and crew? It's madness!"

"Beggin' your pardon, sir," Fox persisted, "but no boat can live in these waves and weather."

"I've sailed the world over in far worse conditions, Mr. Fox."

"That you may have done on the open ocean, Captain. But not while crossin' the world's most treacherous bar. The way wind, tide, and current fight one another here, she's pure white-water chop for miles, sir, with no way to know how the channel winds. It's late in the day and the light is poor. Let's go out to sea for the night, hopin' for calmer weather tomorrow."

"Don't tell me how to sail my ship, Mr. Fox!"

Alexander McKay, who had come to respect Fox for his seamanship as well as for his qualities as a man, spoke up in the First Mate's defense, saying angrily, "The mon is right, Captain Thorn! Sending him out to check the bar with as poor a crew and boat as ye're giving him is the next thing to murder!"

47

"This is *my* ship and *my* command, Mr. McKay! I'll thank you to remember that!"

"What's the harm in waitin' another day, sir?" Fox asked. "By mornin', the wind and waves may be calmer—"

Wheeling sharply around, Captain Thorn gave the First Mate a look filled with scorn, then sneered:

"Mr. Fox, if you are afraid of water, you should have remained in Boston. Either carry out the order I gave you or take the consequences for your mutinous act—which I warn you will be severe."

Ben saw the First Mate's shoulders sag as he accepted the inevitable. Several years older than Thomas Warren, Ebenezer Fox was a kindly man wise in the ways of the sea, liked by the Astor partners, by his fellow officers, and by the men who served under him. There were tears in his eyes as he shook hands with the partners and said a final good-bye.

"My uncle was drowned here not many years ago. Now I am going to lay my bones with his."

Stepping into the boat with the other members of the crew, he waved as it was lowered toward the heaving surface of the sea. "Farewell, my friends! We will perhaps meet in the next world."

Climbing halfway up the foremast and watching the small boat push off from the ship, Ben saw that First Mate Fox was steering, Seaman Peter Vershel and voyageurs Michel LaFramboise and Giles Leclerc were rowing, while the old, lame-backed Frenchman, Antoine Belleau, who could do little physical labor, sat in the bow holding the white signal flag, which he had been told to wave in a forward-and-back pattern if a navigable channel was found or in a side-to-side motion in case of shoaling water or distress.

From the beginning, it was plain to Ben and the other watchers that the seas were too rough and boisterous for the small boat to negotiate them. Rising and falling on the swells and in the troughs, it became unmanageable before it had gone one hundred yards from the ship's side, whirling around like a top, broaching broadside to the foaming surges. Seeing the white flag being waved frantically from side to side in an obvious signal of distress, Ben shouted down:

"The boat's in trouble, sir! She's asking for help!"

"You've got to save her, Captain Thorn!" Alexander McKay shouted up at the quarter deck. "Sail closer and give her quieter water in your lee while you throw her a line and haul her in."

Peering intently in the direction of the tossing small boat for a moment, Captain Thorn turned back and called down:

"About ship! Raise sail and beat out to sea!"

"For God's sake, ye're not leavin' them, are you?"

Duncan McDougall cried out in sudden anguish. "There's five men aboard that boat!"

"Mr. Mumford! Mr. Warren! About ship, I say!"

Sick at heart but aware of the fact that he could not disobey orders given him by the Second and Third Mates, Ben performed his assigned duties as the ship came around, trimmed sails for the new course, and moved out to sea in the growing gloom of the afternoon. Staying clear of the rocky, dangerous coast, the *Tonquin* tacked back and forth through the long, dark night, keeping to the safety of deep water. Though Ben did not hear the angry words that passed between Captain Thorn and Second Mate John Mumford shortly after the "about ship" order was given, he guessed that Mr. Mumford had protested strongly against the abandonment of First Mate Fox and the small boat, with Captain Thorn again ordering Mumford below decks in punishment. This left Third Mate Thomas Warren as the only working officer, a responsibility he accepted with such a grim look on his face that Ben dared not question him regarding the cause of the altercation between Captain Thorn and the Second Mate.

Whether the captain judged the term of Mumford's punishment long enough or simply needed his services on deck, Ben did not know. But in mid-morning next day, the Second Mate resumed his duties and came topside. Looking just as grim as Thomas Warren, he supervised the *Tonquin*'s crew as the ship again approached the coast, dropping anchor in fourteen fathoms of water a mile outside the breakers. Though Ben dared not discuss Captain Thorn's desertion of the small boat and its crew the previous afternoon with the Astor people, he did listen with interest as Alexander Ross told him what he had read about the nature of the bar.

The mouth of the Columbia River was remarkable, Ross said, for its sandbars and high surf at all seasons, but most particularly in the spring and fall, during the equinoctial gales. The sandbars frequently shifted, with the channel moving accordingly, which rendered the passage at all times extremely dangerous. The chain of sandbars over which the huge waves and foaming breakers roared was three miles broad and extended in a white, foaming sheet for many miles more, both south and north of the mouth of the river, forming an almost impassable barrier to the entrance.

"What makes it particularly difficult," Ross said, "is that the channel keeps changing from season to season, week to week, even day to day, according to the amount of freshwater brought down the river and the volume of saltwater brought in by the tides. What few charts have been made soon become useless."

"How wide is the bar?"

"That's all according to where you measure it."

At its mouth, the Columbia River was four-and-a-half miles broad, he said, confined by Cape Disappointment on the north and Point Adams on the south. The Cape was a rocky cliff, rising three hundred feet above the sea and covered on the top with a few scattered trees of stunted growth. Point Adams was a low, sandy beach, jutting out five hundred yards into the river directly south of and opposite to Cape Disappointment. The deepest water was near the Cape, but the channel was narrow, intricate, and constantly changing. Few white navigators had mapped it.

"What about the local Indians?" Ben asked. "Don't they know it?"

"According to the Lewis and Clark journals, the Chinook Indians on the north side of the river and the Clatsops on the south side know it very well. In fact, they make the most seaworthy canoes and are the finest boatmen on the Northwest Coast. If Captain Thorn had a brain in his head, he'd contact one of the local chiefs and ask him to supply a pilot across the bar. But as he proved yesterday afternoon, he's a hopeless idiot."

With the sea now calm and the wind light, Alexander McKay, David Stuart, and Alexander Ross approached Second Mate John Mumford with a proposal they felt Captain Thorn could not refuse.

"If he'll gi' us the long boat, with four good seamen to man the oars and you to steer," McKay told Mumford, "we'll seek out the channel and the men lost yesterday. Will ye tell him our offer?"

"Aye, that I will."

"If you've no objection, Mr. Mumford," Ben said eagerly, "I'd like to be a member of your crew."

"By all means, take him along," Alexander Ross said with an approving smile. "He's got a strong back and a weak mind—just like me."

Mumford nodded. "That's fine with me. If the captain approves, we'll take Seamen Ben Warren, Adam Fisher, John White, and Robert Hill to man the oars in the long boat. That will give us a good crew and seaworthy craft."

Grunting his curt approval to the plan, Captain Jonathan Thorn stood gazing down from the quarter deck as the four seamen, three partners, and Second Mate Mumford took their places in the long boat, which then was lowered into the water under the watchful direction of Third Mate Thomas Warren. For the first mile of rolling ocean between the ship's side and the breaking surf, the long boat moved smoothly through the sea. But on approaching the bar, the power of the chain of breakers made itself felt.

As the waves rolled in one after another in quick succession, the conflict between the outflowing current and the incoming seas created a suction so irresistible that, before the crew in the long boat was fully aware of it, the boat was drawn into the breakers at an angle, becoming completely unmanageable. Realizing what was happening before anyone else did, Mr. Mumford, who was at the helm, called out:

"Turn back, men! We can't fight this surf!"

In turning around, the boat broached broadside to the incoming rollers. Ben felt a surge of sheer terror, for the long boat seemed in imminent danger of turning turtle and casting its human cargo into the raging seas.

"Pull men, pull!" Mumford shouted. "Pull for your lives—or we're all dead men!"

Ben pulled and prayed.

Unable to do anything useful so far as saving the boat was concerned, Alexander Ross took out his pocket watch, he later told Ben sheepishly, noted the minute First Mate Mumford ordered the boat to turn around and the minute it finally fought its way clear of the suction of the perilous surf, then totaled them up.

"Would you believe we were on the verge of being swamped for precisely twelve minutes?" he told Ben.

"You don't say! To me, it seemed more like twelve hours!"

Outside the line of breaking surf still two miles from land, the long boat and its crew cautiously probed the wide mouth of the river for several hours, seeking but not finding a passage across the bar. Returning to the ship just before darkness fell, the tired boat crew rested while Captain Thorn, Second Mate Mumford, and Third Mate Warren reviewed the effort that had been made today, studied what few charts they had of this part of the coast, and made plans for a further examination of the bar the next morning.

Early in the morning of the 25th, John Mumford, Ben Warren, and the other three seamen ventured out again in the long boat, though this time Captain Thorn insisted that Alexander McKay, David Stuart, and Alexander Ross stay behind. Taking a more southerly direction, the boat party made several attempts to cross the bar, failing in all of them, finally getting so entangled with the breakers that disaster was averted only by the Second Mate's skill as a helmsman and the strong oar work by the seamen.

Giving it up for the day as a bad job, the boat crew returned to the *Tonquin*, where the captain greeted Mumford with contempt and scorn.

"Failed again, did ye, Mr. Mumford? Yet ye call yourself a seaman!"

"I'm sorry to displease you, sir. Tomorrow I'll try to do better."

Rolling his eyes upward, Captain Thorn appeared to be calling upon the Good Lord to witness how patient he had been in his tolerance toward his inept ship's officers. Then, lowering his gaze, he glared at Third Mate Warren.

"Mr. Warren, you have sailed the world's seas for many years."

"That I have, sir."

"Though you've not been on this coast before, you do know that the Columbia River bar has been crossed many times by many ships from many nations, don't you?"

"Aye, sir. So I've been told."

"Are you navigator enough to find me a passage across the bar?"

Ben saw his father hesitate before answering. By now, it was three o'clock in the afternoon, far too late in the day to begin another attempt to find the channel. But Captain Thorn was so beside himself with anger and frustration that he had lost all sense of time. Aware of the captain's mood, the Third Mate replied cautiously.

"Perhaps."

"Good! Take Job Aikens, John Coles, Stephen Weeks, and two of the Sandwich Islanders in the pinnace. See if you can't find a channel with at least eight fathoms of water."

"Aye, sir."

"Steer a more northerly direction than that fool Mr. Mumford did. Step lively now, Mr. Warren! Daylight's fading."

As the men selected moved toward the pinnace and prepared

to lower it over the side, Ben Warren said urgently, "Take me along, Father!"

"Be quiet, lad. The captain did not call your name."

"But you don't have a real seaman in the crew, sir. Job Aikens is a rigger, John Coles a sailmaker, and Stephen Weeks an armorer. Neither one of the Kanakas has ever rowed a small boat. You need me!"

"Be still, I say! Only a fool volunteers for small-boat duty off a stormy shore."

Irritably, Captain Thorn called down from the quarter deck, "What is your son pestering you about, Mr. Warren?"

"He wants to go along, sir."

"D'ye want to take him?"

"No, sir. He's worn out from rowing most of the day. I need fresh men."

Ben gave Third Mate Warren a stricken look. "Father! I'm not a bit tired and you know it!"

"Will your keep your mouth shut, you impudent young fool? We agreed when we signed on that aboard ship we'd not be father and son. Let's keep it that way."

Hurt to the very center of his being, Ben turned away, his eyes blurring with tears. Never in his whole life had his father spoken to him in such a harsh tone of voice. Before stepping into the pinnace as the last man aboard, Thomas Warren took hold of Ben's upper arm, squeezed it briefly, then murmured:

"You mean well, I know, lad. But so do I. Please understand that. So do I ..."

Since it was now the turn of the tide, with a light breeze blowing toward the shore, the pinnace made good progress out from the side of the ship. As agreed on, Third Mate Warren raised a flag, indicating he had found eight fathoms of water in a channel leading across the bar. Weighing anchor and hoisting just enough sail for steering-way, the *Tonquin* cautiously followed. A few hundred yards short of the line of breakers which marked the passage across the bar, the pinnace pulled to one side in order to let the ship pass. Laying on their oars in quiet water, the boat crew waited to be thrown a line and taken aboard. At the point where the two vessels passed, they would be within twenty yards of each other, so the pickup would be no problem.

From his perch halfway up the foremast, which he had climbed to unfurl a sail, Ben saw his father smiling and waving as he stood in the pinnace indicating with the flag the direction of deep water in the channel ahead. On the quarter deck of the *Tonquin*, Captain Thorn stood beside the helmsman, gazing intently ahead.

As the *Tonquin* came abeam of the pinnace, Ben suddenly realized that no crew member was standing by preparing to throw the small boat a line. Certainly he could not do it himself, for by the time he descended the foremast, ran along the port rail toward the stern, seized a line, and tossed it over the side, it would be too late.

"Look alive below!" he yelled. "Throw the pinnace a line!"

Peering ahead through the growing gloom, Captain Thorn gave no indication that he heard Ben's cry. Seeing no member of the ship's crew responding, Alexander McKay shouted in alarm:

"Who's going to throw a line to the boat?"

Still, Captain Thorn made no reply. By this time, the pinnace had fallen astern and all the partners were calling out: "The boat! The boat! Throw a line to the boat!"

"In the name of God, Captain Thorn!" Duncan McDougall cried up at the quarter deck. "Throw a line to the boat!"

His eyes fixed on the channel ahead, Captain Thorn said coldly, "I can give them no assistance."

"It'll only take a moment to back a sail!" Second Mate Mumford called up to the captain. "If you'll let me give the order—"

"Belay that talk, Mr. Mumford! I will not endanger the ship."

Stunned by the callous way the master of the *Tonquin* was abandoning the pinnace and its people, Ben scurried down off the foremast, ran to the port rail near the stern, and tossed a line overboard. Even as it unrolled on the heaving surface of the sea, he knew that his action had come too late, for by this time the pinnace, whose crew had picked up their oars and started rowing desperately, was two hundred yards astern.

The ship was into the breakers now, which were giving the keel a tremendous pounding. Vaguely aware that Captain Thorn and Second Mate Mumford were shouting conflicting orders to drop anchors and shorten sail, Ben paid them no heed as he climbed up the mainmast and stared astern, trying to find the pinnace in the growing darkness. As he climbed, the ship struck hard on an underwater reef of sand, shuddered clear, then struck again, the repeated shocks nearly making him lose his grip on the mast.

"Let go the stern anchor!" Captain Thorn was shouting. "She's broaching to!"

"Broach and be damned!" Ben sobbed as he climbed.

"Let go the bow anchor!" Second Mate Mumford yelled. "If she strikes again, we're done for!"

"Neither anchor is holding, sir!" a seaman shouted. "She's ripping her bottom out!"

"*Holy Mary, Mother of Jesus!*" a voyageur cried. "*We're all going to die!*"

Now as high as he could get on the mainmast, Ben gazed astern, seeing nothing but blackness and a welter of heaving white-topped waves. If the ship herself was in mortal danger—as she certainly seemed to be—there was no hope for the pinnace to survive in these wild waters.

"Captain Thorn, you son-of-a-bitch!" Ben shouted at the top of his voice. "I'll kill you for this! If my father is drowned, you'll not live another day!"

6.

ONLY BLIND LUCK saved the *Tonquin*, for from the moment the ship entered the breakers after passing the pinnace, she was out of control. Striking at least half a dozen times on the shoaling sands, her sails were of no use because the following wind died and what fickle breezes arose during the next hour or two came first from one direction, then from another, giving no steering-way impetus whatsoever.

Dropped in quick succession, both the aft and forward anchors failed to hold, the waves from astern driving the ship forward while the current striking her bow pushed her back. As a result, after lurching clear of the sandbars into deeper water, she had no forward motion at all, spinning around and around in the pitch-black darkness like a wood chip tossed into the swirling vortex of a tidal pool.

Time and again, ten-foot-high waves rolled over the ship's taffrail, cascading the length of the deck, forcing the sailors trying to work the ship to abandon their tasks and climb into the rigging, where they hung on for dear life lest they be swept overboard. How long the chaos lasted, Ben did not know. Hours, he guessed, for his hands and arms ached from the strain of hanging on, while his chilled, soaked body grew numb with cold.

On several occasions as he clung to the mainmast, he saw flickers of what appeared to be torch-light off the port rail—which would be the north side of the river. From that same direction, he heard drums beating and voices calling in some unrecognizable tongue. Remembering what Alexander Ross had told him about the Chinook Indians who lived north of the entrance to the Columbia, he wondered if they had ventured out into the dangerous waters beyond the bar, or if, by sheer good fortune, the *Tonquin* had been carried by the incoming flood tide into the safety of quieter waters within the mouth of the river.

Indeed, the latter seemed to be the case, for the ship had stopped pitching now and the deck was stable. Waves no longer rolled in from astern. The anchors seemed to be holding. Somewhere below him, a jubilant voice cried out:

"We're inside the bar! We're anchored in Baker Bay!"

For the time being, Ben was so cold, numb, and exhausted that he did not care where the ship was anchored, so long as it was safe. Climbing down from his perch on the mainmast, he groped his way across the deck to the fo'c's'le hatch, went below, climbed into his hammock, and immediately fell into a deep, dreamless sleep …

When he came on deck next morning after waking shortly after daylight, a fine, mist-like rain was falling from a low gray sky. The deck was a shambles of broken gear, while above, tattered strips of shredded sails made the usually neat ship look like it had been wrecked and abandoned for weeks. Seeing him, Second Mate Mumford, who was supervising a crew working aloft, crossed the deck and spoke to him in an urgent voice.

"I'd like a word with you, lad."

"About what, sir?"

"Mr. McKay, Mr. Ross, and Captain Thorn are taking a party ashore to look for survivors of the boat crews, if any there be. Would you like to go along?"

"I most certainly would."

"What Mr. McKay plans to do is ask the head chief of the Chinooks for a guide who knows the coast. If our boats did make it to shore, the Indians will know where they're likely to be."

"Do you think there's any chance my father survived?"

Casting a quick, furtive look up at the quarter deck, where Captain Thorn stood gazing at the steep, timbered hills north of the river, Second Mate Mumford shook his head. "We can only hope for the best, son. But a word of warning about the threat you made against the captain last night …"

Though Ben remembered vividly enough the way he had cursed Captain Thorn and threatened to kill him, he was not aware that anyone else onboard the *Tonquin* had heard him shout his vow into the wind and dark. But he *had* kept on shouting it as he climbed down off the mainmast and staggered across the deck toward the fo'c's'le, Mumford told him grimly, not appearing to care who heard him.

"You were beside yourself with grief, I know," Mumford said sympathetically. "Still, 'twas a terrible thing to say."

"There were eleven men in those two boats, Mr. Mumford," Ben staid stubbornly. "If they're drowned, Captain Thorn should be charged with murder."

"Not by you, lad. Coming from you in this time and place, such a charge would be an act of mutiny."

"I really don't give a damn, sir. If my father is drowned—"

"Which he may not be. Promise me this, Ben. You'll go with the search party, keeping your mouth shut and your feelin's to yourself, until you find out what's happened to the missing men. Can't you at least do that?"

Ben nodded reluctantly. "Yes, sir. I'll promise you that much. But if my father is dead, I'll find some way to make the captain answer for his crimes."

"Good enough. My prayers go with you."

Rowed ashore in the long boat by Seamen John Anderson and Egbert Vanderhuff, who then returned to resume their cleanup work aboard the *Tonquin*, Captain Thorn, Alexander McKay, Alexander Ross, and Ben Warren were greeted as they came ashore by a swarm of the strangest-looking natives Ben ever had seen. Scarcely five feet tall, bandy-legged, barrel-chested, and with powerfully muscled arms, their heads were grotesquely deformed, being slanted back to a cone-like point from a spot just above the eyes to the back of the head. Staring at them with unconcealed astonishment, Ben heard Ross chuckle beside him.

"Amazing, aren't they?"

"I've never seen anything like it in my life! Are they born that way?"

"From what I've read, the heads of the babies are normal enough at birth. But soon thereafter, the mother reshapes her child's cranium as a sign of distinction."

"How?"

"She ties boards fore and aft, then binds them together with rawhide thongs, which she tightens day by day while the baby grows. After a year or so, the skull takes on the fashionable shape she wants— and remains so the rest of the child's life."

"Does it hurt?"

"Only the baby knows. And by the time it's old enough to talk, it's probably forgotten."

"What a heathen practice! You'd think it would scramble their brains."

"Maybe it does. But these are the people we've got to live and trade with."

Aboard ship, Ben had had few direct dealings with Captain Thorn, whose orders always were passed down through the ship's officers, so it did not surprise him that the captain should pay no attention to him now. Striding ahead in stiff-backed dignity while the crowd of natives swarmed around them, the captain kept taking his handkerchief out of the sleeve of his coat and dabbing it at his nose, as if trying to keep the rank, oily smell of the Chinooks from entering his nostrils.

Atop a rise of land a hundred yards away from the river, a number of buildings made of split cedar planks stood against the hillside. Called "longhouses," Ross said, they were thirty feet wide, sixty feet long, and twenty feet high, half of their height being below ground level. Each of the dwellings housed fifty or so natives, so the inhabitants of this village must number close to one thousand. The most impressive of the dwellings, toward which the party was headed, was the residence of Chief Concomly, Ross said, who had lost one eye in a boyhood accident some years ago but was reputed to be a shrewd, powerful man.

Split lengthways down the middle at the ridgepole, a two-foot-wide slot let out the smoke of the fires burning within each longhouse, while a narrow entrance in front gave access to the buildings. Flea-ridden, smelly, but warm, they provided safe, comfortable quarters for the strongest, most far-ranging tribe living on the American part of the Northwest Coast.

Onboard the *Tonquin*, Captain Thorn had made it crystal clear from the first day of the voyage that he was the ship's master whose privileged space on the starboard side of the quarter deck was not to be infringed on by anyone at any time. But now that the party had come ashore, a curious change in the relationship between the captain and Alexander McKay took place, for McKay's long years of experience in dealing with Indians made him the master of the present circumstances. Pausing outside the entrance to Chief Concomly's longhouse, Captain Thorn seemed glad to let McKay assume charge of the party. "D'ye know how to converse with the slant-headed rascals, Mr. McKay? D'ye talk their lingo?"

For the past several months aboard ship, Ben knew, McKay, Ross, and David Stuart had spent many hours poring over a dictionary of the regional trade language, Chinook Jargon. Ross said the dictionary had been compiled by a British sailor named John Jewitt, who had been a captive of the Nootka Indians on Vancouver Island for several years around 1800, and by Lewis and Clark during their stay on the Northwest Coast in 1805–6. Using a basic vocabulary of Indian, French, Spanish, and English words, Chinook Jargon could be learned quickly and had been in wide use ever since trade between Indians and whites in the Northwest began some twenty years ago.

"I know Jargon well enough to get by," McKay answered Captain Thorn. "But dinnae call these people rascals, sir. Savage though he may be by your standards, Concomly is a proud man. We dare not offend him."

"Oh, God forbid that we hurt his feelings, Mr. McKay!" Captain Thorn sneered, again dabbing his handkerchief to his nose. "To make sure I do nothing wrong, I'll stay outside in the fresh air and let you do all the talking."

"Mayhap that would be best."

If Captain Thorn had heard Ben's threat and intended to discipline him for it, the captain certainly would not try to do so until the fate of the boat crews had been determined, Ben guessed. Nor would the captain attempt to take any sort of punitive action ashore, for this clearly was the domain of the Astor Company partners. All the same, Ben stepped warily as he moved past the captain, careful to make no eye contact with him at all.

Following McKay and Ross down the smooth, hewn wooden entrance steps into the smoky gloom of the longhouse, Ben found the atmosphere inside as rank and pungent as air could be. Which was saying a great deal, for after six months at sea with the hatches closed most of the time the atmosphere of the crew's cramped fo'c's'le quarters got pretty raunchy itself. But here in the longhouse, where several dozen families were living, smoke from fires built for warmth and cooking, body odors from sleeping shelves along each wall, smells of fish, game, and pelts hanging from the rafters overhead, combined to create an atmosphere so overpowering it could almost be cut with a knife.

Leading the way to the far end of the longhouse, Alexander McKay approached a man sitting cross-legged on a low platform apparently meant to resemble a throne. Incongruously dressed in sealskin leggings, a long, double-breasted, black ship captain's coat like the one worn for dress-up occasions by Captain Thorn, and the cocked hat of a British naval admiral, the man was peering crookedly at McKay out of a left eye sparkling with spirit and curiosity, while the right eye showed only a blank socket.

"*Hyas tyee!*" the man cried out jovially to McKay. "Greetings, great chief!"

Sinking to a cross-legged sitting position immediately in front of the one-eyed Chinook chief, McKay politely inclined his head, choosing his words with studied care.

"*Mika kumtuks Boston wawa?*"

Looking pleased that his white guest had at least tried to speak to him in the local tongue, Concomly made it clear that he was an accomplished linguist himself.

"Do I talk English? You damn betcha! We make good *wawa* in any tongue you want. We be *skookum tillicums hyas tum-tums* quick. Good friends with warm hearts. Now you tell me what you need?"

"We lost two boats and several men trying to find a passage across the bar. Can you help us find the survivors, if any there be?"

"*Cultus skookum chuck,*" Concomly said with a scowl, waving a hand to the northwest in the direction of Cape Disappointment. "Bad, strong currents and tides at river mouth. Very foolish for Bostons to try to cross the bar when wind and tide are wrong. We saw Boston sailors in boats and tried to wave them away."

"Aye, we saw you waving at us," McKay said, nodding. "But we could nae tell what you meant. Will you give us a guide who will help us find our people?"

"You betcha! Give you *hyas kumtux* guide."

Motioning a young Indian sitting at his elbow to come forward, Concomly smiled and said, "Give you my son, Conco. Him smart—almost like me. Him *wawa* Boston good—almost like me. If your people still alive, he will find them."

Slant-headed like all the rest of his people, the young man Chief Concomly introduced as his son smiled shyly at McKay, Ross, and Ben Warren before lowering his gaze, which lingered a moment longer on Ben than on the others. He appeared to be about Ben's age, and though his misshapen forehead still struck Ben as odd, there was a glint of character and intelligence in his face that somehow transcended appearance and race. After listening to his father's instructions for a moment, he nodded, then said:

"We go first to beach, north of *skookum chuck*. Likely that where they be."

From the contemptuous look Captain Thorn gave them as they came out of the longhouse with their young Chinook guide, it was plain to see that he did not think much of the assistance being provided the search party. Dogtrotting ahead along a well-worn path through the dripping ferns and bushes which covered the thickly timbered slope beyond the village, where massive trees towered upward over two hundred feet into the rainy day, Conco led them around the steep slope of the hill called Cape Disappointment, beyond which the shoreline of the ocean came in view. Because Ben was more agile and more eager to stay close on the heels of their guide than the three older white men, a gap of fifty or so yards formed between Ben, Conco, and the others as the beach came in sight.

"Wait," Ben called out to Conco. "Let them catch up."

Pausing while the other men scrambled up the hillside, Conco smiled and gave Ben a deprecating shrug, saying clearly with his hands that older men could not be expected to keep up on steep hillside trails with youths their age and must be waited for. As they paused, he touched Ben's shoulder and motioned for him to turn around and look back, a direction Ben assumed to be south. Though visibility was limited to only a mile or two, Ben could see the mouth of the river, the line of breakers sweeping off into the distance, and the immense rolling gray sea to the west. With his left hand, Conco made a flowing gesture clearly representing the current of the great river, then, with his right hand, a chopping, incoming gesture, meaning white-crested surf meeting that current. When Ben nodded that he understood, Conco then moved both his hands together and turned his body to the north as he vividly showed how these two conflicting forces would inevitably drive any craft caught by them northward up the coast.

"I understand," Ben said. "If the boats survived, they'd be driven ashore to the north."

Moving on across the lower slope of the hill after the others caught up, the search party descended to the beach, turned north, and had gone only a few hundred yards when it rounded a bluff and found a half-dead survivor shivering as he huddled among the rocks, where he had sought shelter from the rain and cold. The man was the armorer, Stephen Weeks, who, with Third Mate Thomas Warren, rigger Job Aikens, sailmaker John Coles, and two Kanakas had embarked in the pinnace late yesterday afternoon in search of a passage across the bar.

Even as the members of the search party stripped off their jackets and gave him brandy to warm him, Weeks launched into a bitter tirade against Captain Thorn.

"You done it on purpose!" he cried. "We couldn't believe you'd desert us like that! We kept thinkin' you'd stop to pick us up, but you didn't care! You deliberately left us to drown!"

Whether he had been stunned into silence by the accusation and the miserable appearance of the man, Ben did not know, but Captain Thorn made no reply, though his face turned red with either embarrassment or anger. Again, Ben was struck by the fact that ashore the captain was a far less forceful man than he was aboard his ship. But at the moment Ben cared about only one thing—the fate of his father.

"Are any others left?" he asked urgently. "Did my father make it?"

Shivering uncontrollably, Stephen Weeks shook his head in a lost, bewildered fashion, went into a prolonged spasm of coughing, then stared at Ben as if not sure who he was. A man in his mid-forties, Weeks had a thin, pinched face, pale blue eyes, and stringy white hair. Never a strong man physically, he seemed only vaguely aware of his surroundings.

"Others left, you ask? Aye, there's another one around here somewhere. Maybe two. But one of them is dead ..."

"Tell us what happened," McKay said patiently.

"After the ship passed us, we pulled hard to follow her," Weeks said, "thinking every moment you would take us aboard. But when we saw her enter the breakers, we considered ourselves lost. We saw the ship make two or three heavy plunges, then we ourselves were struck with the boiling surf and the boat went reeling in all directions—"

"My father!" Ben blurted. "What happened to my father?"

"Easy, lad," McKay said gently. "He's doing the best he can."

"A heavy sea swamped us and we turned over," Weeks mumbled. "I never saw Job Aikens, John Coles, or Thomas Warren again. As soon as I got above the surface of the water, I kept tossing about at the mercy of the waves. Then I saw the two Sandwich Islanders struggling nearby and noticed that they were shedding their clothes to keep from being dragged under. They were both good swimmers, and somehow they got to the boat, turned her over, bailed her out with their hands, and managed to get aboard ..."

With the one oar that remained in the pinnace, Weeks said, one of the Kanakas started rowing in an attempt to get free of the breakers. Weeks himself caught hold of another oar he found floating nearby and used it to support his body in the water. Seeing him, the two Kanakas rowed toward him, took hold of his wet clothes, and tried to pull him into the boat, finally succeeding when one of them leaned out and took hold of his clothes with his teeth, his fingers being too cold to maintain a grip.

"We then stood out to sea as night set in," Weeks continued, "and a darker one I never saw. Without clothes, wet, cold, and numb, the two Hawaiians seemed to lose all hope, just lying there in the bottom of the boat without moving or making a sound. Sometime during the night, one of them died, while the other one lay there, barely breathing. Then the tide turned and the sound of breakers ahead got louder and louder. I knew we were in mortal danger ..."

Probably it was that realization that kept him alive, Weeks said, for he knew if the pinnace got entangled in the breakers, all was lost. Rowing desperately the rest of the night in an effort to keep the boat out to sea, he saw at daylight that he was within a quarter-mile of the surf and about twice that distance from the Cape itself. Deciding it would be better to expend his waning energy in one final desperate effort to reach the shore rather than suffer a prolonged death at sea, he headed the pinnace for the breakers.

"Providence favored my choice," he said, "and the sun had scarcely risen when the boat was thrown up high and dry on the beach. Seeing one of the Islanders dead in the boat and the other alive but insensible, I hauled both bodies out of the boat and carried them up to the edge of the woods, where I covered them with leaves. They can't be far away. While gathering the leaves, I came upon a beaten path, which brought me here."

Feeling numb and sick at heart, Ben turned away. At the moment, thoughts of revenge were far from his mind, for the full extent of the tragedy was beginning to soak in on him. Unless other survivors were found—which seemed unlikely—nine men had been lost due to the bad judgment of Captain Jonathan Thorn. In this alien land the breadth of a continent away from American law or a court of justice, no means of filing charges against him existed. When and if such charges were filed, little credence would be given to the testimony of a sixteen-year-old Ordinary Seaman that a naval officer with Thorn's experience had been guilty of criminal negligence.

If they chose to do so, the Astor Company partners could testify against the captain, of course, but Ben doubted they would. Now that the long voyage was over, their main interest was in choosing a site for the trading post to be built near the mouth of the Columbia, getting supplies for it unloaded, then sending the *Tonquin* and the choleric-tempered captain, who had been such a "Thorn" in their flesh literally, on his way north to trade for sea otter and beaver with the Nootka Indians on the Strait of Juan de Fuca and the inlets of Vancouver Island.

Probably, Mr. McKay would go along to supervise dealings with the Indians, Ross had told Ben, while Duncan McDougall remained behind to build the fort and survey the prospects for fur-gathering not only on the lower Columbia but also in the inland Pacific Northwest. Sometime early next fall, the inland contingent of the Astor venture, which was being commanded by Wilson Price Hunt, would arrive from St. Louis, following which the building of Astor's dream of a fur empire reaching from sea and then on around the world would truly begin. If successful, it would make all the partners in the Pacific Fur Company so wealthy that the loss of a few seamen's lives due to a captain's incompetence would be a small matter.

So be it, Ben thought bitterly. But one thing was clear. Whatever course of action he chose to take, he must act alone. Aboard ship, he would be at the mercy of Captain Thorn, with any threatening word or act against him considered mutiny. Ashore, they would be on more equal terms, for land was the domain of the Astor partners.

While his father lived, Ben had never considered any other career than that of a seaman aboard a merchant ship. Now he was beginning to see other possibilities. Suppose, after the trading post on the lower Columbia was established, he did not sail north with the *Tonquin* as he would have done if his father had lived? What if he accepted the challenge Alexander Ross had made him in jest a few days ago, when the northwest coast of the continent had come in sight through the mists of the gray day:

"There lies Oregon, Ben, waiting to be taken by whichever nation can claim and hold her—England or the United States. Why don't you come ashore with me and join the fight?"

Maybe I'll do that, Ben mused. Just maybe, I will …

7.

$\mathscr{R}$UNNING BACK to the Chinook village to tell Chief Concomly and the people aboard the *Tonquin* that a survivor had been found, Conco soon returned with a dozen natives, blankets, and pole litters on which Stephen Weeks and the Kanaka he said lay unconscious nearby could be carried. While McKay, Ross, and Captain Thorn took Weeks back to the ship, Ben Warren, Conco, and three Chinook Indians searched diligently for over a mile up the coast without finding either the dead or live Kanaka. Returning to the ship before darkness fell, Ben found Weeks stronger and more coherent now, able to give him better directions as to the location of the sheltered cove above tide level into which he had dragged both the corpse and the unconscious Kanaka, then covered their bodies with leaves.

Accompanied next morning by two of the Kanakas in the ship's crew, Ben, Conco, and half a dozen natives resumed the search. This time, with more specific directions, they found the two missing Islanders well hidden among the rocks, one stone dead, the other blue with cold and fatigue, his legs swollen and bleeding. Wrapped in blankets and placed on a litter, the still living Kanaka was carried back to the ship, while the body of his dead comrade was watched over and guarded by one of his shipmates while the other returned to the *Tonquin* to tell the Hawaiians aboard of his fate so that they could come back to this cold, wet, lonely spot on an alien shore later in the day and conduct a proper burial ceremony.

Busy aboard ship, Ben did not attend the ceremony—nor did Captain Thorn, who, for the past two days, had been seen very little outside his cabin, leaving the cleanup and repair work to be supervised by Second Mate Mumford, who now was the only officer aboard. But Gabriel Franchere, who was both sympathetic

67

to and curious about the Sandwich Islanders, did go, later telling Ben about the burial ceremony.

"Whether the Islander guarding the body did it out of respect or to protect it from animals, I don't know," Franchere said, "but when we got there, the corpse had been wrapped in a blanket and hung in the lower limbs of a tree. As last offerings, the Kanakas had brought along some biscuits, lard, and tobacco."

"I heard them asking the ship's storekeeper for those items," Ben said, nodding. "How did they use them?"

"After the grave was dug above high-tide level on the beach, they placed the body in it and turned back the blanket in which it was wrapped. They put the biscuits under one of the arms, the lard under the chin, and the tobacco under the genitals. Then they rewrapped the body, which I suppose they felt now was prepared for the journey into another world, laid it in the grave, and covered it with sand and rocks."

"Did they say a prayer?"

"Sort of. All but one knelt in a double row near the grave, their faces turned to the east. The one who appeared to be officiating as a priest went down to the sea, got some water in his hat, then sprinkled it over the kneeling men. He recited what sounded to me like a litany, with the others responding as we do in church. When the ceremony was finished, they got up and returned to the ship without looking back."

Next day, March 27, the pigs, sheep, and chickens that had survived the storm at sea and the waves that had swept over the poop deck during the crossing of the bar were taken ashore, where Chief Concomly set aside an area outside the village in which the ship's carpenter, John Weeks, could build pens to contain them. Before the carpenter began his work, Conco told Ben he should make sure the pens would protect the animals from predators.

"Such as what?" John Weeks asked.

"*Itswoot* and *hyas pusspuss*," Conco said, pantomiming a black bear and a cougar, then rubbing his belly and smacking his lips to demonstrate how much those animals relished pork, mutton, and chicken.

"Hey, I like them Jargon words!" Weeks chuckled. "You can just bet my pens will be as *itswoot* and *hyas pusspuss*-proof as I can make 'em! Ain't no black bear woofer or big kitty cat cougar gonna eat my animals!"

When the rain lessened and the weather moderated a few days later, Alexander Ross and Clerk Benjamin Pillet paid half a dozen Chinooks a few nails and pieces of copper to row them across the lower Columbia and then guide them forty or so miles south along the coast in a search for other survivors of the ship's crew. None were found, so the search party returned empty-handed. Anxious to select a site for the new trading post, Alexander McKay, David Stuart, and Captain Thorn embarked in the long boat with a crew of four oarsmen, of which Ben Warren was one, in an exploratory trip up the river, which lasted several days.

Though Ben was not at all sure exactly what sort of location the party was looking for, he did notice that any site liked by Captain Thorn was immediately objected to by the two Senior Partners, while any bay, flat, or cove admired by the partners was declared unsuitable by Captain Thorn. Coming back to Baker Bay, McKay and Stuart ordered the captain to weigh anchor and sail the *Tonquin* across the river to a promontory twelve miles above the river's mouth called Point George. In their absence, Duncan McDougall had conferred with the Clatsop Indians, who lived on the south side of the river, and been more impressed with them as potential neighbors than with Chief Concomly and the Chinooks on the north bank of the Columbia.

" 'Twas amongst the Clatsops that Lewis and Clark built their winter camp," McDougall pointed out to David Stuart. "Mayhap we'd do better to settle near them."

"Weel, from what I've seen, their heads are just as slanted as the Chinooks'," Stuart replied. "Wherever we decide to build, we can nae afford to insult Chief Concomly. Let's go over and talk to him."

Taking the long boat and four voyageurs to row it for them, Duncan McDougall and David Stuart crossed the lower river the afternoon of April 5, promising to return by the seventh. When a tremendous storm rolled in from the southwest two days later, whipping the lower river into white-frothed chop, they did not appear. Alarmed, McKay and the rest of the Astor party grew worried, for by now they had come to realize how treacherous the lower river could be when the weather turned bad. On the morning of the eighth, their concern was justified, for a Clatsop Indian coming onboard the ship said he had heard that the partners' boat had capsized while attempting to cross the bay the afternoon before.

Concern turned into relief when the storm subsided three days later and the missing men returned to the *Tonquin*. Escorted by Conco and a crew of Chinook paddlers rowing a big seagoing cedar log canoe, McDougall and Stuart admitted they had had a narrow escape from drowning. Though they gave few details of their near disaster, Conco quietly told Ben what had happened.

"White chiefs tell my father they want to cross river and come back to ship. Him say no go today because winds starting to blow, making *cultus* big waves on *skookoom chuck*. They say they not scared of winds or big waves. They will go anyway. When my father see them start to cross river, he tell me to follow and look after them. We stay close behind them in big seagoing canoe. Pretty soon, they get in trouble, just as my father knew they would. But we save them."

Worming the rest of the story out of McDougall and Stuart, Alexander Ross gleefully repeated it to Ben.

"The long boat turned over half a mile out from Chinook Point, they said, dumping the whole lot of them into the water. Like McDougall, most of the French-Canadians couldn't swim, so without help they would surely have drowned. But Conco and his friends were expecting this very thing to happen, so as soon as the long boat swamped, a dozen of the natives dove into the river and pulled the heads of the whites above water so they could breathe. The other natives righted the long boat, bailed it out, got the whites aboard, and headed back to shore.

"The way the Chinooks handle those big cedar log canoes is something to see, I tell you," Ross said, shaking his head in admiration. "I've watched them in rough water time and again. No matter how big the waves get, they never panic. When a roller strikes the windward side of a canoe, all the men on that side dig their paddles into the water clear up to their armpits, while those on the lee side lift their paddles clear. As soon as the swell passes under the canoe, the men on the lee side dig in at exactly the right instant, keeping the canoe on an even keel. All this, mind you, without anybody giving an order or a signal. They just instinctively know what to do and when to do it. They're the best canoe paddlers I've ever seen."

"Neither McDougall nor Stuart have had much to say about their adventure," Ben observed wryly.

"Small wonder!" Ross said with a laugh. "From what I've heard, they were so wet, cold, and scared that after Conco and his friends took them back to his father's longhouse, it took them three days to dry out, warm up, and build up enough courage to cross the river again."

"Did they give the Chinooks a few presents for saving their lives?"

"Grudgingly, Ben. Tight-fisted as he is, McDougall grumbled that it would not surprise him in the least 'If the cunning, slant-headed rascals dinnae upset another of our boats on purpose, just so they can save us and get more presents.' "

With the decision finally made to build the post on the south side of the river, the task of unloading supplies from the ship began. Among these were the precut timbers for a thirty-ton schooner designed after the style of the Hudson River craft back in New York, which plied that river between Albany and lower Manhattan. Though its building would be postponed until the construction of the fort was well under way, it soon became obvious to Ben that the Astor Company partners, the voyageurs, the clerks, and the captain of the *Tonquin* wanted nothing to do with the schooner, for none of them knew exactly what kind of fish, fowl, or beast it was going to be.

Inspecting the precut planks and the blueprint detailing how they should be assembled, Carpenter John Weeks said he'd never built a boat before and was too old to learn how now. Told by Captain Thorn that he would be in command of the schooner, which was to be employed collecting furs from Indian tribes living in the lower one hundred miles of the Columbia River, Second Mate John Mumford at first was pleased that this might mean he would not have to sail north with the ship under a captain he heartily disliked. Later he decided that the prospect of commanding an ungainly schooner in the treacherous currents and fickle winds of a river he knew nothing about while supervising trading with slant-headed savages he did not understand or trust might not be enjoyable either.

When Mumford complained about the task assigned him, Ben volunteered to help. "Sir, I've sailed small schooners on Long Island Sound and the Hudson River. In light winds and currents, they're not hard to handle."

"Would you like to work with me on this one?"

Since the alternative was to become a faller of trees and a beast of burden as the towering cedar, spruce, and fir trees to be used in the building of Fort Astoria—as the post was to be called—were cut down, split, trimmed, and dragged to the site, Ben did not hesitate for a minute.

"I'd be glad to help you, Mr. Mumford. Especially if it means I won't have to ship out on the *Tonquin* again."

Like any craft yet to be launched, the sailing qualities of the thirty-ton schooner could not be determined until she had been put into the water. Broad of beam compared to her length, with a shallow keel, and fat, barge-like lines above water, she appeared designed more for carrying capacity than for sailing grace. Having read in a New York City paper that Mr. Astor had a nineteen-year-old daughter named "Dolly," Ben suggested that the schooner be named in her honor.

"Why not?" Mumford said with a sardonic chuckle. "From what I've heard, she's on the broad side, too, though a tad less than thirty tons. *Dolly* the schooner will be."

Oddly enough, Conco, with whom Ben had struck up a friendship based on age, a mutual interest in the sea, and a curiosity about each other's culture, was far more intrigued with the stack of precut timbers brought ashore from the *Tonquin* and the plans for building the schooner than was Carpenter Weeks or Second Mate Mumford. When he indicated by word and gesture that he wanted to see what the finished craft would look like, Ben showed him the blueprints. These made no sense to him, so Ben turned over a sheet, took a pencil, and drew a sketch of a Hudson River schooner, which Conco immediately understood.

After studying the sketch for several moments, he began shaking his head, criticizing the craft's design. By now, Ben had learned that Chinook Jargon used many English and French words just as they were, though often modifying the names of animals or birds to imitate the cries they uttered. A duck, for instance, was a *quack-quack*, a cow a *moos-moos*, a crow a *caw-caw*, an owl a *hool-hool*, and a cat a *pft-pft or a puss-puss*. In Jargon, an Indian canoe was called a *canim*, while a white man's boat simply was called a boat.

"Boat too *klukulh*," Conco said, indicating with his hands that the schooner was too broad for its length. "Come big wind, make *cultus kalaple*. Roll bad, maybe turn over."

"It does look unstable to me," Ben said, nodding in agreement. "Maybe we can correct that by adding more depth to the keel. Which brings up a thing I've been curious about. I've never seen one of your big seagoing canoes out of the water. How much of a keel does it have?"

"If you want to see one being made, we cross the river and I show you."

"I'd like that."

"Tomorrow I take you to my father's longhouse. I ask him permission to let you meet our *canim tyee*, Chief Canoe-maker of tribe. He is very great man, come from many generations of tribal canoe-makers."

Given Mr. Mumford's approval to absent himself from the building site of Fort Astoria, where the voyageurs, clerks, and mechanics now were suffering the indignity of being hitched like oxen in teams of eight to drag downed logs out of the forest where they had been cut, Ben spent several days in the Chinook village on the north bank of the river, learning how canoes were built. Laboring under the watchful eye of the wizened old *canim tyee* in charge, the native craftsmen and their tools bore no resemblance to those employed in a New England shipyard. But Ben suspected that the results would not have displeased the most meticulous master builder of a New Bedford whaler back home.

Though canoes of several sizes now were being built in a clearing just above the river, the process for each was the same, Ben learned, with the *canim tyee* in charge of every minute detail. To begin with, the *tyee* chose a huge cedar tree as flawless as possible for seventy or eighty feet of its length, then had it felled with what Conco called a *pe-yah-cud*. Examining the blade of the primitive ax, Ben saw that it was of a black volcanic material called obsidian and was incredibly sharp.

After his helpers felled the tree, the *canim tyee* scored the bark, then the workmen trimmed the branches and peeled the trunk. The hull of the big seagoing canoe was shaped slowly and carefully. After hot rocks had been used to burn out the interior and the hull had been roughly formed, the *tyee* went over it inch by inch, supervising his helpers as they used hand-chisels to remove a chip here and another there in a process taking whatever amount of time was required until the vessel took the shape he wanted.

In its design, no blueprints or drawings of any kind existed, so far as Ben could tell, the complete plan for the craft existing only in the *tyee*'s mind. Normally sixty feet long when finished, with a raised stern and a high-peaked prow ornamented with the symbolic figure of a raven, a whale, or a mythical thunderbird, each seagoing canoe would be manned by fifty paddlers kneeling abreast twenty-five on each side, could carry what Ben estimated to be five tons of cargo, and could move through the roughest kind of water with incredible ease and speed.

The balance of the canoes was perfect, achieved expertly by the skilled eye and judgment of the *canim tyee*, who insisted that a wood chip be taken out here, another there, and still others at key points throughout the hull until the trim was exactly what he wanted. Crucial in the construction process, Conco told Ben, was the spreading of the craft's interior in order to make it exactly the right width, which was a delicate balance between load capacity and seaworthiness.

After the hull was hollowed out, it was filled with water which then was heated with red-hot stones. As the still unseasoned wood softened, carefully measured thwarts were placed so that they would act as spreaders, producing a flare. Too little spread reduced stability in heavy seas; too much might split the wood. Working without blueprints or printed directions, the only guide was the judgment of the *tyee*, whose skills had been handed down to him through a long line of canoe-builders.

When Ben asked how long the big seagoing canoes could be expected to last, Conco told him that the one he had been using the day he rescued the McDougall-Stuart party had been built by the grandfather-grandfather of today's *canim tyee*, which, by Ben's calculation, meant it must be at least a hundred years old.

"How do you preserve the wood that long?" Ben asked incredulously. "How do you keep it from cracking above water or getting so waterlogged below that it no longer will float?"

"Glease. Just lub with glease."

By now, Ben had learned that one of several letters that the Chinooks could not articulate was "r," so he had no difficulty figuring out that what Conco was saying was that the cedar canoes were rubbed with grease or a similar substance such as oil. But finding out what kind of grease or oil Conco meant required a bit more linguistic probing.

The first word Conco used was *kamooks*, which Ben knew meant "dog." Even before Ben could ask if that meant dog grease or dog oil,

Conco hastily added the word *pish*, which Ben knew meant "fish," then concluded with the word *hyas*, which Ben knew meant "big." Putting the three words together, Ben came up with the combination "big-dog-fish," a name which whites and Indians alike applied to a three-foot-long shark called a dogfish, which was frequently found in these waters. Regarded as a nuisance by both whites and natives, its flesh was so distasteful that it was eaten only by starving people. But the oil of its liver—which smelled to high heaven—excelled in its preservative qualities.

Noticing that the lines of the big seagoing canoes he had seen in current use by the Chinooks differed in subtle ways from those now under construction, Ben suddenly began to suspect that the changes in lines were related to the time when the Chinooks and the white explorers first had come in contact with one another.

"You say your big canoe was designed and built a hundred years ago. Which would have been before your people saw ships sailed by white men."

"This is true."

"But since then—in the last twenty years, say—your *canim tyee* has seen and liked some of the features of British warships and American whalers that have visited the Northwest Coast. So he's borrowed the lines that have pleased him and is using them in the canoes he's building now. Right?"

Though at first having difficulty understanding what Ben was driving at, Conco at last grasped the concept, smiled, and nodded.

"We see a thing is *cultus*—bad—we *mahsh*—throw it away. We see it is *kloshe*—good—we *iskum*—take and use it. Is same with all Indian people. We take what we like of the white man's ways and throw away what is bad. At least, this is what we try to do."

"Not a bad idea at all," Ben murmured thoughtfully. "And do you know something, Conco? I think there's a lot of good things the whites can learn from you."

8.

*I*MPATIENT AS CAPTAIN THORN WAS to get the supplies for the new trading post unloaded so that he and Alexander McKay could sail north to Vancouver Island and start trading with the Nootka Indians for sea otter furs, it would have been folly to leave the lower Columbia River area until the building of Fort Astoria was well under way. The people and goods being left there needed a roof over their heads, a stockade, and protection against possibly hostile natives. But even as construction of the post began, the short-sighted policies of Duncan McDougall, who had refused to provide any shelter for the mechanics and clerks from the chill, endless rain, angered half a dozen of them so much that they stole muskets, blankets, and food, appropriated a small boat from the *Tonquin*, and headed upriver, vowing to make their way back to the United States, though they had no idea of how to get there.

To Ben's surprise, Chief Concomly responded to McDougall's complaint that the men were missing by sending Conco and twenty warriors after them in a swift Indian canoe. Within three days' time, the Chinooks overtook the party of deserters, which had progressed only thirty miles upriver, and persuaded them to return to the site of the fort.

"Actually, it didn't take much talking to convince the poor devils to come back," Alexander Ross told Ben. "They were awfully cold, wet, and miserable."

"What I don't understand is why Chief Concomly sent his people after them."

"What's the Chinook Jargon word for money—*chikamin*?"

"Or *dolla*."

"That's why Chief Concomly did it. He figured McDougall would reward him for it."

"Did McDougall pay him?"

"My guess is he did, though he won't admit it. He's been mighty chummy with the one-eyed rascal since he and David Stuart spent three nights in the longhouse. In fact, I heard that one of Concomly's daughters kept McDougall's back warm nights while he was there. Maybe his front, too."

That a former North West Company trader should bed an Indian woman did not surprise Ben. Senior Partner Alexander McKay made no secret of the fact that he had had a lasting relationship back in Canada with a Cree woman, who had borne him a son. Now thirteen years old, the boy, Thomas McKay, had accompanied his father on the *Tonquin*. Listed as a clerk with the Astor Company, Thomas McKay was tall, slim, and quiet-mannered, with soft black eyes and dark brown skin. He'd been hoping that his father would take him along when the ship sailed north, he told Ben, but his father had said he would learn more about the Pacific Fur Company business by staying here and working for Duncan McDougall and David Stuart than he would aboard ship with his father.

The scope of Conco's knowledge about the Nootka Indians, whose domain lay five hundred miles to the north, surprised Ben.

"For a long time, we and the Nootkans fought whenever we met," Conco said. "Then their great Chief Maquina and our great Chief Concomly had a truce talk. They said: 'Why should we fight when what we really want to do is trade?' So now, we trade instead of fight."

"What do you trade?"

"*Haiqua* and *mistchimas*. Shells and slaves."

"Who has the shells and who has the slaves?"

"In the shallow waters of Nootka Sound grows a small sea creature with a very beautiful white shell the length of a little finger. It is called *haiqua* and treasured by all coastal Indians—like gold and silver are valued by white people. But the labor of gathering these shells is very great. So the Nootkas need slaves."

"Which the Chinooks supply, I gather. Where do you get them?"

"Wherever our war canoes go up and down the coast. Most round-headed Indians are not good fighters. Whenever we attack a village, we usually kill all the warriors who do not run away, then take their wives and children prisoners. So we always have lots of slaves to trade for *haiqua*."

Conco's use of the term "round-headed Indians" explained a

77

mystery that had puzzled Ben. Apparently all the women and children with normal heads that he had seen doing menial chores in the Chinook village were slaves. Because they were regarded as inferior to the Chinooks, they were not permitted to bear the mark of royalty, just as in China peasant girl babies were not allowed to have their feet bound, as were higher-class females. As for the Chinook practice of taking slaves and then trading them to the Nootkans for seashells, he supposed that was no worse than the white practice of enslaving Africans and trading them for gold.

"You say your people travel up and down the coast. Have you crossed the bar and gone out to sea yourself?"

"Many times. Often with my people I have gone out to sea so far the land cannot be seen. The ocean does not scare me."

Though Captain Thorn was so incensed by the deserters' theft of the ship's boat that he would gladly have tried them for mutiny and hanged them to the yardarm, no harm had been done, Alexander McKay pointed out. Furthermore, the clerks and mechanics were employed by the Pacific Fur Company, not by the master of the *Tonquin*, thus were not subject to his discipline. As a result of their rebellion, McDougall did provide them with tents to keep off the rain, sheet-iron stoves to keep them warm, and enough nourishing food to replenish the energy they were expending hauling and raising the post's timbers. What he did not provide, Alexander Ross pointed out indignantly, was the medical care to which they were entitled.

"It's outrageous how Mr. Astor has neglected the physical well-being of his people," Ross told Ben. "Nothing more clearly proves his indifference than his not providing a medical man either aboard ship or in his colony. It shows how callous he is."

Already, Duncan McDougall had begun trading with the Indians for furs. But after an initial offering of beaver and sea otter pelts by the Clatsops, Tillamooks, Nahcotas, and Cathlamets, all these lower Columbia tribes stopped bringing in skins and became so sullen that the whites feared they were plotting an attack. Only Chief Concomly remained friendly. Only the Chinooks continued to bring in furs, though the prices they now demanded were three times what they had been before. Seeking the cause for this change in attitude, Alexander Ross soon discovered what had brought it about.

"I was asked by a Cathlamet the other day how much we were paying for prime beaver pelts," Ross said. "When I quoted our current price, he put his hand over his mouth in surprise, then said that was three times as much as he'd been paid for some he'd just sold to Concomly. When I asked him why he hadn't brought them to us, he said Concomly had told him it was *cultus huy-huy* to trade with us. You know what that means?"

"Sure. That it's 'bad business to trade' with us."

"Exactly. Chief Concomly apparently has told all the lower Columbia tribes that he's made a deal with the whites that furs can be sold only to him. Then he triples the price and resells them to us."

"Just as we do when we ship them to market in China or England," Ben said with a smile. "Conco was telling me the other day that his people reject what they don't like of white culture and adopt what they think is good. To Chief Concomly, making a big profit trading furs is good."

"From his point of view, I suppose. But who does he think he is—John Jacob Astor?"

Though Ben Warren managed to avoid being employed as a beast of burden to help drag the big timbers used in the building of the fort down out of the woods, he did help for several warm, sunny days in the work of planting potatoes and seeds in a vegetable garden, which it was hoped would flourish and supply a portion of the post's food. When Conco expressed curiosity as to what kind of vegetables the seeds and dried potato eyes would produce, Ben could only demonstrate their size and shape with his hands, while at the same time rubbing his stomach, smacking his lips, and saying *klosche muckamuck*—"tastes good"—in Chinook Jargon.

Nodding that he understood, Conco showed up a couple of days later carrying a basket filled with several kinds of bulb-like roots, berries, and fruits which he identified as *wapato, camas, solemie, powitsch, shot olallie,* and *salal olallie.* Though some were fresh and some dried, upon tasting them Ben thought the *wapato* resembled a potato, the *camas* a sweet squash, the *solemie* a crab apple, the *shot olallie* a cranberry, and the *salal olallie* a blueberry. All grew wild in profusion nearby, Conco said, and were harvested in season by female round-headed slaves. Since harvesting and gathering were beneath the dignity of men in his tribe, he could not understand why the white men

would go to so much work digging up the cold, wet ground and planting their potato eyes and seeds.

"You've got a good point there," Ben said. "Why don't you tell it
to *Tyee* McDougall?"

In addition to the ship's carpenter, John Weeks, the Astor party
employed a cooper named George Bell, a blacksmith named Auguste
Roussil, and a carpenter of their own named Johann Koaster. Hoping
to get the keel of the *Dolly* laid and the building of the schooner
started so that they could begin cruising the lower river, Second Mate
Mumford did persuade John Weeks to help him select a site where the
timbers could be laid out on the river's bank, while Ben tried to explain to Johann Koaster, who was part Swiss, part Russian, and a good
part thick-headed ox, what needed to be done to build the craft.

Because Koaster had no imagination whatsoever and spoke English so poorly that every last detail of the job had to be demonstrated
to him several times before he would pick up a hammer, maul, or saw,
getting him started in the right direction was almost as difficult as getting him stopped before he could drive a nail or saw off a board in the
wrong place. But bit by bit, the building of the schooner proceeded,
while at the same time the construction of the fort went on.

By the middle of May, the most important structure in the com-
plex, a storage building twenty-six feet wide and sixty feet long, had
been completed, and most of the supplies aboard the *Tonquin* had
been brought ashore. Though the stockade would not be completed
for another month or so, the people being left at Fort Astoria had
enough muskets and pistols to defend themselves, while a pair of six-
pounder cannons were placed on blocks in the yard, where hopefully
they would intimidate the natives until corner bastions were completed and they could be mounted on the walls.

With the ship scheduled to head north within the next ten days, it
was decided that Mr. Mumford and Seaman Ben Warren would be
left behind to complete the schooner and gather furs on the lower
river under the supervision of Senior Partner Duncan McDougall.
Sometime next month, David Stuart and Alexander Ross would head
a party bound up the Columbia to the upper reaches of the river,
where a post would be established near the mouth of the Okanogan
River. Traveling with his father as far as the big bend of the Columbia
350 miles inland, Robert Stuart and a small group would travel east
via the inland route across the Blue Mountains, the Snake River

desert, and the Rocky Mountains carrying news of the enterprise back to Mr. Astor in New York.

Sailing north with the *Tonquin*, Senior Partner Alexander McKay would be in charge of trading with the Indians at Nootka Sound. The prospect did not particularly please him, Ross said, for he feared he would have trouble controlling Captain Thorn in their dealings with a band of Indians known to be moody and dangerous. When McKay learned that a personal friendship existed between Chief Concomly and Chief Maquina of the Nootkans, he asked Ben and Conco to meet with him and Ross to discuss several things that were troubling him.

"We've been offered the services of a Coast Indian called Lamansee," he told them. "He claims he's related to the Vancouver Island tribes and can speak their language. Do you think he can be trusted?"

"*Tenas*," Conco said, with a shrug. "You can trust him a little—but not too much."

Filling and lighting his long-stemmed redstone pipe, as he always did when considering serious matters, McKay scowled at Conco. "Weel, now, ye must tell me more about where he can and can nae be trusted. For instance, does he know the channel across the bar well enough to guide the *Tonquin* out to sea?"

"*Wake, wake!*" Conco exclaimed, shaking his head in a violent negative. "Do not trust him to do that! He is a round-headed Indian from the Makah and Nootka tribes far to the north. He may know the waters in that country, but he does not know the mouth of the great river as we Chinooks do."

"Ye seem to do well enough crossing the bar in your big seagoing canoes," McKay admitted. "But a sailing ship is a much larger craft. Could you find a safe channel for the *Tonquin* across the bar?"

Nodding vigorously, Conco said proudly, "When the first Boston captain brought his ship into the river many years ago, it was guided by a Chinook canoe commanded by my father. Ben knows the name of the Boston captain and when it was he came …"

"Captain Robert Gray in the ship *Columbia Redidiva*, in 1792," Ben said. "But this is the first time I've heard that Chief Concomly was his bar pilot."

"He was," Conco said. "From that time on, every ship that has entered or left the river, whether commanded by a Boston or a King

0

George captain, has been guided by a Chinook pilot trained by my father."

"That's good enough for me," McKay said, nodding. "I'll pass the information on to Captain Thorn. Likely he'll want you aboard to give directions to the helmsman, with Ben as an interpreter, when we cross the bar and head out to sea in a week or so."

"Sir," Ben said quietly, "if I ever set foot on the quarter deck of the *Tonquin* again, it won't be to guide her across the bar. It will be to kill Captain Thorn for sending my father to his death."

"I understand your feelings, lad. But you're not a member of the *Tonquin*'s crew now. Nor are you under Captain Thorn's discipline."

"I will be the moment I go aboard, sir. He knows I've made threats against him. After I've guided his ship across the bar, he'll probably put me in irons."

"Suppose I promise I'd nae stand for that? Would ye come aboard gi'en my promise?"

"It's not your ship, Mr. McKay. It's his. He proved that to you months ago."

"Aye, that he did," McKay admitted wryly. "But we do need a pilot, lad, I'm convinced of that. I doubt that Captain Thorn will risk his ship to a slant-headed young Indian whose language he can nae understand. Before he'll do that, he'll try to cross the bar without a pilot, no matter what the cost."

"There's another way to accomplish the same result, sir. When the *Tonquin* is ready to sail, Conco and I will tell you the time of day when the current and tide will be right. We'll have a crew of paddlers in a big seagoing canoe, which will lead the ship through the proper channel. I'll be standing in the stern with a white flag on a staff, just as my father stood in the pinnace when Captain Thorn left him and the others to drown. We'll guide the *Tonquin* safely out to sea."

"Fair enough," McKay said, nodding. "Captain Thorn won't like it, I'm sure, but I'll tell him it's the only way I'll consent to sail." After a moment's silence, during which he looked more melancholy than Ben had ever seen him, McKay turned to Alexander Ross. "I must confess I have no liking for the way this part of our venture is beginning, Alex."

"Why not, sir?"

"With the fort still not finished and poorly defended, we're sailing
0
north to establish trade with a tribe known for its treachery. Now that

Mr. Mumford is being left behind, we have not a single ship's officer
aboard. The only Astor Company people I'll have with me will be
Clerk Lewis and two French-Canadian voyageurs, so I'll have little
backing if Captain Thorn throws another of his temper tantrums—as
I fear he will."

"Surely he won't question your decisions when it comes to trading
with the Nootkans. He has no experience in that part of the business."

"Which will not deter him, I fear, once his vile temper takes over."
Tapping the dottle out of his pipe, McKay sighed. "Ah, weel, there's
naught can be done about it. But if you ever see us safe back here, it
will be a miracle. Take good care of my son, Alex. And you, Ben, gi'
Thomas your friendship and special concern, as I know ye will. He's
of mixed blood, ye know, so will need a friend who understands him
as ye've shown ye do."

Even though word drifted back to Ben from members of the *Tonquin*'s
crew that Captain Thorn had stormed and raged when told by Alexander McKay the terms under which the ship would be guided across
the bar, when faced with the Senior Partner's flat refusal to sail unless
they were met, Thorn finally agreed. Weighing anchor at Fort Astoria June 1, 1811, the ship crossed the lower river to Baker Bay offshore
from the Chinook village, then waited until weather, tide, and current
were favorable in mid-morning, June 5.

Under jib, spanker, and close-hauled mainsail, the Tonquin followed the big Chinook canoe through a channel on the Cape Disappointment side of the river that never measured less than eight fathoms
in depth according to Ben's soundings in the stern, while Conco, in
the bow, who was setting the course by eye, instinct, and long experience, never appeared to doubt for a moment that the ship following
had plenty of water under her keel.

Six miles offshore with the headlands of the Cape only faintly visible through the noontime heat haze, which was beginning to rise off
the edge of the continent, Conco waved back to Ben and called:

"*Mamook kopet!* Finished! Enough water now!"

In the stern of the canoe, Ben waved the white flag he was holding
back and forth several times, then extended its staff at a forty-five-
degree angle to the north, indicating the direction in which the ship

now was free to sail. Aboard the *Tonquin*, a sailor in the bow evidently had been taking soundings, too, and had already sent a message to the quarter deck that the ship was in deep water. A full rack of sails had been shaken out and the billowing white canvas was filling with the strong southwest wind as the ship heeled around on her new course.

As a matter of simple marine courtesy, the American flag flying atop the mainmast should have been dipped and raised three times—as Captain Thorn had insisted be done when saying farewell to the *Constitution* ten months and 21,265 miles ago, according to Gabriel Franchere's journal and the ship's log. But the colors stayed in place. After all, Captain Jonathan Thorn probably was thinking, our escort is not a premier ship of the line of the United States Navy. It is just a dugout canoe manned by fifty slant-headed Indians and a sixteen-year-old white sailor who, if I had my way, would be put in irons, lashed to the mainmast and given fifty lashes, or even hanged to the yardarm for his mutinous thoughts and words.

"And good-bye to you, Captain Thorn," Ben murmured as he saluted the stern of the *Tonquin*. "If I never see your ugly face again, it will be a lifetime too soon ..."

9.

FULLY OCCUPIED trying to get the *Dolly* built at the same time construction of the living quarters and palisade surrounding Fort Astoria went on, Ben did not pay nearly as much attention as Alexander Ross did to the way the local Indians lived and the things they valued as items of trade. Conco had told him about *haiqua*, the seashell found only in Nootka Sound, which was prized so highly by all the coastal tribes, but he had not seen the shell itself until Ross acquired several pieces and showed them to him.

"Would you believe this is what circulates as money in their society?" Ross said in amazement.

"So Conco tells me. The Chinooks trade slaves to the Nootkans for it."

Though the most common variety of *haiqua* was a small white shell about two inches long, convex in shape, and hollow in the center, it ranged from one-quarter to three inches in length and was light and durable. According to Ross, who had done some bargaining with the Indians, its value increased with the number of shells required to make a fathom-long string, a fathom being the equivalent of two outstretched arms, or six feet.

"The Chinooks set such a high price on it," Ross told Ben, "that I've seen a native offer to trade a new gun for six strings and get turned down. Lord knows what the equivalent would be in round-headed slaves."

Noting that both the Clatsops and Chinooks were a well-fed people, who lived by both hunting and fishing, Ross told Ben that he thought the lower Columbia River fishery, on which the natives relied as their major food supply, was the finest in the world.

"There are at least half a dozen different species of salmon which run up the river ten months out of the year, they tell me. The biggest

I've seen caught weighed fifty pounds, though the Indians say the fish are often much larger than that. I would estimate if we set up a commercial fishery to catch, ice, and ship salmon back East, we could count on the Indians supplying us at least a thousand tons a year."

Also to be found in the lower river were monstrous white sturgeon, whose meat was sweet and delicious no matter how old or large the fish got. Seven-hundred-pound sturgeon were common, Ross said, while one monster fish that he had measured and weighed was thirteen feet, nine inches in length, and weighed 1,130 pounds.

"Then there's a small fish they call a *ulichan*, which resembles a smelt or herring," Ross told Ben. "They come into the Cowlitz in such immense numbers to spawn each spring that they can be scooped up in baskets. They're so rich in oil that when they're dried they can be lighted and burned, just like candles."

"I've seen and smelled them in the longhouses," Ben said. "They're so plentiful that the Chinooks stitch them together, smoke, and sell them in fathom-long strings as items of trade. Conco calls them 'fathom-fish.' "

"Or 'candle-fish.' They smell and taste terrible, unless you like undiluted fish oil. But they do seem to have a lot of nourishment in them."

Another curious fact Ross had learned was that none of the lower Columbia River or coastal tribes ever went out to sea and hunted whales as the Makahs did further north near the entrance to the Strait of Juan de Fuca. It was not that the Chinooks or Clatsops feared crossing the bar, for they did this often. More likely, they did not hunt whales because they had a plentiful supply of fish, oil, oysters, and clams in the lower river and shallow bays up and down the coast, so had never needed to develop whale-hunting skills as the Makahs did.

"Lewis and Clark wrote about seeing a hundred-foot-long whale that the Tillamooks butchered after it died and washed up on the beach near Fort Clatsop," Ross said. "In fact, their Shoshone Indian girl guide, Sacajawea, complained that it was a cruel thing she could not go see the 'big fish' that had washed up on the beach, after coming all the way from Mandan country to the Pacific Ocean. So Lewis and Clark took her with them to the beach and gave her a bite of the piece of blubber they bought and cooked. Clark said it tasted like fat pork. But the Tillamooks hadn't killed the whale. They'd just butchered it after it died and washed up on the beach."

Senior Partner David Stuart's plan to lead an expedition inland in midsummer was postponed when on July 15 a large canoe carrying a flag was sighted rounding Tongue Point. Expecting the overland contingent under Wilson Price Hunt, which was supposed to have left St. Louis ten months ago, the Astorians were surprised and disappointed to discover that the flag being carried in the canoe was British, not American. Led by David Thompson of the Montreal-based North West Company, the nine boatmen in the crew were French-Canadian voyageurs who greeted their compatriots in the Astor party like long-lost friends, as indeed they were. The exuberant warmth with which dour-natured Duncan McDougall welcomed David Thompson alarmed Alexander Ross, who confided his suspicions to Ben.

"It seems very strange that Mr. Thompson, a veteran fur trader for a British-owned company, should cross Canada and show up at the mouth of the Columbia only a couple of months after we arrived. He must have known we would be here."

"From what he's told Mr. McDougall," Ben said, "he'd have been here much sooner, if he'd had his way."

"So I gather. Apparently he crossed the Canadian Rockies to the headwaters of the Columbia late last fall. When half of his men deserted him, he went into camp for the winter, built a canoe this spring, then came on the rest of the way this summer."

"He's carrying a sextant with him, I notice, and has taken several astronomical observations since he got here. Why would a man who claims to be a fur trader do that?"

"Because he's more geographer than fur trader, would be my guess. He's keeping a journal of his travels, too. I'd like to read it and find out what he's really up to."

"Maybe you could work out a trade with him," Ben said with a grin. "Let him read yours if he'll let you read his."

"There's no way I'd consent to that," Ross said, shaking his head. "When I signed on with Mr. Astor, I became a half-share partner in the Pacific Fur Company, which is American. My loyalty is to the United States, not to Great Britain. But Duncan McDougall is so friendly to Thompson, I have to wonder where *his* loyalties lie."

Five days after the arrival of the party of Nor'westers, Duncan

87

McDougall stunned the Astorians by announcing that he was going to marry one of Chief Concomly's daughters, a maiden of fourteen. When he heard that, Alexander Ross snorted.

"If that don't take the cake! Do you suppose she's the little beauty who kept his back warm the nights he spent in the chief's longhouse?"

"Could be."

"Ask Conco if he knows the details of how and when his sister's romance with Laird McDougall began."

"I already did. His father has seven wives, Conco says. The girl McDougall is marrying has a different mother than he does, so she's only a half sister. To Chinook women, being bedded by a white man is no big deal. Conco doesn't know what McDougall gave his father in the way of payment for her, what his father promised McDougall in return, or how the marriage will affect relations between us and them."

"Well, it certainly won't hurt Chief Concomly's monopoly of the local fur market. At least not until you get the *Dolly* finished and start gathering furs upriver. How's it coming?"

"Very slowly," Ben said. "But we hope to launch it in a month or so."

Shaking his head, Alexander Ross gave Ben a sidelong look, then said, "Have you seen the bride-to-be?"

"Yes."

"As an expert judge of local beauties, what do you think of her looks?"

"Not bad—considering."

"Considering that she's slant-headed, smells to high heaven of fish oil, is short, pudgy, and bandy-legged? Considering all that, you say 'not bad'?"

Ben laughed. "It's Mr. McDougall that's marrying her, Alex, not me. What his feelings will be when he beds her in the dark, I won't venture to guess. But in broad daylight what he'll be thinking is that she's Chief Concomly's daughter—which makes him a son-in-law of the most powerful Indian chief in this part of the country. To a Scotch fur trader like Duncan McDougall, that's money in the bank."

In late July, David Stuart, Alexander Ross, and half a dozen voyageurs finally left Fort Astoria for the interior, planning to examine the country near the mouth of the Okanogan River to see if building a post there would be feasible. Apparently part of the price McDougall had paid Concomly for his bride was a swallow-tailed, double-breasted, brass-buttoned black frock coat, plus a tall beaver top hat whose crown was pierced with three feathers, one red, one yellow, and one green. The first time Gabriel Franchere saw the costume, he laughed and said:

"It's a wonder McDougall didn't give him a tartan and a kilt. Wouldn't that look great at the wedding, with bagpipes playing 'Here Comes the Bride'?"

Whatever the weather, Chief Concomly always wore this costume when he came to the fort, which he did at least three times a week. In early August, he brought bad news.

"This man, him name Calpo," he told McDougall and Gabriel Franchere as he introduced a Chinook Indian he had brought into the fort with him. "Him just get back from Makah country, across *skookum chuck* from Nootka Sound. Him tell you what he hear about your ship."

What Calpo had heard, Franchere told Ben, was a garbled story to the effect that the *Tonquin* had been destroyed.

"When we pressed him for details," Franchere said, "he gave us to understand by signs and gestures that a large ship with white people in it had been blown up in Nootka Sound."

"Blown up? How? By who?"

"He didn't make that clear. But he got very excited when he told us about it, throwing his hands up in the air to show pieces of the ship flying all over, puffing out his cheeks, then indicating with loud grunts that there had been a tremendous explosion."

"It's hard to believe that the *Tonquin* has been destroyed."

"Certainly we don't want to believe it. Mr. McDougall has asked Chief Concomly to do some checking and see if he can find out anything more."

By mid-September, the living quarters at Fort Astoria had been completed, a stockade built, the two six-pounders mounted on corner bastions, and the *Dolly* finally had been skidded into the river and launched. Returning from upriver, David Stuart and Alexander Ross reported two facts that David Thompson—who with his voyageurs had left the fort several weeks ago—had not bothered to mention: first, that on his way downriver in early July he had stuck a flagstaff in the sand near the juncture of the Snake and Columbia Rivers proclaiming all the country over which he had just passed the domain of His Royal Britannic Majesty by right of its prior discovery by himself, David Thompson; and, second, that the North West Company was planning to establish a fur trading post nearby in the very near future.

"We cannae waste time building our post in the Okanogan country," David Stuart said urgently. "If we delay too long, there'll be no furs left for us upriver next spring."

On the maiden voyage of the *Dolly* up the Columbia, the schooner would transport the trade goods and building materials for Fort Okanogan as far as the Lower Cascades, 145 miles up the river. From that point, the goods would be portaged around the rapids, then carried in several medium-sized Chinook canoes the rest of the way. Both the *Dolly* and the fleet of canoes would be under the command of Second Mate John Mumford, with Ben taking charge of the schooner for its return trip to Fort Astoria. Hopefully, he would be able to persuade some of the Indians encountered along the way to trade directly with the white Astorians rather than through Chief Concomly.

From the beginning, it was clear that the schooner was a very poor sailer. Though she could carry thirty tons of cargo easily enough, drew only three feet of water, and was rigged with fore and aft sails on swinging booms, she would not answer her helm against even the slightest adverse current or wind. Demonstrating a marked tendency to scoot sideways rather than forward when the wind was abeam, she went aground on an incoming tide in a slough on the south shore only twenty miles up the river. Two days later, a strong quartering wind drove her into a mud bank at the mouth of the Cowlitz River on the north shore. Then, as if determined to prove that she was unsailable in any current or wind, she went aground behind what Lewis and Clark had named "Image Canoe Island"—later called "Sauvie Island"—whose nine-mile length masked the entrance to a large river coming in from the south called "Multnomah" by the local Indians, "Willamette" by the whites.

By any name, the silt-filled channel behind the island was a bad place to go aground, for the Multnomah, Kalama, Washougal, and half a dozen other local tribes soon came swarming around, trying to clamber aboard and help themselves to the trade goods, building materials, and tools the schooner was carrying, without offering any furs in return. Since there was no escaping the avaricious natives until the *Dolly* could be refloated, the only thing the small party of whites could do to defend themselves was put up anti-boarding nets, point rifles and pistols at the Indians, and threaten to shoot them if they did not back off. While thus occupied, the whites could do nothing to work the schooner free of the mudflats, being forced to wait and pray for a favorable wind, current, or tide.

In the end, it was Conco who saved the *Dolly* and its cargo. Curious to learn how the white man's sailing ship operated, he had joined Ben, Second Mate Mumford, and two Kanaka crew members aboard; but he also had taken the precaution of being followed by a big seagoing cedar canoe manned by thirty Chinook paddlers. What he quickly learned about the white man's sailing ship was that it spent more time aground than afloat; and that his native craft and crew could paddle rings around it in any kind of wind and weather.

Because the thirty Chinook paddlers were warriors and well equipped with weapons and the thick leather shields which the Chinooks wore when going into battle, they were formidable fighting men. When the first signs of hostility were displayed by the local Indians, Conco signaled to his paddlers, who immediately donned their armor and picked up their weapons, causing a sudden, precipitous retreat of the local natives from the vicinity of the schooner. At that point, Second Mate Mumford gave up on the *Dolly*.

"She ain't a boat—she's a goddam fat waddlin' duck," he exclaimed disgustedly to Ben. "She's all yours, lad. I'll have no more to do with her."

"What about the supplies for the fort, sir?"

"We were planning on transferring them to canoes at the Lower Cascades anyway," David Stuart said. "Now we'll have to do it here. Lightening her load will let you refloat her. Then you can take her back to Fort Astoria."

"Or sink her in the middle of the river," Mumford muttered. "Just so you get her out of my sight."

Watching the building materials and trade goods destined for Fort Okanogan being transferred from the *Dolly* to the dugout canoes, the local Indians began to produce the beaver pelts they had accumulated and had been instructed to sell only to Chief Concomly. Since they knew Conco was the chief's son and assumed he had the authority to speak for his father, they began bargaining with him and with Ben. When Ben suggested to David Stuart that he be given a stock of trade goods and be allowed to offer the local Indians a higher price than Chief Concomly had been paying them, though somewhat less than they would receive from the whites at Fort Astoria, both David Stuart and Alexander Ross approved the idea.

"Aye, trade wi' 'em if ye can," Stuart said. "It's time we taught Concomly a lesson."

"Maybe you'll do better as a trader than you've done as a sailor," Ross chuckled. "The *Dolly* hasn't behaved very well as your first command."

"When I get her back to the fort," Ben said wryly, "our sailing days together are done. But I do believe Conco and I can do some business trading for pelts on the lower river. Instead of the *Dolly*, we'll use Chinook canoes to carry our trade goods and furs, taking along enough warriors to make sure we're not attacked and robbed. None of the lower river Indians will dare to challenge Chief Concomly's son."

Taking the *Dolly* downriver turned out to be much easier than sailing her upriver had been, for she floated well enough when going with the current. Dropping her anchor just below Tongue Point, Ben told her good-bye without tears, perfectly willing to let her rot in peace, her career on the river limited to a single voyage. Since both Duncan McDougall and Chief Concomly approved the fur-gathering enterprise undertaken by Ben and Conco, the two young friends now were free to do what they liked best: explore the coves, bays, and inlets of the lower river as they desired.

As Ben expected would happen, Second Mate John Mumford became discontented with the upriver expedition almost as quickly as David Stuart and Alexander Ross grew exasperated with him. Though Ben learned no details of the quarrel that brought about a parting of the ways, he suspected Mr. Mumford told the truth when he declared upon his return to Fort Astoria after a week upriver:

"I've been too long at sea, lad, to live away from the smell of salt air. Damn all, but them French-Canadian voyageurs are an untidy lot, with no sense of discipline in their happy-go-lucky nature. A pox take them and the fur-tradin' business, I said, and come downriver."

"I can understand that you'd miss the sea, Mr. Mumford."

"How're you getting along with the *Dolly*?"

"Great—now that she's anchored."

"Any word yet on what happened to the *Tonquin*?"

"Rumors, that's all. Mr. McDougall finally persuaded Chief Concomly to send three runners north a week ago to see what they can find out. We should be hearing from them soon."

Toward the end of October, the three Indians returned in a high state of excitement, for in Makah country they had encountered Lamansee, the interpreter who had sailed north with the *Tonquin* last June 5. Bringing him back with them, they insisted that he tell Concomly the story he had told them. Next day, Chief Concomly, accompanied by his son Conco and several canoe loads of Chinook warriors, brought Lamansee to the fort, where he repeated his horror-filled story to the assembled white men …

It had taken eighteen days for the *Tonquin* to sail north to Nootka Sound, Lamansee said, where the ship dropped anchor in a sheltered bay offshore from a large Indian village. Knowing that Alexander McKay was a veteran white trader representing the rich *Tyee* John Jacob Astor, as well a good friend of Chief Concomly, the head man of the Nootkans, Chief Maquina, invited McKay to come ashore and spend a couple of nights in his village. Well treated and entertained while there, McKay was told by Chief Maquina that the Nootkans possessed a great number of fine sea otter furs which they were willing to sell at reasonable prices to the whites. But since he was growing old and infirm, he would not go aboard ship himself, leaving the trading to a shrewd, experienced, more active chief named Nookamis.

This meant, Lamansee said, that for the first two days Captain Thorn was the only white man aboard the *Tonquin* who could set prices regarding the amount of blankets, knives, beads, hawks-bells, pots, pans, and other trade goods that would be given in exchange for furs.

"From the beginning, he made the Indians feel bad because he refused to bargain. He would pay just one set price for all furs, he said. A blanket. A jackknife. A string of beads. All the same price for the same-size fur. But the Indians were not used to trading that way. Chief Nookamis said: 'We will not trade yet. We will talk some more.' "

At first, Captain Thorn was cautious, Lamansee said, hanging anti-boarding nets around the ship to control access over the rails, permitting no more than ten natives at a time to come aboard. Though these were standard precautions for white trading vessels when in the area, the Nootkans refused to take them seriously. In fact, they made a game of seeing how far they could go in getting the whites to relax their rules. After first one and then another of the natives cut holes in the netting and clambered aboard the ship from all directions, Captain Thorn finally ordered the anti-boarding nets pulled in and the restrictions relaxed.

"T' hell with the rules!" he declared to Clerk James Lewis. "The filthy beggars are so eager to trade, they'll give me all the furs I want for whatever price I choose to pay 'em!"

From that time on, Lamansee said, no limit was set as to the number of natives permitted onboard at any one time. By noon of the second day—with Alexander McKay still ashore in the village—fifty or more Nootkans were swarming over the deck of the vessel. Still, very few furs were being traded, for Captain Thorn stubbornly refused to give ground on his set-price policy, while Chief Nookamis would not lower his demands.

"Damn your greedy soul, I meant what I said!" the captain raged angrily. "One blanket or one jackknife for a prime pelt. That's all I'll pay."

"But these are beautiful furs!" Nookamis protested, picking up a couple of prime sea otter pelts that Captain Thorn had contemptuously thrown down and kicked aside. "See how silky and thick the hairs are! Feel the smoothness of the fur! Give us one blanket and two jackknives—"

"One blanket or one jackknife!" Thorn roared, his face reddening. "Take it or leave it!"

"We will compromise. Give us one blanket and one jackknife. That is a fair price." Thrusting a pelt under the captain's chin, Nookamis laughed good-naturedly. "Feel it, captain! So smooth! So fine!"

"Goddam it, I'm sick and tired of your shilly-shallying! I'll 'smooth and fine you'—you foul-smellin', dirty heathen! Since you don't like my price, you can just eat your goddam sea otter pelts! Now get your greasy, fat ass off my ship!"

Snatching the pelt out of the chief's hand, Captain Thorn ground it viciously into the Indian's face, threw it down, then wheeled and walked away. As he mounted the ladder to the quarter deck, the chatter of the natives aboard ceased, Lamansee said. Hands covered mouths in astonishment and shock. A deathly silence fell.

"This was a very bad insult to Chief Nookamis. We all knew that. We saw him make a cutting-off sign, meaning *kopet*—it is finished. Trading was done for the day. Without another word, all the Indians aboard the ship picked up their furs, got into their canoes, and went back to the village."

Early the next morning, Alexander McKay, looking solemn and grim, returned to the *Tonquin*. Going immediately to Captain Thorn's cabin, he exchanged strong words with the captain, saying that the Indians who had come ashore were badly upset, that Chief Nookamis had been gravely insulted, and that trading with the Nootkans had come to a standstill.

"In God's name, Captain Thorn, why did ye treat the chief as ye did?"

"Because I was sick and tired of the old beggar's whining. For a day and a half, I'd been tellin' him how much we'd pay and how he could take it or leave it. But the ignorant old bastard wouldn't listen."

"Ye've got to have patience when trading with Indians, Captain Thorn. Ye've got to treat them with respect. Above all, ye must never touch the person of an Indian—particularly his face. It's an insult he'll nae abide!"

"God's blood, Mr. McKay, I've dealt with natives the wide world over! If there's one thing I've learned, it's that they respect firmness and strength. Which was what I showed 'em."

"There are three hundred warriors in their village," McKay said gravely. "We have only twenty-seven men aboard this ship. We're at the mercy of these people, Captain Thorn."

"The devil we are! We've got muskets, pistols, and cannons, while they have only knives and spears. If it comes to a fight, we'll give them bloody hell!"

"Which will end our chances for trade wi' them and all the other Indians on the Northwest Coast, I'm sure. If ye dinnae curb that flaming temper of yours, Captain Thorn, you'll doom our venture to failure."

"Don't tell me how to behave aboard my own ship!" Captain Thorn exploded. "It's only to Mr. Astor, not to you, I'll answer for my conduct."

❧

Shortly after daybreak, next morning, canoes began coming out to the *Tonquin* from the Indian village, Lamansee said. The day was clear, the sea calm, the air warm. Sitting near the taffrail at the stern of the ship, Alexander McKay looked grim as he sucked on his long-stemmed redstone pipe. Coming out of his cabin, Captain Thorn paused on the quarter deck, shading his eyes against the morning sun with his hand as he gazed down at the approaching canoes. He called down cheerfully to McKay:

"They're coming back, Mr. McKay, just as I told you they would. They're bringing lots of furs. They've learned their lesson, I'll wager."

"Mayhap they have, Captain Thorn," McKay answered skeptically. "But to be on the safe side, you'd best put up the anti-boarding nets and limit the number you let on deck to ten at a time."

"Why bother? They're meek as lambs this mornin'. Why, they've even brought along their wives and babies. Hostile people never do that."

Indeed, the mood of the Nootkans had changed drastically from what it had been the day before, Lamansee said. As the boats swarmed around the ship, the Indians were laughing and calling out cheerful greetings in Chinook Jargon to the sailors aboard the *Tonquin*.

"*Mahkook!* Trade! *Huy-huy!* We come to trade!"

While Senior Partner Alexander McKay watched disapprovingly, Captain Thorn ordered the hatches opened and a large supply of trade goods brought on deck, with the Nootkans being permitted to come aboard without restriction to their number. Bales of blankets, a bushel basket of jackknives, strings of beads, buckets of hawks-bells, bolts of bright-colored cloth, pots, pans, iron skillets, and trinkets of all kinds were strewn across the poop deck, where Clerk James Lewis and half a dozen sailors traded with laughing, good-natured Indians.

Watching the activity from the quarter deck, Captain Thorn appeared to be delighted, Lamansee said, as well he might be. Not only had he shown Mr. McKay what a superior trader he was, he also was making a fabulous profit for Mr. Astor and himself. In exchange for each two-dollar blanket or fifty-cent jackknife, he was obtaining a premium sea otter fur that later could be sold to a wealthy Chinese mandarin for spices, silks, tea, or even gold worth a thousand dollars in England or America. If the rest of this venture—which was to include a voyage north to Sitka and Russian Alaska—were as successful as it now appeared trading with the Nootkans was going to be, Captain Thorn would be a wealthy man upon completion of the *Tonquin*'s two-year trip around the world.

As the morning passed, more and more Indians swarmed aboard, each one carrying a bundle of beautiful furs. In contrast to the haggling of the first two days, no time was wasted today in arguing over price. One fur for one blanket? Fine! A fur for a jackknife? That would be fine, too, the Indians said, for only a limited number of blankets were needed for warmth in the longhouses, while extra jackknives always were useful.

Watching the trading as he sat on a coil of rope near the taffrail, Alexander McKay puffed on his long-stemmed pipe and made no effort to interfere, Lamansee said, though he still looked grim. By noon, most of the blankets were gone, tossed over the side of the ship to native women waiting with their babies in the dozens of canoes surrounding the *Tonquin*. All the Indians were trading for jackknives now, with the supply of them getting low. Coming down off the quarter deck, Captain Thorn pushed his way through the crowd of Nootkans—which now numbered two hundred or so—to the taffrail where McKay was sitting.

"D'ye still dislike my way of trading, Mr. McKay?" Thorn demanded. "D'ye still think my methods are wrong?"

"What I think is," McKay answered, shaking his head, "ye should not push your luck too far. Ye'd best clear the deck, I say, and get the ship underway."

"Aye, we seem to have bought most of their furs," Thorn answered, nodding. Turning to the crew members who were dragging piles of furs toward the open hatch and tossing them down for storage in the hold, Thorn cried out:

"Belay that! Prepare to raise anchor! Lay six men aloft to raise sail!"

As three sailors started climbing the rigging to unfurl sails on the mainmast, while three more scrambled up the foremast, a pair of men moved toward the capstan, where they started undogging the links controlling the bow anchor chain.

"*Mahkook huy-huy kopet!*" Captain Thorn called out to the Indians pressing around him on the poop deck. Making an imperious, dismissive gesture to Chief Nookamis, he shouted, "Trading is done! Get your people over the side, you greasy old fool!"

It was then, Lamansee said, that the Nootka trading chief gave what must have been a prearranged signal known to all the Indians who had come aboard since early that morning. Throwing open his blanket coat, Nookamis lifted a carved wooden whistle to his lips with his left hand, blew a shrill blast that could be heard all over the ship and among the dozens of circling canoes, then drew a knife from his belt with his right hand and lunged toward Captain Thorn.

"Only a shot from one of Mr. McKay's pistols saved the captain from being killed by the chief's first thrust," Lamansee said. "Later, I was told that when the Nootkans plotted their revenge, Chief Maquina made them promise they would not kill Mr. McKay, for he was their friend. But Mr. McKay must have suspected something was going to happen, for the moment Nookamis blew on the whistle, McKay jumped to his feet and drew two pistols he had hidden under his coat. His first shot missed Nookamis, killing another Indian nearby. When the Indians surrounding McKay drew their knives and charged him, he fired again, killing two more Nootkans. By then, they were on him, stabbing him again and again. Then they picked him up and threw him over the side, where the women in the canoes finished him off with war clubs and spears."

"Where were you while all this was going on?" Duncan McDougall interrupted.

"In the rigging," Lamansee answered evasively. "I was helping with the sails."

"Is that why they didn't kill you?" Gabriel Franchere asked. "Or did you know what they planned to do, so climbed the lines in order to get out of harm's way?"

No, Lamansee said hastily, he had no idea what the Nootkans planned to do. If he had known, he certainly would have warned the white men. Once the killing started, of course, the fact that he had Nootkan blood in his veins and relatives living in the native village no doubt induced the natives to spare his life, so long as he took no active part in defending the white men. Surely the Astorians could understand that.

"Weel, it cannae matter a tinker's dam now," McDougall said somberly. "Finish your tale. What happened then?"

With at least two hundred Indians swarming over the ship, Lamansee said, the fight was short and bloody. Drawing his own jackknife, Captain Thorn fought bravely and fiercely, killing or wounding several Indians before he himself was struck down. Descending from the rigging, three of the six sailors who had been aloft were attacked and killed, while the other three managed to fight their way toward the forecastle hatch leading to the magazine where the gunpowder and arms were stored, which Clerk James Lewis and Armorer Stephen Weeks had gotten to and opened.

"The white men barricaded themselves, found pistols and muskets, and began shooting at the Indians. With no guns themselves, the Nootkans gave up the attack. By then, all the other white men aboard had been killed. So the Indians got into their canoes and went ashore."

"Including you?" Franchere asked.

"Yes, for there was nothing else I could do. I knew I was lucky to be alive."

In the village ashore the rest of that afternoon and all through the night, the victorious Nootkans sang, danced, and celebrated, Lamansee said, for they felt they had won a great battle. Shortly after midnight, while he was asleep in his sister's longhouse, a group of warriors who had been watching the *Tonquin* spotted a small boat being lowered over the side. Several of the sailors who had survived the massacre apparently had decided to attempt to escape by stealthily launching the boat and rowing it toward a point of land enclosing the inner harbor. Knowing that they could not raise the anchor and work the ship by themselves, they felt that their only chance for survival was to slip away in the small boat.

But the Nootkan warriors were more familiar with the local currents and tides than the white men were. Alerted to the escape attempt, the Indians set out in pursuit, caught up with the small boat a couple of miles down the coast, and made captives of the hapless sailors. Still feeling the blood-lust of revenge, the band of warriors tortured the white men in unspeakable ways for a few hours, then put them to death.

"It was from these white sailors," Lamansee said, "that the Indians learned that a wounded man too badly hurt to travel still remained aboard the ship. From what they said about him, I am not sure who he was. The clerk, James Lewis, perhaps. Or the armorer, Stephen Weeks. Whoever he was, the Indians decided that they had better be careful when they went aboard the Tonquin next morning to see what they could salvage in the way of trade goods, guns, and powder."

A little after dawn, next day, a large number of Nootkans launched their canoes and paddled out toward the still-anchored ship, whose partially unfurled sails flapped in the rising breeze. Circling warily around the ship, the warriors had not yet decided whether to risk going aboard, when a lone white man appeared on the poop deck and started waving at them in a friendly fashion.

"*Mahkook okoke sun!*" he cried invitingly. "Trade some more today! *Huy-huy kloshe okoke sun!* We have good trade today!"

With the bodies of the ship's captain and crew still lying where they had fallen all across the deck, the puzzled Nootkans could only conclude that the man had gone *pelton*—crazy—driven out of his mind by the violence and death he had witnessed the day before. But the thing that mattered was he appeared to be unarmed, friendly, and in no mood to do them harm. So canoe by canoe, the Indians closed in on the ship.

By the time the first group climbed aboard, the man had vanished. All the ship's hatches were closed. When the Indians tried to open them, they found the hatches barred from the inside. Whoever the crazy man was, he had disappeared.

Well, no matter. All sorts of trade goods, sea otter furs, ship's gear, and other valuable treasures lay scattered about the deck, with no white men to prevent the Indians from helping themselves. Canoe after canoe load of Nootkans climbed the ship's rope ladders or scrambled over the rails, until every able-bodied person living in the village was on the deck of the *Tonquin* or hanging in the rigging. Even Lamansee himself had come aboard, he admitted, taking a perch at the very top of the foremast so that he could see what was happening below.

"It was then," he said, "that the ship went *boom*."

"You mean," McDougall said, "it exploded?"

Yes, that was what happened, Lamansee answered. It exploded with such force that he was thrown high into the air and far out beyond the bow, falling into the water so stunned that he had no recollection of what had happened. Later, he was told that he had been pulled out of the sea, gotten his lungs emptied of water, and then was taken ashore, where he began to realize that he was lucky to be alive when so many other natives had been killed or horribly mutilated by the explosion.

"How many?" Franchere asked.

"*Mokst tukamonuk,*" Lamansee answered, raising two fingers on each hand, then spreading them wide to indicate a multiplication factor of ten. "Two hundred *memaloose*—die—at least. Maybe more."

"*Two hundred Indians were killed?*" Franchere exclaimed incredulously. "That doesn't seem possible!"

"What happened to the *Tonquin* itself?" McDougall asked.

"Ship gone. All gone. Nothing left but little pieces of wood."

For long moments, an awed silence lay over the trading room in which the whites and Indians had gathered to listen to Lamansee's story. Looking like he'd been struck between the eyes with an axe, Duncan McDougall shook his head in stunned disbelief.

"A three-hundred-ton ship blown into splinters so small there's nothing left but little pieces of wood! How could such a thing happen?"

Though it was not his place to speak up in the presence of men much older than he and with so much more invested in the enterprise, Ben Warren said:

"Easy enough, sir. The *Tonquin* had four-and-a-half tons of gunpowder stored in her hold. If the charge were set by a man who knew his business, that would blow any ship to Kingdom Come."

"Eh?" McDougall snorted. "How would you know that?"

"Armorer Stephen Weeks told me."

"When?"

"Over a year ago, sir, the day the voyage began. We were talking about Captain Thorn and what might happen if a British man-of-war threatened to capture us. Stephen Weeks said that before Captain Thorn would surrender his first command, he might order Weeks to blow up the ship with all the men left aboard."

"You think that's what he did?"

"If he were the last man aboard left alive—as I suspect he was—I'm sure he would have done it, sir. Because when I asked him if he would carry out such an order, his answer was quick and clear. 'I'd have no choice,' he said. 'Might as well be dead by my own hand as his—for he'd kill any man that disobeyed an order, quick as he'd kill a fly. That's his naval training.' "

10.

$\mathscr{L}$AMANSEE'S ACCOUNT of the explosion that had destroyed the *Tonquin* was confirmed during the next few weeks by stories told by other regional Indian tribes. Though the accounts conflicted in a few details with Lamansee's narrative, the bleak truth so far as the Astorians were concerned was that their supply vessel and half of their people had been wiped out. Planning to return to the mouth of the Columbia after the trading mission to the Nootkans and Russian Alaska had been completed, the *Tonquin* had unloaded only a small portion of its supplies such as powder, lead, firearms, and trade goods before sailing north. This left Fort Astoria on short rations until next year's ship arrived from New York, which would not be until April or May.

The Astorians also were wondering what had happened to the overland contingent under the leadership of Wilson Price Hunt. Scheduled to leave St. Louis a year ago, none of its people had arrived yet nor had any word of its progress been received.

With the United States and Great Britain on the verge of war a year ago, no news had been received as to whether hostilities had broken out or if some sort of a compromise that would lead to peace had been arranged. Certainly the confident attitude shown by David Thompson and the French-Canadian voyageurs upon their arrival last summer indicated that they expected war to come and for the Pacific Northwest to fall under British control.

As the only American citizens among the mixture of Nor'westers, French-Canadians, and Kanakas now living at Fort Astoria, Ben Warren and John Mumford felt isolated from their home and countrymen. So far as he was concerned, Mumford grumbled, the fur-trading business held no interest; he intended to get out of it just as soon as he possibly could.

"If ever a ship crosses the bar," he told Ben, "I intend to be on her deck when she leaves, no matter where she's bound."

"Even if she's British?"

"It's naught I'll care what flag she's flying, lad, just so she takes me off this heathen coast. What about you?"

"After my experiences on the *Tonquin*, I'm in no hurry to go to sea again. I have no family left back East. The truth is, I'm beginning to like it here."

"You've taken young Thomas McKay under your wing, I notice, tryin' to befriend him, even though he's a half-breed."

"With his father gone, he's a lost soul. I promised Mr. McKay I'd look after him."

During the weeks since Lamansee had told his story about the destruction of the *Tonquin*, a marked change had taken place in the attitude of the Clatsops and most of the other lower Columbia River tribes toward the Astorians. With the exception of the Chinooks, who still were friendly, they had become rude, demanding, and arrogant. Duncan McDougall was not long in discerning the cause for their hostility nor in devising a cure for it.

"They think we're weak and defenseless, now that our ship and half of our people have been destroyed," he said dourly. "Weel, I'll soon teach 'em a lesson about that."

Calling a council of all the chiefs of the lower Columbia River tribes in the yard within the stockade one afternoon, McDougall served them a treat of well-sugared hot tea, gave them presents of blue beads and pieces of red cloth, then said he had an announcement of great importance to make.

"The white men among you are few in number," he said. "But we are mighty in medicine." Taking a small black bottle out of his pocket, he held it up so that all the assembled Indians could see it. "In this bottle I hold the smallpox, safely corked up. I have but to draw the cork and let loose the pestilence, which will sweep every man, woman, and child from the face of the earth."

Horrified by the threat of a disease which in time past had wiped out more than half the natives through whose villages it had raged, the Indians present were stricken with abject terror. Imploring *Tyee* McDougall not to uncork the bottle, all the local chiefs fervently swore that they were firm friends of the white men and would always remain so. Surely *Tyee* McDougall would not be so unjust, they said, as to punish his staunch Indian friends living in this area for crimes committed by the Nootkans far to the north.

"Weel, ye've convinced me for now that ye want to be friends," McDougall said, holding the bottle up so that they all could see it was still firmly corked. "I'll nae let loose the disease today. But just remember, I have the phial and can draw the cork the moment ye threaten to harm us."

From that day on, Duncan McDougall would be known and feared by all the natives as "The Great Smallpox Chief." Chief Concomly was so badly shaken by the threat, Ben noticed, that as soon as he had sworn how friendly his people were, he left the fort and recrossed the river to his village as hastily as the other leaders returned to theirs. Lingering behind, Conco expressed his concern to Ben.

"Would *Tyee* McDougall really do such a terrible thing?"

Much as Ben wanted to reassure his friend, he could not do so, for the truth was he did not know. Even the best white doctors were helpless when epidemic diseases such as cholera and smallpox swept through a community, though of recent years medical men in France and the eastern United States had had some success in giving people immunity to smallpox by injecting their arms with pus taken from a person infected with the so-called milkmaid's disease called "cowpox."

Though Ben seriously doubted that the corked black bottle with which McDougall had threatened the Indians really contained the fatal essence of whatever it was that caused smallpox, he had heard stories of how white traders in New England and Canada had sold blankets contaminated by smallpox-infected white people to Indians for the express purpose of killing off the natives, none of whom had been vaccinated or possessed any natural immunity whatsoever, with deadly results.

"All I can tell you, Conco," Ben said, "is that as long as we are friends, he will not uncork the bottle. I wish he had not made the threat. But he felt he had to."

Though Ben had expected winter at Fort Astoria to be much like it was back on the New England coast, the weather through November, December, and early January brought very little snow and few freezing days. What it did bring was rain in every possible variety:

light, gentle mist; steady drizzle; sudden downpours during which
huge drops fell as if dumped from buckets; with now and then gale-
force winds from the southwest that drove the rain in horizontally
with such violence that it turned the sea outside the bar and the river
within to such a maelstrom of seething waves that not even a Chinook
canoe dared venture into the water.

As if unwilling to end the year on a gloomy note, the sky cleared
and the sun shone brightly the afternoon of December 31, 1811. On
January 1, 1812, Senior Partner Duncan McDougall ordered a light
charge of powder placed in the cannons, a small ration of rum served
to the men, work suspended for the day, and the New Year properly
saluted, causing Gabriel Franchere to note in his journal:

> The day was passed in gaiety, every one amusing himself as much
> as possible.

Next day, both the steady rain and the work resumed. While Ben
and Conco took their canoe and crew of paddlers to the longhouses of
the lower river Indians and bartered for pelts, some of the workmen
cut timbers for building materials while others made charcoal for the
forge of blacksmith Auguste Roussil. Carpenters John Weeks and Johann Koaster built a barge, while cooper George Bell fashioned barrels for the trading posts to be established upriver with the coming of
spring.

Though called a "barge," the craft being put together by the two
carpenters was a utilitarian sort of boat designed by Ben Warren,
Duncan McDougall, John Mumford, and several river-wise voyageurs
as a cargo-carrying trailer to be towed behind a dugout or bark canoe.
When necessary, it could also move independently where the waters
were calm. Not nearly as big as the useless *Dolly*, it was oblong in
shape, with a square stern, a pointed bow, and a flat bottom with a
modified keel. Capable of carrying seven tons of freight, it could be
paddled by eight voyageurs, had a steering oar in the stern, and a well
amidships in which the mast for a small square sail could be stepped
when the wind was favorable. Unlike the thirty-ton schooner, it was
not too heavy to be placed on log rollers and pulled around portages
upriver, if enough strong backs were available. In the lower river or
even outside the bar, it could be used to transport cargo when the seas
were moderate.

In midwinter, the monotony of rain and work was interrupted by a long-looked-forward-to event: the arrival of the first contingent of the overland section of the Astor party. Because McDougall was confined to his room with a hacking cough and a bad cold, which his young Chinook bride was treating with hot rum and tea, mustard poultices, and tender loving care, Gabriel Franchere was privileged to greet two canoe loads of travelers, which arrived the afternoon of January 18, 1812.

"Welcome, gentlemen," Franchere exclaimed heartily. "Where in God's name have you been?"

In due course, the new arrivals told the first installment of a long, harrowing story. Two of the men were Senior Partners, Donald McKenzie and Robert McClellan. With them were Clerk John Reed and eight French-Canadian boatmen. Second in rank to Wilson Price Hunt, Donald McKenzie was a huge, red-bearded man, standing well over six feet tall and weighing over three hundred pounds—not an ounce of which was fat. For all his impressive size, he was a quiet man, so disinclined to talk that it was Partner Robert McClellan who told the party's story, which began about the same time the *Tonquin* had set sail from New York in early September 1810 ...

Unable to hire a sufficient number of experienced Americans for the overland section of the party, John Jacob Astor had employed and taken in as partners a number of French-Canadians, Scotsmen, Irishmen, and Englishmen, whose loyalties inclined more toward the North West Company than toward his own fledgling Pacific Fur Company. Placed in charge of the overland contingent was an American, Wilson Price Hunt, whose loyalty to Astor was complete, but whose leadership decisions tended toward vacillation and weakness.

The overland party included sixty-four men, a large quantity of trade goods, traps, ammunition, and baggage. Most of its members were seasoned frontiersmen or voyageurs. Originally planning to ascend the Missouri River, as Lewis and Clark had done, fear of the Blackfeet induced Hunt to abandon that route in the land of the Arickaras and cross the Rockies further south. Taking a leisurely month to trade his boats and extra supplies for horses, his group traveled west through the Bighorn Mountains and the Wind River country, entering Jackson Hole by way of the Hoback River. Because of their slow pace, it was now late September, so Hunt detached four men to remain there for the winter.

The party reached an abandoned trading post west of the Tetons on Henry's Fork October 8, 1811. It was here that Hunt committed what was later recognized to be the great mistake of the expedition. One hundred miles to the west over relatively easy terrain lay Lolo Pass and the trail blazed earlier by Lewis and Clark. With 118 horses, the well-mounted Hunt party could easily have reached the land of the Shoshones in four days' time. A friendly tribe, the Shoshones would have gladly guided them across the Bitter Root Mountains into the land of the even more hospitable Nez Perces, who would have helped them build dugout canoes as Lewis and Clark had done, so that they could float down the Clearwater, Snake, and Columbia to the sea.

But to the river-oriented French-Canadians, Henry's Fork looked very inviting. Hunt knew nothing about the country ahead except that the southward-flowing river joined the Snake southwest of Jackson Hole, and that the Snake flowed west, then north, then west again until it joined the mighty Columbia. The local Indians warned him that the river was unnavigable, but the voyageurs in his employ were regarded as the finest rivermen in North America. What could the Indians know about navigating white water compared to what *they* knew?

"Of course, what really influenced Mr. Hunt's decision," Robert McClellan said as he accepted a refill for his now empty mug of rum, "was that one of our leaders—whose name I'll nae reveal—was suffering from an ailment that made riding a torture—"

"Piles," Donald McKenzie grunted, also holding out his cup. "He had a bad case of the piles."

"So Mr. Hunt yielded to the desires of the party, abandoned the horses, and decided to trust to the river the rest of the way. We set about manufacturing a flotilla of canoes, a task we completed in ten days."

Detaching four more trappers to winter in the vicinity, plus Partner Joseph Miller, who had grown so disgusted with the enterprise that he had decided to give up his share and quit, the party left its horses in the care of two Snake Indians on October 19, and embarked in fifteen canoes. At first, travel on the strong, dark, rapid stream was very pleasant, the party making good time and congratulating itself for having chosen this mode of transportation. But their mood soon changed.

As the river's true nature revealed itself, McClellan said, the voyageurs changed its name from "Mad River," which they at first had called it, to *La Maudite Rivière Enragée*, "The Accursed Mad River." In rock-strewn gorges and white-water rapids expressively named the Devil's Scuttle Hole and Caldron Linn, a boat was wrecked and a voyageur named Antoine Clappine was drowned. Belatedly, Hunt suspended further attempts at navigation until the downstream hazards could be appraised. His own inspection of a forty-mile stretch convinced him that the rapids could not be negotiated. Other members of the party thought differently, tried the river again, and quickly lost four more boats, though the voyageurs managed to scramble ashore.

"Mr. Hunt then called what I must describe as a most bewildered council," McClellan said. "It was now early November, we were in the midst of the Snake River desert, and winter was at hand. Mr. Hunt decided to split the party into four groups. The first would stay where we were, dig caves, and cache the extra supplies. The second would return to Henry's Fork for the horses left there. The third would proceed down the river. The fourth—which was ours—would travel northwest toward Nez Perce country."

"Where were they supposed to meet?" Franchere asked.

"*Och mon*, that was a matter left mostly to God and chance," McClellan said with a shrug. "Since we knew nothing about the country, we could make no plans."

"Weel, *I* knew where the Nez Perce country was, for I'd carried a map of the route followed by Lewis and Clark in my head ever since we'd left St. Louis," Donald McKenzie muttered, his words half lost in his raised mug. "But Hunt nae would listen when I said I could take us there."

"He's telling God's truth, Donald is," McClellan agreed with a nod of his head. "Traveling across desert and mountain country he'd never seen before, he took us to the Clearwater and the Nez Perces in just twenty-one days. To help us come on down to the lower Columbia, they gave us food and two dugout canoes against Donald's promise to come back and establish a trading post in their country later this year."

"Which I'll damn sure do," McKenzie grunted. "They're fine people."

The second installment of the story was revealed on February 15, when Wilson Price Hunt himself and most of the rest of his people arrived at Fort Astoria. As details of the party's adventures were revealed, Ben Warren agreed with Gabriel Franchere that the leadership shown by Hunt had been very poor.

Three days after being sent back to Henry's Fork to pick up the horses, Hunt said, the members of that group declared their mission too risky, so they rejoined the men digging caches. Several days later, the group that had continued downriver returned, too, reporting the Snake's waters absolutely unnavigable. Now, Hunt decided to travel in two groups, one on each bank of the river. By then, it was November 9, and winter had come.

Suffering greatly from cold, starvation, and illness, the two parties followed the Snake until it turned north and buried itself in a deep canyon where it no longer was possible to travel along its banks. There, the two parties united, leaving behind half a dozen men who were too weak or ill to travel and the body of Baptiste Prevost, who had become so frenzied at the sight of food, Hunt said, that he "danced in a delirium of joy" while in a canoe, upset it, and drowned.

Also missing from the party was the hunter, John Day, and Senior Partner Ramsey Crooks, who had gotten lost in the snow-covered heights near the river while in search of game. The rest of the party crossed the Blue Mountains over a trail used for generations by the local Indians, striking the Columbia River a few miles below the mouth of the Snake, then following it on west to Fort Astoria …

In May 1812, the final installment of the saga was revealed when a party of Astorians heading upriver to Fort Okanogan was hailed from across the river by two half-starved whites, who turned out to be the two lost men, Ramsey Crooks and John Day. While wandering around in the wilds of the Blue Mountains, they said, they eventually were found by a friendly band of Umatilla Indians, who fed and sheltered them for several weeks, then put them on a trail that was supposed to lead them down to the Columbia.

Mistaking their way, the two men came further west than they should, got lost in desert country, struck a north-flowing stream, and were following it down toward the Columbia when they encountered another Indian tribe, the Wishram, who treated them very badly, taking their guns and clothing and leaving them to die of exposure. Before that could happen, they managed to make their way to the mouth of the desert river and the Columbia, where the Astorians found them naked, starving, and destitute.

After being taken to Fort Astoria, Ramsey Crooks recovered his health in a few weeks, but John Day became mentally deranged and did not regain his sanity and strength for many months …

Expecting either an American supply ship from New York or a British man-of-war bearing news that hostels had begun, Duncan McDougall had arranged with his Chinook father-in-law, Chief Concomly, to lay materials for a bonfire which would be lighted on the heights of Cape Disappointment whenever a ship was sighted off the coast, and for a square of white cloth hung near the top of a tall tree to be flown to show that white people were living in the area.

At ten o'clock in the morning, May 8, 1812, a wave of excitement ran over Fort Astoria, for faintly in the distance to the northwest the low, rolling boom of a cannon was heard. Repeated three times, the sound could mean only one thing.

"A ship!" Duncan McDougall cried, snatching up a spyglass and running up the steps to the catwalk inside the stockade. After peering intently toward the heights of Cape Disappointment, which was clearly visible on this bright, sunny day even though fifteen miles away, he shouted jubilantly, "Aye, the signal fire has been lighted! I can see a column of smoke rising! Charge the bastion pieces, Mr. Mumford, and fire a proper reply!"

"Aye, sir, charge the pieces it is!"

While the two six-pounders which had been installed at opposite corners of the fort were being loaded, Ben Warren, who came running up from the dock where he had been working on the newly completed barge, yelled at Mumford:

"Do you suppose it's one of ours?"

"God knows, lad. But at least it's a ship."

Fired alternately, the two fort cannons gave a measured three-
salute reply which sounded ear-piercingly loud inside the stockade
after echoing off the face of the steep hill behind the fort, but which
Ben feared might be lost against the mild southwesterly breeze blowing inshore. But much to the delight of the eager listeners within the
fort, after an interval of a minute or so three more booms of the ship's
cannons were heard in the distance.

"'Tis a ship makin' a friendly reply," McDougall exulted. "Can ye
take us out in the barge to greet her, Ben, to make sure her captain
knows we're here?"

"Likely Conco and his father are already on their way, sir. The
Chinooks always go out to meet the ships."

"That I know, lad. But I'd still like to gi' them a welcome, if we
can."

With the barge docked just below Tongue Point on the south side
of the Columbia twelve miles above its mouth, it would take two or
three hours to reach the bar, Ben knew, and another hour to lay alongside the ship, which would be anchored in deep water off the coast. By
then, the tide would have ebbed, then would turn in mid-afternoon
and set inshore, creating ideal conditions for sailing the ship through
the narrow channel below Cape Disappointment and into the quiet
waters of Baker Bay. Since the Chinook village on the north side of
the river was much closer to the bar, the natives' canoe no doubt
would reach the ship much sooner, but whether the ship's captain
would trust the Indians or accept their help was questionable.

"No reason why we can't go out, sir. The barge is a good sailer in
calm weather, and we've got a nice day for it."

"Good! Pick your crew and get ready to go. Mr. Mumford!"

"Aye, sir?"

"Break out an American flag and be prepared to sit in the bow of
the barge wavin' it at the ship as we close wi' her. If she's American,
she'll know we're friendly. If she's British, we'll surrender—gi'en honorable terms."

With Duncan McDougall and John Mumford sitting in the bow of
the barge and Ben at the tiller, the awkward-looking but surprisingly
maneuverable craft left the dock, manned by eight strong-backed
voyageurs. Once out of the lee of the hill behind Fort Astoria, Ben ordered the square sail set, which, quartered to the southwest breeze,
helped the paddlers push the barge down and across the river.

At one o'clock in the afternoon, the barge entered the channel leading out across the bar just in time to utilize the last of the ebbing tide. Though the breeze had lessened, it now came from dead ahead, so Ben ordered the square sail hauled down, leaving the paddlers to propel the boat on their own. Steadying his spyglass against the rocking of the craft, Duncan McDougall studied the ship lying at anchor a few hundred yards away.

"She's a merchant ship, clear enough. Praise God, she's flyin' an American flag. I make her name out to be the *Beaver*. Gi' her a friendly sign, Mr. Mumford!"

"Aye, sir! That I'll do!"

Waving the flag back and forth as the barge moved into the lee of the big merchant ship, Mumford scowled at a large Chinook canoe nearby, which contained some thirty paddlers and appeared to be trying to close with the ship whose near rail was lined with white men armed with muskets leveled at the Indians.

"In God's name, Ben, tell your Indian friends to sheer off! The ship's crew thinks they're under attack!"

Indeed, that seemed to be the case, for as the barge drew nearer to the ship, the wild cries of the Indians in the fast-moving canoe as it darted in and out, the shouts of the whites aboard, and the way the muskets stayed trained on the Indians made it obvious to Ben that the exuberant, well-meant greetings of the Chinooks were being mistaken by the whites as a prelude to an attack. Catching the attention of Conco, who was standing in the stern of the canoe, while his father, Chief Concomly, waved, jumped up and down, and shouted with increasing anger and indignation at the ship, Ben waved and called:

"*Wake, wake!* No, No! They think you're bad Indians, Conco! Back off! Back off, I say!"

Making a full-arm gesture indicating that he understood, Conco signaled to his paddlers and cramped the steering oar around, changing the course of the big canoe so abruptly that his father nearly fell overboard, being saved only at the last instant by a pair of husky Chinooks who caught his falling body and managed to keep him inside the canoe. As it swept past, Ben could hear Chief Concomly howling in outrage.

"God's blood, don't he know he almost started a war!" McDougall muttered. "I'll have to talk wi' the old fool."

Sight of the American flag and the white men in the barge calmed the apprehensions of the master of the *Beaver* to the extent that he let the Astorians pull alongside and come aboard. After introductions were made, he invited Duncan McDougall, John Mumford, and Ben Warren into his cabin for a tot of rum, while the voyageurs were served and mingled with the crew on deck.

Commanded by stout, gray-haired, middle-aged Captain Cornelius Sowle, from Tiverton, Rhode Island, the *Beaver* indeed was an Astor-chartered ship. Leaving New York six months ago, the 480-ton vessel had made a fairly routine trip to the Northwest Coast, save for the melancholy fact that she had lost one sailor to black scurvy—with which he apparently had been afflicted when he came aboard—and two men washed overboard by a monstrous following sea during a stormy passage around Cape Horn.

"What d'ye ken of war between the United States and Great Britain?" McDougall asked.

"We were still at peace when we left New York in October," Captain Sowle answered. "The British still are making threats and impressing sailors they claim are nationals. With so many French-Canadians aboard, we skipped calling at Cape Verde Island, as all American vessels are doing these days."

"D'ye know of the *Tonquin* loss?"

"Yes, we heard when we stopped at the Sandwich Islands that the *Tonquin* and its crew had been destroyed by Indians. That was why we were so suspicious of the way the natives greeted us here."

"Did ye nae see our signal fire and hear our cannon?"

"That we did, sir," Captain Sowle answered stiffly. "But for all we knew, the hideous-looking Indians who were greeting us could have murdered you, taken over the fort, then lighted the signal fire and shot off the cannon in order to lure us into their clutches. They're such evil-looking wretches, I'd judge them capable of anything."

"*Och mon*, they were just tryin' to be friendly," McDougall muttered uncomfortably. "They were offerin' to pilot you in across the bar."

"Indeed?" Sowle said skeptically. "One of my crew members who understands their jargon did say that their leader told him that white men were living in a house they had built near the mouth of the river. But after getting a close-up look at the one-eyed old rascal when he tried to climb aboard, I knew he was not to be trusted. So we made him stand clear of the ship while we sent First Mate Rhodes out in a boat to sound and place marker buoys along the channel."

Though Ben hardly expected Duncan McDougall to volunteer the information that the villainous-looking, one-eyed Indian leader the captain referred to was his father-in-law, he doubted that McDougall's prolonged fit of coughing was caused by the potency of the rum.

"Begging your pardon, Captain Sowle," Ben said politely, "but Chief Concomly and the Chinook Indians know the bar far better than white sailors do. They've been guiding ships across it for twenty years."

Studying Ben as if suddenly becoming aware of his presence for the first time, Captain Sowle smiled superciliously. "Is that so? How did you become such an authority on the subject?"

"Sir, the lad was a seaman on the *Tonquin*," Second Mate John Mumford interposed hastily. "No doubt you knew his father, Captain Thomas Warren, of Gloucester, Massachusetts."

"Indeed I did. An able captain and a fine man."

"He was one of nine men lost in trying to find a passage across the bar for the *Tonquin*. Since then, his son, Ben, has been working as a pilot with the Astor Company. None of our people know these waters as well as he does."

Regarding Ben with a bit more respect, Captain Sowle, who appeared to be a very nervous man, asked, "Can you take us to safe anchorage in Baker Bay?"

"Yes, sir. I'm sure I can."

"How soon?"

"The wind is favorable now, sir. The tide will be turning within the hour. I suggest you weigh anchor and get underway by mid-afternoon. That way, we'll have plenty of daylight left for the passage."

"Very well." Captain Sowle turned and looked at Mumford. "But I want you standing beside the helmsman with him, Mr. Mumford, just to make sure his steering directions are sound. And I won't permit that villainous-looking old chief to come aboard, as he seems to want to do. Keep him out of my sight."

By now, Ben had come to the conclusion that Captain Cornelius Sowle was as timid and unsure of himself as Jonathan Thorn had been bold and self-confident. But he kept his thoughts to himself as preparations were made to weigh anchor, raise sail, and cross the bar.

Because of the ideal weather conditions—a steady following wind, a favorable tide, and a mild chop—Ben was not surprised that the crossing was made with few problems. Towing the barge, the *Beaver* raised only the jib, spanker, and close-furled mainsail. All he needed to do, Ben knew, was follow the big Chinook canoe, which was being guided by Chief Concomly in the bow and steered by Conco in the stern, into the deep-water channel lying near the north side of the river's mouth. True, it took much longer to change course in a 480-ton sailing ship than it did in a seagoing Chinook canoe, but his months aboard the *Tonquin* had prepared him for that, and with Second Mate John Mumford beside him the passage was marred by only two minor incidents.

Fussy and nervous as a mother hen guarding a newly hatched brood of chicks, Captain Sowle stood to the left of the helmsman; Second Mate John Mumford stood to the right; while Ben stood to the right of Mumford. Whether the incidents that so upset Captain Sowle were the fault of Ben, John Mumford, or the helmsman, Ben did not know, but during the relaying of sailing directions misunderstandings occurred on two occasions, causing the *Beaver*'s keel to touch the sloping sands of the channel first on the port, then on the starboard side. Each time this happened, Captain Sowle reacted violently.

"My God, we've struck! You've put us aground!"

"No, sir. We just touched a bit of sand, that's all. See there! Already we've floated free."

Though to both Ben Warren and John Mumford, the brief "kiss-and-run" contacts with the sand were so minor that they knew no damage could possibly have been done to the keel, the momentary groundings had so shaken Captain Sowle that by the time the *Beaver* entered the river and dropped anchor in Baker Bay, he seemed on the verge of a nervous breakdown. His hands were trembling as he pulled a handkerchief out of his pocket and mopped his perspiring forehead.

"Never again! I swear it! If ever I manage to cross this damnable bar and get safely out to sea, I'll never drop anchor inside the mouth of the Columbia River again!"

At the time, Ben felt the captain's vow was one he would soon forget. But he misjudged his man.

11.

CAPTIVATED BY John Jacob Astor's glowing promises of their becoming rich men in a few years, still another Senior Partner, John
Clarke, who had invested enough money to buy a full share, and six
clerks, who were to be paid one hundred dollars a year and then
would be given half-shares after five years if their service was satisfac-
tory, were passengers aboard the *Beaver*. Along with a dozen artisans,
two dozen voyageurs, and a shipload of supplies, they were a welcome
reinforcement to Fort Astoria.

As usually happened when a ship called at the Sandwich Islands
following a long voyage from the East Coast, losses and gains in personnel had been incurred, Ben learned. The sailor who had died of
scurvy and the two seamen washed overboard during a storm off the
Horn had been replaced by the hiring of twenty-six Kanakas, sixteen
of whom were to work for the Company while the other ten were to
be employed as sailors. Paid ten dollars a month, the Company employees would take orders from Duncan McDougall, while the ten native sailors, who spoke no English, would be taught their tasks by a
muscular, humorless old Islander called "Bos'n Tom." Having picked
up a smattering of English by sailing on British and American whaling
ships, where he also had learned how to discipline the easygoing
Kanakas with a rope end applied to their bare backs, he would be re-
warded for this added responsibility by being paid fifteen dollars a
month.

To John Mumford's delight, the *Beaver* needed an officer, having
lost Third Mate Walter Dean in Hawaii because he had quarreled
with Captain Cornelius Sowle over the definition of his duties.

"What happened was the captain bought sixty hogs and a batch of
sugarcane to feed 'em in pens on the poop deck," Mumford told Ben.
"As you well know, live hogs can be mighty messy. Since he'd paid a

lot of money for the hogs and wanted to take 'em to Astoria in good shape, Captain Sowle told Third Mate Dean it would be his personal responsibility to see that they were given good care."

"And Dean objected?"

"Long and loud. First, he tried to get Bos'n Tom to look after the hogs. But Tom claimed his job was to boss sailors, not to care for hogs. So Dean went back to the captain and said his mate's papers qualified him as a sailor, not as a swineherder. 'You'll do what I tell you to do,' says the captain, 'or I'll put you ashore.' 'Well, if you tell me I've got to wade ankle deep in hog shit,' says Dean, 'I *will* go ashore.' And he did."

"So the captain left him in the Sandwich Islands?"

"Right. Now I've got the Third Mate's job."

One of the six clerks who had come out on the *Beaver* was a stocky, brash, nineteen-year-old Irishman named Ross Cox. Straight off the streets of Dublin, he took an immediate liking to Ben, bombarding him with endless questions about the fur-trading business, the Indians, and the nature of the inland country he hoped soon to see. Like Alexander Ross and Gabriel Franchere, he was keeping a detailed journal of his adventures, he told Ben, whose publication he expected to make him as famous as his eventual full partnership in the Pacific Fur Company would make him rich.

"I'm told parties will be going inland to establish trading posts in the upriver country," Cox informed Ben. "I hope to start as an assistant at one of them, then take charge after I've learned the trade. What will you do?"

"Keep running the barge in the lower river, I suppose. Mr. Mumford thinks there'll be a need for a pilot who knows the bar, as ship traffic increases. He says I should charge for my services, like harbor pilots do back East."

With six Senior Partners and 140 employees now in residence at Fort Astoria, Wilson Price Hunt and Duncan McDougall were anxious to get the *Beaver* unloaded so that the parties headed upriver could be on their way. In accordance with his instructions from Astor, Hunt then would go aboard the ship and sail north to Sitka, Alaska, where he would pay a visit to Governor Alexander Baranov. Hoping to establish a good working relationship with the Russians, who controlled the fur-gathering business from the Bering Sea in the far north to Bodega Bay in central California, Astor had stocked the hold of the

Beaver with a choice supply of goods badly needed by the isolated post, which Hunt hoped to exchange for valuable sea otter, seal, and other furs.

If their meeting went well, Hunt not only would make a substantial profit for the Pacific Fur Company but would also enlist Russian America as a powerful ally against Great Britain, in case of war. Gossip around Fort Astoria had it that Mr. Hunt was worried about how he would fare with the boisterous, earthy Russian, Count Baranov, who habitually challenged his dinner guests to a drinking contest to determine which one of them could consume the most rum and still stay on his feet and keep his senses—a competition he seldom lost. Though not a teetotaler by any means, Mr. Hunt did not like to mix drinking with business.

Before winter came, the *Beaver* would bring Hunt back to Fort Astoria, collect whatever pelts the inland posts had sent downriver, then would sail west to the Sandwich Islands, China, India, England, and on around the world. All this was dependent, of course, on a state of peace continuing to exist between Great Britain and the United States. If war broke out, other arrangements would have to be made.

But right now, the speedy unloading of supplies for Fort Astoria appeared to be the last thing on Captain Sowle's mind. After carrying several barge loads of tinned foods, guns, ammunition, and Indian trade goods from the anchorage at Baker Bay to the Fort Astoria dock four miles across and twelve miles upriver—a slow, time-consuming process—Ben asked John Mumford when Captain Sowle planned to move the ship.

"First, he says he wants to take soundings of the lower river," Mumford said evasively, "just to make sure we'll have plenty of water under her keel when we do move her."

"He doesn't need to worry about that, sir. At flood tide, the river's thirty feet deep all the way across, with not a rock in her anywhere."

"I know. All the same, he wants to play it safe. Tomorrow morning, he's sending First Mate Rhodes and a boat crew out to make soundings and place marker buoys."

"That'll take at least a week," Ben protested. "Mr. Hunt wants the supplies off-loaded right away."

"So I've told Captain Sowle, lad. But he's bound and determined to do it his way."

"It's a mighty stupid way, if you ask me. He's as fussy as an old maid!"

"That he well may be. But his orders from Mr. Astor, he says, give him full charge of the way he handles his ship."

Ben turned away in disgust. "Captain Thorn said the same thing. Look what happened to him."

"Patience, lad, patience."

"Well, all I can do is keep off-loading the supplies with the barge, I suppose, slow as it is."

"Oh, there is one thing Captain Sowle wants you to off-load right away, Ben."

"What's that?"

"The hogs. In this hot weather, they're making quite a stink. He'd like you to start in the morning."

Much against his better judgment, Ben undertook the job. On the face of it, a barge capable of carrying seven tons of freight, manned by six husky voyageurs, should have been able to carry a substantial cargo of potential pork chops from the deck of the *Beaver* to the Fort Astoria dock. In fact, Ben tried to jolly his French-Canadian crew into a pleasant mood by reminding them that they often were called *mangeurs du porc* because of their fondness for that kind of meat.

"In appreciation for the job you're doing for him," Ben said, "maybe you can persuade the fort cook to barbecue the first hog we deliver and serve it to us for supper."

What neither Ben nor the voyageurs realized was that transporting ten squirming, squealing, seasick, constantly defecating hogs at a time in the limited confines of the barge—even with their legs "hog-tied"—was not nearly as simple as carrying the same dead weight of pork encased in barrels of brine. In the end, he had to agree with one of the voyageurs, who exclaimed:

"Eaters of pork, we may be, *M'sieu*. But waders in *merde du porc*, we refuse to become. Before we will wade in hog shit again, *Mon Capitan*, we will throw both you and the hogs overboard and let you drown together."

Telling Third Mate Mumford he had a mutiny on his hands, Ben finally persuaded Captain Sowle to take advantage of an incoming tide, a sunny day, and a mild westerly wind to hoist anchor and sail cautiously across and up the river to a spot just below the Fort Astoria dock. With the seasick hogs finally put ashore, the deck hosed clean, and the hatches opened, off-loading the rest of the supplies went much more quickly. On June 29, 1812, the *Beaver* was ready to sail north to Russian Alaska.

The process of piloting the *Beaver* outbound across the bar was much like that of bringing her in, Ben found, save for the fact that this time Conco rather than his father was in command of the Chinook canoe which led the way. Chief Concomly's feelings had been hurt, Conco told Ben, because Captain Sowle had failed to reward him for guiding the ship in with the gift of a dress uniform and hat to add to his extensive collection. Heaping insult on injury, the captain also had refused to accept Concomly's well-meant present of a nubile, willing, well-greased maiden to share his bed and keep his back warm while his ship was in port. Though too proud of his reputation for guiding ships safely across the bar for twenty years to wish for a shipwreck, Chief Concomly made it clear to his son-in-law, Duncan McDougall, that he would regard it as no great tragedy if the ship went aground on a sandbar and got stuck there for a week.

On an ebbing tide before a stiff offshore breeze, the *Beaver* moved smartly down and across the river, falling in two hundred yards astern of the Chinook canoe in Conco's charge as it kept to the deep-water channel near the north side of the Columbia just below Cape Disappointment. Having learned how long a response time the ship required to answer her helm, as well as being more knowledgeable about wind-drift and river current factors now, Ben let the ship's keel kiss sand only once—and that very lightly. But again, Captain Sowle's reaction was hysterical.

"Never again will I cross this damnable bar! I take oath to that! Next time, I'll lay offshore and drop anchor in deep water, where I won't be putting my ship in mortal danger!"

With the *Beaver* clear of the mouth of the river and ready to raise a full rack of sails, Ben accepted the captain's curt grunt of dismissal with a brief salute and a polite wish for fair winds and a pleasant voyage, then left the quarter deck and walked with Third Mate John Mumford toward the lee rail, below which Conco and his native paddlers were holding the big dugout canoe that would take him ashore.

"Did I do all right, sir?"

"You did fine, lad. I'd hire you as my pilot any day."

"I've been thinking on what you said about my becoming a bar pilot, Mr. Mumford. Since I work for the Company, I can't expect pay for this job, I know. But if I were a professional, what would my pilot services be worth?"

"Why, it seems to me, Ben, that considering the size of the ship, the value of its cargo, and the degree of knowledge and skill involved, two hundred dollars would not be too much."

"Good Lord!" Ben exclaimed. "That's twice the yearly wage of a half-share clerk!"

"Why shouldn't it be? There's a lot more riding on your judgment piloting a ship across the bar than on a clerk's deciding which side of a ledger page to enter the price paid for a bale of furs." Mumford held out his hand, which Ben clasped fervently. "God be with you, lad. With luck, I'll see you again in November."

During the rest of the summer and into the early fall, three posts were established in the upriver country, which, from what he had heard of it, Ben had no desire to see. Under the direction of David Stuart and his assistant Alexander Ross, the first party went to Fort Okanogan, 450 miles up the Columbia in semi-desert country, to complete the post there. John Clarke, who seemed to be a very capable man even though in appearance he was something of a dandy, went into the Spokane country and established a post 150 miles directly east of Fort Okanogan. Keeping his promise to the Nez Perces, Donald McKenzie took a third party up the Columbia and the Snake to the mouth of the Clearwater, with Ross Cox along as an assistant, to build a post called Fort Nez Perces.

Feeling it was high time that word of the enterprise be taken to Astor, young Robert Stuart led a group overland, which included Senior Partner Robert McClellan, who had become so displeased with the venture that he decided to return to civilization.

Remaining at Fort Astoria with Duncan McDougal, were Ben Warren, Gabriel Franchere, forty-five clerks and artisans. Having proven himself to be very useful because of his linguistic talents and his diplomatic way of doing business with the natives, Gabriel Franchere now was McDougall's right-hand man. Though it was becoming increasingly clear that he would be granted a full-share partnership in the Company long before the term of his apprenticeship was up, Franchere confided to Ben that he might not accept it, for he was getting desperately homesick for friends, family, and a special young lady he had left back in Montreal.

August warmth gave way to the coolness of September, then to the rain and chill of October, and finally to the cold, blustery windstorms of November. By then, the lack of news regarding relations between the United States and England or how the *Beaver* was faring in Russian Alaska began to take on an ominous meaning.

Truth was, the news on both counts was bad …

Called New Archangel by the Russians or Sitka by the natives, the island trading post from which Alexander Baranov ruled his Alaskan fur empire with an iron hand was half a world away from St. Petersburg to the west, just as Fort Astoria was half a world removed from New York to the east. In each case, six months' travel by sea or land was required to transport vital supplies to the posts, while the return exchange of furs or communications took just as long.

At the time of Hunt's arrival in late summer, Baranov was badly in need of supplies and in a mood to entertain visitors. During the summer, hostilities finally had broken out between Great Britain and the United States, Baranov had heard. No longer willing to accept the impressment of its sailors, the United States had declared war on England June 18, 1812, though word of the declaration was months reaching the Pacific. Ship traffic on the high seas was sharply curtailed. Though Russia was taking no part in the war, Yankee ships all over the Pacific were scuttling for safety in neutral ports such as Honolulu, Bodega Bay, and Canton, in order to be out of the reach of British raiders. So far, the *Beaver* was the only American bottom to drop anchor in Sitka's spectacular, mountain-surrounded harbor. Since it was carrying both badly needed supplies and the Senior Partner of the Pacific Fur Company, the ship's visit should have been as fruitful as Astor had hoped it would be.

"Above all, I vant you und Count Baranov should become goot friends," Astor had told Wilson Price Hunt before their parting over a year ago. "A great deal depends on how you get along togedder …"

Astor then went on to explain that if war came, Hunt should consider seeking refuge for his ships, people, and goods in Russian Alaska. Heavy drinker though he was, Baranov had a universal reputation for integrity. Drunk or sober, when he gave his word, he kept it. But drunk or sober, he would not give his word to any man he did not like. Though he was prepared to like Hunt, the personalities of the two men were so diametrically opposed that they found it impossible to agree on anything.

To begin with, Hunt found the news of war between the United States and England—which at that moment had not been confirmed—very disturbing. Alarmed by the preponderance of men of British allegiance residing at Sitka, he was anxious to do his trading and be on his way. But to Count Baranov, who was eager to hear the latest news of the world, entertainment must precede business—and his kind of entertainment included night after night of heavy drinking.

A man of conservative habits, Hunt disliked having excessive drinking thrust upon him. Not being a world traveler familiar with the dissipations of the St. Petersburg court as Baranov was, he had the American businessman's distaste for haggling. Sure that his Yankee shrewdness would enable him to handle any foreigner with whom he was forced to trade, he mistrusted bargains made by a man in his cups.

This proved to be a fatal mistake, so far as his relations with Baranov were concerned. Though the cargo carried on the *Beaver* contained many items badly needed by the Russian post—cornmeal, rice, sugar, tobacco, tar, handkerchiefs, 733 pairs of shoes, and hundreds of other articles—for which Hunt probably could have obtained a large quantity of excellent furs in a package deal made during a single falling-down-drunk evening with Baranov, his sanctimonious insistence on cold sober, item-by-item haggling bought him nothing from an annoyed, amused Count Baranov but two months of daily quibbling that in the end drove Hunt to his knees, trade-wise.

After giving Hunt only a fraction of the value in furs that he had expected to receive for the ship's cargo, Baranov then granted him the dubious privilege of sailing northwest to the Bering Sea, where, in the storm-wracked, ice-girt Pribilov Islands, he was permitted to collect a limited number of sealskins by killing and skinning a few hundred seals on his own. In late October, he found the area to be no playground for ships.

Arriving at the lonely, fog-draped sealing station on October 31, Hunt and the ship's boat party landed on Pribilov Island with the greatest difficulty in the violent surf just before a gale blew up and drove the Beaver out to sea beyond the horizon. For days, Hunt lived in miserably primitive conditions with seven resident Russian *promysh-leniki*—seal-hunters—and a hundred natives in their gloomy huts, which were made of whalebones covered with old sealskins and earth. When the *Beaver* finally returned, Hunt paid off the surly hunters and natives, carried his sodden, half-frozen sealskins out to the ship, and sailed away with a fervent prayer that he never would see Russian Alaska or do business with Alexander Baranov again.

"Thank God we're heading back to Fort Astoria!" he exclaimed, as the *Beaver* took a bone in her teeth and headed south before a strong arctic wind. "Things must be going better there."

After three days' running before the wind, with the sailmaker exhausting the ship's supply of spare canvas in order to replace sails shredded or lost in northern gales, while below decks the carpenter and his crew labored to shore up strained bulkheads and plug leaks in the hull caused by collisions with icebergs and the pounding of violent seas, Captain Sowle grimly gave Hunt the bad news.

"We're not gong back to Fort Astoria."

"Why not?"

"Because in my judgment the ship is in no condition to endure the stress of winter storms off that treacherous coast or the extreme danger of crossing that terrible bar."

"We have to go back to Fort Astoria," Hunt protested. "They're counting on us to pick up their furs. Your contract with the Company requires you to return me to that post."

"No, it does not," Captain Sowle said firmly. "My written orders from Mr. Astor state quite clearly that in the event of war, or if, in my judgment, the ship would be endangered by my calling at a dangerous port, I am not required to do so."

Though Hunt pointed out that the war news had not been confirmed, that the *Beaver* need not cross the bar but could anchor in deep water offshore while he was taken off and the collected furs were brought aboard by barge or Chinook canoe, no argument he could make altered the captain's decision.

"Put your protest in writing, if you like, Mr. Hunt. I'll not risk my ship to capture by the British or destruction by the elements. In her present condition, the Beaver sails poorly in any direction except before the wind. That's why I've laid out a SSE course straight for the Sandwich Islands, which not only will give us our best chance to avoid

British men-of-war but also to avoid having to make westing off the coast of North America to Hawaii, as we would have to do if we called at Fort Astoria."

"You're sailing southeast to the Sandwich Islands?" Hunt said with a frown. "Don't they lie to the west of where we are?"

"Look at the map, Mr. Hunt. I've laid out our course on the chart."

During the next few minutes, Captain Sowle gave Hunt a lesson in geography and navigation, proving that under the present circumstances there was no alternative to the decision the captain had made. Vaguely under the impression that the bulk of Russian Alaska lay directly north of the mouth of the Columbia, Hunt now saw on the map that the island on which Sitka was located angled to the northwest, while the seven-hundred-mile-long chain of the Aleutian Islands forming the lower tail of Alaska stretched southwest to Siberia, with the Pribilov Islands, which were in the Bering Sea north of the Aleutians, actually located at 170 degrees West Longitude, while Hawaii lay at 158 degrees West, 12 degrees to the east.

"In miles, what are we talking about," Hunt asked, "so far as sailing directly to Hawaii or going by way of Astoria is concerned?"

However timid he may have been where sailing his ship across a dangerous river bar was concerned, Captain Sowle was supremely confident of his ability as a deep-sea sailor.

"As I've calculated the course, from the Pribilov Islands to Oahu, we'll have to sail 2,820 nautical miles, SSE. To the mouth of the Columbia from the Pribilovs, the distance is 1,859 miles, SE. From the Columbia to Hawaii, we would have 1,376 miles in a southwesterly direction. Which in the ship's present condition, poses a problem."

"Why?"

"At this time of year, most of the heavy windstorms come from the southwest—which means we'd be sailing directly into the teeth of a constant gale most of the way. The *Beaver* is in no condition to contend with tacking or wearing ship day after day. She'd fall apart."

"In that case, we'll do what you think best, of course," Hunt said bleakly. "If British raiders do come to the Sandwich Islands, we should be safe from seizure there, for I doubt if even Great Britain would dare challenge the sovereignty of King Kamehameha."

In that supposition, Wilson Price Hunt was right, for he found upon the arrival of the Beaver in Oahu early in January 1813 that a number of merchant ships from the United States, England, Portugal, and half a dozen other European countries were lying at anchor there, waiting to see how the war would affect their travels. Though an official state of war was now confirmed beyond any doubt, with the British said to have at least two twenty-gun sloops and one forty-gun frigate-of-war prowling the Pacific looking for prizes, none as yet had called at the Sandwich Islands.

Kamehameha's resident advisor, Captain Reginald Barker, who had served in the British Navy himself, told Hunt that the Hawaiian king had declared he would take no guff from either the King George men or the Bostons.

"If a warship from either country calls at the Sandwich Islands, it will be seized and immobilized," Barker said. "His Majesty vows he'll be neutral in the war."

"Captain Sowle says he won't take me back to Astoria, even after the ship is refitted and repaired."

"A wise decision, I would say, Mr. Hunt. If a British man-of-war caught the *Beaver* in the lower Columbia, there'd be no escape."

"He wants to go on to Canton, where he feels he can sell the furs even if the ship is interned. But I've got to get back to Fort Astoria. Do you think there's any chance I could charter a ship from a neutral country to take me there?"

"I'll ask around," Captain Barker said genially. "Meanwhile, why don't you come to my palace and be my guest while you're waiting? There are worse places to spend a few months, you know."

"Indeed, I do," Hunt agreed fervently. "And one of them is Sitka, Alaska."

12.

$\mathcal{I}$T WAS NOT UNTIL APRIL 11, 1813, that the Astorians learned a state of war had existed between the United States and Great Britain for almost ten months. Brought overland from Montreal by a party led by John McTavish of the North West Company, the news was made even worse by the arrogant statement made by McTavish that England soon would control this part of the country.

"Why d'ye say that?" McDougall demanded.

"*Och mon*, it's as plain as the nose on yer face, Laird McDougall. Over a month ago, the merchant ship *Isaac Todd* was scheduled to sail from London, bound for the lower Columbia. Keeping her company was the armed frigate *Phoebe* and two sloops of war, the *Cherub* and the *Raccoon*. After sailin' around the Horn, they will come north, sweepin' the Pacific Ocean clean of American shipping, after which the British Navy will take possession of all hostile settlements on the West Coast."

"Seems like a grand show of power," Duncan McDougall observed skeptically, "to conquer such a wee trading post as ours. Ye'll forgive me doobts, John, till I see it happen."

"Oh, it will happen, surely enough," John McTavish chortled. "Ye'd best accept that and make yer peace with the North West Company, which will call the piper's tune in the fur trade for all of North America."

"Weel, the North West Company does nae call the tune in this part of the country yet," McDougall said angrily. " 'Tis owned by Mr. Astor and the Pacific Fur Company, in which I'm one of the Senior Partners. So just ye put a bridle on yer tongue, John, and cease yer braggin'."

"I've got twenty men in my party, Duncan, wi' fifty more on their way. Ye'd best mind yer manners and make us welcome."

"Weel, *I've* got one hundred and forty men at my beck and call, wi' eight hundred Chinooks, five hundred Clatsops, and the thousands of Nez Perce, Spokane, and Okanogan Indians that Donald McKenzie, John Clarke, and David Stuart can muster to support them. So if it's war ye want, we'll gi' ye a belly full."

"We dinnae want to fight ye, Duncan," McTavish said placatingly. "After all, we're countrymen, ye and me, who once worked for the same company—"

"But dinnae work for the same company now, I remind ye. As long as I take my pay from Astor, I'll nae betray him."

"More honor to ye for that, Laird McDougall. When I met wi' yer partners upriver, they said the same thing. Business is business, said John Clarke, Donald McKenzie, and David Stuart—which is a thing every Scotsman understands. But we also understood what I said to yer partners in return—that ere long all the business in this part of the country will be in the hands of the North West Company. Ye'd best accept that."

Indeed, the three partners in charge of the upriver posts did realize that they might have little choice but to deal with the North West Company, now that hostilities had begun. Already, the war appeared to be going badly for the United States. Eventually achieving independence for the Thirteen Colonies after waging a long, tedious land war that never did have wholehearted British support, was one thing. Defeating England at sea, where its navy had long reigned supreme—which the United States must do if it were to maintain its hold on such a distant outpost as Fort Astoria—was quite something else.

Coming downriver in early June, David Stuart, John Clarke, and Donald McKenzie held a grim council with Duncan McDougall, as the four Senior Partners argued over what to do.

"We lost most of the supplies that were on the *Tonquin*," Donald McKenzie pointed out. "The *Beaver* has been gone for a year wi' no word from Hunt, so we must assume that it's lost, too. The chances for this year's supply ship to reach us across a sea swarmin' with British raiders are very small. So let's face it, gentlemen, we're marooned on a lonely coast."

"I agree that our situation is hopeless," David Stuart said, wearily nodding his head. "Since the papers of organization for the Pacific Fur Company state that if, in the opinion of a majority of the Senior Partners in the field, it is felt that the enterprise cannot succeed, we may abandon it after five years. I suggest we do just that."

" 'Tis nae five years yet," McDougall said stubbornly. " 'Tis only three."

"If we do fold up, what will we do?" John Clarke asked. "Sell out to the North West Company?"

"They've nae made us an offer yet," McDougall said. "My feeling is, they're hopin' a British man-of-war will show up soon. Then they'll take possession of the fort wi'out payin' us a dollar for it. But if that's their game, I've got a way to stop it."

"How?" McKenzie asked.

"All the furs we've gathered are packed into small bales we can load into canoes and disperse upriver long before a man-of-war can cross the bar and force us to surrender the fort. To make sure we'll have plenty of time, Ben Warren has promised me he won't pilot a hostile ship across the bar wi'out my say-so. Neither will Conco or his father. In fact, Chief Concomly says he's got eight hundred warriors who'll fight on our side, if we choose to do battle with the King George men."

"God almighty, *mon*, ye can't be thinkin' of startin' an Indian-white war, can ye?"

"Not a bit of it. I'm just tellin' ye, Donald, we're nae as defenseless as John McTavish takes us to be. In the old country, as ye may recall, a McDougall could whip three McTavishes in a fight."

"As could a McKenzie, when it came to that. Mayhap a Stuart could do as well."

"Since we seem to be evenly divided regarding what we should do," John Clarke said, "I suggest we postpone our final decision until fall. Why don't we go back to our posts and continue to trade with the Indians until the middle of September? Then we'll bring our furs downriver and decide what's to be done next. Can we all agree to that?"

The four partners said they could …

Having promised Duncan McDougall that he would not guide a British man-of-war across the bar without first notifying the factor that he was doing so, Ben had told Conco to keep a sharp eye out for approaching ships and to let him know the moment he saw one off the river's mouth. On August 4, Conco came hurrying across to Fort Astoria in a Chinook canoe and told Ben that from the lookout atop Cape Disappointment he had sighted a sailing ship lying offshore signaling for a pilot to guide it across the bar.

"Could you make out its flag?" Ben asked.

"With the big spyglass you gave me, I could see it very well," Conco, answered, spreading out a sketch he had made on a piece of bleached deerskin so that Ben could see it. "As you taught me to do, I noted its colors and design." He pointed with a finger. "Here near the staff, it is green in the smaller part, while the larger part to the right is red. Between the parts, there is a circle with a yellow rim. Inside the circle itself it is green on one half, red on the other, around a white shield which bears four small blue squares."

"You've got mighty sharp eyes, Conco, to have seen all that."

"With the big spyglass, it is easy, for the flag is brought very close. Do you know which nation it is?"

"Portugal," Ben said. "These days, a lot of the world's merchant ships are sailing under the Portuguese flag because that's a nation none of the belligerents want to offend."

"Will you pilot the ship in?"

"No reason why not. Let me check with Mr. McDougall first, to make sure he approves. Then we'll go out and meet her."

Pulling alongside the waiting ship in mid-afternoon, Ben was pleasantly surprised to find Wilson Price Hunt aboard, as anxious for news of Fort Astoria as the people there were for word of him. The small square-rigger was called the *Albatross*, having left Baltimore a couple of years ago under another name and mixed British-American ownership, sailing easterly around the world by way of Lisbon, Capetown, Madagascar, Bombay, Canton, and Honolulu. Stranded there after Captain Sowle had insisted on sailing the *Beaver* on to China, Mr. Hunt had chartered the ship to bring him to Astoria as a passenger, though the swarthy Portuguese captain who was now acting as master of the *Albatross* had bluntly refused to pick up any Pacific Fur Company cargo that might jeopardize his ship's neutrality.

Since Mr. Hunt seemed in no mood to engage in small talk and Ben was preoccupied with giving directions to the helmsmen—who did not understand English very well—little conversation passed between them as Ben followed Conco and the Chinook canoe along the tricky channel leading across the bar. Finally, Hunt asked:

"You've heard about the outbreak of war?"

"Yes, sir. An overland party of Nor'westers told us about it last April. Mr. McDougall thinks they want to buy us out."

"Have any British ships of war showed up?"

"No, sir. But the Nor'westers keep saying they will." After several minutes of silence, Ben asked, "How was Russian Alaska?"

"Cold," Hunt said curtly. "But I must say I was well treated in Hawaii by Captain Reginald Barker, even though he is an Englishman. It's the garden spot of the Pacific, so far as I'm concerned. My only complaint is that I was stuck there so long waiting for a ship that would bring me to Astoria."

Though he was not present during the meetings between Hunt, McDougall, and Franchere, Ben heard enough gossip among the Astorians to learn what was going on. With seventy-five members of the North West Company now camped near the fort like vultures waiting for a wounded animal to die, Hunt agreed with McDougall's arm's-length policy of selling John McTavish and his people only enough gunpowder, lead, salt, and dry food staples to let them hunt wild meat and trade with the local Indians for the salmon, clams, and oysters needed to keep them alive. But where furs were concerned, they were to be frozen out of the local trade.

Defending Fort Astoria against an attack by a British man-of-war would be a difficult matter, Hunt agreed, which he would leave to the judgment of the Senior Partners on the scene.

"Since there really is nothing I can do here at the moment," Hunt said. "I'll be sailing back to Hawaii in a couple of weeks. Being Portuguese and chartered, the *Albatross* is not under my command. When I get back to Hawaii, perhaps I can buy a sloop or schooner that I can control."

"Now that war has broken out," McDougall asked, "cannae Mr.

Astor persuade his friends in high places to send an armed ship out to the Pacific to protect his interests? Or can he nae buy and arm one himself?"

"I've heard a rumor that the United States does have a warship operating in the South Pacific," Hunt said. "I've also heard a rumor the British have sunk her. The most depressing rumor that has reached Hawaii is that when asked how he intended to protect his people and interests in Astoria, Mr. Astor just shrugged and grunted, 'I don't. Let the United States flag protect them.' "

"Small comfort that'll be to us," McDougall muttered sourly, "when a twenty-gun British man-of-war sails across the bar and fires a broadside at the fort. I'll do me best to look after the Company's investment, Mr. Hunt. But I nae will fight His Majesty's Navy."

By the end of September, the three upriver posts had been closed, their remaining supplies and accumulated furs brought to Fort Astoria, and the four Senior Partners faced the decision which they had postponed last June. Having heard nothing further from Hunt, the partners assumed they could expect no help from him or an American warship. Though no British vessels had showed up yet, John McTavish and his big party of Nor'westers seemed increasingly confident that a man-of-war would appear any day. Irritated by their arrogance, Duncan McDougall improved on his emergency plan to disperse all the baled furs upriver by adding all the transportable supplies in the fort. If he were forced to surrender Astoria, he swore, nothing would be left inside its walls but an empty shell.

"Which we'll set afire before we go," he told John McTavish grimly, "just to make sure ye get nothin' but ashes."

"*Och mon*, that'd be a sore waste of all yer labors," John McTavish complained. "Can we nae take an inventory of yer supplies and furs, then set a price and negotiate a civilized sale?"

"Makin' an inventory and settin' a price will nae be a problem, John. But if we did agree to sell, how would ye pay?"

"Wi' a draft on a Montreal bank, of course. We're honorable men."

"Would you sign it?"

"Aye, that I would."

"Makin' the draft payable to John Jacob Astor in New York?"

"If that's the way ye want it, aye."

Taking the offer to the other three partners, McDougall found them all willing to accept it. As they pointed out, the accumulated furs were worth nothing here with no ship available to carry them to market. Because the war might last for years, there would be no way of resupplying the upriver trading posts until the blockade was lifted. Donald McKenzie did raise one important point.

"D'ye think his offer is made in good faith? Or is it just a way of stallin' till a warship comes?"

"That, we'll see, Donald. But once I get the rascal's verbal agreement, I'll find a way to make him keep it, ye may be sure."

Taking an inventory of the furs and supplies on hand at Fort Astoria required ten days, with the final list completed and priced on October 16, 1813. After half a day of haggling, John McTavish and Duncan McDougall agreed that a ten percent markup on the value of the goods, plus transportation charges, was fair enough. When totaled up, the whole sale came to $80,500 in American money, to be paid in the form of a draft on a Montreal bank.

After Gabriel Franchere, who wrote a very clear hand, had penned three copies of the sale agreement, McDougall said to McTavish:

"Now if ye'll make out and sign the bank draft, John, I'll date and sign the agreement. Then the deed will be done."

"I dinnae have a bank draft wi' me, Duncan. Tomorrow I'll bring one. Meantime, if ye'll sign my copy of the agreement, I'll have my associates look it over—just to make sure all the 't's' are crossed and the 'i's' are dotted."

"Ye'll nae get a signed agreement from me, John McTavish, till I see a signed bank draft from you. I'll expect ye to bring it to me right after breakfast tomorrow mornin'."

"Surely, I'll do that, Duncan. Unless it rains. In which case, I'll drop over shortly after dinner. If the sun shines, that is ..."

After almost a month of shilly-shallying on the Nor'westers' part, during which John McTavish found first one and then another reason for postponing the signing of the agreement and delivering the bank draft, while he waited for the expected British man-of-war to show up, Duncan McDougall decided he had had enough. With the Nor'westers camped on the flat two hundred yards downhill from the fort,

McDougall implemented the promise he had made the partners to see that the commitment made by John McTavish in behalf of the North West Company was honored by doing three things:

First, he sent Gabriel Franchere into the Nor'wester camp, where the young clerk announced quietly but firmly that all credit for food and supplies was being cut off, beginning now.

Second, he put the voyageurs to work carrying bales of furs and supplies down to the fleet of canoes assembled at the Fort Astoria dock, their route taking them through the heart of the Nor'westers' camp.

Third, he sent Donald McKenzie up to the catwalk nearest the camp, where he gave notice in his deep, far-carrying voice that, as a measure of self-defense, the fort cannons mounted on the corner bastions were going to begin a firing exercise at eleven o'clock—two hours from now—in order to check the accuracy and range of the six-pounders. Since it was now nine A.M., the exercise would be canceled, of course, if the agreement were signed, the promised bank draft delivered, and ownership of the post changed hands before the deadline.

That ultimatum got the desired action.

At eleven o'clock in the morning November 12, 1813, the transaction was completed to the satisfaction of all those present. From that moment on, the North West Company became the owners of Fort Astoria, with its current employees either switching allegiance or making preparations to leave this part of the country.

With one exception.

The exception was Ben Warren—who swore he would do neither.

13.

As the only former member of the *Tonquin's* crew now living at Fort Astoria, Ben Warren felt isolated, with no friends except Conco, the six voyageurs in his barge crew, and Gabriel Franchere. Having been employed as a seaman, he had no interest in the fur business other than cruising the lower river and collecting pelts from the natives. Who would pay him for that job now, he did not know. In fact, the transfer of ownership of the post from American to British had come so suddenly that even the four Senior Partners were not sure where their loyalties lay, while the employees of lower rank were completely confused.

Most of the Americans at the post said they wanted to quit their jobs and return to the "United States," as soon as transportation could be arranged. But so far as Ben was concerned, this part of the country *was* the United States, despite the fact that the British flag now flew from the staff within the palisade yard.

At the insistence of John McTavish, the post was renamed Fort George. When McTavish told Duncan McDougall that the North West Company wanted him to continue as factor, McDougall accepted the offer so quickly that John Jacob Astor later accused him of conniving with the North West Company to sell out his interests at ten cents on the dollar, despite the fact that McDougall had gone to great lengths to make the best deal he could under trying circumstances.

After David Stuart, John Clarke, and Donald McKenzie returned to the East and delivered the $80,500 draft which McDougall had obtained in payment for Astoria, the New York merchant made the same unjust accusation against them. This made McKenzie so angry that he declared:

"Weel, if that's how he feels, I'll gi' the fat little bastard a *real* dose of physic to swallow! I'll offer my services to the North West Company, go back to my Nez Perce friends in the Clearwater country, and show the ungrateful old fool how the fur business should be run!"

Both Ross Cox and Alexander Ross declared their willingness to switch allegiance and employers in exchange for an opportunity to make their fortune in the fur trade.

Though Gabriel Franchere wanted to get out of the business and return to Montreal immediately, Duncan McDougall persuaded him to stay on until next spring, pointing out that the trails in the high country of the upper Columbia and across Canada would be covered with snow until June anyway, so he might as well put his time to good use helping the North West Company get started in the local trade.

Conco told Ben that the change in ownership had puzzled his father, Chief Concomly.

"He wonders if the Bostons will become slaves of the King George men. Mr. McDougall says no, that this was simply a business transaction. But my father says if any of the Bostons need help, he will be glad to give it to them."

"Most of the Americans plan to quit and go home," Ben said. "Except for me."

"You will stay in our country?"

"Damn right, I will. This is my country, too."

"Will you go to work for the King George men?"

"Not if I can help it, Conco. I want to be my own man, though I'm not sure what I'll do or where I'll live."

"Come to my village and live with me. You will never be cold or hungry there."

"Thanks for the offer, friend. I'll stay at the fort for the time being. Maybe something will turn up."

While still unsure of what he was going to do, a long-anticipated event occurred that gave Ben an opportunity to heed a piece of advice given him by the former Second Mate of the *Tonquin*, John Mumford. Crossing the river to Fort George on a gray, rainy morning December 1, 1813, Conco told Ben that from the viewpoint atop Cape Disappointment he had sighted a ship lying off the mouth of the Columbia. After listening to Conco describe it, Ben nodded and said:

"Sounds like one of the ships the Nor'westers have been expecting for months. Or it could be an American naval vessel or Mr. Hunt coming back. I'll check with McDougall and see what he wants me to do."

What the newly hired factor of Fort George wanted Ben to do, it developed, depended to a great extent on what his employer, John McTavish, requested of him. Not surprisingly, the Nor'wester was as skittish about the possibility that the ship lying off the mouth of the river might be an American man-of-war as McDougall had been earlier that Hunt's *Albatross* might be a British naval vessel.

"Could you see her flag?" McTavish asked Conco. "Does she carry any guns?"

Because of the fog lying off the coast, Conco said, all he could see of the ship was its vague outline. Whether it was British or American, a merchant ship or a man-of-war, he simply could not tell. All he knew was that it had fired three rounds with its cannon, the universal signal requesting a pilot across the bar.

Whatever the ship's nature or nationality, it would have to be guided into the river, McTavish admitted. But if it turned out to be the American naval vessel reputed to be cruising the Pacific, he did not intend to lose his recently purchased furs.

"What I want ye to do, Duncan," he told McDougall, "is load all the pelts into boats—as ye did before—and have the voyageurs take them upriver a few miles beyond Tongue Point, where they'll stay till we know whether the ship is hostile or friendly."

"That I can do, John."

"You, Ben, weel go out wi' Conco and his Chinook paddlers in a native canoe and tell the captain ye'll pilot his ship across the bar when the weather and tide are right—which, if the ship is unfriendly, need not be for days."

"I won't be able to fool a deep-water captain very long, Mr. McTavish. Nor will I try."

"Weel, this you can do, lad, to help us a bit. If the ship flies the American flag, tell her captain that the Astor Company's Duncan McDougall is still in charge of the trading post—which is nae a lie—so there's no reason to attack the fort. If it's a British ship, of course, ye can bring her in straightaway."

"I won't lie for you, sir. But if you want me to pilot the ship in, I will promise you this much—I'll say nothing at all about who owns the post."

"Good enough! That'll gi' us a bit more time."

"One more thing, sir. Neither the North West Company nor Astor is paying my salary now. So if Conco and I are to be employed as bar pilots, somebody will have to pay our fee."

John McTavish stared at him. "A fee? Ye'd charge money for guidin' a ship across the bar?"

"Yes, sir. It's a common practice in ports where local knowledge is needed to keep a ship from going aground."

"He's right, John," McDougall said, nodding. "A pilot's fee is a small price to pay for protecting a ship from being wrecked in dangerous waters."

"How much of a fee?" McTavish asked.

"If the ship is American, two hundred dollars in silver coin. If she's British, forty guineas in gold."

"That's a large sum of money, lad."

"Guiding a ship across what many captains call the most dangerous bar in the world is a large responsibility, sir," Ben answered stubbornly. "Any ship's master will tell you that."

"Weel, then, can ye nae make the ship's captain pay yer fee?"

"I can try, Mr. McTavish. But since I don't know who the captain will be—and I do know you—I'm asking you to guarantee I'll get my money."

Finding no sympathy in Duncan McDougall's dour face, which was showing the ghost of a smile, John McTavish shrugged in resignation.

"Very well, lad. I'll gi' ye my word. But tell me somethin', Ben. Yer da', Thomas Warren, was a Welshman born and bred, that I know. But did he nae have a bit of Scotch blood in his veins—most of which he passed on to you?"

Cold, raw fog, intermittent showers of rain, gusts of wind coming first from one direction and then from another, plus a nasty chop running diagonally across the bar, made Ben glad that the craft taking him out to meet the ship was a seagoing Chinook canoe under the direction of Conco rather than the fort's less manageable barge manned by voyageurs. In this weather, bringing the ship in today looked doubtful, for only two hours of daylight would remain when the turn of the tide made the attempt possible.

"I'll leave it to your judgment as to whether we should risk it or not," he told Conco. "If we run out of daylight, you can put me aboard the ship and leave me there for the night or however long it may take for weather and tide to be favorable. Agreed?"

After a brief glance up at the sky, Conco smiled and nodded. "Sure, Ben. But I think the weather will be fine to cross just before dark."

By now, Ben had learned never to question Conco's judgment where weather predictions were concerned. On several occasions when conditions on the lower river seemed perfectly calm, he had known Conco to become very agitated, turn the canoe he was steering toward sheltered waters, and get it out of harm's way only minutes before a violent storm struck. At other times when the wind, waves, and rain were at their height and seemed bound to last for hours, Conco would order his crew to put their canoe into the water, pile aboard, and head out across the river, whose white-capped, turbulent surface soon would turn calm and tranquil. Asking him what signs he read to make his predictions was as useless, Ben knew, as requesting a veteran Gloucester fisherman to tell you why he had decided to seek codfish a certain distance and direction from shore on any particular day. Just as the Gloucester fisherman knew from long experience where the codfish were likely to be, so Conco knew about the weather.

By the time the Chinook canoe came abeam of the waiting ship, the fog had lifted and a wan winter sun shone through scattered clouds. Hailing the ship and being invited aboard, Ben found himself on the quarter deck of the British corvette, *Raccoon*, a twenty-six-gun naval vessel. Licensed as a privateer and carrying 120 prize-hungry sailors, the ship was commanded by Captain William Black, who was quite surprised to see a young white man climb out of a big cedar log canoe manned by thirty slant-headed Chinook paddlers.

"How in God's name did you ever get mixed up with such an odd-looking lot of savages?" Captain Black demanded after Ben had introduced himself. "They look like devils straight out of Dante's Inferno!"

"They're Chinook Indians, sir. No one knows this coast as well as they do."

"Indeed? How did you become so friendly with them?"

"I was a seaman aboard the *Tonquin*. Since I've gone ashore, I've been working with Conco, the chief's son, guiding ships into the river."

"You're an American?"

"Yes, sir. And these are American waters, I remind you."

A slim, dapper man, with long, dark sideburns and a bristling mustache, Captain Black laughed good-naturedly. Taking Ben by the elbow, he steered him into the warmth of his cabin, where he set out cups, hot water, and rum.

"We'll suspend hostilities for the time being, Mr. Warren, while we share a hot rum."

"If it's all the same to you, sir, I'll settle for hot tea."

"Hot tea it is for you then, though I'll have rum myself." After serving the drinks, Captain Black sat down on the other side of the small table. "Now tell me how you propose to take my ship across the bar and into the fabled Columbia River."

"We'll follow behind the Chinook canoe, which is commanded by my partner, Conco. But we'll have to wait two hours for the tide to turn."

"Why do we have to follow an Indian canoe? Don't you know the channel?"

"Yes, sir, I do, but it changes every day. To be on the safe side, I want Conco guiding us in. He and his father have been piloting ships across the bar for twenty years."

"Exacting a tribute, no doubt."

"Just as Conco and I still do, Captain Black, though we call it a business. The fee for your ship will be forty guineas."

"What if I refuse to pay?"

"Then I'll thank you kindly for the tea, sir, get back into the canoe with Conco, and wish you luck in finding your own way across the bar. Which you will need, I assure you."

Shaking his head in amazement, Captain Black exclaimed:

"Is there no limit to Yankee enterprise? I've sailed halfway around the world seeking prizes and glory, only to be held up by a beached American sailor and his slant-headed Indian partner, who've declared a monopoly on the mouth of the mighty Columbia River! I'm flabbergasted!"

Ben got to his feet. "As I said, Captain, you're free to find your own passage across the bar. But I do advise you to wait for the incoming tide."

"Oh, I'll pay your piddling pilot's fee gladly enough," Captain Black said impatiently. "It's just that you surprised me by setting up shop in what I took to be a howling wilderness. Sit down, damn it! Sit down and let me hot up your tea."

"Thank you, sir. It does taste good."

"Sure you won't have a stick of rum in it?"

"Plain tea is fine, thank you."

"What about your Indian boat crew? Won't they freeze their bottoms off sitting out there for two hours in the rain and cold?"

"They're used to it."

"If you guarantee their good behavior, I'll tell the mate he can let them come aboard a few at a time. My sailors are eager to get a closer look at the slant-headed rascals. We might even give them something hot to drink, so long as it's not rum, which I know drives Indians crazy."

"None of the Chinooks will touch alcohol, Captain. They think it's poison. But hot, well-sugared tea would be a real treat to them. My partner, Conco, will make sure they behave."

After stepping out of the cabin and giving the order to the First Mate, Captain Black returned, sat down, and poured himself another hot rum. When Ben asked for the latest news about the war between Great Britain and the United States, the captain was glad to oblige.

As the Nor'westers had told the Astorians months ago, the *Raccoon* had left England in company with the armed frigate *Phoebe*, the corvette *Cherub*, and the merchant ship, *Isaac Todd*. Though the four ships had kept in sight of one another between Rio de Janeiro and Cape Horn, they became separated during a storm near the Strait of Magellan. At the appointed rendezvous location in the South Pacific, Juan Fernandez Island, the three warships got together again, then waited for the merchant vessel, *Isaac Todd*, to join them.

"After a couple of weeks, we heard that an American raider, the *Porter*, was playing the very devil with the British whaling fleet in the Pacific. So Commodore Hillier decided the *Phoebe* and the *Cherub* would go after the *Porter*, while I came north in the *Raccoon* and destroyed the American trading post at the mouth of the Columbia. Nothing personal about it, you understand, Mr. Warren. Just the fortunes of war."

"I understand perfectly, sir," Ben said with a straight face. "You must do your duty, I know."

"As a matter of fact, we have yet to capture a prize, for the pickings are slim in these waters. Truth to tell, you Americans have done a damn sight better in the war than we expected you'd do. The performance of the *Constitution*, for instance, has been brilliant."

Remembering his last sight of the U.S.S. *Constitution* as an escort two days after the beginning of the voyage, Ben's interest quickened.

"What did she do?"

"What didn't she do, is a better way to put it! She outsailed and outfought every warship we put against her. For example, in early Jul, 1812, off the New Jersey coast she mistook five British ships for friendlies and sailed right into the middle of them. Discovering her mistake and being heavily outgunned, she turned on her heels and ran for Boston under full sail. Not one of our ships could catch her."

"I've heard she's the fastest frigate in our navy."

"Two weeks later off the coast of Nova Scotia, she destroyed one of our warships and captured another. Ten days after that, we thought we had her trapped near the mouth of the St. Lawrence when one of our forty-four-gun frigates took her gauge to windward and started pounding the devil out of her hull with solid shot. But damned if it didn't bounce off her and fall harmlessly into the water. Our gunners were so amazed, they said her sides must be made of iron."

"I've been told she's well built."

"She certainly is. In fact, the Americans now call her 'Old Ironsides.' "

"How did the battle end?"

"The Americans won, I'm ashamed to say. Thirty minutes after the engagement began, the British captain struck his colors and surrendered. Which does not mean you Americans are going to win the war, of course. But considering the small size of your fleet and your lack of naval tradition, you Colonists are putting on a jolly good show."

Not being much of a drinking man himself, Ben hardly qualified as an expert judge of how much rum a ship's captain could consume in the space of two hours and still keep his wits about him. Certainly by the time the tide turned and the *Raccoon* got underway following the Chinook canoe into the channel in the low-angled southwestern sunlight of the dying day, Captain William Black's tongue had become so thick as he stood on the quarter deck shouting sailing instructions to the First Mate that Ben could not understand a word he said.

Fortunately for the safe passage of the ship across the bar, the mate either understood the commands well enough—or gave proper commands of his own—to keep the ship under control. Standing beside the helmsmen giving him corrections in course while trying to keep the Chinook canoe in sight in the increasingly poor light, Ben did get a bit irritated at the captain's persistent questions regarding the status of the trading post he had orders to destroy.

"Where is it located?"

"On the south side of the Columbia, twelve miles upriver."

"How many people are in it?"

"Two hundred or so."

"Is it well defended?"

"I can't say."

"Is its outer stockade built of logs or stone?"

"I can't say."

"Are cannon mounted on its corner bastions?"

"I can't say."

"How big are they? What is their maximum range? Will they be firing grape or solid shot?"

Preoccupied giving directions to the helmsman in the trickiest part of the channel, Ben did not answer. Accidentally lunging against him as the ship heeled over and he lost his balance, Captain Black said angrily:

"Did you hear me, Mr. Warren?"

"Yes, sir," Ben said curtly. "The answer still is, I don't know."

"For a young man as bright as you pretend to be," Captain Black sneered, "you don't know much of anything, do you?"

"On the contrary, Captain," Ben said quietly, "there is one thing I know very well."

"What's that, pray tell?"

"If you don't quit asking me foolish questions while I'm trying to do my job, I know I can put your ship aground in the next minute or two. I suggest you shut up and leave me alone."

Captain Black's face turned beet red. For a moment, Ben thought the master of the *Raccoon* was going to take a swing at him. Then the captain's strict British naval training—which had taught him long ago that a pilot was never to be interfered with while taking a ship through dangerous waters—took over. Standing stiff, straight, and appearing suddenly very sober, Captain Black nodded and said crisply:

"Point well taken, Mr. Warren. Carry on!"

Full dark had fallen by the time the ship reached the quiet waters of Baker Bay just offshore from the Chinook village on the north side of the river. From this point on, Ben did not need a guide to show him the way upriver to the anchorage just below Fort George, for enough afterglow lingered in the night sky to outline the headlands and hilltops he would use as markers. Before dismissing Conco and his crew of Chinook paddlers, Ben told Captain Black what his choices were.

143

"We can drop anchor here in Baker Bay," Ben said, "then go on up the river to the fort around noon tomorrow. Or we can use the rest of the incoming tide to sail upriver tonight."

"Can you find your way safely?"

"Yes, sir. I know the lower river very well."

"You certainly brought us in over the bar neatly enough, I'll admit. How long will it take us to reach an anchorage below the fort?"

"Three or four hours."

"Which would put us right on the doorstep of our prize while the defenders are sound asleep. I like that, Mr. Warren! Can't you just imagine their surprise when they wake up tomorrow morning and find a twenty-six-gun British man-of-war lying just below the fort? They'll be frightened out of their britches!"

"Yes, sir. I imagine they will."

"Mind you, we'll not fire unless fired upon, Mr. Warren. In the interest of avoiding bloodshed, I hope you'll go ashore and tell the post's commander that resistance is futile. Will you consider doing that?"

Still keeping a straight face, Ben said he would …

By the time the *Raccoon* dropped anchor half a mile below the fort and Ben had been rowed ashore, it was midnight. Having heard ship noises out in the dark, Duncan McDougall and John McTavish were still up and very much aware of the fact that a ship had arrived, though it was not until Ben joined them in the Fort George counting room that they learned its identity and mission.

"British, ye say?" McTavish exclaimed. "Praise the Lord! We'll nae lose our furs after all!"

"Don't be too sure about that, sir. Captain Black says he has orders to destroy the fort."

"To what?"

"But he did promise me he'd give you a chance to surrender before he opens fire. You can talk to him about it in the morning." Ben yawned and stretched sleepily. "Now if you'll excuse me, gentlemen, I'm going to bed. I've had a long, busy day."

14.

$\mathcal{F}$ROM WHAT BEN OBSERVED of the confrontation between Duncan McDougall, John McTavish, and Captain William Black next morning, the master of the *Raccoon* was far more shocked by what he found on the site of the fort than the Nor'westers were surprised to see a twenty-six-gun man-of-war anchored on their doorstep. Trying to make clear to the captain that the trading post already was in friendly hands and need not be destroyed as enemy property, the two fur company men sent a boat out to the ship, brought the captain to the stockade, and pointed out the British flag flying within the enclosure.

"We've gi'en the post a good British name," McDougall said proudly. "Instead of Astoria, it's now called Fort George."

"Yes, yes, that's all very well!" Captain Black said impatiently. "But where is the monstrous American fort I was ordered to destroy?"

"Here," McDougall grunted. " 'Tis right here."

"*This* dinky little place is Fort Astoria?" the captain demanded. "It can't be!"

"But it is, sir," McTavish said. "As we've been tryin' to tell ye, after the sale we renamed it Fort George."

"What sale?"

"The one by which we paid the Astor Company 80,500 American dollars for all the buildings, supplies, and furs it owned, transferrin' title to the North West Company. Havin' bought them out, we then raised the British flag and renamed the post."

"Well, I'll be blessed! This is the fort that was represented to me as so great! Good Lord, I could have knocked it over in two hours with a four-pounder!"

Because Captain William Black and his 120-man crew had been counting on making their fortunes by capturing valuable prizes at sea or on land under their license as privateers, their disappointment was keen. As the captain had told Ben yesterday, they had taken no American merchant ships during their long voyage. Since they were carrying goods designated for the North West Company, for whose transport they could not even charge freight, and could not condemn the furs and supplies on hand at Fort George as prizes of war, their voyage so far had been a total loss.

To make matters worse, as soon as Chief Concomly was told by his son that a British man-of-war had arrived, the chief ordered his people to arm themselves in their stiff sealskin war jackets and cedar bark shields, then assembled a fleet of war canoes, and came storming across the river prepared to do battle against the invaders. Assembling his warriors in strategic locations between Fort George and the anchored ship, he called his son-in-law, Duncan McDougall, out in the palisade yard and made a ringingly patriotic speech.

"Ever since the Americans came to live among us, my people and I have become very fond of them. We do not like the King George men. When the Canadian trader John McTavish came down the river with his followers last summer, they were very poor; they had no powder, lead, or food, and were starving to death. We wanted to send them away or kill them, but you would not let us. We could not understand this."

"They're our people, in a way," McDougall said uncomfortably. "They offered to buy the fort."

"I know they did. You were afraid of them, so you delivered your fort, your furs, and all your goods to their leader. Now the King George men have sent a warship to put you in chains and carry you off as slaves. But we will not let them. Since the Americans are our friends and allies, we will fight on their side. We will hide in the bushes and among the trees near the landing, then when the soldiers from the ship come ashore, we will rush down and kill them."

Shaking his head, McDougall said nervously, "No, Chief Concomly, ye cannae do that. We sold the fort to the Nor'westers, true enough, but 'twas a legal business transaction. The master of the *Raccoon* was given orders to destroy the fort if it was still in American hands, but he knows now that the British own it. He'll do us no harm."

"You do not want us to fight the King George men?" Chief Concomly asked in bewilderment.

"Nay, we do not."

"You are afraid of them!" Chief Concomly said scornfully. "My daughter did not marry a *hyas tyee*—a great white leader. She married a woman who dresses in a man's clothes!"

In an effort to lessen the chief's contempt, Duncan McDougall flattered Concomly's vanity by making him a present of a new suit of clothes, gave him a basketful of beads, bells, and baubles for his wives, and sincerely thanked him for his concern.

Rebuffed in his effort to help his American friends, Concomly visited the *Raccoon* and paid his respects to Captain Black, who was in his cabin nursing a hot rum as he tried to figure out a way to salvage something from what so far had been a financially disastrous voyage.

"It is a great joy to meet you," Concomly said cheerfully after being ushered into the cabin. "I am very glad that I have lived long enough to see a great ship of my brother, King George, enter the river. I have known for a long time that the Americans have no ships with as many guns as those of the King George men."

"Why, thank you, sir," Captain Black muttered. "Very decent of you to say so."

"As a token of my esteem, I want to make you a present," Concomly went on, displaying a beautiful sea otter fur, which he then placed in the captain's hands. "If ever you want help fighting the Americans, I have eight hundred warriors ready to do battle on your side."

Even though unfamiliar with trading policy on this coast—whose "potlatch" custom dictated that a present given required one of equal value in return—Captain Black knew that common courtesy demanded some sort of response. Aware of the fact that he had a cup in his hands while his guest did not, he said hastily:

"I say, old chap, would you like a tot of rum?"

"No *lum*," Conco said firmly, for among the Chinooks neither the use of alcohol nor the enunciation of the letter "r" was tolerated. "Just hot tea, well sugared, if you please."

While fixing the chief the requested drink, Captain Black thought of a way to respond to the sea otter fur present.

"At noon tomorrow, sir, we plan to conduct a ceremony officially transferring possession of Astoria from the United States to Great Britain. I would like you to be there as the leading representative of the native population of the region. Will you do that for me, Chief Concomly?"

"Oh, yes! I will be honored to!"

"To make sure you are properly attired," the captain continued, getting to his feet and opening a clothes wardrobe in the corner of the cabin, "I shall give you this gold-braided coat, cocked hat, and sword, which once belonged to an admiral in the British Navy. Also, a British flag, which I hereby authorize you to fly on a staff in front of your longhouse in order that you may show your loyalty to the Crown."

Taking the presents, Chief Concomly got to his feet and said solemnly, "You are a *hyas tyee*, Captain—a great white leader—who has done me a great honor. Long may you wave!"

Though Duncan McDougall, John McTavish, Ben Warren, the two hundred white employees, and the thousand or so Chinook, Clatsop, and assorted Indians of other lower Columbia River tribes who were present for the occasion did not have the slightest notion what the ceremony beginning at high noon the next day was all about, all those present had to admit it was very impressive. When Captain Black declared he was taking possession of Astoria and the "whole country" lying thereabouts, Ben wondered if he meant the Columbia River, the Pacific Coast, or the entire region lying west of the Rocky Mountains. Whatever he meant, the declaration sounded grand. Not in the least surprised that his father-in-law had switched allegiance and clothing for the ceremony, Duncan McDougall dourly admitted that the secondhand admiral's coat, cocked hat, and sword looked far better on Chief Concomly than the suit he had given him did, for the suit had been two sizes too large.

But both he and John McTavish *were* surprised when, following the ceremony, Captain Black insisted that an inventory be taken of all the furs, supplies, firearms, boats, tools, trade goods, and possessions of the fort, with three fair copies to be made of the completed list.

"Whatever for?" McDougall asked.

"Because naval regulations and my license as a privateer require it," Captain Black said stiffly. "Spoils of war and all that, you know."

"Spoils of war, ye say?" McTavish protested. "But we're on the same side, for God's sake! You didn't take the goddam fort—the North West Company bought it!"

"Still and all, this sort of thing must be done in proper form, old chap. When the final adjudication of prize money is made after the war, the list will be important."

Since the assets of Fort Astoria already had been inventoried before the sale was made to the North West Company, having Gabriel Franchere copy the list three more times was no problem. Cynical soul that he was, John McTavish suspected that Captain Black wanted the list made as groundwork for possible legal action after the war, when he might put in a claim for compensation as a privateer for property he had captured and thus saved for the Crown.

Whatever the captain's motive for the inventory may have been, his sudden decision after three weeks to leave Fort George and go out to sea without engaging Ben and Conco's services to pilot the *Raccoon* across the bar certainly was far from rational. Consulting neither man, miscalculating the weather, the wind, and the tide, the unfortunate captain appeared merely to aim his vessel at the open sea across the broadest part of the river's mouth—a sure formula for disaster—then drove the ship with all sails set before an offshore wind of near gale force.

Ben himself was not on hand to observe what happened. But Conco, from the lookout atop Cape Disappointment, kept the ship in sight with the big spyglass for most of its half-day struggle with the waves, current, and wind. Later, he told Ben that by the time the *Raccoon* finally cleared the bar and got out to sea, she was a floating shipwreck completely out of control.

"She grounded at least half a dozen times," Conco said. "She was careening like a drunken man who keeps falling down, getting up, and then falling down again. Why do you suppose he tried to cross the bar without a pilot?"

"Maybe our forty-guinea fee was too rich for his blood, once he found out he'd get no reward for destroying Astoria," Ben answered with a shrug. "Or maybe he'd had a few too many hot rums."

Whatever the reason, Ben heard later that Conco's calling the vessel a floating shipwreck had been accurate. Next to helpless on the stormy winter sea as she limped south down the coast to Bodega Bay, the *Raccoon* had seven feet of water in her hold when she finally made harbor. Finding it impossible to procure the necessary materials to repair the damage there, the unfortunate Captain Black and his crew were about to abandon the vessel and proceed overland to the Gulf of Mexico, where they might find a ship that would take them back to England, when the captain's luck changed.

Calling at the same port was the long-lost British merchant ship, the *Isaac Todd*, with whose assistance they succeeded in stopping the

149

leaks and putting the *Raccoon* in good sailing order again. But neither she nor her dapper captain ever returned to the Columbia River …

So far as bad luck went, it was not just the British who had it. In early February 1814, Wilson Price Hunt returned to the Columbia with a tale of misfortune that closed out the Astor venture once and for all.

After returning to Hawaii last August, Hunt had purchased the brig *Pedlar* and was about to come back to Astoria when he received news of the *Lark*, the third annual supply ship sent out from New York by John Jacob Astor. Unfortunately, the news was bad. After evading several British warships, the *Lark* had made a successful passage around Cape Horn, only to have a sudden violent squall strike her three hundred miles from Oahu, throwing her on her beam's end.

In the wreck, the second mate and four crew members perished. By cutting away the masts, the captain and the rest of the crew managed to save and right the ship, but by then she was completely waterlogged. Hoisting a small jury-rigged sail on the foremast, the survivors salvaged a case of wine and some fishing gear out of the cabin, managed to catch a shark during thirteen days of helpless drifting, and on its raw flesh and the wine stayed alive until wind and waves drove the wreck ashore on a rocky outer island of the Hawaiian chain.

Though the natives there saved the captain and crew and treated them kindly enough, they afterward claimed salvage rights, plundering all that was left of the ship and its cargo. Hearing of the wreck, Wilson Price Hunt sailed the *Pedlar* to the site, took Captain Northrop and his men aboard the brig, and brought them to what had been Fort Astoria last August but now was Fort George.

Since there was nothing else he could do, Hunt took the news of the transfer of ownership quietly enough. He told McDougall and McTavish:

"I wish you well. As for the employees of the Pacific Fur Company, all their wage contracts will be paid unless they wish to transfer their allegiance to the North West Company. Those who want to return to the United States overland may do so. Those preferring to go by sea may come aboard the *Pedlar*, which will be sailing in a week or so."

Given the choice of a six-month-long, wartime sea voyage on a small ship or a possibly more dangerous but shorter trip by land, most of the older employees chose to go by ship, while the younger men opted for the overland route. When Hunt asked Ben which choice he would make, Ben shook his head.

"Neither, sir. I'm staying here."

"You're going to work for the North West Company?"

"No, sir. I'm going to work for myself."

"Doing what?"

"Piloting ships across the bar. Conco and I are going into the business together."

Hunt smiled. "That accounts for Duncan McDougall's asking if you'd made me pay for your bringing the *Pedlar* across the bar—which you didn't."

"After all the bad luck you've had, Mr. Hunt, I didn't have the heart to charge you for something I was glad to do for nothing."

Though Wilson Price Hunt was not so weak a man as to blame everything that had gone wrong with the Astor venture on bad luck, it certainly had played a part. The loss of the *Tonquin* and the *Lark*, the misfortunes of the overland party in the wild waters of the Snake River, the more recent attacks by Indians in the desert section of the Oregon country, and the drowning of half a dozen voyageurs in the lower Columbia just a few months ago when their boat capsized in a sudden storm—all had combined in the space of three years to raise the total of men lost since the beginning of the venture to sixty-five.

In contrast, the Lewis and Clark Expedition from St. Louis to the Pacific and back over a similar period of time had lost only one man to illness.

Certainly some of the losses incurred by the Astorians had been caused by bad judgment on the part of the leaders—with Hunt perhaps responsible for a few of the miscalculations. But overall, the failure of the venture could not be charged solely to him.

"I appreciate your thoughtfulness, Ben," Hunt said quietly, "but your pilot's fee won't bankrupt Mr. Astor. Since you won't be working for the North West Company, I assume you'll be building a house of your own, right?"

"Yes, sir. I've already picked out a spot atop the highest hill above the fort, with a good view of Cape Disappointment to the northwest, the bar to the west, and the river to the east. I plan to clear it and start building my cabin right away."

"Good for you! I'll give you a draft for your pilot's fee bringing the *Pedlar* in and taking her out, which you can spend for materials at the

Fort George store. It will be nice to know that at least one loyal American is left on the Columbia River."

"That worries me, sir. How do you think the war between the United States and Great Britain will end?"

"From all I've heard, we've fought their navy to a standstill wherever we've met it on our coastal seas. As far as land engagements are concerned, we tried to invade Canada and got repulsed, while they struck at Washington, then pulled back after burning a few government buildings that weren't worth much anyway. My guess is that the people of both countries will get so sick and tired of paying for a war that none of them really want, we'll stop fighting and find a compromise we can both live with."

"Will we give them the Pacific Northwest?"

"That's as unlikely, Ben, as the possibility that they will give us Canada. North America is a big continent. Somehow, we'll find a way to share it."

"Then there is one thing you could do for me, sir."

"What's that?"

"When the North West Company took over Astoria and changed its name to Fort George, they pulled down the American flag and stored it. I'd like to have the flag they took down."

"To fly on top of your own hill?"

"That's right, sir. If I'm going to be the only American living in this part of the country, I want every ship that enters the river to know I'm here."

"Bless you, lad! You shall have it! Pray God you never have to lower it to any nation!"

15.

$\mathcal{A}$NTICIPATING THAT the trading post at the mouth of the Columbia might be in British hands by the time the ship arrived, the *Isaac
Todd* sailed from London in March 1813, in company with the *Phoebe*,
Cherub, and *Raccoon*. After getting separated from the men-of-war off
Cape Horn, she touched at Juan Fernandez Island, the Galapagos,
and the Spanish settlement of Monterey, California, where Captain
Horace Smith learned that the badly damaged *Raccoon* was at anchor
in nearby Bodega Bay. Hastening there, the *Isaac Todd* lent the *Raccoon*
the assistance needed to put the warship into sailing condition again
so that Captain Black could resume his quest for prizes and glory.

Moving north, the *Isaac Todd* reached the Columbia and was
brought across the bar by Ben and Conco, dropping her hook in the
river just off Fort George April 17, 1814. By then, Ben had moved out
of Fort George and cut down enough trees atop his hill overlooking
the fort to give him a good view of the lower river. He had built a
solid cabin with a stone fireplace and attached privy, which he planned
to add onto later as his time and resources allowed. He took pride in
the fact that his would be the first permanent American dwelling place
to be built in the Pacific Northwest, for its predecessor, Fort Clatsop,
which the Lewis and Clark party had built a few miles to the southwest in late December 1805, had been abandoned on March 22, 1806,
when the party started its return trip to St. Louis, and now was falling
into ruin.

Though his hilltop was half a mile away from Fort George, Ben
kept in touch with the trading post and still had friends there. The
closest of these was the stocky Dublin Irishman, Ross Cox, lately returned from the Spokane country where the North West Company
had put him in charge of a post trading with the natives of the upper
Columbia River. A couple of days after the arrival of the *Isaac Todd*, **153**

Cox paid Ben a visit, excitedly telling him about the wonderful cargo of luxury goods brought out from England by the ship: casks of delicious porter; wheels of excellent cheese; a fine supply of newspapers, magazines, and books; and prime English beef preserved so well in tins that it tasted just as good a year and a half after being canned as it did fresh.

"But most marvelous of all," Cox said, "is that there's a young lady aboard. A pert, lively, blonde lass named Jane Barnes."

"How did they preserve her?" Ben asked with a smile. "In tins?"

"The way I got the story, the ship's master, Captain Horace Smith, has quite an eye for the ladies. While the ship was bein' loaded, he spent his spare time in a Portsmouth tavern where Jane Barnes worked as a barmaid. As a man and a lass will do, they got to jollyin' each other over this and that, until finally she says, 'Where're you bound this trip?' To which he replies, 'The North West Coast of America.' She says, 'Law, that sounds like a grand adventure. If I was a man I'd love to go with you.' Then says he, 'Why, dearie, ye don't have to be a man—ye just have t' want to go.' "

"And she said she did?"

"Quick as a flash. So he wasted no time takin' her aboard."

"Did he marry her?"

"That was no part of the bargain. He already has a wife and a brood of children in Liverpool, it seems, which would complicate matters if he did want to commit marriage with Jane Barnes, which he didn't. But from what I've heard of her, she's not the kind to fret over that. Anyway, she shared the captain's cabin for thirteen months on the voyage out from England. And here she is."

Indeed, Miss Jane Barnes was very much present at Fort George, for she made a point of coming ashore each afternoon and parading from the dock to the stockade yard, where all the white employees of the fort and the curious Indian hangers-on could get a good look at her. Following this display of her physical charms, she would join John McTavish, Duncan McDougall, his Chinook wife, and whatever other dignitaries were present in the Fort George counting room for high tea and a bit of cultured conversation. Like most of the other men, Ben often found business to transact at the fort in late afternoon, so managed to see and admire what had to be the most interesting female visitor the fort had entertained during its existence under the British flag.

Whether Miss Barnes's dresses—which she changed every day—were from her own wardrobe or part of the ship's stock of luxury goods destined for the Hawaiian and Chinese trade, Ben did not know. But they certainly were stunning, extravagant, and rich, designed to display her plump, saucy figure to its best advantage. One day, she would wear a hat decorated with a spectacular array of feathers and flowers; the next, her long, shining blonde hair would be uncovered in all its glory, accentuated by jeweled combs and bright silk ribbons. Trailing her around, young Indian women would beg to be permitted to touch some part of her hair, face, clothing, or person, which she allowed them to do on a limited basis. For these favors, their gratitude knew no bounds.

As for the awed, drooling Indian men, all they were permitted to do was follow Miss Barnes at a reasonable distance, their bulging eyes in their slanted foreheads nearly falling out of their sockets with wonderment.

At teatime, most of the white men living at the fort treated Miss Barnes politely enough; but Duncan McDougall, who was well grounded in literature and poetry, decided one day to sound out the lady's intellectual depths, which he found to be extremely shallow. Later, he told Ben about their conversation.

"Whilst carryin' on a discussion with her, somethin' was said regardin' the intelligence of Indian women, to one of whom—as ye well know—I am married. Rather superciliously, she says, 'What d'ye mean by intelligence, Mr. McDougall? Far as I can see, the Indian women hereabouts haven't got any. How could a Chinook woman even have room for a brain, what with her slanted head and all?'

" 'Well, Miss Barnes,' says I, 'some white ladies I know are brainless, too, even with lots of room in their heads, for there's nothin' rattlin' around in their skulls but silly notions of fancy clothes, jewelry, an' hairdos.' 'Handsome is as handsome does,' as the poets say. Bein' fond of quotations herself—and most always gettin' 'em wrong—she quips, 'Oh, Mr. McDougall, as Shakespeare says, every woman is a rake at heart.' To which I answers, 'Pope, madam, Pope! If ye must quote the classics, at least get the name of the man who wrote the verse right.' "

" 'Pope?' says she with a lofty air. 'There never was no Catholic Pope as I knew of wrote poetry. So I'm sure you must be mistaken. It was Shakespeare who wrote that line, I have no doubt.' "

" 'Alexander Pope!' shouts I. 'Didn't you ever hear of him?' 'No,' says she, 'I can't say as I have. So he must not have amounted to much.' Then she pours herself another cup of tea, leans back, picks up a copy of the *London Times,* and pretends to read it. Only she's holdin' the bloomin' paper upside down. Why, I tell you, Ben, the damned illiterate bitch don't know 'B' from 'Buffalo.' "

However dim the marital prospects of Miss Jane Barnes may have been so far as the master of the *Isaac Todd* was concerned, she soon was offered a dazzling proposal ashore. It came from Conco's older brother, Cassakas, whom one of the Astorians facetiously had named "Prince of Wales" a couple of years ago because of his pompous way of putting on airs. Reluctantly, Conco passed the proposal on to Ben, explaining that his brother wanted Ben to negotiate its details with Miss Barnes. When Conco finished outlining the offer, Ben frowned and asked:

"Is he really serious about this?"

"Very serious, I fear."

"Even though he already has four wives?"

"They will not affect this marriage, he says. If the beautiful white lady will become his bride, she will be the number one wife in his household, with all the privileges that will give her."

Because Duncan McDougall already had set a precedent by marrying one of Chief Concomly's daughters and taking her into his house, Ben knew that a flat, tactless rejection of the proposal could have serious consequences, so far as relations between the white traders and the Chinook Indians were concerned. Though he would have preferred to have nothing to do with the negotiations, he decided that the best way to handle them and save face all around would be to set up a meeting of the principals in his cabin, where a greater degree of privacy could be obtained.

Getting the eager would-be bridegroom, Cassakas, to agree to the arrangement was no problem, though the Indian did insist that he not meet his intended face to face in the beginning. He preferred that Conco explain the terms of the offer to Ben in Miss Barnes's presence, he said, with Ben then passing them on to her with a strong recommendation that they be accepted. While the dickering was taking place inside the cabin, he would remain outside, pretending not to know or care about what was going on until a decision had been made and he was officially notified.

Persuading Jane Barnes to accompany Ben to his hilltop cabin and

156

sit quietly listening while the proposal was explained, turned out to be a more difficult matter. First, Ben had to make clear to her that the offer of marriage—which caught her interest the moment the word was mentioned—came not from him but from a third party. Second, he required her pledge that she would keep the proposal secret because exposure to ridicule might wound the pride of Chief Concomly's eldest son so deeply that irreparable damage would be done to regional Indian-white relations. Third, bringing a young, attractive, sexually appealing white female into what until now had been his lonely male domain stirred thoughts and desires that lately had become increasingly troublesome.

Telling Duncan McDougall what he was about to do, Ben asked the factor to prepare Jane Barnes for the discussion by stressing its delicacy and importance. Even after McDougall had done so in Ben's presence, the young lady still did not seem to understand what was at stake. Nevertheless, right after teatime at the fort next day Ben invited her to take a walk with him to his hilltop cabin to meet Cassakas and Conco, the pretext being that he wanted to show her his spectacular view of the lower river.

"Oh, my goodness, Mr. Warren!" she exclaimed. "I do love spectacular views! A stroll on such a lovely day does sound like a fine lark! Will I be safe from wild animals when we're out in the woods?"

"As safe as ye were in Captain Smith's cabin for thirteen months," McDougall growled. "Ben is a gentleman."

"It was four-legged animals I was worried about, Mr. McDougall, not men," Miss Barnes said archly. "I've yet to meet a man I can't handle."

"That's God's truth, I'll wager!"

"You say a rich, important Indian chief will be there?" she asked McDougall.

"Aye, wi' a proposal ye must consider carefully. We must nae hurt his feelings."

"Law, Mr. McDougall, I'd never do that!" Taking Ben's arm, she smiled and blinked her long eyelashes coquettishly. "Lead the way, sir. It's been ages since I've strolled in the woods with a handsome young man."

When they reached his cabin after a short uphill walk, Cassakas allowed them only a brief glimpse of his richly attired, whale-oil-smeared body and his paint-bedaubed face as he paced at the edge of

BILL GULICK

the clearing, then fled in nervous panic into the bushes nearby. Giving him a puzzled look, Miss Barnes whispered to Ben:

"Is that *him*?"

"In the flesh, ma'am. He's Chief Concomly's oldest son, Cassakas, known to white men as the Prince of Wales."

"Well, he don't look much like a prince to me," Jane Barnes giggled. "He just looks like a greasy savage with a pointed head."

"Wait till you hear his offer, Miss Barnes. It might make you change your mind."

Going into the cabin, where Conco was waiting uneasily, Ben fixed and served tea for the three of them, then translated as Conco stated the terms of his older brother's offer.

"First, Cassakas wants you to know that he is Chief Concomly's eldest son, so will become the most important man in the tribe when his father dies. Though he already has four wives, he will always let you lie next to him in his bed, he says. As a wedding present, he will send one hundred prime sea otter furs to your relations. You will never have to carry wood, draw water, dig for roots, or hunt for provisions—"

"Law, think of that!" Jane murmured, stifling a snicker.

"He will make you mistress over his other wives, he says, and permit you to sit at ease from morning to night, with nothing to do except wear a different dress every day. He will make sure that you always have an abundance of fat salmon, anchovies, and elk meat, and you will be permitted to smoke as many pipefuls of tobacco a day as you think proper. In a word, you will be treated like a queen for as long as you live. What do you say to that?"

To her credit, Miss Barnes swallowed a giggle, gave Conco a dignified nod of appreciation, then said politely to Ben:

"Tell him I'm honored by his proposal. But I must say no."

"He'll want a reason."

"Tell him I'm already promised to someone else."

"He'll ask who."

"Lord love me, Mr. Warren, how can I answer that? I've been propositioned by dozens of men in the Portsmouth tavern where I worked, by Captain Smith, by a Spanish Grandee in Monterey, and by any number of naval officers aboard the *Phoebe*, *Cherub*, and *Raccoon*."

"I have no doubt you've been propositioned often enough, Miss Barnes. But being 'promised' to a man implies a proposal of marriage. Can you give me the name of a man who's done that?"

158

"Oh, just tell him any name that pops into your head," she answered petulantly. "Say I'm promised to a fat Hawaiian prince in the Sandwich Islands or to a rich mandarin in China. To Captain Smith, if you like. Or even to you. All I know is, I don't want to marry a slant-headed savage and spend the rest of my life in this heathen land."

Ben looked inquiringly at Conco. "Do you think he'll accept that?"

"What I think is that my brother is a fool even to want to marry a white woman," Conco answered stiffly. "But I do not blame her for turning him down. She would not like living with him and his four other wives."

"Will he be angry?"

"Probably. But he will get over it after she leaves. Unless she marries you and stays here, that is, as she says she might."

Ben felt his face turn red. "She was joking, Conco. At least, I think she was." He looked at her. "Weren't you, Miss Barnes?"

Giving Ben an enigmatic smile, Jane Barnes tossed her head and answered coyly:

"Why, I'm not sure, Mr. Warren. Jollyin' with men has always been a weakness of mine, gettin' me into all kinds of trouble. But now that you mention it, I will say you're handsome enough to suit me. If you were rich and lived in a fine house, I might take a proposal from you very seriously. But you aren't and you don't, so I'll have to say no—I won't be promised to you."

"To Captain Smith, then?"

"Might as well name him as anybody. But do thank the Prince of Wales for his most generous offer and give him my sincere regrets."

Despite Ben's efforts to keep the proposal Cassakas had made to Jane Barnes secret, the offer and refusal soon became common knowledge around Fort George and in the Chinook village across the river. In an attempt to save face, Cassakas first angrily declared that he would not come near the fort again as long as she was there, then said a group of his warrior friends were planning to kidnap her the next time she went for her usual afternoon walk on the beach.

Though the kidnap threat probably was just a bluff, Miss Barnes did curtail her afternoon strolls the rest of the time the ship lay at its anchorage. Apparently growing as weary of the lady as she was of him, Captain Horace Smith raised no objections to Duncan McDougall's suggestion that Jane Barnes join an overland party of Nor'westers planning to leave for Montreal in early June, from which city she then could take ship back to London. But Miss Barnes quickly scotched that idea, saying that much as she might enjoy an occasional half-mile stroll in the woods with a handsome man, traveling three thousand miles by canoe, horse, and foot was not her cup of tea.

So when the *Isaac Todd* sailed after a month's stay at Fort George, Jane Barnes was still aboard as a guest in Captain Smith's cabin. Concerned that Ben might regret the loss of the only white woman to have visited the lower Columbia during the past four years, Conco offered to ease his sorrow by supplying him with his pick of the choicest maidens in the Chinook village—for a night, a week, or however long he might need her to keep his back warm.

"Thanks, Conco," Ben said gratefully. "But for now I'll get along with a good fire and a couple of blankets."

"You need a woman of your own race as a wife, I know. Where will you find her?"

"Oh, sooner or later someone a sight better than a used English barmaid will wash up on the beach, I imagine. Meanwhile, I'll live alone and wait."

Some months later, word of two momentous events reached Fort George by means of the well-traveled *Albatross*, which had called at Bombay, Canton, and Oahu, and now was stopping on the lower Columbia before heading around Cape Horn for New York. The first part of the news was that when the *Isaac Todd* reached Canton, two wealthy suitors had vied fiercely with each other for the honor of making an honest woman of Miss Jane Barnes: one, a rich, elderly Chinese mandarin; the other, a recently widowed, lonely, well-to-do Britisher who owned a substantial number of shares in the East-India Company.

The Englishman had won.

The second part of the news was that the war between the United States and England was over. As Wilson Price Hunt had predicted, it had ended up pretty much a draw. On the high seas, the two nations had agreed to stop fighting, to respect each other's rights regarding the impressment of sailors, and to resume trade. On land, in the eastern part of North America, Great Britain would retain Canada while the United States would keep the lands won during the Revolutionary War.

So far as the Pacific Northwest was concerned, a compromise unique among nations was being worked out under the Treaty of Ghent. By its terms, citizens of both England and the United States would be allowed to travel, live, and do business in any part of the region lying west of the Rocky Mountains to the Pacific Ocean and north from Spanish California to Russian Alaska.

Called "Joint Occupancy," this policy was to last ten years.

When that period of time had elapsed, one of three things would happen: (1) Ownership of the region would be decided by a majority vote of the people living in it; (2) the Joint Occupancy doctrine would be extended for another ten years, or (3) the war would be resumed.

"Fair enough," Ben told Duncan McDougall. "All we Americans ask is a fair chance to take over the country."

"Ye're a brave lad, Ben, to say that. But the odds are agin' ye two hundred to one. How can ye possibly take over this part of the country alone?"

"Well, to start with, Duncan, the Treaty of Ghent requires that all property seized during the war be returned to its rightful owner. Since Captain Black took over Astoria in the name of the British Crown, we Americans now demand that you give it back. I'll be glad to accept its return on behalf of Mr. Astor ..."

16.

W HEN JOHN MCTAVISH vehemently protested that returning the post to American ownership, then affirming its purchase by the North West Company and giving it back to the British, would be a meaningless ceremony, Ben had a sharp answer ready for him.

"If you don't comply with the terms of the Treaty of Ghent, sir, you'll risk clouding the North West Company's legal title to Fort George."

"How so?"

"As I understand it, the key question is does sale or seizure take precedence? What Mr. Astor's attorneys will argue is that seizure does."

"They'll be dead wrong there, lad. As ye must recall, the sale agreement was signed and our bank draft gi'en in payment to Mr. Astor three weeks before Captain Black made us go through his ridiculous seizure ceremony."

"True. But the bank draft wasn't delivered to Mr. Astor until months later. When it was, he claimed the sale was made under duress at ten cents on the dollar. What I also recall is that the North West Company stalled as long as it could in anticipation of a British warship's arrival. In fact, it wasn't until Duncan McDougall threatened your people with the fort's cannons that you finally signed the agreement and delivered the bank draft."

"Weel, ye may have a point there," McTavish said uncomfortably. "What would ye have us do?"

"Set up another ceremony like the one Captain Black conducted, with all the Company employees and the local Indian chiefs present as witnesses. On behalf of the North West Company, you'll lower the British flag and run my American flag up to the top of the mast. On behalf of the Astor Company, I'll accept the terms of the sale, after which you'll lower the American flag, give it back to me, and run the British flag up in its place."

"Very well, we'll do it. But it still seems like a pack of nonsense to me."

Nonsensical though the flag-lowering-and-raising ceremony three afternoons later may have seemed to John McTavish, Duncan McDougall, and the employees of the North West Company, Ben noticed that it made Chief Concomly, Conco, and the other local Indians regard him with new respect—which as the only American resident in the region he had hoped it would do. For twenty-five years, the natives had been aware of the fact that the King George men and the Bostons came from different nations of whites. But now they could see visual symbols in the form of two different flags flying above two separate, distinct establishments.

Certainly, Fort George, with its numerous buildings, stockade, cannons, and two hundred employees here and upriver, had the advantage of numbers. But the hilltop cabin and flagstaff raised by the young American sailor who now made a business of guiding ships of all nations across the bar were solid evidence that the United States was a nation to be respected, for a few years ago it had sent the Lewis and Clark party across the continent, then, more recently, had fought Great Britain to a draw that had forced that country to concede access to the Pacific Northwest to citizens of both nations on equal terms.

Ben's pride in being the only American currently living in the area, plus the simple fact that he liked to keep busy and work with his hands, inspired him to enlarge on his living quarters. During the next two years, he made several impressive additions to what had begun as a one-room cabin, expanding it into a substantial house in whose appearance and amenities he took considerable pride.

In selecting the location, he had made sure that the hilltop site rose a hundred feet higher than Fort George, so that the American flag flying near the top of a fir tree in its yard could be clearly seen by any ship entering the river. Sticking to his policy of charging each ship he guided across the bar a pilot's fee of forty guineas or two hundred American dollars, he could afford to make substantial purchases at the

Fort George store. Now and then when a ship carried goods he particularly wanted, he would bargain instead of charging a pilot's fee; by this means he acquired a set of dishes, cooking utensils, a suit of clothes, a musket, a brace of pistols, and even some quality pieces of household furniture.

From the captain of a British merchant ship, he bought a real treasure in the form of a nineteen-power brass marine telescope that could be mounted on a swiveling metal table so that it would sweep all the points of the compass. After bringing it home, he spent several days deciding where and how he wanted to mount it, his eventual conclusion being that he first must build a second story on his house, then, above that, a sheltered platform with a 360-degree vision line from which he could scan all the horizons of the lower river.

Because the extent of this building project was beyond his skills with a hammer and saw, he hired several craftsmen from Fort George, who were delighted to be paid for their work in gold or silver coins rather than in the stingy credits given them at the North West Company store. From what they told him, things were going badly so far as trade with the local Indians was concerned. John McTavish had been called back to Montreal, while Duncan McDougall was being sent north to a post on the west coast of British Columbia. Whether the decision to separate was his idea or hers, no one could say; but his wife of four years—Chief Concomly's daughter—was being left behind.

Sent out by the North West Company to take charge of Fort George was another Scotchman, James Keith. Unlike his much bolder predecessors, he seemed content to remain within the stockade walls, spending Company funds consuming tinned beef, flour, meal, rum, jams, and other expensive supplies imported from England rather than sending out hunters and fishermen to live off the country or at least trade with the natives for foodstuffs.

"A Director back in Montreal complained that living on shipped-in supplies 'is like eating gold,' " one of the carpenters told Ben. "James Keith don't seem to care that the Indians hereabouts have gotten so many knives, guns, and blankets in exchange for their sea otter furs, they've quit bringing them in."

"Conco says sea otters are getting scarce along the coast," Ben said. "At least in places where they're easy to kill."

"That may be true. But the Indians aren't bringing in any seal, beaver, or other furs that are there for the taking. As you know from your own pelt-gathering days, most natives in this part of the country are too lazy to do much trapping on their own."

More and more, Ross Cox said, it was becoming evident that the large volume of furs needed to make a trading post profitable in this part of the country could not be acquired simply by buying those brought in by the Indians. Whether lazy or simply lacking the white man's greed, the average local native refused to exert himself once his relatively simple needs for the white man's trade goods were satisfied. Even if he were persuaded to hunt or trap, he set such a high price on the pelts he brought in that the rate of profit expected from the trade by Company stockholders in Montreal and London fell far below the minimum twenty percent per annum figure to which they long had been accustomed.

"The two posts upriver, Fort Okanogan and Spokane House, are doing well," Cox told Ben. "There, we send trapping parties led by white men or French-Canadians into the mountains every season to trap directly for the Company at set wages. Sure, some of the local Indians go along. But since we supply their guns, traps, food, and gear, we keep them under tight control. If they don't produce, we quit supplying them and send them home."

"I hear Donald McKenzie has signed on with the North West Company and has come back to Fort George."

"So he has. He keeps telling Keith that if the North West Company will give him the money and men to build a new post in the Nez Perce country, with Alex Ross as his assistant, he'll mount a fur-gathering expedition that'll put us all in the shade. So far, Keith has turned him down. But I suspect Big Mac will have his way sooner or later."

Taking a liking to the red-bearded giant from the first day he met him, Ben felt that if anyone ever deserved the description "big enough to go bear-hunting with a switch," Donald McKenzie was that man. Standing several inches above six feet and weighing a solid 312 pounds—not an ounce of which was fat—McKenzie was so full of energy that he was like an avalanche rumbling down a steep mountain slope, so unstoppable in whatever he undertook to do that few men opposed him for long. But as his close friend Alexander Ross wrote in his journal, Donald McKenzie did have one weakness:

Capable of enduring fatigue and privations, he found no labor too great, no hardship too severe; but he had a great aversion to writing, preferring to leave the details of his adventures to the pen of others.

To travel a day's journey on snowshoes was his delight; but he detested spending five minutes scribbling in a journal. His traveling notes were often kept on a beaver skin written hieroglyphically with a pencil or a piece of coal, and he would often complain of the drudgery of keeping accounts. When asked why he did not like to write, his answer was, "We must have something for others to do."

Few men could fathom his mind, yet his inquisitiveness to know the minds and opinions of others knew no bounds. Every man he met was his companion; and when not asleep, he was always on foot strolling backward and forward full of plans and projects, and so peculiar was this pedestrian habit that he went by the name of "Perpetual Motion."

After several months of bickering with James Keith and the Directors of the North West Company, Donald McKenzie finally found a piece of writing that persuaded the holders of the pursestrings to let him have his way—the bottom line on the profit-and-loss page in the ledger book. Though not normally a man to brag about his accomplishments, he did crow a bit during a visit to Ben's house over a glass of rum shared in celebration.

"What I did, lad, was show the powers-that-be how much profit the Fort Okanogan and Spokane House operations had made during the past three years, compared to the horrific losses James Keith had suffered at Fort George. 'Gi me the men and money to build a post amongst the Nez Perces,' I said, 'and I guarantee to equal the profit made from both of them during the same period of time.' "

"And they did?"

"Wi' scarcely the blink of an eyelash, Ben. Oh, there was some quibbling over where the post should be located, with me wantin' to put it in the heart of Nez Perce country where the Clearwater joins the Snake, and them sayin' it ought to be built in a safer place on the west side of the Columbia where it makes its big bend to the north. Weak sister that he is, Keith said placing it there would keep the river between us and the Nez Perces, in case they started trouble. But I said, 'I'll nae insult my fine Nez Perce friends by puttin' a river between us. I'll build the post at the bend of the Columbia, if ye insist, but it'll be on the east side of the river inside the boundaries of their lands.' "

Given enough money and men to build a large post to be called

Fort Nez Perces, Donald McKenzie told Ben before leaving for the interior country that there were two important matters that must be addressed before the British-Canadian fur business could operate successfully.

"First, the Nor'westers and the Hudson's Bay Company, which have been fighting a bloody battle all across Canada for years, will have to settle their differences and merge as one company. Second, Fort George must close its post here and move up the Columbia a hundred miles or so—say to Point Vancouver—where the soil and climate are better for farming and stock-raising and there's not so many trees covering the land."

"You'd have them desert the mouth of the Columbia?"

"This is a port of entry, lad, no more. Here, shipping, fishing, and the timber business will always be important. But it's no place for a trading post."

Not being interested in the fur business himself, Ben was inclined to agree with Donald McKenzie. Now that the war had ended and trade was being resumed, the Columbia River bar and the 145 miles of navigable water upriver to the Lower Cascades teemed with the ships of many nations. Having heard of the hazards of the bar and learning from other captains that a knowledgeable pilot was available, the masters of ships visiting the coast for the first time often expressed their desire for guidance by laying to in deep water off Cape Disappointment and signaling by cannon or masthead flag that they wanted aid.

During a six-month period, Ben logged piloting jobs from the North West Company coastal trading schooners *Colonel Allen* and *Columbia*; two Russian vessels, the *Ilmen* and the *Chirekoff*; the American schooner *Lydia*; the old-timer *Albatross*; and two full-rigged ships from the East Coast, the *Sultan* and the *Atlas*. Also recorded in his log were the French ship *Bordelais* and the American brigs *Brutus* and *Clarion*.

During the summer of 1818, what would turn out to be the most important ship of his life since the *Tonquin* entered the river. This was the American sloop-of-war *Ontario*. Commanded by an arrogant, stiff-necked naval officer from Boston, Captain Franklin Biddle, the American warship was accompanied by the British frigate-of-war, H.M.S. *Blossom*, whose Captain Winston Hickey proved to be just as prim and stuffy as his American counterpart.

The official business upon which they had come, Ben learned, was making sure that the terms of the Treaty of Ghent were being honored to the letter, insofar as the wartime seizure and peacetime return of American property were concerned. Ben's assurance that the terms had been properly observed did not influence their behavior in the least.

"Would ye believe that yer American Captain Biddle demands that we have another ceremony," James Keith said indignantly, "lowering the British flag, following which the American flag will be raised in its place?"

"Yes," Ben said with a smile, "I'd believe that, for he told me. Would *you* believe that he asked to borrow *my* flag for the ceremony— and I told him no?"

"Why did ye turn him down?"

"Because I've been the only American citizen living in this part of the country since the Astorians left. Damned if I'll lower my flag to any man or nation, I told him, even temporarily. Finally, he agreed to issue a new flag out of ship's stores and raise it over Fort George."

"Then we lower it and raise the Union Jack in its place?"

"So far as both captains are concerned," Ben said, shaking his head, "they have no interest in who owns the post or what it's called. Under the terms of the Joint Occupancy Treaty, the flags of both nations can fly wherever an American or a Britisher chooses to raise them."

"Weel, I certainly won't fly both flags on the same mast. I'm a British subject and this is a British post."

"True, Mr. Keith. But according to the Treaty, you and I are joint occupants of this country now. So I suggest you let both flags fly from the same staff until the warships are gone. Then, if you like, you can lower Captain Biddle's new American flag and give it to me. The one I have is getting badly faded and worn."

By mutual consent following the flag-lowering-and-raising ceremony October 6, 1818, both the British frigate H.M.S. *Blossom* and the American sloop-of-war *Ontario* weighed anchor and crossed the bar before a stiffening northeast wind that was rising steadily toward gale force. Leading the British vessel through the channel, Conco and his crew of Chinook paddlers guided the *Blossom* out to deep water, then turned back to pick up Ben off the *Ontario*, which had followed two miles behind, after the American ship used the last of the ebbing tide and daylight to clear the bar.

Laying to under close-reefed sails, the *Ontario* and Captain Biddle maneuvered with all their considerable naval skills to make a lee for the Chinook canoe so that it could take Ben aboard. Time and again in the choppy, dangerous seas, the effort failed. Finally, with daylight almost gone and the wind and seas continuing to rise, Ben waved his right arm in a thrusting-away gesture, indicating to Conco and his crew of natives that they should head back to shore while they still had a decent chance of a safe passage, returning for him after daylight tomorrow morning. Signaling that he understood, Conco and the canoe sheered off and soon were lost in the fading light.

Over the booming surf and roaring wind, Captain Biddle shouted in Ben's ear, "They'll not try again?"

"It's too risky, sir. If the weather improves, they'll be back tomorrow."

"The bottom has dropped out of the glass, Mr. Warren, and it's still falling. This has the look of a major storm."

"Likely you're right, Captain. We'll just have to wait it out."

"How long?"

"Two days. Maybe three. At this time of year, a storm out of the northeast could last for a week."

"Good Lord, man! You can't ask me to lay to for a week just because you missed your pilot boat! This is a naval ship of the line!"

"Well, I can't walk on water, Captain."

"I'll not ask you to. But much as I do feel obliged to help a pilot, I'm committed to be in Hawaii by the first of November. With this strong following wind, we should make landfall at Oahu within three weeks."

"Are you inviting me to go along?"

"As a guest of the United States Navy, Mr. Warren. With as much sea traffic sailing from Hawaii to the mainland as there is nowadays, you should have no trouble catching a ship back in a week or so. Of course, if we sight a vessel bound for the lower Columbia in the next few days, we'll hail her and put you aboard."

Knowing that this was one of the hazards of the trade, Ben took it philosophically. With a cold, rainy winter at hand on the Northwest Coast, the prospect of spending a few weeks in a balmy clime was not unpleasant.

"Captain Biddle, I accept your invitation. This should be a nice time of year to visit Hawaii ..."

17.

$\mathcal{T}$HOUGH NO EASTBOUND SHIPS were encountered during the swift voyage to what some mariners still called the Sandwich Islands, Ben Warren had no regrets, for being a passenger aboard the naval sloop-of-war U.S.S. *Ontario* instead of a working Ordinary Seaman on the merchant ship *Tonquin*, as he had been seven years ago, was a real treat. After arriving at Oahu, whose lovely harbor teemed with ships of many nations, Ben could have taken passage for the Columbia River on an American merchant ship bound there within a week's time.

But as he would say in years to come, a funny thing happened to him in Hawaii, causing what should have been a week-long stay to lengthen into one of four months.

First, Captain Biddle accepted the invitation of King Kamehameha to come to a state dinner at the royal palace and to bring along the young American pilot he had carried to Oahu as a passenger. At the state dinner, the two Americans met a number of interesting guests, the most intriguing of whom was the former British Naval Captain Reginald Barker. Twenty years ago, Captain Barker had gone ashore in Hawaii and taken such a liking to the Islands that he quit His Majesty's Navy and became King Kamehameha's principal advisor.

This had been at the time when two extremely important events in local history were taking place: first, the consolidation of power in the hands of a single king instead of being fragmented among a number of warring chieftains; second, the rejection of an attempt by England to establish sovereignty over the Islands and make them part of the British Empire.

Legend had it that it was Captain Reginald Barker's sage advice that helped King Kamehameha achieve both goals. Certainly, Great Britain should have known it could not conquer and annex the Islands simply by naming them after the Earl of Sandwich and pronouncing them British. A generation earlier, the outwardly placid natives had shown they were not to be trifled with by killing and eating the British explorer Captain James Cook. Guided by his shrewd English advisor, King Kamehameha used the more civilized and more potent weapon of trade to reject the feeble takeover attempt. Sitting at the crossroads of the Pacific as it did, the port of Oahu ruled the vast region lying west of Cape Horn east to the China Sea and from Antarctica in the frozen south to the Bering Sea in the far north. With Captain Barker quietly advising him in the background, the Hawaiian monarch played one power against another to keep the kingdom over which he ruled as an absolute monarch both prosperous and free.

As a reward for his services, Kamehameha had given Captain Barker an exalted title, a large grant of land, and the hand of his most beautiful daughter in marriage. To this marriage, three handsome sons and three lovely daughters had been born. The oldest of these daughters, Lolanee, was a tall, supple, stunning girl of nineteen, whom Ben met at the dinner that night.

From the moment he saw her, he knew that she was the woman he wanted to marry. But it took him four months of excruciating, stormy courtship to persuade her to accept his proposal.

Certainly, he encountered no objections from Lolanee's father or mother, for they both liked him from the start. With the U.S.S. *Ontario* scheduled to sail two weeks after the ship's arrival in Oahu, Captain Barker invited Ben to be a houseguest in their home in the hills above the beach, which not only permitted him to see Lolanee and her family every day but also gave him the advantage of her parents' advice as to what he should do to win her favor.

"I've done the best I could to educate and raise Lolanee right," Captain Barker told Ben one evening, as they sat sipping a rum and pineapple drink on the palm-shaded lanai overlooking the turquoise sea. "Of course, her mother has spoiled her rotten."

"Hah!" the mother snorted, overhearing her husband's remark as she passed by. "With six children to raise, a household to run, and a husband to keep happy, when would I find time to spoil anyone but you?"

"They're a curious race of people, these Hawaiians," Captain Barker went on, pretending he had not heard his wife's remark, though from the way he smiled fondly at her Ben knew he had. "Ordinarily, they're the most mild-natured people on earth. But say or do the wrong thing to them, they turn into tigers. Whatever you do, Ben, make sure you stroke Lolanee the right way."

"How do I tell which is the wrong way?"

"She'll let you know, lad. Believe me, she'll let you know."

Unlike the New England girls he had known back home, who dressed and behaved so primly that they never showed an ankle or raised their voice in indiscreet shouts or peals of laughter, Lolanee and her brothers and sisters were uninhibited, active, and loud. All of them swam like fish, climbed like monkeys, and rode the tough, scrubby Island ponies with reckless abandon over the roughest kind of terrain, sitting astride without a saddle.

Though both Lolanee and her mother had been dressed in long, beautifully tailored white satin gowns, dignified shoes, and diamond-studded tiaras—as befitted members of the royal family—when Ben first met them at Kamehameha's state dinner, when he next saw them at their home, they had discarded their shoes and most of their clothes, going barefoot and lightly clad as long as he was there.

Most shocking to him was the fact that when Lolanee invited him to go for an early morning swim with her and the rest of the family, he found that, after he had taken off his shoes and stripped naked to the waist before running down to the beach with them, they had done likewise, the whole family going shoeless and topless—including Lolanee and her mother.

Well, he thought philosophically after his breathing and heartbeat returned to normal, in this balmy air and water, it wasn't likely they would catch cold.

As the weeks passed and he began to feel more and more like a member of the family, he came to understand why Reginald Barker had found life in the Islands so appealing, even though some aspects of it were distasteful to his orderly British mind.

"They're a warm, loving people, so far as their family is concerned," Captain Barker told Ben. "But they have no concept of what the world is like beyond their shores. Until twenty years ago, the notion that the tribal chieftains should quit fighting one another and unite under an all-powerful king never entered their minds. That's what I did for Kamehameha. I showed him how to pull the Islands together and stand up to the civilized world."

"Which you had left?"

"With no regrets, lad. During the past two hundred years, England has gotten so buried under the stuffy ash of tradition that it's lost its energy and incentive to improve the lives of its people. Through sheer stupidity, it lost the United States. In another fifty years, I'll wager, it will lose Canada. By the Treaty of Ghent, it did keep a foothold in the Pacific Northwest under the Joint Occupancy agreement for ten years. But I can tell you what will happen then."

"What?" Ben asked.

"The people who live in the country will throw the bloody rascals out and form a government of their own. They'll be so sick and tired of having their lives ruled from London, they'll insist on making their own laws."

"You may be right, sir. But at the moment I'm the only American resident among two hundred British citizens."

"Don't worry about that, Ben," Captain Barker said with a smile. "When you marry Lolanee and take her to America, the odds will be only two hundred to two. She'll have no trouble dealing with that."

During his courtship with Lolanee, Ben had barely managed to persuade her to make one concession at a time: first, that she would marry him; second, that the ceremony would take place early next spring; third, that she would let him continue his career as a pilot. Until now, she had not agreed to leave her home and family in Hawaii and move with him to the wilds of North America.

"It's news to me, sir, that she *will* live in America."

"Oh, she decided that long ago. She's thrilled to death with the idea. She's been telling her mother and me about the fine, big house you've built, how the two of you will rule over thousands of slant-headed savages, and how she'll be queen of the Pacific Northwest, just as her grandmother is queen of Hawaii."

"I'm afraid she's expecting a lot more than I can give her. In many ways, the Pacific Northwest is a primitive place."

"So is Hawaii, Ben. But she's got the blood of two tough, intelligent races in her veins. She'll make you as good a wife as you'll make her a husband."

A week after their marriage, Ben and Lolanee sailed aboard the American merchant ship *Eagle*, departing Oahu April 6, 1819, and making landfall off Cape Disappointment on May 1. Even if Ben had been inclined to spend the time preparing his bride for the harsh weather and uncomfortable living conditions she was going to encounter in the new world, she was too enthralled with the ship, the sea, and the novelty of watching the sailors work during the day, while he was so engrossed with the pleasures of marriage and the joys of making love to her at night, that the future seemed of no importance.

As usually happened when a ship called at Oahu, the *Eagle* had filled vacancies in the crew with a dozen happy-go-lucky Kanakas, who regarded Lolanee with a curious mixture of familiarity and respect. On the one hand, they teased and exchanged jokes with her as if she were one of their kind; on the other, they treated her with the formal courtesy reserved for royalty. Well tutored in languages by her father, she could converse in Spanish or French with sailors of those nationalities, just as easily as she could talk to the Kanakas in the pidgin English that was used by Hawaiians and Orientals in this part of the world.

Like many New England skippers who read extensively to pass the time, Captain Thomas Meek was an avid student of literature and poetry. So when he invited the newlyweds to dine with him and Lolanee found his shipboard library well stocked with the works of Shakespeare and a number of English poets, they both were delighted to share their interests. But the real treasure to Lolanee was the captain's collection of Boston, New York, and Philadelphia newspapers and magazines, which he had accumulated over the years.

During spells of bad weather when she was confined to the cabin, Lolanee pored over such publications as *Poor Richard's Almanac* and eastern newspapers advertising the latest American inventions. Marking those that caught her eye, she then gave Ben no rest until he had promised to obtain them for her from the merchant ships that called at the lower Columbia or order them sent out on the next packet.

Remembering what a surprise freezing weather, snow, and ice had been to the warmth-loving Kanaka sailors when the *Tonquin* neared the coast eight years ago, Ben was prepared to cushion the shock of cold weather for Lolanee by bundling her up in a long sea otter fur coat, hat, and gloves. But when the *Eagle* lay to off Cape Disappointment in late afternoon the first day of May, the weather was mild, the sky clear, and hardly a breath of wind stirred. By ten o'clock next morning, when the tide turned and Ben told Captain Meek that conditions were right to cross the bar, the sea was as smooth as glass, a gentle, balmy wind was blowing toward the mouth of the river, and the air temperature was only a few degrees lower than it had been when the *Eagle* left Hawaii.

"If this is the foul weather you've been warning me about," said Captain Meek, who was making his first voyage to the Northwest Coast, "I'd love to be here when it turns fair."

"In all my eight years here, sir," Ben said in amazement, "I've never seen a day as nice as this one."

"Give the credit to your bride, lad," the captain said with a smile. "Even the weather welcomes her to America."

Before raising anchor and moving into the channel, the ship was approached by a seagoing Chinook canoe manned by thirty paddlers. As Ben had expected, Conco was in command of the craft, beaming from ear to ear with a happy smile as he stood in the stern and waved an enthusiastic greeting. Invited to come aboard, he briefly acknowledged his introduction to Captain Meek, then clapped a hand over his open mouth in awe and embarrassment as he stared shyly at Lolanee.

"Conco," Ben said, "this is my wife, Lolanee. Lolanee, this is my friend and partner, Conco."

To Ben's delight, she immediately set the nervous Indian at ease by giving him a stunning smile and extending her hand.

"I'm glad to meet you, Conco. Ben has told me many good things about you."

"Thank you, Mrs. Warren. I heard he was bringing home a wife. But I did not know she would be so beautiful."

So as simply as that it was made clear to Ben that the two most important people in his life at the moment were going to be friends. Though Captain Barker had jokingly told Ben that Lolanee's mother had spoiled her rotten, she gave no evidence of that during her first weeks as mistress of the hilltop house overlooking the lower Columbia River. Admittedly, there were many things she did not know how to do when it came to running a household, but she soon proved herself to be a quick learner.

Building a fire in a hearth or cookstove was a new experience, because until now servants had done these tasks. Cooking was a new chore, too. When this required both laying a fire and then getting the heat to the right place in the right degree for the right amount of time, while using pots, pans, and utensils she never had seen before, the process and the results ranged from uncertain to disastrous. But the sunny nature she had inherited from her mother, coupled with the stubbornness of her father, kept her going until she got mad—then Heaven help whoever or whatever got in her way.

Before leaving the Fort George anchorage, Captain Meek gave Lolanee his collection of magazines and newspapers, as well as his promise to ship her several items that had caught her fancy. Knowing that at home she had had many servants, Ben kept her supplied with more Indian helpers than she could possibly use, most of whom she soon discharged, telling him it was far easier to do a task herself than explain it to a native woman.

Communication with the local Indians was no problem to her, for the Chinook Jargon used by the lower river tribes had so many similarities to the tongues and dialects she already knew that she soon became as fluent in it as Ben himself. As to the change in climate, it was fortunate that he had brought her here at this time of year, for late spring and early summer could be incredibly beautiful in the lower Columbia area—and this year nature was at her very best.

At Fort George, the local fur business was still poor, Ben learned, for James Keith still persisted in his narrow-minded policy of buying only the pelts brought in by the local Indians while refusing to send out parties of whites to trap on their own. Upriver, the interior posts were doing well and soon would be doing even better, for, after completing the new post Fort Nez Perces at the northward bend of the Columbia and putting Alexander Ross in charge, Donald McKenzie had led a large party east into the Snake River country with a promise not to return until the hundred or so horses taken into the mountain wilderness were so laden with beaver pelts that they could barely walk.

With plenty of ship traffic crossing the bar, Ben and Conco had all the pilot work they could handle. But as Ben discovered one morning on a visit to the Chinook village on the north side of the river, Conco was having trouble handling a domestic problem within his own household.

It had long been a matter of regret that the first three children born to Conco's wife had been girls, Ben knew, but just two weeks ago Conco had been delighted to announce that his wife had borne him a boy. Giving it the affectionate diminutive name *Sitkum*, which meant

"half" or "little treasure" in the Chinook tongue, Conco had beamed
with pride whenever he spoke of the child. But when Ben asked him
about the baby this morning, his face turned gloomy.

"My wife is angry at me over him."

"Because of the name you gave him?"

"No. Because of what I made her do to his head."

"What was that?"

"I told her not to flatten it."

Among all the coastal tribes, head-flattening was a mark of royalty,
Ben knew, with only slaves permitted to bear the stigma of growing up
with naturally rounded heads.

"Why on earth did you do that?"

Before Conco could answer, a young woman carrying a baby and
followed by Chief Concomly himself came running down to the
beach. Ben recognized her as Conco's wife. Crying hysterically, she
poured out a torrent of angry words, while Chief Concomly nodded
his head vigorously in support, waving his hands in impassioned gestures as he backed up everything she said. Both of them kept pointing
at the infant's head, where the imprint of a recently removed head-
press could be seen.

"No!" Conco shouted angrily in the Chinook tongue. "You are my
wife and you will obey me! No!"

"I am your father!" Chief Concomly cried. "You will obey *me*! I
will not let you disgrace your firstborn son! I say yes!"

"This is a new day, father. We must learn new ways. I still say no!"

For the first time since he had lived among the Chinook Indians, a
usually polite young native woman turned on Ben and scolded him violently to his face. "This is your fault, Boston man!" Conco's wife
screamed. "It is because of you that my husband brings dishonor to
his son and his people!"

"Enough!" Conco cried, seizing his wife savagely by the shoulders
and spinning her around. "You disgrace me by your bad behavior! Go
back to the longhouse and do not defy me further!"

Even Chief Concomly gave way before the rage in Conco's voice,
for the father knew that his son had been pushed as far as he would go.
After they had left the beach, Conco was silent for a long while, a deep
misery in his eyes, then he looked at Ben and said in a low voice:

"What she said is not true. It is not your fault."

"Then why did you do it?"

"It has been eight years since the Bostons came to our country. Of all the white men I have known, you are the only one who has become my friend. I have learned much from you."

"As I have from you, Conco."

"But I know there is a great difference between your race and mine. Is it because of the shape of our heads, I wonder?"

"It's what's inside one's head that counts, Conco. You're not lacking anything there."

"I hope this is true. But I want my son to have a chance in what I know will be a different world. So I made my wife leave his head alone. If he grows up to look like you, perhaps he will *be* like you. I do not want white men to judge him by the shape of his head."

18.

FROM THE MOMENT she first saw the hilltop house her husband had built overlooking the lower Columbia, Lolanee knew it had been designed by a man. Ben's description of it as a "fine, big house" was accurate, so far as size and the quality of the materials put into it went. But a woman's touch was sorely lacking.

The first floor, which had been the original cabin, was twenty-five feet wide by fifty feet long, with the kitchen and a massive iron cook-stove taking up a quarter of the space. The rest was occupied by a big, sprawling, undivided room containing bunkbeds around three walls, a long table, and half a dozen chairs made of small, peeled logs. The floor was of twelve-inch split cedar logs with their trimmed side up and their round side down; though solid enough, its surface had set-tled unevenly so that grass and moss grew up through the cracks, making it impossible to keep clean.

Above the cookstove, the black tin pipe venting the smoke made a ninety-degree "L" where it went through the wall, fitting so poorly and so lacking in insulation that it leaked badly when it rained and got so hot in dry weather it threatened to set the house on fire.

A massive stone fireplace fully six feet wide supplied heat for the big room on the ground floor, while another directly above, which was only four feet wide, was supposed to heat the undivided room on the second floor. Above it was a roofed-over third floor, open on all sides, which served as an observatory where Ben had mounted the brass telescope with which he scanned the lower river and the bar.

Because he frequently brought home Indian friends, such as Conco and his father, employees of the North West Company, such as Don-ald McKenzie and Alexander Ross, and the officers of ships he and Conco had guided across the bar, the big room downstairs was where he entertained and Lolanee fed them. Since she had come home with him, he had turned the second floor into their personal living quarters, installing a large feather bed, a bureau, and some finished chairs imported from England in the section away from the fireplace, while near it he had raised a partition and enclosed a space where she could have some privacy and read by the light of a whale-oil lamp while he associated with his noisy guests on the floor below.

With plenty of three-foot-long lengths of fir and pine cut and stacked outside, hauling enough firewood in to build a roaring blaze and keep the downstairs toasty and warm was no problem, for Ben and his visitors had the strength to carry the log sections inside. But for her or the female Indian servants to drag the logs upstairs was a problem, for the stairs were only two feet wide, the wood was often wet, heavy, and burned poorly, and fire-building was an art she had not mastered. Often after she had labored for hours preparing and putting food on the table for half a dozen hungry men, whom Ben never notified her were coming because their arrival depended on the weather and the tide, she would wearily climb the stairs and sit down to read and rest a bit before going to bed, only to find that the upstairs fire had gone out, that the room was freezingly cold and depressingly damp, leaving her no choice but to crawl into the big, cold bed, then lie there alone and shivering while the smoking, drinking, and roistering went on downstairs.

If she had felt like it, of course, she could have called downstairs to Ben and told him that she was cold and would he please bring up some dry wood and rebuild the fire. He would have done so without complaint immediately, she knew, for he never failed to do whatever she asked of him. But damn his eyes, she thought angrily, once in a while he should know without her telling him that she was cold and lonely. Particularly now during this bleak January weather of early darkness and endless rain, with her so far from her family and the warm Island climate—and pregnant for the first time.

Of course, he did not know that yet. By her reckoning, she was four months along and not yet beginning to show. But he should have noticed she was putting on weight, experiencing morning sickness, and, after working as hard as she had tonight, suffering from an occasional headache. Well, yes, she could have told him. And she *would* tell him when he gave her the right opportunity. But what did he expect her to do, for Heaven's sake? Trip down the stairs, pick up the fireplace poker, rap on the table for silence, and then scream at the top of her voice:

"Now hear this, you dumb, uncaring men! I'm pregnant! I'm going to have a baby! And I need some tender, loving attention from my stupid husband!"

No, she could not do that. But she had reached the point where she could no longer bear Ben's neglect in silence. Tonight, with the fire dead, the room too cold to read, and the thought of going to bed alone just as dreadful as the prospect of sitting up and shivering for another hour or two, she was torn between an overpowering urge to scream or cry.

Downstairs, the loud talking and laughter had subsided as the hour grew late; presently, she heard the sound of Ben's footsteps on the stairs. By then, she had decided that instead of screaming or crying, she was just going to get very mad and give him a piece of her mind. So when he greeted her in a cheerful tone of voice, made more than a little mellow by a few hot rums, she was ready for him.

"Hey, Lanee—you're still up!"

"Yes," she answered curtly. "I'm still up."

He began unbuttoning his shirt. "Big Mac and Conco are staying over for the night. Told 'em they could bunk below, where it's nice and warm. Can't expect 'em to go out in this kind of weather."

"No. You can't expect them to do that."

"Say, it's cold up here. What happened to the fire?"

"It went out."

"Why didn't you yell? I'd have brought up some wood and built it up for you."

Lolanee got stiffly to her feet, her breathing shallow and harsh as she glared at him.

"Oh, I wouldn't dream of asking you to do that, dear. Not when you're enjoying yourself so much drinking and telling stories with your friends. I'd much rather sit here in a cold, damp room, shivering and freezing to death."

"Lanee!"

"Don't you ever think of anyone but yourself? You wait until it's so late in the day that I'm sure you won't be coming home, so I let the servants leave. Then you barge in with half a dozen friends and expect me to feed them, while you sit around drinking and laughing and talking about the great times you've had bringing a ship in across the bar or gathering furs that are going to make the Company a fortune—"

"Hey, Lanee! You know my business depends on the weather and the tides—"

"Then after I've worked hours cooking and serving you food, you smoke and drink and laugh some more while I stagger up the stairs to a cold, damp room with icicles instead of a caring husband in the bed—"

"For God's sake, Lanee!" Ben exclaimed, trying to put his arms around her. "You *are* upset. If you'd only told me—"

"Why should I tell you? You wouldn't care!"

"That's not true! I love you, Lanee. Everything I do is for you."

"You don't care! You let me be cold and lonely while you make sure your Indian friends and your ship's officers and your big Scotch trader get the best of everything, making me work my fingers to the bone to feed them—"

"Now wait a minute, Lanee!" Ben said angrily. "This is part of the business. You knew that before I brought you here."

"Well, I certainly didn't know you'd put their welfare ahead of mine."

"I've never done that, Lanee! It's damned unfair of you to say I have."

She sniffled. "Now you're swearing at me."

"Only because you're being so unreasonable. Sure, this is a bad time of year for you, with the wind and the cold and the rain—particularly for a girl who's used to a milder climate."

"It's not the weather I'm unhappy about. It's the way you take me for granted."

"You *are* unhappy, then?"

"I didn't say that, Ben! What I said was—"

"Yes, you did. You said it's me you're unhappy about, not the weather. Do you think I'm deaf?"

"No—but I think you're dumb. So inconsiderate—"

"Well, maybe I *was* dumb to bring a girl from a climate where food falls off trees to a country where a man has to work for a living! But this is America, Lanee, where it takes a tough breed of people to survive."

"Don't brag to me about how tough you are, you … you … *haole!*"

"What does that mean?"

"An outsider. A foreigner. A person who thinks he's better than the Island people just because he comes from what he calls a more civilized country."

"Don't you like America?"

"I didn't say that!"

"Do you want to go back to Hawaii?"

"I didn't say that, either!"

"Because if you do, I can damn sure arrange it!" he raged furiously. "I married you and brought you to America hoping you would love it and me enough to want to make a life together here—"

"I do, Ben! *I do!*"

"But if you don't, I can put you on the next ship out and send you home. Then you can spend the rest of your life sipping tea with the British side of your family and eating fat roast pigs and skinny white sea captains with your native relatives, letting me make my own life here. Is that what you want?"

Shocked into silence by the ridiculous things they both had said in the heat of their sudden argument, she lowered her head and began to cry. Pulling her to him, he murmured tenderly:

"For God's sake, Lanee! I didn't mean a word of that!"

"Neither did I!"

"Something's wrong. What is it?"

"Well, for one thing, I'm pregnant ..."

"Oh, my God! When did this happen?"

She giggled. "You should know. You were there."

"I've got to take better care of you. You need to stay warm and get your rest. You shouldn't be working so hard. I'll get you more help—"

"Oh, for Heaven's sake, Ben, I'm not going to have a baby tomorrow. Most of the time, I feel fine."

"When do you think it will be?"

"Not for five months or so. But there are a few things I wish you'd do."

"Whatever you want, Lanee. Just name it."

"I know your work depends on the weather and the tides. But if you'd try to give me some idea of when you'll be coming home and how many of your friends will be with you, it would be a great help."

"I'll do that, Lanee. I swear, I will. What else?"

"This room is so big and hard to heat, I can't ever get warm in it. The logs are too heavy for me or the women servants to drag up the stairs—"

"I'll hire a couple of husky men to make sure you've got a good fire going whenever you want it. I'll order them to be handy day and night."

"No, Ben. I've got a better solution."

"What's that?"

"A Franklin stove."

He frowned. "A which?"

Crossing the room to the small table under the wall-hung whale-oil lamp, she picked up a copy of a two-year-old Philadelphia newspaper folded to show a pen-and-ink sketch in an advertisement at which she had been gazing longingly for weeks.

"A stove invented and patented by your namesake, Benjamin Franklin, which is guaranteed to heat a room much better than the best fireplace ever built. Here's a drawing and an advertisement telling all about it."

Taking the newspaper out of her hand, then pulling her down to sit on his lap while he kept one arm around her, Ben read the advertisement aloud:

LADIES!

HEAT WITHOUT A HASSLE

Invented and Recommended

By the Greatest American of His Day—

BENJAMIN FRANKLIN HIMSELF!

HARRIED HOUSEWIVES!

No Longer Do You Need to Nag Your Husband

to Bring in More Wood for the Big, Smoky, Inefficient Fireplace!

Instead Just Nag Him to Buy You a

FRANKLIN STOVE

"Hmm, this is interesting," Ben said. "According to experiments made by Benjamin Franklin, over half the heat put out by a fireplace goes up the chimney. With his patent stove, ninety percent of it radiates out into the room."

"And the pieces of wood you put into it are much smaller," Lolanee said, leaning her chin on his shoulder. "If you would have a man cut it to the right size, I could carry it up the stairs by myself …"

"You can take a piece of sheet iron, it says here, close off most of the fireplace opening, then let the smoke go up the fireplace chimney, without losing nearly as much of the heat. That makes sense …"

"Oh, Ben, it would be so wonderful to be warm again! If you would order a Franklin stove for me—"

"I can do better than that, Lanee. Just yesterday I saw half a dozen of these very stoves in the cargo hold of the Russian ship, *Chirekoff*, bound for Alaska. Count Baranov in Sitka ordered them for his castle."

"Ben! Could you buy one of them for me?"

"Buy, steal, beg, or threaten to run his ship aground if he won't let me have it—I'll get you one, Lanee. Before his ship leaves the lower river, Captain Ivan Kratoski is going to be minus one Franklin stove. We've got to keep you and the baby warm."

"Oh, Ben!" Lolanee exclaimed, kissing him fervently. "That would be wonderful!"

Stroking her back with one hand while the other moved gently across the soft swell of her breasts, he chuckled. "Funny thing, Lanee. Your back feels cool but your front feels warm. What causes that?"

"My mixed English and Hawaiian blood, probably," she said with a laugh. "They give me an uneven body temperature."

"With a warm side and a cool side, you mean?"

"Something like that. In England, they like cool rooms, I'm told. In Hawaii, we like rooms warm. So maybe my back side does feel cooler than my front side to you. But the Hawaiian blood inside me— including the baby—wants the air on the outside to be warm."

"Well, for the sake of your beautiful, cool backside, your warm, soft front side, and the baby-to-be inside, Lanee, I'll get you a Franklin stove and keep all sides toasty and warm. Now, is there anything else bothering you?"

"Well, yes. I want you to make me a promise about the baby. Now, you'll probably think me silly to ask this—"

"Silly or not, I'll do whatever you want. What's the promise?"

"That our baby won't have a slanted head like all the Indian babies in this part of the country do."

"Of course it won't! Whatever gave you that idea?"

"Well, I just got to wondering if there's something about the air or climate in this part of the country that shapes the heads of Indian babies so that they're slanted. Is there any danger *our* baby will look like theirs do?"

"Lord no!"

"How can you be so sure?"

"Because I know it to be a fact that all the local Indian babies are born with normal heads, Lanee. But among the coastal tribes, it's considered a mark of royalty to change the shape of the baby's head. So after it's born, it's put in a head-press and given a slanted look while the bone is soft."

"What a horrible thing to do!"

"To us, yes. To them, it's just like foot-binding is to the Chinese. But since white men came to their country, they're beginning to abandon the practice. As a matter of fact, Conco and his wife had a big fight a while back over putting their firstborn son's head into a press."

"You mean, he wanted to do it and she didn't?"

"No, the other way around. And he won. He said he wanted his son to grow up to look like me."

"So do I, Ben," she whispered, snuggling up and kissing him again. "So do I! Now take me to bed and make me feel warm! When you're here, you're better than a Franklin stove."

19.

Born June 30, 1820, the healthy male baby brought into the world by Lolanee Warren had a perfectly shaped, normal head. Present in the room with her upstairs were Conco's wife and two female Clatsop Indian servants, while handy downstairs in case they were needed were her husband, Ben, and a distinguished visitor to Fort George, Dr. John McLoughlin. Though it was not the custom in that place and time to have a medical doctor in the room during the birthing process, it was a comfort to Ben to have Dr. McLoughlin in the house, for his training as a surgeon in Montreal made him as knowledgeable in such matters as a doctor could be.

Summoned upstairs soon after the child was born, Ben sat gingerly on the side of the bed while his wife cradled the new baby on her breast, smiling up at him with warmth and joy.

"Isn't he beautiful, Ben?"

"Yes. But not as beautiful as you."

"We'll name him Thomas, after your father."

"And Reginald, after yours."

"Could we add Kamehameha for my grandfather?"

"If you like, Lanee." Staring down at the wrinkled red face of the baby, Ben smiled and shook his head. "Thomas Reginald Kamehameha Warren. That's a lot of names for a baby boy to carry. So we'll probably just call him Tommy."

Arriving from Montreal a week ago on the bark *William and Ann*, Dr. John McLoughlin was a tall man, standing several inches over six feet, with piercing gray eyes, prematurely white hair, and a stern manner that Ben soon learned concealed a basically kind nature. Though originally he had worked as a factor for the North West Company, he recently had switched allegiance to the Hudson's Bay Company. The purpose of his trip out to Fort George was not clear; gossip had it that he had come to achieve some sort of agreement between the two companies in settlement of their long, often bloody conflict over which was to control the fur business in North America.

Because of the relative youth, energy, and aggressiveness of its people in the field, the North West Company had dominated the trade for the past ten years, thus appeared likely to be the eventual winner. But the "Ancient and Honorable Society of Gentlemen," as the Hudson's Bay Company was described in its charter from the Crown, had been in business since 1670, knew its way around the seats of power in the British Parliament, and was not to be defeated by a ruffian band of brash Canadians.

Instead of driving the H.B.C.—"Here Before Christ"—company out of business, it now appeared that a face-saving merger of the two companies would take place, following which, after a decent interval of time, it would be the North West Company that would vanish without a trace.

During his stay at Fort George, Ben heard, Dr. McLoughlin examined the North West Company's books very closely and questioned Factor James Keith on every detail of the post's operation. In the end, he reached the same conclusion that Donald McKenzie had come to a couple of years ago: first, that the post's expenses greatly exceeded its income; second, that parties must be sent out into the field to gather furs if the yield were to be increased; and third, that the Fort George location near the mouth of the Columbia River was a poor one because it was in what would probably become American territory eventually and could not sustain itself with agricultural production.

"Tell me, Mr. Warren," Dr. McLoughlin asked Ben one day, "can a ship the size of the *William and Ann* sail any distance up the Columbia?"

"It certainly can, sir. Properly handled, a seagoing ship can sail as far upriver as Point Vancouver on the north shore. That's over a hundred miles."

"Would you pilot the *William and Ann* there?"

"I'll be glad to."

Because the river was running high now in early summer flood, the only problems Ben had taking the ship upriver were with the wind and the tide, for when both were adverse no progress could be made. But on an incoming tide with a following wind, sailing upriver was easy. Dropping anchor off Point Vancouver two days later, a ship's party in a small boat took Dr. McLoughlin, Ben, and Conco north up the broad, flat, open valley adjacent to the Cowlitz River, where McLoughlin spent several days examining the quality of the soil, the native grasses, the trees, and the water power sources available.

By then, Ben had learned that the doctor was well versed in Indian ways, for he had married first a Chippewa woman, who had borne him one son, Joseph McLoughlin, then a Cree woman named Margaret Boudin, who some years ago had lived long enough with the Astor Company Senior Partner, the late Alexander McKay, to bear him a son, Thomas McKay, who now lived at Fort George.

Though Dr. McLoughlin did not confide in Ben regarding whatever conclusions he may have reached, gossip after he returned to Fort George had it that the days of the post near the mouth of the Columbia were numbered—as was the employment of James Keith by the newly merged company.

Before weighing anchor and crossing the bar outward bound on its way around Cape Horn and up the east coast to Montreal, the master of the *William and Ann*, Captain Samuel Iverson, told Ben he would not need his pilot services for the passage.

"I logged the route quite closely on the way in," he said in his clipped, precise voice. "I'm sure I can find the way."

"Whatever you say, captain."

Overhearing Ben's attempted dismissal, Dr. John McLoughlin exploded in a sudden display of the violent temper for which Donald McKenzie had told Ben he was famous.

"You're dispensing with the pilot, you say? Nonsense, Captain Iverson! Surely you're not that big a fool!"

"But, sir," the captain protested, "his charge is forty guineas. And I *do* know the way!"

"What's this ship insured for with Lloyds, captain?"

"Oh, five thousand pounds, I imagine."

"So to save the trifling sum of forty guineas you'd gamble that one crossing of the most dangerous bar in the world makes you as much of an expert as a man who has piloted ships across it for ten years?"

"Well, if you put it that way—"

"I most certainly do!" McLoughlin turned to Ben and growled.

"Take us out to sea, Mr. Warren. I've seen enough of your work to respect your skill."

After piloting the ship out across the bar, Ben asked Dr. McLoughlin the question that was on the lips of every person connected with the fur trade on the lower river.

"Will you be coming back, Doctor?"

McLoughlin's smile was as warm as his scowl had been frosty. "I'm sure I will, Ben. This time, to stay."

By the summer of 1821, the absorption of the North West Company by the Hudson's Bay Company was complete; most of the wounds inflicted by the bitter fur trade wars had been bandaged, if not healed. Put in charge of operations in North America was a dynamo of a man called a "rare genius" by some, "a real bastard" by others. Truth to tell, he was both, Ben learned when Sir George Simpson paid a visit to Fort George in company with Dr. John McLoughlin after a rapid trip across Canada on foot, by horse, and by canoe, for he had been born out of wedlock and was a man whose ambition knew no bounds.

Typical of Sir George was the fact that though he had taken a half-blood Indian girl into his bed, who had borne him four children without benefit of marriage, he remained contemptuous all his life of white men who did marry Indian women or treated them with respect, while he himself continually sought to find a lily-white British lady who would marry him and give him an aura of respectability.

Short, plump, and vain, he was a man in his mid-thirties who insisted on traveling in style wherever he went, even to the extent of having the elite corps of voyageur canoe paddlers with whom he traveled pause a few miles short of the trading post at which he and his party would soon arrive so that he could freshen up his clothes and be sure that the fort's ceremonial cannon and corps of Scottish bagpipers would be prepared to meet him in proper style.

Though Ben was not aware of the political maneuvering that had been going on between Great Britain and the United States since the Joint Occupancy Treaty had been made, he had an uncomfortable feeling of isolation as the lone American resident living in the Pacific Northwest. Since the days of Thomas Jefferson, the presidents that succeeded him—James Madison, James Monroe, and John Quincy Adams—seemed to have had little interest in the Pacific Northwest, apparently being quite willing to let an empire-sized piece of magnificent country go to the British by default.

According to articles in the London newspapers reaching him after being well traveled and read, British diplomats now felt that recognizing American claims to Astoria in the Treaty of Ghent had been an egregious error. Since it had been made, they intended to encourage the fur traders to retreat no further, using the Columbia River as a natural boundary between the two countries. This meant that Fort George must be abandoned and a newer, larger, more self-sustaining post be built upriver on the north side of the Columbia. Because of the vast distance between London and the Pacific Northwest, Sir George Simpson would be given unlimited powers to govern Canada, while Dr. John McLoughlin would act as chief factor and resident manager of the Columbia District.

Traveling across Canada together in Simpson's usual flamboyant style, he and McLoughlin reached Spokane House in mid-October, briefly checked to see how Alexander Ross was handling matters there, then came on down the Columbia to Fort George. To say that Simpson was displeased with the way the managers were running Fort George was an understatement. He was incensed by their profligate ways and incredible stupidity. In a report to the London shareholders, he wrote caustically:

> From the earliest days of Astoria, the Columbia traders have slipped willingly into habits of improvidence. The Nor'westers imported suits of mail; and for God knows what exotic reasons, laid in supplies of ostrich plumes. Despite the change in management the company's servants remained cheerfully unreconstructed, consuming quantities of European provisions brought in at enormous costs.

In his view, the fittings and appointments at Fort George were "altogether too grand" and its current head trader, John Dease, was a man "overly addicted to tea."

Calling Alexander Ross "empty-headed and bombastic," he recognized his organizational talent and ability to bring in furs, but reinforced the field leaders by bringing west tough, energetic Peter Skene Ogden. So notoriously difficult to discipline that the only way he could be brought under control was to appoint him leader of the meanest party of trappers in the field, Ogden celebrated his new responsibility by physically whipping the three worst malcontents in the trapping party, forcing them to respect and obey him. By his own admission, Peter Skene Ogden lived by the rule:

"In my moral primer, necessity has no law."

Economies must be pursued on all fronts, Simpson decreed, which meant that drastic cuts must be made in personnel. A thriving coastal trade should be established north to Puget Sound, the Fraser River, and British Columbia, he told Dr. McLoughlin, while fur-gathering brigades were to be sent south to California on a regular basis. Most important of all, Fort George had to be closed and a new post to be called Fort Vancouver built a hundred miles upriver from the mouth of the Columbia. Though its chief factor, Dr. John McLoughlin, would be supplied with all the money, materials, and craftsmen needed to build the post, Sir George Simpson expected it to be self-sustaining soon after its completion.

Though Ben at first feared that closing Fort George would mean abandoning the white settlement near the mouth of the Columbia, he found that ship traffic in and out of the river increased rather than lessened. Needing materials with which to build a forge, a sawmill, a gristmill, and a large farming and factory community, Dr. McLoughlin patronized American as well as British workmen and companies. While the post was being built, ships of both nations frequently required pilots across the bar and on up the river.

Ever since its discovery in 1792, the lower Columbia River had been noted worldwide for the size and quality of the trees growing close to tidewater, so Astoria—as the settlement now was called—did a thriving business cutting and fitting masts and spars.

Shrewd judge of men that he was, Dr. McLoughlin disdained hiring the slothful ex-employees of Fort George as workmen, choosing instead to hire Americans with typical Yankee skills, energy, and ingenuity, using some as millwrights and blacksmiths, and others in the coastal trade because of their knowledge of native dialects and willingness to work harder than British or Irish immigrants off big-city streets.

Quick to see and take advantage of opportunities for foreign trade, McLoughlin established a thriving business shipping lumber and salmon to the Spaniards in California and the Hawaiians in the Islands. All this activity increased traffic on the lower river.

The dedication of Fort Vancouver was scheduled to take place March 19, 1825. Since this was to be a big event attended by many dignitaries, Ben asked Lolanee if she would like to go.

"Are we invited?"

"Certainly. We're on the list of honored guests."

"Can we take Tommy?"

"I don't know why not. We'll be aboard the *William and Ann* while we're on the river, with plenty of comfortable living quarters ashore at Fort Vancouver itself. Quite a few Kanakas are living there now, I hear. You might like to visit them, since they're your people."

"It would be fun to show them Tommy. All right, Ben. We'll go."

Not quite five years old now, Tommy was a brown-eyed, chubby, energetic boy, just beginning to lose his baby fat, as full of mischief and curiosity as a child raised by Lolanee's relaxed Hawaiian standards and Ben's more strict New England precepts could be. Both parents agreed that a child should be loved without limit; beyond that, Lolanee's philosophy was to leave the boy alone, while Ben's was to train his mind in the direction he wanted it to go.

From the time he began to toddle, Tommy could swim like a fish, thus had absolutely no fear of water. From the time he learned to talk, he was interested in boats, making the slackwater lagoons, the river shore, and the harbor his playgrounds. Frequently taken by Ben across the lower Columbia to the Chinook village, where Conco's son, Sitkum, now was a year older, Tommy pleased both parents by becoming bosom friends with the Chinook boy. Like most children when left to their own devices, the two boys recognized no language barriers, yelling, arguing, and laughing together in their water-oriented play in whatever combination of English, Hawaiian, Chinook Jargon, or Pidgin English best suited the message they wished to convey.

Sailing up the river to Fort Vancouver aboard the *William and Ann* was Tommy's first voyage aboard a seagoing ship. The solemnity of the occasion made him behave himself for only the first fifteen minutes after going aboard, then he began looking for something exciting to do. With her usual casual attitude toward keeping him out of trouble, Lolanee assumed that since ships were Ben's world, he would take on the responsibility of looking after Tommy, making sure he did not fall overboard, get entangled with the anchor chain as it was being hauled in, or climb to the top of the mainmast—all of which he tried to do—while she enjoyed herself standing at the rail gazing at the passing scenery.

Ordering Tommy to hold on to his hand, stand still, and not bother Captain Samuel Iverson—who did not seem to like little boys—Ben stood beside the helmsman as the ship made its way upriver, quietly warning him of a nearing sandbar, an adverse current, or a crossing point where quieter water or a better breeze could be found. Pacing back and forth across the quarter deck, Captain Iverson scowled his disapproval, then gave essentially the same instructions to the helmsman a few moments later.

Dr. McLoughlin's orders to all British sea captains that they must employ Ben, Conco, or Chief Concomly as a pilot when crossing the bar or cruising the lower reaches of the Columbia galled Captain Iverson, Ben knew. Snobbish where ship navigation was concerned, he could not accept the fact that a slant-headed Indian or an American sailor half his age could handle the ship better than he could in dangerous waters. Adding insult to injury was the fact that the little uniform made by Lolanee to show off Tommy to her Hawaiian friends at Fort Vancouver was an exact replica of the black broadcloth trousers, coat, white shirt, black string tie, and billed cap worn by British merchant ship captains such as Captain Iverson.

Since marrying Lolanee, Ben had come to understand what her father, Captain Reginald Barker, had meant when he said that he had left England because that country had become so buried under the stuffy ash of tradition that it had lost its energy and incentive to improve the lives of its people. Captain Samuel Iverson was a perfect example of that stuffiness. To him, Ben knew, any person not of pure, undiluted, white, Anglo-Saxon blood was inferior to an Englishman like himself. French-Canadians, Americans, Hawaiians, Indians, and mixed-bloods such as Lolanee and Tommy all rated far down the scale, so far as he was concerned, and the less he had to do with them, the better.

Well, Ben mused, *the feeling is mutual. But I'd better make sure Tommy minds his manners while we're aboard.*

The extent of the Fort Vancouver establishment planned and developed during the past two years under the direction of Dr. John McLoughlin was truly amazing, justifying its description as "the most civilized British trading post west of London." If it were not yet self-sufficient, it soon would be, for the fields of grain and vegetables on the extensive plain outside the fort walls, the cattle, sheep, swine, work oxen and horses, the numerous living quarters built to accommodate the French-Canadian trappers, voyageurs, workmen, and their Indian wives and children covered hundreds of acres.

Counting the Kanakas who had worked for the Astor, then the North West, and now the Hudson's Bay Company, at least three hundred Hawaiians had spent some time in the region, a majority of whom had liked it well enough to stay. The present residents of "Kanaka Village," as it was called, numbered just under two hundred, Ben was told. Given quarters to themselves in a small, newly completed cabin at the edge of the village, Ben, Lolanee, and Tommy were pleased with their accommodations, though Ben realized that their placement outside the stockade walls of the fort itself was a subtle recognition of the fact that their social rating was several notches down the scale from that of the resident managers and senior clerks.

The fact that Lolanee was not invited to sit as an honored guest at the formal dinner which highlighted the dedication did not surprise Ben, for he knew that protocol at Hudson's Bay Company "Society of Gentlemen" affairs banned women. At first, he was concerned that Lolanee would feel insulted and give the so-called Gentlemen a piece of her mind, as only she could do. But as matters turned out, she did not even notice the slight, for she was having far more fun with the ladies in the kitchen than she could possibly have had as the lone female in such stuffy male company.

Served in the dining room of Dr. McLoughlin's well-appointed home, the dinner, at which Sir George Simpson was the honored guest, was equal in the quality of its wine, food, and the excellence with which it was served to the best to be found in an exclusive London club. Present were three members of the Hudson's Bay Company board of directors visiting from England; two British, one Russian, and one American sea captain; and such senior field directors as Alexander Ross from Spokane House, Finan McDonald from Flathead Post, and Peter Skene Ogden from Fort Nez Perces. Also seated at the table were half a dozen junior clerks who seemed more intent on not choosing the wrong fork or spoon, not taking a sip too much wine, and not saying anything that might give offense to their superiors than on enjoying the dinner.

It was an indication of his status, Ben knew, that he should be seated between the oldest of the junior clerks and the youngest of the field directors, Peter Skene Ogden. Unlike the clerks, Ogden, a chunky, muscular, blunt-mannered man, made no attempt to choose the right piece of silverware or to restrain his wine intake, for he ate like a starving man, emptied every glass of wine set before him with incredible rapidity, and said exactly what was on his mind.

Upon learning that Ben was an American, he laughed roughly and exclaimed: "Used to be a damned Yankee myself, by God! But my father fixed that."

"Oh?" Ben said. "How?"

"I was born in New Jersey a few years before the Revolutionary War. But my father was a Tory and thought his American neighbors were worthless rabble. So he moved the family to Montreal and we became Britishers." Grinning crookedly at Ben, Ogden emptied another glass of wine and signaled for a refill. "Not that I have anything against Americans, you understand."

"Nor do I have anything against Britishers," Ben said stiffly. "But as I recall, the rabble did win the first war, then fought England to a draw in the second. Under the Joint Occupancy Treaty, as I'm sure you know, we have as much right to this part of the country as you do."

"You're outnumbered, my friend. So you'd better learn how to sing *God Save the King*."

"Before I'll do that, Mr. Ogden, I suspect I'll join the rabble in going to war and whipping you British again."

"Look, I don't mean to insult you, Mr. Warren. I really don't give a tinker's dam about politics or who owns this part of the country, d'ye understand? All I care about is beaver. What else is there of value out here?"

Because the American merchant ship captain—who by now was dozing in his chair—was the only fellow countryman at the table, Ben did not feel inclined to pursue the argument any further. But the supercilious attitude of the Britishers at the table irritated him. After the dessert plates were taken away and after dinner port was served, cigars were lighted and a general discussion of future Hudson's Bay Company policy in the Pacific Northwest began. Sir George Simpson did most of the talking.

"The completion of Fort Vancouver gives us an ideal base of operation," he was saying. "The next step is to control the supply of beaver. We must make sure the Americans have no reason to cross the Rocky Mountains."

"Have they made such an attempt?" asked one of the London directors, a florid-faced, white-haired man with muttonchop whiskers.

"Only in their usual disorganized, dog-eat-dog fashion. Since the abject failure of his venture on the lower Columbia, Astor has sent a few American Fur Company trapping parties to the headwaters of the Missouri. The Rocky Mountain Fur Company put together by the Sublette brothers has sent men across the Divide into the Snake River country. The most serious threat so far has come from William Ashley's young field leader, Jedidiah Smith, in the Salt Lake area." Glancing down the table, Simpson spoke sharply to Peter Skene Ogden. "You've had trouble with him, I understand."

"Aye, that I have," Ogden growled. "For a Bible-toter, he's a tough son-of-a-bitch."

"But you did refrain from violence, Mr. Ogden?"

Ogden nodded and grunted, "Had to. We were outnumbered."

"In my opinion, there are two rules we must make sure our trapping parties obey at all times," Simpson continued. "The first is that the Americans are to be discouraged by all means short of violence. The second is when we're trapping in country where Americans might try to compete with us, our people are to strip it bare. By that I mean not a single furbearing animal of any variety, size, or sex is to be left alive—no matter how worthless their pelts may be."

"Isn't this contrary to usual Company policy?" another of the London directors asked with a scowl. "What I mean to say is, don't we usually take only the mature animals and leave the rest for seed?"

"That's correct, sir. Since its founding, the Hudson's Bay Company has followed the sensible policy of trapping a beaver stream only once every four years, taking only the mature males as far as possible. Following this practice, our trappers leave the stream untouched so that four years later its beaver population will replenish itself and it then can be harvested again."

"But you're abandoning this policy now?"

"Yes, sir. At least in all the regions west of the Rockies into which American trappers are tempted to come. Since the only commodity of value in that country is beaver, I want to make sure that the Americans have no reason to enter it. When the time comes for the Joint Occupancy Treaty to be settled by the people living in the Pacific Northwest, I want to make sure the British outnumber the Americans by an overwhelming margin."

Pleased with the impeccable logic of that line of reasoning, the muttonchop director proposed that the assembled guests at the table drink a toast to Sir George Simpson's leadership. By now, the American merchant ship captain was sound asleep and Ben did not feel like raising his own glass. So there were two abstentions from the toast, a breach of etiquette noticed and accepted by Dr. John McLoughlin with a wry smile in Ben's direction.

Sailing downriver two days later on the *William and Ann*, which put Lolanee and Tommy ashore near the landing below their home, with Ben then piloting the ship across the bar and saying a stiff farewell to Captain Samuel Iverson and the three London directors, Ben dropped into the Chinook canoe commanded by Conco and returned to the lower river. Curious about the big dedication ceremony at Fort Vancouver, to which neither he nor his father had been invited, Conco asked Ben how he and his family had enjoyed it.

"Well, Lolanee and Tommy had a good time," Ben said thoughtfully. "And I learned a few things."

"Such as?"

"That the only thing of value in this part of the country is beaver. And that when the time comes to decide who owns it, the British will win by a big margin."

"Do you believe that?"

"To hear Sir George Simpson spout off, it's the only thing that can possibly happen. But somehow I've got a feeling he's overlooking something. Give me a little time, Conco, and maybe I'll figure out what it is."

20.

ONE OF THE THINGS Sir George Simpson was overlooking, Ben learned soon after the dedication of Fort Vancouver, was the tendency of reckless young Americans to explore whatever new country interested them, accepting no national boundaries to their travels. Recalling that Simpson had asked Peter Skene Ogden about having had trouble with a field leader named Jedidiah Smith, to which Ogden had replied, "For a Bible-toter, he's a tough son-of-a bitch," Ben asked his longtime friend, Alexander Ross, if he knew anything about Smith. Ross flinched visibly.

"Unfortunately, I do. There's no one like him in the fur trade. You'll probably not believe this, Ben, but it's all true …"

Going to work for William Ashley in St. Louis at the age of eighteen, Jedidiah Smith had proved his courage in dangerous circumstances at nineteen, and became a trusted leader of men at twenty. But it was neither his youth nor his courage that made him stand out from the crowd.

It was his religion.

"He's a bold, outspoken, practicing Christian," Ross said, "the only one I've ever known in the fur trade. No person that has ever had dealings with him can doubt his piety. Wherever he goes, he carries a Bible and a hymnbook and will preach to anyone that will listen on the slightest provocation."

"What brand of religion does he hold to?"

"Wesleyan Methodist, I'm told, though I'm no expert on such matters."

"Where did you meet him?"

"At Flathead Post a year or so ago. He and half a dozen of his men were playing hide-and-seek with Peter Skene Ogden and a party of his trappers …"

What had happened, Ross said, was that Jedidiah Smith and six of his men had spent the previous summer and fall along the headwaters of the Snake. By accident or design, they showed up at Flathead Post shortly before Ogden set out December 20, 1824, on a trapping expedition in the high mountain country to the west of the Continental Divide. Since the seven Americans and the twenty-two lodges of Hudson's Bay Company *engagées*, freemen, Indian guides, and women camp helpers all planned to travel in the same direction, it seemed a good idea to travel together.

At least, to the Americans, it did. Being familiar with British ground rules that the Americans were to be discouraged by any means short of violence, Ogden did not protest, but one of his assistants, William Kittson, thought good manners should have their limits. After moving up the Bitter Root Valley and crossing over to the North Fork of the Salmon February 11, 1825, Kittson was happy to report at long last the imminent separation with the Americans, noting in his journal:

> The seven Americans are preparing to leave us and try to make their way to the Snake River … well satisfied, I hope, with the care and attention we paid them … One Jedidiah S. Smith is at the head of them, a sly, cunning Yankey … Mr. Ogden has ordered me to notice the way they went …

Now there began a game common to trappers and gold-seekers—a game of fool the other fellow, fake him into unproductive territory, or, if he does make a strike, move in quickly and get your share. When in beaver country, Ross said, trappers worked in teams of two or three, one team working this creek, another that, with meeting places arranged from whence the party as a whole would move on once the area was trapped out. Since this was on the edge of Blackfoot country, a constant watch must be kept for hostiles.

A party of seven men was more mobile than one of twenty-two lodges; it was also more vulnerable. The ground rules did not permit the betrayal of one party to hostiles by the other; still, if the trappers got careless and lost their scalps, it was *their* hair to lose. Exactly what happened to the two trapping parties as they worked their way south toward the Salt Lake area, Alexander Ross did not know. What he did know was that a group of Iroquois Indians from eastern Canada, which he himself had equipped and trained as trappers for the Hudson's Bay Company, was attacked by hostiles, saved their scalps, but got themselves hopelessly lost in unfamiliar country.

Jedidiah Smith and his small band of Americans, who did know the country, found them. Delighted to see friendly white faces, the confused band of Iroquois asked Jedidiah Smith if he would be so kind as to guide them back to Pierre's Hole, where they were supposed to meet Ross and the main party.

"As a practicing Christian," Ross said sourly, "Smith told them he was delighted to be of help. However, since they had managed to save a hundred beaver plews, he would charge a slight fee for his services. Say, a hundred beaver plews?"

"Did they pay it?"

"What else could they do? And I thanked him politely when he brought them back to me, though the truth was I wouldn't have minded too much if he hadn't. To add insult to injury, he led them in Bible-reading and hymn-singing every night he stayed in our camp. Though they were all good Catholics when he met them, I swear he would have made Methodists of them if he'd stayed another week."

Later, down in the Bear River country, William Ashley and Jedidiah Smith managed to persuade a dozen or so of Peter Skene Ogden's trappers to desert him and sell their furs to the American rather than the British company in a clash that got so confused and heated it very nearly erupted into violence. Though he had tried to explain to Simpson and McLoughlin that he was acting under duress, Ogden was still under a cloud, so far as Simpson was concerned, regarding his loyalty to the Hudson's Bay Company.

Now, surprisingly, Jedidiah Smith had shown up on the coast in the southern part of the Oregon Country, and was appealing to Dr. John McLoughlin for help. Ben heard about it from his friend and protegé, Thomas McKay.

Two years Ben's junior, the black-eyed, brown-skinned young man, who was half Cree and half Scotch, had inherited the intelligence of his father and the wilderness instincts of his mother, becoming a valued employee of first the North West, then the Hudson's Bay Company. Having become one of Peter Skene Ogden's assistants, he was well acquainted with Jedidiah Smith and his wide-roving band of American trappers, which managed to get into trouble wherever it went.

After a profitable season trapping the headwaters of the Snake near Jackson Hole, Smith proposed an ambitious journey which hopefully would open new territory in the Southwest, territory nominally controlled by the Spaniards. In 1827, the Joint Occupancy Treaty between Great Britain and the United States had been renewed for another ten years. South of the forty-second parallel, the Spaniards had no interest in beaver, Smith knew. So he decided that he would take a look at that part of the country, which he and the fifteen trappers in his party would be the first Americans to explore.

Yes, the treaty with Spain excluded Americans from the region. But since when did a sly, cunning Yankee have to pay attention to a treaty, if a profit were to be made—even if he were a pious, practicing Christian?

Taking the better part of a year to cross the desert and mountains west of Salt Lake, Jedidiah Smith found California rich in beaver and horses, to which he and the trappers in his party helped themselves. Understandably, the Spanish authorities took a dim few of the invasion of their territory, arrested Smith and his friends, and threw them in jail. This taught the Americans a lesson, though not quite the one the easygoing Spaniards intended. In essence, the lesson was that if you stole horses or beaver in Spanish territory, you should be careful not to get caught.

Released from jail finally in central California, Smith and his band of Americans headed north toward the Oregon Country, trapping no beaver and stealing no horses until they were sure they were out of reach of the Spanish authorities, then proceeding to do again what they had done before. By the time they reached the domain of the Umpqua Indians near the southern Oregon coast, they had accumulated a number of excellent horses and valuable furs.

There, Jedidiah Smith and his partner Arthur Black made the serious mistake of trusting a band of Indians notorious for their treachery. Attacked while sleeping, the fifteen trapper members of the party were killed to the last man; all their horses and furs were taken; and only the two leaders of the party escaped alive to carry their tale of horror northeast through the rugged, mountainous country to Fort Vancouver.

"Sir George Simpson happened to be visiting the post the day Smith and Black showed up," Thomas McKay told Ben. "It's long been Company policy that the killing of white men by Indians must always be punished immediately and severely. So I was put in charge of a heavily armed party of Hudson's Bay Company employees, with orders to go to the Umpqua country, find and discipline the Indians who had committed the crime, and retrieve the lost horses and furs."

"Which you did?"

"Yes. That band of Indians will never molest white men again."

The curious thing about the whole episode, Ben learned later, was that Dr. McLoughlin—with Simpson's approval—charged Jedidiah Smith for the recovery effort only at the value of the men's time at the rate of sixty dollars a year and four dollars apiece for horses lost during the trip. He then purchased Smith's furs, amounting to $20,000 worth, at the market price, giving him a draft on London in payment.

Even more curious was Smith's reaction to the Company's generosity. Having seen how scrupulously Peter Skene Ogden, Dr. John McLoughlin, and Sir George Simpson had obeyed the ground rules, he demonstrated that even a sly, cunning Yankee could have moral scruples. As a contemporary wrote:

> Smith's Christian nature would not permit McLoughlin to outdo him in generosity, and he insisted that the fall hunt of himself and his associates be made east of the Continental Divide, so as not to trespass upon the territory which the Hudson's Bay Company claimed as belonging commercially to them.

Unilaterally, Jedidiah S. Smith had abrogated the Joint Occupancy Treaty and resigned from the competition.

Honorable though he may have been in promising never to compete with the British company again, Jedidiah Smith did innocently plant a seed among the Indians of the eastern part of the Oregon country that eventually would grow and flower in a manner never dreamed of by Sir George Simpson. Pausing for a few days at Flathead Post to enjoy the grudging hospitality of Alexander Ross, Smith could not resist leading the local Indians, whom he genuinely liked, in a few evenings of hymn-singing and Bible reading. But the question he put in their primitive minds had little to do with the white man's religion.

That question was: *Does the white man's Bible contain such secrets as how to make rifles and gunpowder? Where must we go to get the Bible?*

21.

*T*HE ACTIVITIES INITIATED at Fort Vancouver under the bold leadership of Dr. John McLoughlin contrasted so sharply with the inertia of the managers at Fort George that it became clear to Ben that the British were dead serious about their intentions to take over the Pacific Northwest. In 1826, a crew of skilled shipwrights and carpenters brought to the post from the Orkney Islands built the schooner *Vancouver*, which became the first vessel ever constructed from scratch in the region, though earlier Ben had helped assemble the thirty-ton *Dolly*, whose precut timbers had been carried to the Columbia aboard the *Tonquin*.

Approximately the same size, the two-masted schooner *Vancouver* was much better designed than the broad-beamed *Dolly* had been, proving to be a good sailer in these waters, making a number of trips across the bar and north as far as Russian Alaska.

Though both British and American sea captains felt that the hazards of the bar and the lower river made navigation dangerous for any ship over two hundred tons, it was Ben's opinion that it was the way the ship was handled—not its size—that was important. Tragically, this was proved by the loss of the *William and Ann* with its captain and all hands in late February 1828.

Exactly what happened never was clear to Ben or anyone else on the scene, for neither sailors nor the ship's log survived to tell the tale. Arriving on a gray, rainy afternoon, with a storm making and seas rising out of the southwest, the *William and Ann* was sailing in company with the American schooner, *Convoy*. Responding to a signal requesting a pilot, Ben went out with Conco and his crew of Chinook paddlers, got aboard the *Convoy*, then brought her in across the bar to the safety of Baker Bay.

He had assumed that Captain Samuel Iverson, who was still master of the *William and Ann*, would follow at a safe interval, but when the *Convoy* reached quiet water and dropped her hook, the other ship was not in sight. By then, full darkness had fallen, so Ben supposed that Captain Iverson had decided not to risk making the crossing in the failing light and worsening weather, beating out to sea and the safety of deep water, where he would wait for daylight and lessening winds before making another attempt.

But next day, which dawned clear with a strong wind still blowing from the southwest, the sea off the coast was empty, showing no sign of the missing ship. Hearing through Conco and the native grapevine that wreckage had been seen washing ashore on Clatsop Spit—the long neck of sandy beach guarding the south entrance to the Columbia—it was assumed that the missing ship had gone aground there. The often belligerent Clatsop leader, Chief Kilamook, had been heard bragging, Conco said, about killing the survivors who had managed to escape the wreck and make it to shore, after which he and his braves had stolen the ship's cargo.

Placing guilt on the Clatsops for killing the survivors and stealing the ship's stores was not nearly as important to Ben as discovering the cause of the wreck. He well remembered how arrogant Captain Iverson had been a few years ago and how strongly he had resented Dr. McLoughlin's order that he pay a pilot to take his ship in and out of the river's mouth. With a strong southwest wind blowing onto a lee shore late yesterday afternoon, Ben felt that the *William and Ann* either should have followed very closely after the *Convoy*, or, if the light were too poor and the weather too bad to cross the bar before darkness fell, should have sheered off sharply to the northwest and gone well out to sea before laying to for the night.

The fact that the ship had gone aground southwest of the river mouth meant that Captain Iverson had either gotten caught by wind and tide in the broad mouth of the bar and found it impossible to turn and sail to the northwest, or that he had been so sure of his ability to read the waters that he had attempted to bring his ship in through an unsafe passage. In either case, bad seamanship was involved. Paying for his folly, he had been driven onto the sands of Clatsop Spit and the *William and Ann* had been lost with all hands. When the news reached Fort Vancouver, Dr. McLoughlin was furious.

"Do you know what happened?" he asked Ben.

"I was aboard the *Convoy*, sir, bringing her in across the bar. We thought the *William and Ann* was a mile or so astern, but we lost her in the darkness and rain. After we dropped anchor in Baker Bay, the captain of the *Convoy* sent a crew back in a ship's boat to find her and give her what assistance they could. But the wind kept getting stronger and the day darker, so they had to give up and come back."

"Chief Kilamook claims that when the ship was wrecked, there were no survivors. But the Clatsops in his village have hauled a lot of the cargo ashore and are claiming it as salvage."

"So Conco tells me."

"Do you suppose they killed the survivors, then stole the cargo?"

"I wouldn't put it past them. They're known to be an ornery lot."

"Well, I'll teach them better!" Dr. McLoughlin growled angrily. "I'm sending the *Vancouver* downriver with orders to question Chief Kilamook and recover the cargo. If the arrogant old rascal won't comply, I'll make him regret it."

Though he was not on the scene to witness the action, Ben learned that Dr. McLoughlin kept his word. When questioned by the captain of the *Vancouver*, Chief Kilamook bluntly denied that the Clatsops had murdered survivors of the *William and Ann* wreck, then flatly refused to give up any of the ship's stores he and his people had salvaged, even though they were the property of the Hudson's Bay Company. When the captain threatened to bring a party of armed men ashore and search the village, Chief Kilamook's response was to order his warriors to don their leather shields and masks, seize their weapons, and prepare to attack the ship's captain and boat crew.

Having been authorized by Dr. McLoughlin to meet force with force, the captain trained the six-pounder in the bow on the village, fired several rounds, and reduced the village to rubble. During the barrage, Chief Kilamook and several Clatsop Indians were killed, while half a dozen more were badly wounded. Though the survivors fled into the nearby woods in panic, taking their stolen loot with them, the "White-Haired Eagle"—as the natives called Dr. McLoughlin—again had taught the Indians that the vengeance of the Hudson's Bay Company against transgressors was quick and severe.

Meanwhile, as ship traffic on the lower Columbia continued to increase, an interesting bit of news from the interior post of Spokane

House indicated that Sir George Simpson was taking measures to consolidate the hold of the Hudson's Bay Company on the loyalty of the region's Indians by instructing them in both education and religion. Selecting three bright, fourteen-year-old boys from the Spokane and Kootenay tribes, Simpson had taken them to Winnipeg, where they were given a good secular education and taught the Church of England religion. When they returned to their people, Simpson hoped, they would be prepared to combat the heresy spread by roving religious trappers such as Jedidiah Smith.

During their five years at Winnipeg, two of the boys died. But the third—an intelligent young man named Spokane Garry—returned to his people so full of wisdom and piety that Indians from as far away as the Flathead and Nez Perce country felt compelled to send their own *shamans*, *tewats*, or whatever name they called their tribal medicine men, to Spokane House, where they spent days listening to the nineteen-year-old spellbinder tell them about the white man's magic, some of which he read them aloud from what he called "The White Man's Book of Heaven."

Returning to their own country, the Flatheads and Nez Perces—who were closely related—decided that they, too, would like to acquire the white man's technical skills, which enabled him to make such wonderful things as guns and tools of iron, even if that meant learning how to read the printed words in the mysterious "Book of Heaven." But instead of sending several bright young boys east to be educated by the King George men—whom they mistrusted—the Flatheads and Nez Perces would delegate half a dozen adult men to go to St. Louis, where their old American friend, William Clark, who had visited them twenty-five years ago, now was Superintendent of Indian Affairs for the Far West.

When they saw him in St. Louis, they said, they would ask him to send American *tai-tam-nats*—Holy Men—west to live among and teach the Indians in their own country. How would the delegation find its way? By following the instructions Jedidiah Smith had given them a few years ago at Flathead Post: going first to the early summer fur rendezvous just west of the Continental Divide, then traveling back to St. Louis with the returning brigade.

Incredible as all this sounded to Ben Warren in his remote hilltop home overlooking the lower Columbia, he realized that it did happen, adding one more link to the chain of inconceivable events Sir George

Simpson had overlooked when he formulated his policy of "stripping the country bare" of beaver so that there would be nothing of value left in the Pacific Northwest to attract Americans to the region.

A curiosity to explore new land—which had motivated Jedidiah Smith—was one factor Simpson had overlooked. But now an even more powerful motive—missionary zeal to save heathen souls—had gone to work. Back in New England, Ben read in newspapers reaching Astoria, religious missionary societies were being organized at such a feverish pitch that one upper New York State region was being called "The Burnt District" because it had been struck and scorched so often by bolts of "God's Lightning," inspiring missionaries to obey the Great Command: *Go ye therefore, and teach all nations, baptizing them in the name of the Father, and of the Son, and of the Holy Ghost.* MATTHEW 28:19.

From what Dr. John McLoughlin told Ben at Fort Vancouver, inspiration for the American missionary movement had begun with an article published in an eastern religious newspaper which had told about the visit of the Flathead and Nez Perce delegation to St. Louis, then shown a sketch of an Indian with a sharply pointed head, who, it was claimed, had been a member of the delegation. That the article was wildly inaccurate did not matter to the religious zealots whom it inspired.

"I have deep respect for believers of all faiths," McLoughlin told Ben. "But the premise of this article was completely false. As you and I well know, the Flatheads do not flatten their heads, nor do the Nez Perces pierce their noses. But religious zeal seems to overwhelm truth."

"Do you think American missionaries will come out to this part of the country?"

"They're already on their way. A party of Methodists led by the Reverend Jason Lee arrived at the American fur rendezvous on Green River early this summer, I'm told. According to an express dispatch I've just received from Thomas McKay, who went there as a representative of the Hudson's Bay Company, they've been invited to establish a mission on the Clearwater in Nez Perce country. He's trying to persuade them to come on west to the lower Columbia instead."

"Do you want them here?"

"If they're going to come to the Oregon Country, I prefer that they live where the Hudson's Bay Company can keep an eye on them. My feeling is they ought to settle in the Willamette Valley, south of the Columbia. That's good farming and stock-raising country, where a number of retired Hudson's Bay Company employees already are living."

"So I've noticed. Will there be any conflict between your people and the American missionaries?"

"I see no reason why there should be. Most of the Company men are French-Canadians, who have taken Indian wives and are raising families. The Company is glad to help them. We'll be happy to help the Americans, too."

"Even though Sir George Simpson may not approve?"

Shaking his head, McLoughlin said stiffly, "I have to live in this country, Ben. Sir George Simpson doesn't. To me, Joint Occupancy means that I must treat Americans with the same courtesy and respect that I do British subjects. If they respond in kind—as Jedidiah Smith did—I'm pleased. If they do not, I resent it, of course. But I cannot respond to their rudeness in kind, much as I might wish to do so."

During the past two years, Ben knew, a pair of Americans motivated neither by beaver nor religion had shown up at Fort Vancouver, sorely trying the patience of Dr. McLoughlin. The first was a rabid New England visionary named Hall Jackson Kelley, who proposed throwing the British out of the Pacific Northwest, colonizing the Oregon Country at government expense, and giving each and every unemployed American resident living on the Eastern Seaboard a square mile of fertile Oregon land. The second was Nathaniel Wyeth, a practical man who had quickly tired of Kelley's words and had struck out for Oregon on his own.

Having been a successful ice merchant and businessman in Boston, he organized a company that planned to march overland to Oregon, where it would meet his chartered brig, the *Sultana*, which would sail around the Horn carrying a cargo of trade goods for the Indians and a thousand empty barrels. When it reached the lower Columbia, Wyeth would employ the Indians to catch enough fat salmon to fill the barrels, salt and ice them down, then the ship would return to Boston, where he would sell the fish and make a fortune.

Like Astor's by-land and by-sea expeditions twenty years earlier, the scheme was a good one in concept. Also like Astor's, it failed in its execution because of a series of misfortunes which the man who devised it could not have foreseen.

Wrecked on a South American reef, the *Sultana* never reached the Columbia. Wyeth's second chartered ship, the *May Dacre*, which

Ben piloted across the bar, fared better, making her way up the Columbia and dropping anchor a few miles upriver from Fort Vancouver. There, she opened her hold and exposed the thousand empty barrels while she waited in vain for them to be filled with fish.

Though plenty of fat, gleaming salmon were running in the river, which the Indians caught in great quantity for the Hudson's Bay Company, they refused to catch a single fish for Nathaniel Wyeth. The reason for this, he soon discovered, was that Dr. John McLoughlin had quietly told the Indians that any person who fished for or traded with the American company would never do business with the Hudson's Bay Company again.

Try as he might, the New England ice merchant found he could not teach the necessary salmon-catching skills to the increasingly disgusted white members of his party, many of whom deserted him and struck out as trappers, farmers, schoolteachers, or tradesmen on their own. After two months of largely wasted effort, Wyeth had no choice but to send the *May Dacre* back to Boston with not enough cargo in its hold to pay its charter.

In an attempt to compete with the Hudson's Bay Company for furs in the Snake River country a thousand miles to the east, Wyeth built a desert trading post named Fort Boise. In response, Dr. McLoughlin—with Simpson's approval—had Thomas McKay build a larger, better stocked post named Fort Boise 250 miles to the west. Though just "good-neighboring distance" in that vast country, exchanging neighborly visits was not the purpose of the post. Like the Indian boycott of Wyeth's salmon-fishing venture in the lower Columbia, it was just one more weapon in the Hudson's Bay Company policy to combat American expansion into the Oregon Country "by all means short of violence."

Defeated at every turn and finally forced to give up and go back to Boston, Wyeth still had good things to say about his competitor, writing just before he left the Oregon Country that he: "… found Dr. McLoughlin a fine old gentleman, truly philanthropic in his ideas …"

Not so complimentary to the resident manager of the Hudson's Bay Company was the crazed, wild-eyed zealot Hall Jackson Kelley, whose impassioned writings extolling the virtues of the Pacific Northwest had been rolling off the presses for years. Finally inspired to move himself, Kelley had taken ship to the east coast of Mexico, crossed overland to Acapulco on the west coast, then sailed north to

the Spanish settlement of Bodega Bay in central California. There, he
picked up half a dozen ragtag American followers interested in traveling with him to Oregon, one of whom was an ex-trapper named
Ewing Young. By then, Kelley had caught a bad case of malaria. By
the time he reached Fort Vancouver and was taken to Dr. McLoughlin to be cared for, he was even further out of his mind than his normally half-crazed state.

For years in his writings, he had portrayed the Hudson's Bay Company as being the mortal enemy of American expansion into the Oregon Country. Now, finding himself in the care of this huge,
white-haired, fierce-eyed doctor who called himself manager of the
British establishment, Kelley was convinced that his fever-weakened
body had been delivered by his enemies into the presence of the devil
himself. To further complicate matters, the party of Americans led
north from California had picked up a couple of dozen loose horses en
route. Acting on the complaints of local citizens, the Governor of California had sent a message to Dr. McLoughlin stating that the Ewing
Young party were horsethieves and that he would be obliged if the good
doctor would arrest them and return them to Bodega Bay for trial.

Under these circumstances, Ben learned later, it was not surprising
that instead of being given quarters in the McLoughlin home and a
place of honor at the gentlemen's table, Kelley was housed in the
smallest, meanest, most poorly furnished shack to be found on the
edge of the Fort Vancouver grounds. Finally convinced that Ewing
Young, at least, was not a horse thief, Dr. McLoughlin politely told
the Governor of California that he would return the animals but did
not have the authority to arrest American citizens and transport them
to Spanish California for trial.

After telling Ewing Young he was free to settle anywhere he liked
in the Oregon Country, Dr. McLoughlin put the still-complaining,
still-suspicious Hall Jackson Kelley aboard an American merchant
ship bound for Boston, and paid for his passage home.

As a relieved footnote to the incident, Dr. McLoughlin solemnly
told Ben:

"Even if Mr. Kelley had not been accused of consorting with
thieves, he could not have eaten with the gentlemen at my table. He
was not the right sort, you know."

22.

During the first ten years of their marriage, Lolanee often accused Ben of having a better memory for the dates of shipwrecks on the lower Columbia than for the birthdays of their children. This was true, he admitted, but it was partially her fault, for shipwrecks were always terrible disasters, while the birth of each child as Lolanee managed it was always an occasion for great joy.

Their second child, a girl, was born August 4, 1823. Agreeing that each of their children should have both an American and a Hawaiian name, Ben and Lolanee called the baby Sarah, after Ben's mother, and Allamanda, after Lolanee's favorite bright yellow Hawaiian flower. When their third child, also a girl, was born November 19, 1825, Lolanee insisted that the Hawaiian part of her name, Hina, come first, while the American part, Flora, after Ben's aunt, be placed second.

"Hina was the beautiful goddess mother of Molokai, the most enchanting of all the islands," Lolanee told Ben. "My mother's family loves that name."

"Did Hina the goddess have a husband?" Ben asked. "Or was it a virgin birth?"

"If a *haole* like you had asked that question in Hawaii when my grandfather was alive," Lolanee answered sharply, "King Kamehameha would have ordered your heart cut out and had you buried under a corner post in a heathen temple, whose very name would be taboo for a hundred years."

"By that, I gather she did have a husband."

"She certainly did—a man so handsome he would have made Apollo look like a pig. His name was Wakea, which means 'Father of the Islands.'"

"So if our next child happens to be a boy, we could name him

Emil, after my youngest brother, and Wakea, after the father of Molokai. That way, Hina will have a soulmate."

"What a sweet idea, Ben! We'll do it!"

Ben had learned by now that when Lolanee put her mind to something, it always got done; so he was not in the least surprised when she gave birth to a boy child February 23, 1828. To help him remember the date, it was just two days later that the *William and Ann* was wrecked on Clatsop Spit.

More and more of recent years, captains who had crossed the bar a number of times grew overconfident of their ability to read the waters. Dispensing with the services of a pilot, they sometimes came to grief when they miscalculated the effects of wind, current, and tide. In a particularly foolish case, Captain Patrick Ryan of the American merchant ship *Isabella* lost his vessel unnecessarily when the use of a pilot or better judgment would have saved it.

Ironically, it was not the bar itself that proved to be a hazard, but the shoal called Sand Island, which was well inside the mouth of the river. Crossing the bar through the deep water channel just below Cape Disappointment in calm weather the afternoon of May 23, 1830, Captain Ryan carelessly let his ship drift too far to the south, putting it aground on the sloping sandy bottom just offshore from the Clatsop village once ruled by Chief Kilamook, which had been rebuilt since his death.

Because the ship grounded gently on the sloping sandy bottom on the ebb tide, with no structural damage done to the keel, the *Isabella* was in no trouble and probably could have been refloated by judicious kedging on the flood tide. But Captain Ryan panicked. Recalling the disaster of the *William and Ann* two years earlier, when a storm drove that ship ashore and Chief Kilamook and his warriors allegedly murdered the survivors and appropriated the cargo, the captain ordered the ship abandoned at nightfall. After he and the crew took to boats and rowed ashore at Fort George, the unmanned ship—which the Clatsops did not molest—was left to the mercy of the elements, pulled loose her poorly set anchors on the flood tide, drifted out across the bar on the ebb, and eventually became a total loss.

Though the appearance of Americans such as Jedidiah Smith, Nathaniel Wyeth, Hall Kelley, and Jason Lee in the Oregon Country indicated that the United States was beginning to take an interest in the Pacific Northwest, it was not until 1836 that serious competition to the Hudson's Bay Company monopoly appeared at Fort Vancouver. This came in the form of Protestant missionaries Dr. Marcus and Narcissa Whitman and the Reverend Henry and Eliza Spalding. Sponsored by the American Board for Foreign Missions, a joint venture of the Congregational and Presbyterian churches, these *tai-tam-nats*, as the Nez Perces called them, were not to be diverted to the Willamette Valley, as the Jason Lee party had been, nor were the ladies to be denied seats at Dr. McLoughlin's dining room table, as Lolanee had been ten years earlier, though neither she nor Ben had considered it an insult at the time.

What the Whitmans and Spaldings intended to do, they told Dr. McLoughlin, was establish two missions several hundred miles to the east, one among the Cayuse Indians in the Walla Walla Valley, the other among the Nez Perces, in the Clearwater country. Giving him a long list of the tools and supplies they would need to buy from the Hudson's Bay Company, Marcus Whitman and Henry Spalding flatly refused to settle south of the Columbia where the British company could keep an eye on them, though their wives would accept Dr. McLoughlin's hospitality and stay at Fort Vancouver for six weeks or so while their husbands went inland and supervised the building of mission houses.

"What can I do?" McLoughlin complained to Ben, without really expecting an answer. "If I refuse to sell them supplies, the Hudson's Bay Company will be regarded as selfish and mean-spirited. If I do supply them, Sir George Simpson will reprimand me severely."

"So what will you do?" Ben asked.

"As I've told you before, I have to live in this country. Sir George Simpson does not. So I'll help them in every way I can, while at the same time warning them of the dangers they'll face settling in such remote country."

The coming of American missionaries to the Oregon Country was not the only epoch event to which Dr. McLoughlin must respond in what had until now been a comfortable, unchanging world. Due to arrive soon in the lower Columbia was the first example of a newfangled invention that he heartily detested—a steam-powered ship.

"It's called the *Beaver*," he told Ben with a snort of disgust as he showed him a newspaper recently received from London. "As I'm sure you know, both British and American inventors have been playing around with steam engines for years. The confounded things are so heavy, undependable and dangerous, that the idea of putting them aboard a ship is ridiculous. But in the case of the *Beaver*, they've done it."

According to the article in the London *Times*, the first-ever steamship built specifically to navigate the waters of the Pacific Northwest had been launched on the Thames in 1835. The article proclaimed:

> It is safe to say that no vessel has attracted anywhere near as much attention as this pioneer of the Pacific. Over 150,000 people, including King William and a large number of the nobility of England, witnessed the launching, and cheers from thousands of throats answered the farewell salute of her guns as she sailed away for a new world.
>
> Much speculation is indulged in as to the success of her cruise. The machinery was placed in position, but the sidewheels were not attached, so she was rigged as a brig and started for her destination under canvas, with Captain Home in command. The bark *Columbia* sailed with her as consort.

Ben looked up with a frown. "From this I gather she'll use windpower, rather than steam, to cross the ocean."

"Of course she will!" Dr. McLoughlin said contemptuously. "She's designed to burn soft coal—the stinking, smelly, smoky stuff that has made all the big cities of England such hellholes to live in for years. Further on in the article, it says her bunkers can hold only enough coal to fire her boilers for two days. How far can she sail in that time?"

"It says she can burn wood, too."

"Aye, that she can. But how many forests grow on the high seas?"

To McLoughlin, it would have been no great loss if the *Beaver* had capsized under the weight of her useless machinery. But Ben, as a seafaring man familiar with the vagaries and limitations of wind power, had long been intrigued by experiments using steam power to move ships. His son Tommy, now sixteen years old, and Conco's son Sitkum, now seventeen, were so excited at the prospect of seeing their first steamboat that they could talk of little else.

Because the two boys possessed the same avid interest in canoes, small boats, and sailing ships that their fathers did, they had learned the ways of the lower river, the bar, and the sea outside at an early age. Sadly, Chief Concomly had died in 1831, full of years and knowledge at the age of sixty, which was old for members of his tribe. Following the new custom first adopted by Conco, who had refused to let his wife or his father force him to deform his son's head, most of the Chinooks, Clatsops, and other lower Columbia River tribes no longer indulged in head-flattening.

Well educated by her British father, as Ben had been by his parents, Lolanee had insisted from her first day in America that there be plenty of books, magazines, and newspapers in the house. With Lolanee teaching him an appreciation of good literature and Ben instructing him in the mathematics needed by seafaring men, Tommy received a well-rounded education. Since both parents insisted that his studies must come first, with free time in which to fool around with water, boats, and his bosom friend Sitkum postponed until his lessons were done, it quickly became a habit in Hilltop House that Sitkum—who was waiting around for Tommy anyway—be included in the instruction. Soon Conco could boast of another first for the youth in his tribe: that his son could read, write, and do sums.

Tall, slim, and handsome, as his father had been at that age, Tommy Warren had inherited his mother's soft brown eyes and darker skin, as well as her sunny disposition, quick wit, and a tendency to flare up when his pride was offended.

A head shorter, Sitkum was stocky, barrel-chested, with strong arms and legs, his normally shaped head featuring thin lips and deep-set black eyes whose slightly Oriental slant confirmed the Chinook tribal tradition that in the far-off mists of the past the "Old People," their ancestors, had migrated across the land bridge from Asia.

Despite their youth, both boys were qualified to pilot ships across the bar, for Ben and Conco had taught them well. But since most captains looked askance at turning so much responsibility over to boys so young, the two older men did most of the bar work, while Tommy and Sitkum specialized in acting as river guides between the mouth of the Columbia and Fort Vancouver.

Having read every article about steam engines and boats that they could get their hands on, Tommy and Sitkum were far more knowledgeable than their fathers regarding the potential of the *Beaver* in Pacific Northwest waters. Even so, when Sitkum crossed the river March 16, 1836, with the exciting news that an odd-looking ship "with a smokestack sticking up from its middle" had dropped anchor off Cape Disappointment and had fired three guns in a signal for a pilot, it was Ben who knew it was the long-awaited steamer.

"Is she alone?" he asked Sitkum.

"Yes, sir. At least I saw no other ship with her."

Including Tommy, Sitkum, and Conco with the crew of Chinook paddlers crossing the bar to meet the *Beaver*, Ben smiled as the two boys recited facts and figures about the ship.

"She's a hundred feet long," Tommy said, "with a twenty-foot beam, an eleven-foot depth, and draws eight feet of water. She's double-planked out of solid English and African oak, has a copper-sheathed bottom, and displaces 187 tons. Her side-wheels, when they're put in place, will be set well forward, and she'll have a top speed of eight knots."

Eyeing the vessel as the Chinook canoe approached it, Ben shook his head. "She's neither fish nor fowl to me, though I will say her brigantine rigging makes her look like she'd be a good sailer. Wonder what happened to her escort, the *Columbia*?"

What had happened, Captain David Home said with excusable pride when Ben, Conco, and the two boys went aboard to pilot the *Beaver* in across the bar, was that from the day the two ships cleared Land's End and moved out into the open sea the *Beaver* proved to be so much better a sailer that time and again she had to reef or lower sails and wait for the *Columbia* to catch up. Whether due to the superior craftsmanship of her designers, the quality of the materials put into her, or sheer luck, Captain Home did not know why she sailed so well. But he boasted that the 163-day passage of the *Beaver* from England to the mouth of the Columbia was a record that would stand for a while. Furthermore, it was an indication that, despite Dr. John McLoughlin's old-fashioned misgivings, the career of the *Beaver* in Northwest waters was going to be a long and happy one.

Anchoring off Fort George—which the Hudson's Bay Company continued to maintain and staff as a minor Indian trading post—a crew from the *Beaver* crossed the river and raised the Union Jack from the flagstaff atop Cape Disappointment as a signal that it had arrived. A week later, on March 21, the tardy *Columbia* showed up and hove to off the Cape, then, after the fog cleared, crossed the bar the next morning.

Because of the early spring runoff, high tides, contrary winds, and constantly shifting sandbars in the lower river, it took both ships two weeks to work their way up to Fort Vancouver, whose blacksmith shop and craftsman skills were needed to bring the paddle wheels, guards, and connecting engine machinery above decks and install them.

Putting Tommy aboard the *Beaver* and *Sitkum* on the *Columbia* to act as river guides in the tedious business of moving the ships upstream, Ben was amused by their reports that it was the *Columbia* that continued to have problems—going aground, having to be kedged out of the mud by the ship's boat, or towed off sandy shoals by the *Beaver*, until at last reaching the anchorage just off Fort Vancouver.

"How does Dr. McLoughlin like the *Beaver*?" Ben asked Tommy.

"Fine, I guess. At least he fired the fort's cannon to salute her arrival."

"That surprises me, son. From the way he's been talking, I thought he'd be firing at her."

23.

*F*ROM THE DAY the *Beaver* first showed up in the river, neither Ben nor Conco saw their sons again unless they happened to go to Fort Vancouver, where the paddle wheels were being installed, or viewed the steamer as she cruised up and down the lower river on test runs. When he did see Tommy, Ben found him talking an alien language that he could not begin to understand.

"The *Beaver* has two Bolton and Watt engines," Tommy told his father, "designed by the man who invented the steam engine, James Watt. They're propelled with a side-lever action. She's got thirteen-foot paddle wheels, with buckets six-and-a-half feet long. Her boilers use low-pressure steam, which will turn the paddle wheels thirty times a minute, driving her along at nine miles an hour in the river or eight knots at sea."

"You seem to have learned a lot about steamers, Tommy."

"Captain Home is a good teacher and seems to like me. He's offered me a berth as third mate. Can I take it, Dad?"

"What about your friend Sitkum?"

"He's been offered a berth, too. He'll be below decks as third engineer. What he'll do mostly is stoke the boiler fires with coal until it runs out, then he'll work in the woodcutting crew ashore."

Talking to Dr. McLoughlin, Ben learned that hiring the two boys had been the factor's idea. Though McLoughlin doubted that the steamer could operate profitably and hated its stink and noise, he admitted that it had made a tremendous impression on the Indians of the lower Columbia. No doubt it would have a similar effect on the natives of Puget Sound, British Columbia, and Russian Alaska. By equipping it with anti-boarding nets, a couple of six-pounders, rifles, and pistols with which the crew could defend itself, the *Beaver* would avoid the kind of disaster that had overwhelmed the *Tonquin*. At the same time, its trading missions to the north would get it out of the factor's sight and smell, as well as impressing the Indians with the might of the Hudson's Bay Company.

"By taking Tommy and Sitkum aboard," McLoughlin said, "Captain Home will have two level-headed young men who know the local waters, the language, and the customs of the country. They should prove very useful to him."

"Well, I know they're both dying to go with him. Of course a third mate and a third engineer aboard a ship as small as the *Beaver* don't have much authority, so far as the rest of the crew is concerned. But they will wear officers' caps, which is all they want anyway."

With only twenty tons of coal in her bunkers and no more of the "black stones that burn"—as the Indians called it—available in this part of the world, two weeks of off-and-on cruising between Fort Vancouver and the mouth of the Columbia exhausted that source of fuel. It was then that Sitkum really began to earn his meager pay as third engineer, for the big-city-raised British crew was only too glad to let him make arrangements with Indian woodcutters ashore and supervise the chopping, splitting and loading of the awesome amount of resin-rich firewood needed to keep the steamer's boilers going.

Because the brigantine rigging was not compatible with steam sailing, the masts, spars, and yards were removed at Fort Vancouver before the paddle wheels were installed. From that time forward, the *Beaver* would move only on steam power. If her experiences in the lower river were any criterion, she would consume forty cords of wood a day when steaming under full power, which would mean that she would steam one day, then lay by two while the necessary quantity of wood to keep her going was cut and brought aboard.

Even so, Ben suspected she would earn her keep, despite Dr. McLoughlin's misgivings, for he observed the role she played in an epoch event in the lower river. Since Tommy and Sitkum also took a part in the historic happening, he told Lolanee about it when he came home to Hilltop House that evening.

"The *Columbia* was anchored off Fort George, getting ready to set sail for England. Dr. McLoughlin wanted to add some furs to her cargo, so he sent word for her to come up to Fort Vancouver and load them. The wind and the current were against her and she could make no progress upriver for two days. So the *Beaver* came downriver, put a line on her, and gave her a tow."

"What's so important about that?"

"Steam power is the future of the river and the Pacific Northwest, Lanee. Tommy and Sitkum are going to be part of it."

"I know how Tommy feels about the *Beaver*," Lolanee said softly. "He's so proud of his third mate's cap, I think he wears it to bed."

"You don't mind that he's going to be gone a lot?"

"Of course I mind. But ships and the sea are the life of my people and yours. Why should we expect him to be different?"

Two events in 1837 and 1841 clearly showed that American interest in the Pacific Northwest was growing and that the Hudson's Bay Company was going to have problems running the Oregon Country. One was the whiskey-selling business started in the Willamette Valley by ex-mountain-man Ewing Young; the other the wreck of the American naval vessel *Peacock* just within the mouth of the river.

Despite the accusations made against him by the Governor of Spanish California a few years ago, former trapper Ewing Young had proved to Dr. McLoughlin's satisfaction that he was not a horse thief. Building a cabin and claiming a piece of land not far from the mission established by Jason Lee, Young had plowed and tilled the fertile soil in an honest effort to settle down and become a farmer. But when he found no market for his bumper crop of rye, wheat, and corn, he did what many another independent-minded, hill-raised Americans had done before him—he built a still and began to sell whiskey, for which there was a ready local cash market.

As a teetotaler, the Methodist minister Jason Lee opposed the still because he felt it would debase the white settlers and wreak havoc among the Indians. Dr. McLoughlin frowned on it because an uncontrolled source of spirits was bound to have a bad effect on the Indian trade. When both men tried to reason with Ewing Young and persuade him to close down the still, he reasoned back with the indisputable argument that he was breaking no law and that he had a right as a free American to do as he damn well pleased.

Conferring on the matter, Lee and McLoughlin agreed on a different approach. What they would do, they decided, was buy Young out—not with cash money but by acting as cosponsors of a venture that would occupy his energy and time, make him and them a profit, and improve the development of the Oregon Country. Ben learned the details of the scheme when he piloted the Yankee brig *Loriot* over the bar outbound for California.

From the first day of its appearance a few months ago, the brig—which arrived empty from Honolulu—and the passenger who had chartered it, William Slacum, had been something of a mystery. Dr. McLoughlin's suspicion that Slacum was a spy turned out to be correct, for he had served as a purser in the American Navy and had been commissioned by President Andrew Jackson to look into Hall Kelley's charges that American settlers in the Oregon Country were being oppressed by the Hudson's Bay Company.

Spending two weeks with Jason Lee, Slacum had assured the missionary that President Jackson and the United States had no intention of letting Great Britain take over the Pacific Northwest. Furthermore, he felt that enterprising Americans such as Ewing Young should be encouraged to develop new businesses, though not necessarily whiskey distilling. Since cattle were in short supply in this part of the Northwest, while California was so overrun with them that they could be purchased for three or four dollars a head, why not form a company, send it to California, buy a mixed herd of cattle, then drive it north to the Willamette Valley?

In charge of the venture, of course, would be ex-mountain-man Ewing Young.

All parties concerned thought the idea a great one. Since the best offer made him to abandon the whiskey business had been $51 and twelve bushels of wheat from the Lee Mission, Young magnanimously dissolved the Young and Carmichael Distilling Company without reimbursement and accepted the presidency of the Willamette Cattle Company.

"Don't know where Bill Slacum gets his money," Young told Ben as the *Loriot* moved out across the bar, "but he gave me $150 to buy a decent outfit, then persuaded Dr. McLoughlin to put up $500 for the Hudson's Bay Company and the Reverend Lee to subscribe $600 for the Mission. Top of all that, me and my crew of drovers are getting free passage south to Bodega Bay."

From what Ben heard later, the cattle-purchasing venture was highly successful, for the lackadaisical ranchers in Spanish California were only too glad to trade hard Yankee coin for wild Mexican cattle, all of which—save for a few blooded bulls—they turned loose to breed, multiply, and roam over the vast grassy plains and hills of the empire-sized *mañana*-land called California.

"First, Señor, you must pay for the number of cattle you want to buy," the ranchers told ex-mountain-man Young and his crew. "Then you can try to catch them and drive them to Oregon without losing too many along the way. In this endeavor, Señor, I can only tell you: *Salud y buen suerte*. Health and good luck."

Unfortunately for posterity, neither Ewing Young nor any of the drovers he employed had the spare time or energy to record their day-to-day adventures during the several late-spring and summer months it took to catch and drive five hundred wild Mexican cattle from the Sacramento Valley north to the Willamette country through thick timber, over rugged mountains, and across raging rivers.

"Loosely speaking," Young recalled later, "we started with five hundred head and we finished with maybe half that many—also loosely speaking. God knows what happened to the rest of the damn critters along the way. They just sort of got loose."

Though never immortalized in story or song, that was the beginning of the cattle industry in Oregon.

So far as the wreck of the *Peacock* was concerned, its basic cause again was the impatience of a captain trying to navigate strange, dangerous waters without a pilot. Beginning to get serious now about contesting British claims to the Pacific Northwest, the United States sent five naval vessels under Commander Charles Wilkes to survey and map the area under the Joint Occupancy Treaty from British Columbia and Puget Sound on the north to the Columbia River and the Oregon coast to the south.

Lieutenant William H. Hudson, skipper of the sloop-of-war *Peacock*, was assigned to enter and survey the lower Columbia. Exactly how he was to accomplish this task was left to his good judgment. But if he exercised any judgment at all, it was deplorably bad. As Ben reminded Lolanee later, her father, Captain Reginald Barker, had once made the sarcastic observation that young British and American naval captains had just one thing in common: "You can always tell when it's their first command—but you can't tell them much."

Wouldn't you think, Ben asked Lolanee, that a naval officer about to risk his ship crossing what was known to be the world's most dangerous bar would have learned something about its history? Wouldn't he be aware of the fact that since the discovery of the Columbia River by Captain Robert Gray in 1792, Chinook Indians had been guiding ships in across the bar for twenty years, while, since the establishment of Fort Astoria, Fort George, and Fort Vancouver, experienced white men who knew the bar and the lower river also had been available as pilots?

"Apparently, all he knew was that the Columbia is a big river with a wide mouth. Since the morning was sunny and warm, with a favorable wind and tide, he just aimed the *Peacock* at what looked like a nice channel and drove her aground with all sails set."

"Did the ship sink?"

"Not at first, Lanee, though eventually she did break up and was lost."

With her keelson driven deep into the sands of a shoal just below Cape Disappointment, the *Peacock* stuck fast all through the daylight hours of July 17, 1841, despite the captain's desperate efforts to work her free. In late afternoon, the wind veered, fog rolled in, and on a strong ebb tide the ship started to pitch and roll. Breakers began pounding her sides, which sprang leaks. A particularly heavy sea smashed the bulwarks, stove in the cutter, flooded the spar deck, and left the gun deck knee-deep in water.

"Captain Hudson insisted on keeping the crew onboard and waited out the night," Ben told Lolanee. "By the time Conco and I found out what had happened and went out to the ship, her situation was hopeless. All we could do, I told the captain, was take his crew ashore. He asked me what kind of accommodations were available there. I told him he'd have to take potluck with the Indians in the Chinook village. He didn't like that much, but he had to accept it."

"Did he pay you and Conco for your services?"

"I got nothing, but he did pay Conco after a fashion. Since this is the height of the fishing season, the Chinook village was full of Indians willing to sell salmon, sturgeon, oysters, clams, moccasins, and mats to the stranded sailors, as well as giving them shelter in the longhouses. The sailors paid off in cotton shirts, Conco says. In the next day or two, he'll take them upriver to Fort Vancouver where they'll wait for Commander Wilkes and the rest of the squadron."

Missing from the crew of the *Peacock* when its roll was called a

week later at Fort Vancouver, Ben heard, was a Negro cook named
James D. Saule. Joining the ship at Callao, Peru on its voyage north,
Saule apparently decided that the naval life was not for him, deserted,
and stayed out of sight until the survey fleet completed its work and
left the region. Surfacing in the Willamette Valley near Jason Lee's
Methodist Mission, he set himself up in business as a small-time, in-
dependent Indian trader.

Exactly what happened there, Ben did not know, but an Indian
named Cockstock claimed he had been cheated by Saule and his
friends in a trade. First an argument, then a fight, broke out, during
which Cockstock and a white man were killed, with others of both
races injured. Found guilty by a people's court of "inciting trouble,"
Saule was banished from the Willamette Valley, came to Astoria, and
was employed as a cook for a time, then moved across the river and
claimed a piece of land between Cape Disappointment and the sandbar now called Peacock Spit on which the ship he had deserted had
been wrecked.

Building a cabin there, he took a Chinook woman—whom he frequently abused—into his bed, then became a thorn in the side of both
the Chinook village nearby and the Hudson's Bay Company at Fort
Vancouver …

Now twenty-one years old and serving as First Mate of the Beaver,
Tommy Warren had given little thought to being one of the very few
native-born Americans currently living in the Joint Occupancy region
of the Pacific Northwest. Though he had heard his father talk about
New England, where he had been born and raised, and his mother
discuss Hawaii, where she had been nurtured, both were alien countries to him. Old enough to vote now, he had yet to live in a country
with an organized government.

In the Fort Vancouver area, a sizable number of Hawaiians com-
monly called "Kanakas" had taken up permanent residence, inter-
marrying with French-Canadian trappers' children, Scotch, Irish, and
English clerks, and occasionally with men or women of Indian blood.
As a child of ten, he once had asked his mother what a Kanaka was.
She had tried to tell him.

"In the Islands, Hawaiians traditionally call themselves *kanaka maoli*, which means 'indigenous people.' I can't use that term myself, of course, for my father, Reginald Barker, was British."

"Does that make you a half-breed?"

"Better not call her that, Tommy," his father said. "When I did the day I tried to rope her and pull her down out of a palm tree, she dropped a coconut on my head."

"Breaking the coconut wide open," Lolanee said, smiling sweetly. "Your father was out of his senses for the rest of the day."

"During which I asked your mother to marry me," Ben said. "Which she did."

"I felt sorry for him because I'd beaned him with the coconut."

Since both parents had taught Tommy the history of his forebears, he knew that he had a British naval captain and a New England whaling ship master as grandfathers and that he carried the name of his great-grandfather, Kamehameha, the Polynesian king who had brought the Hawaiian Islands under the rule of a single all-powerful monarch. But in this part of the world, no formalized code of laws existed, with rules of behavior being enforced among the Indians by their chiefs and council of elders, in the fur trade by Dr. John McLoughlin and the Hudson's Bay Company, and in the Willamette Valley settlement adjacent to the Methodist Mission by Jason Lee and his religious followers.

Generally speaking, the attitude of all the residents of the Oregon Country was that since no pressing need for a government existed, why bother organizing one? When violence and fatalities had followed the dispute between Cockstock and Saule near the Methodist Mission, what most people accepted as justice was achieved by trying Saule in a "people's court" on the charge of "inciting trouble," finding him guilty, then banishing him from the community.

When Ewing Young set himself up in business distilling and selling whisky, an attempt had been made first to reason with him, then to buy him out. Upon the failure of both those efforts, the ex-mountain-man's energies and talents had been diverted into a more productive business by making him president of the Willamette Cattle Company. In this venture, he had succeeded so well that his premature, unanticipated death in the spring of 1841 caused a crisis that not even a "people's court" could resolve.

The gist of the problem was that he had died intestate—leaving neither heirs nor will.

Since he owned a number of cattle, had built a cabin, claimed a square mile of fertile land, and possessed a thousand or so dollars in gold and silver coin, neither the Methodist church, of which he was not a member, nor the Hudson's Bay Company, for which he had never worked, seemed qualified to decide how his assets should be distributed. What was needed, all the Willamette Valley settlers agreed, was a properly constituted court. But since the region had no government, it could have no court.

Getting together to discuss this perplexing situation, the late Ewing Young's ex-mountain-men friends, Americans Joe Meek and Doc Newell, and French-Canadians Etienne Lucier and François X. Matthieu, shared a few snorts of whiskey and some tentative ideas about organizing a local government.

"Let's face it, gents," said Joe Meek, who claimed to be a shirttail relative of President Polk (one of his sisters having married into the Polk family), which made him something of an expert on government. "About half the people livin' in the Willamette Valley would favor an American-style government, if we had one, while the other half would favor a British-style government."

"*Oui, M'sieu Meek,*" agreed Etienne Lucier, with a Gallic shrug. "This in all likelihood is true—if we had a government. Fortunately, we do not. In my opinion, it is much better this way, for when government comes, so do taxes. And taxes I do not like."

"Well, we can't just sit here and let our old friend Ewing Young's assets be frittered away," Doc Newell said. "Since he died, his cattle have gotten wild as deer, scattering every which way into the hills. Ain't hardly a day passes that we don't find a calf killed and eaten by wolves. If we had a government, it could at least put a five-dollar bounty on wolf hides so we could kill off the pests and protect our livestock."

François X. Matthieu nodded and said, "For this, I would pay a reasonable tax. But only if all my neighbors agreed to pay it too, with a sheriff appointed to collect it."

"Well, now, I'd be glad to undertake that chore," Joe Meek volunteered. "Just get the thing organized, gents, and give me the authority. I'll clean out the wolves in the valley in no time at all."

Shortly thereafter, the first of what became known as the "Wolf Meetings" took place in a warehouse owned by the Hudson's Bay Company near a little settlement called Champoeg. Ostensibly, the purpose of the meetings was to set a bounty on wolves, to assess every settler living in the area five dollars a year, and pay Joe Meek to act as the community's authorized wolf-killer. But as often happened when independent-minded men got together in that place and time, the subject soon moved on from wolves to politics, which outraged Hudson's Bay Company employees.

"Why, d'ye know what those men are talking about at their meetings?" exclaimed a British Senior Clerk after attending one of the meetings. "Forming a government, that's what! They're saying the people living in this part of the country ought to be allowed to vote on the matter. Can you imagine such tommyrot!"

"It's the bloody Americans who're stirring things up," agreed a Junior Clerk fresh out of a London slum. "Why, if them blokes 'ad their way, they'd 'uve plotted the Boston Tea Party in Westminster Abbey!"

"Well, I told them straight out," the Senior Clerk snorted, "they could hold no more political meetings on Hudson's Bay Company property."

"What'd they say to that?"

"What you might expect Americans to say—that the Company may own the building but it don't own the land around it. So they've called their next meeting for out-of-doors on French Prairie, which is just a stone's throw away."

Tommy Warren's presence at what would prove to be a historic meeting near Champoeg on French Prairie May 2, 1843, had nothing to do with wolves or politics. What had drawn him to the area on that particular day was a sixteen-year-old girl named Abigail Kennedy, who lived with her parents at the Lee Mission nearby. Though he had not yet reached the point where he had settled his heart and mind on the particular young lady he intended to marry, he recently had told his mother that he was in the process of narrowing the field of prospects down to three girls, of which Abigail Kennedy was one.

Admittedly, the *Beaver* remained his first love. Still the only steam-powered vessel operating in the waters of the Pacific Northwest, the little steamer was doing yeoman service sailing in and out of the Columbia River, up the Pacific Coast to the Strait of Juan de Fuca, into Puget Sound, and on the waters of the Inside Passage as far north as Russian Alaska. With Captain David Home talking of retiring and returning to England in a year or two, it would be only a matter of time before Tommy Warren took over as master of the *Beaver*. Below decks, Sitkum had developed a remarkable talent for keeping the cranky engines of the side-wheeler functioning, for he was better educated and more intelligent than anyone else in the black gang except for Chief Engineer Peter Arthur, who had taken a liking to the young Chinook Indian from the beginning and had taught him everything he knew.

As time passed, Sitkum not only managed to keep the engines chugging but also simplified the woodcutting chore so that now near Indian villages all along the way, stacks of well-cured, furnace-sized chunks of wood cut by natives eager to trade were ready and waiting when the *Beaver* came to call, needing only to be carried aboard, which reduced the time spent unproductively. The relationship between Tommy and Sitkum still was a close one, for each man respected the other for his special field of knowledge. In particular, Tommy trusted Sitkum's instinct for weather, which time and again he found more reliable than his own.

So far as the field of prospective wives went, Tommy was attracted to a perky, well-rounded Kanaka girl living at Fort Vancouver named Noa Okani, as well as to a tall, black-eyed French-Canadian girl named Luisa Gervais, whose family lived near the Falls of the Willamette at Oregon City. As yet, he had not decided whether he liked them or Abigail Kennedy best. But after going to an endless, mind-and-tail-numbing church service at Salem with the prim, strait-laced Abigail Kennedy, he had come to the conclusion that if he had to accept the Methodist religion and its long services in order to win her, he would scratch her off the list of prospects.

Being in the neighborhood and hearing about the meeting being held out-of-doors on French Prairie, Tommy went to it out of simple curiosity, just to see what was going on. Wandering around or chatting in animated groups in a natural open area near a grove of tall Douglas firs, a hundred or so men of assorted ages and loyalties were milling about, listening with varying degrees of attention as Joe Meek, Doc Newell, Etienne Lucier, and François Matthieu harangued the crowd in English and in French.

The distinction of being the oldest settler in the area belonged to a French-Canadian named Joseph Gervais, Tommy knew, who happened to be the grandfather of dark-eyed Luisa Gervais, whom he now had moved up to number two on his list of possible wives. Coming west with the overland section of the Astor party in 1812, Joseph Gervais had transferred his loyalty first to the North West, then to the Hudson's Bay Company, for which he had worked until retiring a couple of years ago to a claim in the lower Willamette Valley. Like most French-Canadians, he and his clan were Catholics, so Tommy supposed he would have to embrace that faith if he married Luisa. From what he had seen of Catholic services, they were much shorter than those of the Methodist religion, so converting to that faith might not be so bad.

On the other hand, both Noa Okani and his mother believed in the old-time Hawaiian religion with its multiple good and evil gods, which Tommy found more exciting, more tolerant, and more fun than any deities in the Methodist or Catholic dogma. As for his father's religion, Tommy had recently heard him say that the same Boston Board of Foreign Missions that had sponsored the Whitmans and the Spaldings had also sent missionaries to Hawaii, whom the natives had greeted without enthusiasm.

"Seems the first thing the missionaries tried to do," Ben said as he and Lolanee sat down to dinner with Tommy and the other children at Hilltop House one evening, "was put clothes on the native girls. After the trouble I had with your mother, I could have told them that wouldn't work."

"From what I've heard from my family," Lolanee said, "the missionaries to Hawaii are a bunch of blue-nosed Calvinist snobs, who are so intolerant of the people they're trying to convert that they won't even let their own children go to school with them, for fear their dried-up little souls might get polluted by native ways. Instead, they send their own children back to Boston to be educated."

"Too bad your grandfather is gone," Ben said. "He'd have put the missionaries in their proper place."

"He certainly would—six feet under the corner posts of a heathen temple."

"Speaking of heathens," Tommy said, "Noa Okani took me to what she called a *luau* in the Kanaka village at Fort Vancouver a while back."

"Did you enjoy it?" his mother asked.

"You bet I did! They barbecued a pig, danced, ate and drank a lot. We had a wonderful time. Noa said a *luau* is sort of a native religious ceremony. Is that true?"

"It certainly is, Tommy. A *luau* is a way of giving thanks for the spiritual and physical gifts that the gods and your fellowman have given you. You're supposed to have fun."

"Well, it sure beats a Catholic mass or a Methodist sermon all hollow as a way to worship. No wonder the missionaries want to stop it."

Today, politics, not religion, claimed Tommy Warren's attention.

Having the loudest voice and the most compelling manner of all the men assembled on French Prairie, Joe Meek had at last gained the attention of the crowd. Though he and his friend Robert "Doc" Newell were relative newcomers to the Willamette Valley, having arrived here just three years ago in the fall of 1840, they had spent twenty years trapping the streams of the West. Like others of their kind, they had seen their livelihood destroyed when the market for beaver collapsed in New York, London, and Paris because silk imported from China was replacing beaver felting as the preferred material for hats, dresses, and coats.

What apparently had been the last great American fur trade rendezvous had been held on the western slope of the Rockies in the summer of 1840, following which Joe Meek, Doc Newell, William Craig, and a number of other mountain men had decided to give up the trade and make their living in other pursuits. Catching up with an inept party of American missionaries who were attempting to cross the continent with three horse-drawn farm wagons, Meek, Newell, and Craig took over the wagons and succeeded in bringing them west to the Whitman Mission, thus could brag that they had blazed the overland trail to the Oregon Country. According to a recent rumor a train of one hundred wagons, one thousand people, and five thousand oxen, cattle, and horses planned to leave Westport in the spring of 1843 and would reach the Willamette Valley sometime in September. Joe Meek and Doc Newell hoped to greet the emigrants with the news that the Oregon Country now was ruled by Americans.

"As most of you people know," Joe Meek was telling the crowd, "we been talkin' government for some time. In February, we held the first meetin', passing a five-dollar tax on each family to pay me for killin' off the wolves, which I did. In March, we had another meetin', at which we voted to appoint a committee of twelve for the purpose of taking measures for the civil and military protection of this colony."

"Don't call us a colony," Doc Newell protested. "We fought a war to end that nonsense."

"A bunch of people, then, tryin' to decide what kind of govern-ment we want to live under. That's what we're here for."

"As I told you before, *M'sieu* Meek!" Etienne Lucier cried. "If we have a government, we will have taxes. I will not vote for that!"

"You voted for the Wolf tax, didn't you?"

"*Oui.* But that was necessary."

"Well, the only thing we're goin' to vote on now, Etienne, is whether we want to be governed by British or American laws. Any taxes we approve will come later."

"Suppose we want no government at all?" François Matthieu de-manded. "Why can't we vote on that?"

"Because we've got no government now and we need one," Meek yelled in exasperation. "That's what this meetin' is all about."

Moving off a short distance from the crowd, he picked up a stick and drew a hundred-foot-long line on the surface of the moist earth.

"Who's for a divide? All in favor of organizing a government in the American style, follow me and step over to this side of the line. If you favor the British style, take your stand on the other side of the line. Come on now, men! Show the world where you stand! Who's for a divide?"

24.

 ＨＥ ＦＩＲＳＴ ＭＯＶＥＭＥＮＴ came quickly, with twenty or so Americans going over to the Joe Meek side of the line, while an equal number of Britishers led by a just-retired ex–Hudson's Bay Company employee named Hamish McPherson assembled on his side of the line. The dividing slowed then, though never stopping completely, as men joshed one another in English and in French:

"Make up yore mind, George—you gonna be a sheep or a goat?"

"What'll yer Injun *klutchman* say, Frenchy, if you choose American an' she favors British?"

"She'll probably kick him out of her bed!"

"Wal, maybe he kin trade her fer a squaw who's joined the church at the Lee Mission, who'll teach him what government by American bluenoses *really* means!"

Watching the band of undecided men grow smaller as it divided into what appeared to be roughly equal groups, Tommy Warren felt that he was here only as an interested spectator, until Joe Meek yelled at him:

"Hey, Cap'n Warren! Where do you stand?"

"On what?"

"On the divide, consarn it! How're you gonna vote?"

"Why, to tell you the truth, Mr. Meek, I hadn't given it a thought. I've never voted in my life."

"You're free, white, and twenty-one, ain't you?"

"Yes, sir."

"Born in Astoria?"

"Yes."

"Yore pa is the bar and river pilot, Benjamin Warren, who came to Astoria on the *Tonquin* in 1811, ain't he?"

"That's right."

"Then you're a born-and-bred American citizen, jest like Doc Newell, me, and at least half the men at this meetin'. Now's the time to stand up and be counted."

"On which government I favor, you mean?"

"You bet! If you want to live under a Provisional Government set up American style, step over to our side of the line. If you want to live under British law, step over to the other."

"Well," Tommy said tentatively, "I suppose if I've got to choose, I'll vote American ..."

"Then move yore feet, boy! Hustle yore butt over to this side of the line!"

After he had done so, Tommy stood with the now silent group of men gathered around Joe Meek and Doc Newell, staring with them at an equally silent group of the same size gathered around Hamish McPherson on the other side of the line. Both Meek and McPherson were circulating around, counting their adherents. After a few moments, Meek called out:

"I tally fifty men on my side, Hamish. What's your count?"

"The same as yours, Joe. I also count fifty."

Standing halfway between the groups, Tommy noticed, there now were just two men: the ex-trappers Etienne Lucier and François X. Matthieu, both of whom had been very active and very vocal at the "Wolf Meetings" held during the past few months. Though both were French-Canadians who had married Indian women and fathered a number of half-blood children, their wives were now dead and their children lived elsewhere in the Willamette Valley or near Fort Vancouver north of the Columbia River. A few years ago, the two old friends had claimed a piece of fertile land and built a comfortable cabin near Champoeg, where they planned to live out their days. A strong supporter of Joe Meek and the "Wolf Tax," François Matthieu was known to favor the freedom of an American-style government, while his partner, Etienne Lucier, liked the idea of no government at all, for to him government meant taxes.

That was the gist of their argument now.

"But I ask you, *mon ami*," Lucier was saying vehemently, "why must we have any government at all? Why can we not leave matters as they are?"

"We need clear title to our land, Etienne. For this, we must have a government."

"If we vote British, the Hudson's Bay Company will still rule the country, *n'est ce pas*? Cannot they give us title to our land?"

"All the Company can do is make rules for us to live by. They can't give us land."

"But the Americans can?"

"According to Joe Meek, the first thing a Provisional Government set up American style will do is give every white or half-white settler in the Oregon Country title to a square mile of land. Not only that, we'll be covered by the United States Constitution, which guarantees all its people rights—such as free speech and the vote."

"*Oui*, I have heard this. It does sound good. But I have also heard that an American government will do bad things, too."

"Like what?"

"Like making settlers pay special taxes for improvements on their cabins. For instance, I hear they will tax *les fenetres*."

"The windows? You mean, they'll tax our cabin's windows?"

"That is what I have heard, *oui*. Because we went to great expense to buy from the Hudson's Bay Company store six glass-paned windows imported from England to put into the walls of our cabin to give us better light, the Americans will make us pay a tax of two dollars a year on each and every window—just like they do in New York City."

Scowling, François Matthieu turned to Joe Meek and demanded: "Is that true, Joe? Do they really tax windows in New York City?"

"Wal, I ain't never been there myself—"

"I have," Doc Newell said. "It's not true, Etienne. Not true at all! No windows in New York City nor anywhere else in the United States are taxed."

"And they damned sure won't be taxed by the Provisional Government in Oregon," Meek declared firmly. "I guarantee that."

After a few moments of hesitation, Etienne smiled, shook hands with his partner, then together the two old friends crossed to the American side of the line. Taking off his battered red felt hat, Joe Meek threw it high in the air, shouting jubilantly:

"The people have spoken, gents! We've voted to go American fifty-two to fifty!"

Being gone frequently with the Beaver during the next few months, Tommy Warren was not present when action was taken to implement the vote. But from what he heard from his father and friends upon his return, Joe Meek and Doc Newell had wasted no time setting up a Provisional Government in the American style. Between early May, when the vote was taken, and mid-September, when the first exhausted travelers of the thousand-member party of American emigrants that had set out from Westport in the early spring of 1843 began to straggle into Fort Vancouver, a government suited to the desires and hungers that had impelled the movers to come to Oregon had been set up and was in working order.

Following the appointment of nine men to draw up a program, the ad hoc committee reported to a mass meeting held at Oregon City on July 5 that it had created four legislative districts. The most central of these, in which the capital would be located, would be called "Champooick," "Champoeg," or some such name, after either the French word champ ("field"), the Indian word pooick ("root"), or both, pronounced by most people "Shampooey." Its vague boundaries included all of the Willamette Valley. The lines defining the other three districts were vaguer still. Thinking big as always, Joe Meek proposed that the Provisional Government claim jurisdiction over all the Joint Occupancy lands north to Russian Alaska, south to Spanish California, and east to the summit of the Rocky Mountains, with the three other districts to cover these areas.

While neither denying nor confirming British claims in the region, the key provision in the new body of laws was that any white or half-white resident of the Oregon Country could claim a square mile of land not previously settled upon by anyone else. Within the next year or two, the Provisional Government would elect a legislative body, set up a Constitution modeled after that of the United States, and send it to the nation's capital with a request that it be approved immediately. The Joint Occupancy Treaty with Great Britain must be terminated, the petitioners demanded, and the boundary question settled on favorable terms. Following this, it was expected that Oregon Territory would be organized within five years, with full statehood to follow within ten.

Talking these matters over with his father one late September evening in Hilltop House, Tommy was surprised to find that in many ways his father was better prepared for the changes in government than he was himself.

"What's happening now," Ben told Tommy, "is exactly the kind of thing that took place after the Revolutionary War when your grandfather was your age. England no longer has the power or the will to hold onto a colony of upstart Americans so far removed from the homeland."

"Will the British be thrown out completely?"

"God knows. For years, Sir George Simpson and Dr. John McLoughlin have been trying to encourage Americans to settle south of the Columbia River, hoping to make it the boundary between the two countries. But if this year's party of emigrants is as large as they say it is, Dr. McLoughlin is going to have a problem keeping all those land-hungry people south of the river."

"Did you know that McLoughlin himself has claimed land and is building a house near Willamette Falls? There's even a rumor floating around that he plans to become an American citizen."

"No, I haven't heard that, Tommy. But it doesn't surprise me. After all, he's made his home in this part of the country for twenty years. He's done more to help American settlers than any other man in a position of power."

"If the northern boundary of the United States is settled at 54–40, as the more rabid American politicians are demanding," Tommy asked, "what will happen to Hudson's Bay Company properties such as Fort Vancouver on the north side of the Columbia, Fort Nisqually on Puget Sound, and Fort Langley in British Columbia? What will happen to ships owned by the Company?"

"My guess is there'll be a lot of blustering by politicians on both sides, with a peaceful settlement made eventually. Certainly we won't be so foolish as to go to war over territory again." His father gave him a quizzical look. "What are your prospects for taking over command of the *Beaver*?"

"Nil, at the moment. The Company doesn't want its only steamship commanded by an American, any more than I want to captain a British ship."

"There's talk of building an American steamer in Astoria, you know."

"So I've heard. If that happens, I'm available."

"You wouldn't consider going back into sail?"

Tommy shook his head. "Not if it means going to sea, Dad. I intend to make my career in coastal waters or on the lower river in steam-powered craft."

"Good for you, Tommy!" his mother exclaimed. "I don't want you going on long voyages to the far corners of the world. Neither will your wife—when you have one."

"What your mother is hinting at, Tommy," Ben Warren said with a chuckle, "is that it's high time you brought us up to date on which of your sweethearts you favor—Noa, Luisa, or Abigail?"

After a moment's hesitation, Tommy gave his mother a sidelong glance, then murmured, "To tell you the truth, Mom, I've met a new girl I like a lot. She came out with the wagon train from Westport."

"An American girl?" Lolanee asked.

"Not exactly. What I mean is, not yet. But she wants to be."

Ben scowled at Tommy. "You'd better explain that one, son."

"Don't rush him, dear," Lolanee said. "Let him tell us about her in his own way." She smiled fondly at Tommy. "What's her name?"

"Freda Svenson," Tommy said. "She came to America from Sweden with her parents, who were planning to emigrate to Oregon. Her father was a gunsmith, who hoped to work at his trade in a newer, freer country. But shortly after they reached Philadelphia, both he and her mother caught the cholera and died, leaving her an orphan."

"Poor girl!" Lolanee said. "How old is she?"

"She's just nineteen, Mom. She didn't know a soul in Philadelphia and spoke very little English. The only place she'd ever heard of in America was Oregon, where her parents planned to go. Since this was their dream, it became hers, too. She decided to go to Oregon by whatever means she could."

"Alone?" Ben said incredulously.

"She's a very strong-minded young lady, Dad. She found a wealthy German-American brewer named Gustav Mueller who needed a servant girl to help his wife Emma mind their four children and do the housework. She indentured herself to them, then headed west for Oregon."

"Wait a minute!" Ben interrupted. "That indentured servant business hasn't been practiced in the United States since the Revolutionary War. Why would she be so foolish as to do a thing like that?"

238   "Because she didn't know any better, Dad. All she knew was that Gustav Mueller planned to go to Oregon and set up a brewery in the

Willamette Valley. His wife needed a dependable servant girl to do the chores and take care of the kids along the way. They told Freda that if she would work for them for five years—with no pay except her keep—they would give her a hundred dollars in gold when her time was up, which she could use as a dowry to find herself a husband."

"A dowry?" Lolanee asked with a scowl. "What on earth is that?"

"It's an old-country custom, dear," Ben said, "by which a young lady is given a cow, a few sheep, or a sum of money which she can use as a lure to catch herself a husband. Unfortunately, it never caught on in backward countries like Hawaii. If it had, your father might have paid me a tidy sum to take you off his hands."

Lolanee gave him a withering look, then turned back to Tommy. "I hope you told her all a young lady needs to attract a husband in this part of the world is character and a capacity for love."

"A pretty face and a shapely figure are useful, too," Ben added. "How does she rate there?"

"Ben, you're incorrigible!" Lolanee exclaimed. "Why I ever married you, I'll never know!"

"Because you had the very qualities you've recommended to Tommy," Ben said. "Plus a pretty face and a shapely figure, which was what really trapped me."

"Freda is pretty enough," Tommy said with a shrug. "But she's stubborn, too. She doesn't understand how we do things in America. For instance, when I told her that if I were married I could claim a square mile of land, she immediately asked, 'How many square miles could Mr. Mueller claim?' When I said, 'Just one, the same as me,' she didn't believe me. 'Mr. Mueller is a rich, important man, who is going to build a big brewery in the Willamette Valley,' she said, 'while you are just a first mate on a little steamboat. Surely the government would not let you have as much land as Mr. Mueller.' "

"How did you answer that?" Ben asked.

"First, I got mad. Then I told her she had a lot to learn about America, and, like it or not, I was going to be her teacher. That made *her* mad, so she said I had a lot to learn about manners, and that maybe *she* would teach *me*."

"You're going to have a problem with that girl, Tommy," Ben said wryly. "Have you proposed to her yet?"

"No—and I won't until she forgets that indentured servant guff and quits working for the Muellers. But she's got her heart set on that hundred-dollar dowry. She says if I'm very polite to the Muellers, maybe he'll give me a job in his brewery, which will be a lot better than my first mate's berth on the *Beaver*."

"How did you respond to that?" Lolanee asked.

"I'm afraid I got a little rude. I told her that the four Mueller kids are spoiled brats, that Gustav Mueller is a stuffed shirt, and that Emma Mueller is a pain in the *okole*."

"Oh my, Tommy!" Lolanee exclaimed with a giggle. "Did you really say that?"

"I'm afraid I did, Mom," Tommy said sheepishly. "And she made me translate it for her."

"My Hawaiian is a bit rusty," Ben said, "but if memory serves me right, one's *okole* is what one sits on—and I don't mean a chair."

"It's more Pidgin English than it is Hawaiian," Lolanee said, "but you are in the right area. And Emma Mueller does sound like a pain in the ass to me." She looked thoughtful for a moment, then smiled and added, "Why don't you bring Freda home with you for a few days, Tommy? Maybe I can teach her a few things about living in the United States that she needs to know."

Tall, willowy, and strong from hard physical work, Freda Svenson had sea-blue eyes, golden hair, and the look of a young woman wise beyond her years. Apparently, Tommy had said exactly the right thing when he had told Freda that he wanted to take her downriver on the *Beaver* to Astoria, where she was invited to spend a week at Hilltop House with his parents. In Sweden, she said, it was very important that a young lady meet the family of her prospective husband.

"You have a brother and two sisters, *ya*? That is a nice size family. To my mother and father, only one child was born—me. But until my parents died, there was much love in our family among the three of us."

"Right now, my sisters are in Hawaii visiting their grandparents," Tommy said. "Only my younger brother, Emil Wakea, is at home. He's fifteen and a real pest."

"How old are your sisters and what are their names?"

"Sarah Allamanda is twenty. Hina Flora is eighteen."

"*Ak fy!*" Freda exclaimed. "What interesting names your brother and your sisters have! Are they Hawaiian?"

Tommy nodded. "It started with me, I'm told, when my parents

decided to honor Dad, and Mom's fathers and her grandfather by sad-
dling me with the name Thomas Reginald Kamehameha Warren.
They never use it, of course. They just call me Tommy."

"Are your sisters married?"

"Not yet. Sarah has a prospect in Hawaii and may get married while she's there. Hina has a boy she's sweet on in the Kanaka village at Fort Vancouver. They're both nice, lovely girls. But they don't hold a candle to my mother. So far as Dad and I are concerned, Mom is queen of the family."

"I look forward very much to meeting her. What have you told her about me?"

"The truth, of course," Tommy said with a grin.

"Which is —?"

"That you're as pretty as you are stubborn. Mother likes that. I'm sure you'll get along well together."

When Freda had asked permission to take a week off from the drudgery of looking after the children and doing the household chores, Mrs. Mueller had flatly denied it, which did not surprise Tommy in the least. Nor was he surprised when Freda bluntly told Mrs. Mueller that she had earned the week off and was going to take it whether Mrs. Mueller liked it or not, for in her view the opportunity to meet the parents of the man she hoped to marry far outweighed the impor- tance of her obligations to the Mueller family.

Fuming at the servant girl's defiance, Mrs. Mueller had demanded that her husband discharge Freda immediately without compensation of any kind.

"Also, as a penalty for her defiance," Mrs. Mueller told her hus- band, "you vill keep the gunsmith tools which belonged to her father that you brought to Oregon for her in our wagon. Dot vay, sale of the tools vill repay us for the food and shelter ve haf given her during the past year."

"A goot idea, Momma. Also, I vill look around for another girl to indenture as a servant."

But this was Oregon, not Philadelphia. Quickly learning that the crude, simple-minded men who had formed the Provisional Govern- ment would not stand for depriving a nineteen-year-old orphan girl of her rightful inherited property or requiring her to work without pay, Gustav Mueller persuaded his wife that it would be best to give Freda   **241**
Svenson the requested week off and not confiscate the gunsmithing tools.

Aboard the *Beaver* on the way downriver, Tommy Warren asked Freda what she intended doing with her father's tools.

"Oh, perhaps after I get married I will open a little shop where I can do gun repairs," she answered. "That was my father's dream, so I will try to do it for him."

"Do you know how to fix guns?"

"But of course I do! From when I was a little girl, my father taught me the skills of his craft."

"He taught gunsmithing to a girl?"

"In Sweden, it is the custom for the father to teach the daughter his skills, if he has no sons. That way, the craft he has learned will stay in the family. When the daughter marries and has sons, she will pass on the secrets of the trade to the next generation."

Coming from a nation of seafarers as she did, Freda was familiar with sailing ships on mountain-girt inland waters, as well on the Atlantic Ocean. But this was her first experience aboard a steam-powered craft, as well as her first view of the Columbia River west of Fort Vancouver. Both the broad, majestic river and the skill with which Tommy handled the steamboat impressed her tremendously. Despite intermittent showers of rain and gusty headwinds which drenched her face and soaked her hair, she stood at the quarter deck rail hour after hour, enthralled by the passing scenery during the day-long trip downriver, bareheaded until Captain Home jokingly appointed her honorary Third Mate and placed a billed cap on her head.

Until now, the only portion of the Columbia River that she had seen had been the bleak sagebrush-covered desert reach 200 miles east of Fort Vancouver, where the Oregon Trail descended from its crossing of the Blue Mountains to water level. There, the westering emigrants had begun the final and most difficult leg of their 2,000-mile journey across the continent. Relatively calm and placid for a while, the river changed its character as it neared the eastern slope of the Cascade Mountains, churning through a rock-strewn chasm only a few hundred yards wide as it tumbled over twenty-foot-high Celilo Falls. Literally turning on edge then, it raced at thirty miles an hour through fourteen miles of white-water rapids to The Dalles, beyond which it broadened and became quieter for fifty miles as it cut its way deeper into the mountains. Through the heart of the 10,000-foot-high Cascade range, another six-mile-long stretch of tossing, foaming water called the Upper, Middle, and Lower Cascades formed a final barrier, until finally the exhausted river reached quieter water forty miles east of Fort Vancouver.

At The Dalles, Freda told Tommy, the thousand-member party of emigrants with which she was traveling had been forced to build log rafts, take the wheels off their wagons, place them on the rafts, and then commit their fate to the mercies of the river, with groups of men ashore holding restraining ropes and attempting to control the rafts as they floated through the rocks, currents, and tumbling white-water hazards of the six-mile-long gorge. Being a well-equipped, well-guided party, Freda's group of people came through with a relatively small loss of equipment and no loss of life, though she heard later that they had been more fortunate than most parties. But for all of them, the experience had been terrifying.

"What is really needed through the gorge," Tommy told Freda, "is a portage railroad around the rapids, which would carry dismantled wagons, goods, and people. Between The Dalles and the Upper Cascades, there's a fifty-mile stretch of quiet river that could be navigated by a steamboat, if somebody would build one."

"You mean a steamboat like this one?"

"Not exactly, Freda. The *Beaver* is a deep-water ship designed to ply the lower river and coastal waters. The kind of boat needed upriver would have a broader beam, draw less water, and be propelled by a stern-wheel rather than side-wheel paddles. That kind of boat could be nosed into sandy shores for loading and unloading and would not need a deep water dock as a side-wheeler does."

"Would you run it?"

"Sure, I'd be glad to," Tommy said. He grinned at Freda. "All I need is somebody to build it for me. Do you suppose your friend Gustav Mueller would finance it?"

Whether her inadequate grasp of English or a tendency to regard all questions seriously was responsible, Tommy did not know. But he had come to realize that Freda did not have much of a sense of humor. After a moment of silent thought, she shook her head.

"No, Tommy, I do not think he would. It is building a brewery that interests him, not building a steamboat. Also, he is not my friend. I am just a servant to his family."

Rowed ashore in the ship's boat when the *Beaver* lay to at the anchorage just below Hilltop House, Tommy and Freda were met by his father, Ben, and his younger brother, Emil, who at fifteen was beginning to take an interest in girls in a general way, thus was intrigued to see what kind of selection his older brother had made in a specific way. Knowing that both his father and brother had a devilish sense of humor, Tommy was concerned that they might shock Freda with the nature of their greeting. But both Ben and Emil were on their best behavior, giving her a formal handshake and a friendly smile as Tommy introduced her to them.

"Freda, this is my father, Ben. And this is my brother, Emil."

"How do you do," Freda said. "I am pleased to meet you."

"Hey!" Emil exclaimed. "You are pretty, just like Tommy said!"

"Welcome to Astoria, Freda," Ben said. "I hope you won't mind a half-mile walk uphill over a wet trail."

"After a 2,000-mile walk west over all kinds of trails, Mr. Warren, I won't mind it at all."

Pausing a moment to watch the ship's boat return to the Beaver, which swung it aboard, then heeled around and began churning its way across the lower river toward Baker Bay, Ben gave the darkening, cloudy evening sky a mariner's glance, then said to Tommy, "Where's she headed this trip?"

"Fort Nisqually and the lower Puget Sound. She'll be back in a couple of weeks."

"Any change in your situation?"

"No. I've still got a berth as long as the Company keeps its headquarters at Fort Vancouver. But if it moves north, we'll part with no hard feelings on either side."

"I took your advice about filing a land claim. While you're here, I'll show you the square mile I picked. It's got nothing on it but trees, so it's not worth much. But it was the only piece of land I could find hereabouts that didn't have a settler living on it."

Moving ahead up the winding trail with Emil, Freda turned and said, "Excuse me, Mr. Warren, but I heard what you said to Tommy. You have filed a claim on a square mile of land?"

"That's right."

"Is it true what Tommy says that any person living in Oregon can own a square mile of land, no matter how rich or how poor he is?"

"The way the Provisional Government wrote the law, Freda, any single man who is white or half-white, now living in Oregon, can claim 320 acres of land. If he's married, he can claim a 640-acre piece, which is a square mile."

"But the land you have claimed, you say, is not worth much because the only thing on it is trees?"

"Right. Not being a farmer, all I'm really interested in is a stand of prime timber that eventually might be worth something as ship masts or sawmill logs. With all the trees growing in this part of the country, it's going to be a long time before a commercial market develops, I'm afraid. But Tommy thought it would be a good idea for me to file a claim while the law is still in effect, just in case it's changed later on."

"I would like to see this piece of land, Mr. Warren."

"Sure, I'll be glad to show it to you, if you don't mind a long walk in the rain and mud."

"In Sweden, it rains, too," Freda said with a merry laugh. "I am not made of sugar or salt to melt because of a little wetness."

Exactly what Freda and Lolanee talked, laughed, and cried about during the five days and nights of their visit together at Hilltop House, Tommy never knew. But from the moment they met, they got along almost like mother and daughter. Because of the growing tension between the United States and Great Britain over how the boundary dispute would be settled, American and English warships were crossing the bar and sailing as far upriver as Fort Vancouver in increasing numbers, which, with the added commercial traffic brought about by the growing settlements in the Willamette Valley and northward toward Puget Sound, kept Ben and Conco extremely busy as pilots.

Glad of the opportunity to refresh his skills at handling sailing ships, Tommy made three trips out and three trips in over the bar in a period of four days with his father. The most interesting of these occurred in late afternoon the fourth day. Before a building gale moving in from the southwest, Ben decided that rather than beating out to sea and laying to for a couple of days in deep water well offshore until the storm subsided, he would take an all-or-nothing gamble by piloting the big three-masted American merchant ship *Sea Lark* into the mouth of the river through the seldom-used South Passage just beyond Clatsop Spit—an area long known as a graveyard for ships because of the constantly shifting sands of its many channels.

Standing beside his father and the ship's nervous captain, Gerald Prudhouse, as Ben peered ahead for his landmarks through the driving rain and failing light, Tommy saw that his father's face was rigid with cold concentration as he called up thirty years of experience in piloting ships across the world's most dangerous bar to bring the vessel through safely. By now, the seas had become so rough and the wheel so hard to handle that Captain Prudhouse had detailed two husky sailors to man it, one on each side, with orders to maintain their grip on the spokes no matter what happened.

Even under the stress of these tense minutes, Ben did not forget that it was experience that made pilots, that he was still the teacher, and that his most apt apprentice stood on the quarter deck beside him. After giving the helmsmen an occasional terse correction in course and making sure it was executed precisely, Ben beckoned Tommy closer, shouting in his ear to make himself heard over the thunder of breaking surf and howling wind:

"We've got a thirty-knot gale astern and a near-record flood tide moving in behind us, Tommy!" he yelled. "Otherwise, I'd never have attempted to use this channel!"

"It looks mighty treacherous to me."

"Under most conditions, it is. But today it's a good gamble. I'm sure we'll make it through."

"What's the bottom like?"

"Nothing but loose, shifting sand. Given our sailing speed and powerful thrust from the incoming tide, if we do go aground we'll have a hundred yards of dry spit under our keel before we stop. We can walk inland from there without getting our feet wet." Giving the alarmed captain a sidelong glance and a quick grin, Ben added. "I'm not planning to go aground, of course. I mean to keep enough water under our bottom to carry us all the way into the lower river."

Twice during the ten-minute passage through the worst of the violently tossing breakers, the fore-and-aft pitching of the Sea Lark made her bow strike so hard when she slammed down into the water that one of the sailors at the wheel shouted, *"We've struck!"* to which the white-faced captain cried, *"Stay with the wheel, sailor! Stay with the wheel!"*

In both instances, Ben did not flinch, merely shaking his head like a street-fighter shrugging off a glancing blow. But just as Tommy was beginning to breathe easier and conclude that the worst of the passage was behind them, the ship rose and fell again, this time slamming its bow down so solidly that there was no doubt it had struck sand, not water. Almost toppled off their feet by the ship's sudden lurch, the two sailors at the wheel were too surprised even to complain, saving all their strength and energy to hold on.

"Come around, damn you! Come around!" Ben pleaded grimly. "You can't cross the bar sideways! Come around!"

Even as it appeared that the *Sea Lark* was going to hang up so badly on the sandbar that the wind and tide would roll her over on her side, she shuddered, turned, came free, and suddenly was moving straight ahead bow-on into calmer, deeper water.

"Good girl!" Ben breathed. Turning, he gave the ashen-faced captain a casually triumphant salute, then smiled at Tommy. "We'll be home for supper tonight after all, Son. I hope you're hungry!"

So far as Lolanee was concerned, she had known from the beginning that Freda Svenson was the right girl for Tommy. In appearance and background, the two women were different in many ways: Lolanee, brown-skinned, full-figured, with black hair and eyes; Freda, light-complexioned, golden-haired, blue-eyed, and slim. Though Lolanee came from a warm country two thousand miles to the west, while Freda came from a cold land the width of a continent and an ocean to the east, they shared the fact that they both were strangers in a new land, where both were destined to spend the rest of their lives with men they loved.

Instinctively, Lolanee knew that nothing she could say to Freda would influence her decision regarding Tommy, just as nothing she could say to Tommy would affect his decision about Freda. After taking the long walk through the wet woods with Ben to look at the piece of land he had chosen to file on, Freda climbed with Tommy to the third-floor, roofed-over observatory on which Ben had mounted the telescope and spent several rare sunny hours of a cool autumn afternoon looking and listening as Tommy pointed out the headlands, broad reach of river mouth, bar, sea, and the shipping moving in and out of the majestic Columbia. During their time together in that spot, they must have reached a decision, for that evening after supper, Tommy said quietly,

"Mom. Dad. We've made up our minds."

Giving Ben a quick glance, Lolanee let her hand lie under his as he covered it, then said, "What did you decide?"

"To get married."

"We're glad for you both," Ben said. "You're right for each other."

"I want very much to be part of your family," Freda murmured softly, a glint of tears filming her eyes. "Since I have no family of my own."

"Set a date yet?" Ben asked.

"As soon Freda settles matters with the Muellers," Tommy answered. "I told her to just quit and forget the hundred-dollars they promised her if she would work for them five years. But she says since she did give them one year, they should pay her twenty dollars for that."

"It is not much of a dowry to bring to our marriage," Freda said shyly. "But at least I will bring something."

"If you ask me," Emil blurted impulsively, "Tommy ain't worth *twenty cents* as a husband! But it's your dowry, Freda, to spend as you please."

"Tommy!" Lolanee exclaimed.

"Just joking, Mom. But he's lucky she'll take him at all."

"Well," Ben said, "I suppose you could make a good case in the Champoeg district court that the Muellers should pay you something for the year's work you've given them, Freda. But I hope you won't let waiting for a judgment on that delay your wedding."

"Oh no, we won't!" Freda said earnestly. "We must get married right away so that we can file a claim on a square mile of land."

"Right. Any idea where you'll locate, Tommy?"

"Upriver, I think. A few miles east of Fort Vancouver, probably, on the Oregon side of the river. My feeling is that when the boundary question is settled, that part of the country is going to develop by leaps and bounds. Sooner or later, there'll be steamboats on the upper river. Maybe a portage railroad around the Cascades and Celilo Falls, too. I want to be close by when it happens."

"What about your Indian friend, Sitkum?"

"Wherever I go, Dad, he'll go with me. He's the best steam engine man in this part of the country."

"We'll miss you when you leave home, Tommy," Lolanee said, her own eyes glistening now. "But with steamboats on the river, we can travel much faster and see one another more often. We wish you both much happiness."

248

25.

Unrest over the boundary question was intensifying. Sent out by the British government to investigate the need for installing fortifications in the Cape Disappointment area, Lieutenants Henry J. Warre and Mervin Vavasour found an ideal site for a battery of cannon on the cape. Unfortunately, it was in the possession of a man who claimed to be an American citizen, James D. Saule. Feeling it best to keep this a civilian matter for the time being, the two officers requested that Peter Skene Ogden, now representing the Hudson's Bay Company at Fort Vancouver, erase Saule's "squatter's rights" as quietly as possible by buying him out.

At that particular time—August 1845—expansionist-minded President William Knox Polk was promoting "Manifest Destiny" with his fiery slogan "54–40 or Fight!" in which he demanded that the Pacific Northwest border of the United States extend to Russian Alaska. Whether motivated by patriotism or simple shrewdness, no one could say, but Saule refused to sell the desired piece of land for a penny less than two hundred dollars. After paying that amount, Ogden took the deed-of-title-transfer to Oregon City, where an office recently had been set up in which to register such transactions, and tried to legalize his purchase.

To his surprise, he learned that instead of owning the property, Saule had merely been occupying it on behalf of its *real* owners, Newton and William McDaniel (who were *real* American citizens). Their price for the desired piece of land, they told Ogden, was $900. But when he asked Lts. Warre and Vavasour to reimburse him, they said they had not authorized him to spend *that* much money and would give him nothing. When he went looking for Saule, the man had vanished.

Feeling his personal honor was at stake, Ogden paid the legal

249

owners their $900 asking price, spent another $200 having the land surveyed, then registered his title to the site with the land office in Oregon City. When and if his country ever wanted to install a battery of cannons with which defend its claim to the Pacific Northwest, he was ready to make a deal.

Meanwhile, on July 18, 1846, yet another American naval vessel, the three-masted, armed schooner *Shark*, appeared off the mouth of the Columbia. Its avowed mission was to survey and chart the bar and mouth of the river, though a number of the more belligerent American settlers—hearing that the ship carried twelve cannons—regarded the survey project as merely a cover for the *Shark's* real mission, which was the bombardment of Fort Vancouver.

As usual, the ship's master, Captain Schenck, was blissfully ignorant of the fact that experienced native or white pilots were available to guide his vessel across the bar, accepting instead a bad piece of local advice. Telling Lolanee about it after he had been called to get the ship out of serious trouble, Ben Warren was livid with anger.

"From what I've seen of the American Navy, Lanee, it must be run by idiots. What apparently happened was that the captain of the *Shark* was hailed by a Negro in a small boat, who claimed to know the river and the bar."

"The man named James Saule?"

"Right. The deserter-cook from the *Peacock*, who recently skinned Peter Ogden out of 200 dollars. Apparently, he's still living with his Chinook woman in a shack near the cape. He told Captain Schenck he has followed the sea for twenty years and has been living on the lower Columbia ever since he went ashore five years ago. He claimed he knew the bar and the river like the lines in the palm of his hand."

"Didn't he have some trouble in Oregon City a while back?"

"Wherever he goes, he's had trouble, Lanee. His only service aboard the *Peacock* was as a cook for a few months between Peru and the mouth of the Columbia. He deserted when the ship was wrecked. All the same, he convinced Captain Schenck that he was an expert pilot, so the captain took him aboard and put the *Shark* in his hands. In less than twenty minutes, he drove her aground on the sands of Chinook Spit."

"Which is when they sent for you?"

"Right. By the time I got to the *Shark*, James Saule had been fired and booted over the side. I told Captain Schenck that Saule had been a cook, not a seaman, and that if he cooked as bad as he piloted, he did the *Peacock* a great favor by deserting before he poisoned the whole crew."

"Did you save the *Shark*?"

"Eventually, yes. With some careful kedging and a lot of help from Conco and his people, we finally worked her free, with no damage done. She'll be around for a few weeks, Captain Schenck says, making a survey of the bar and the lower river, where there are no adequate charts."

"You and Conco got paid, I hope."

"Finally, yes, though I had to scald the captain's hide with some pretty strong language before he would agree to pay us in coin rather than by a draft on the U.S. Treasury. He seems to feel it was our fault his ship got in trouble."

Trouble seemed to follow the *Shark*, for her brief stay on the lower Columbia proved to be a time of turmoil. Early that summer, word had reached the Willamette Valley that the United States had notified Great Britain it wished to end the Joint Occupancy Treaty. This meant that one of two events was imminent: a settlement of the boundary question or war. It was common knowledge that Peter Ogden had paid a large amount of money for a strategic cannon site overlooking the north entrance to the river. Though the Provisional Government approved at Champoeg three years ago had favored American control by a razor-thin 52–50 margin, another vote might reverse the margin in favor of the British. Rather than risk that, most Americans advocated throwing the British out by force. Sea-weary after long months of cramped quarters, low pay, poor food, and rigid naval discipline, the discontented crew members aboard the *Shark* were deserting in increasing numbers and filing land claims both north and south of the Columbia River. Though proclamations for their arrest and modest rewards for their return were posted ashore, few were caught and returned, while replacements were not to be found.

In the Oregon Country, these days, strange new winds of change were blowing, Ben Warren sensed. To land-hungry Americans and ex-Hudson's Bay Company employees, this was a country of freedom and opportunity, where all men were equal. So far as the possibility that the United States and England would go to war over who was going to own this part of the world, Ben could not take that seriously.

"If possession is nine points of the law," he told Lolanee, "most of the Joint Occupancy country already belongs to the United States. The only question left to be settled is how far to the north the line will be drawn."

So far as Captain Schenck was concerned, the crew of the *Shark* had been so reduced by desertions that it lacked the manpower either to complete his charting of the lower river or to make war against Great Britain. In a desperate attempt to salvage his mission, he headed his ship out to sea across the most dangerous part of the river bar— the South Passage—at noon September 10, 1846, without waiting for a favorable tide or a pilot.

The result was disaster.

The first Ben Warren knew of it was when he saw through the telescope atop the Hilltop House observatory that a ship was in trouble on Clatsop Spit. By then, there was nothing he or anybody else could do to save the *Shark*. Striking on the shoals in the middle of the bar, the ship was trapped by the shifting sands and held fast until huge breakers began rolling in and pounding her sides, tearing her apart.

In a desperate effort to save her, Ben heard later, Captain Schenck ordered the three masts chopped down and the twelve cannons cut loose from their mounts and jettisoned. Unfortunately, the ship was so hard aground that even this drastic lightening of her above-deck weight did not save her and she refused to budge from her perch. Reluctantly, Captain Schenck gave the order to abandon ship.

"There was no panic apparently," Ben told Lolanee after he had gotten the rest of the story from the ship's commander. "All hands took their places at the oars of the ship's boats and rowed ashore in good order. The natives in the Clatsop village took them in, he said, and treated them very well. But his ship was a total loss."

"Well, at least our friends at Fort Vancouver won't have to worry about being bombarded now," Lolanee said caustically.

"That's true," Ben agreed with a nod. "But apparently one of the cannons had enough wood under it after it was cut loose to float out over the bar and drift ashore several miles down the coast. The Tillamook Indians that found it are treating it as big medicine, I'm told. They're talking about building themselves a canoe big enough to carry it in case they decide to go to war against the United States."

But news drifting out to this far corner of the Pacific Northwest contained only messages of peace. On November 1, 1846, the most important information of all was received when word came that the United States and England had at last agreed to a boundary separating the two countries.

According to first reports, it would follow the 49th Parallel westward across Canada through the Great Lakes region to Puget Sound, veer southwest of Vancouver Island, and then follow the Strait of Juan de Fuca west to the Pacific. This meant that all the Hudson's Bay Company posts south of that line must eventually be closed and the region opened to American settlement.

"Wal, it ain't President Polk's 54–40 by any means," Joe Meek told his friends at Champoeg, where the Provisional Government was in the process of drawing up yet another memorial to the National Congress urging immediate statehood for Oregon. "But it ain't the 38th Parallel nor the Columbia River, neither. Guess we'd rather settle for that than go to war again …"

End of Book One